The Florentine

The Florentine

by Sandra Shulman

William Morrow & Company, Inc.
NEW YORK 1973

Shulman, Sandra.
    The Florentine.

    Bibliography: p.
    1. Florence—History—1421-1737—Fiction.
2. Medici, Lorenzo de, il Magnifico, 1449-1492—Fiction.
I. Title.
PZ4.S56316Fl   [PS3569.H775]   813'.5'4
ISBN 0-688-00042-8   72-10201

*For my parents
with gratitude*

BOOK I
"Yesterday's Child"

Francesca

It was Franca's favourite hour: the hour before sunset, when evening seemed to creep up beneath the sun. Though the brazen disk was still high in the cloudless blue, a misty lilac light suffused the hills beneath and gave distance the darker tones of twilight.

She looked down across the groves of craggy-trunked, silvery-leaved olive trees into the valley of the Arno. The river was a shining pewter snake, and the city, bathed in shadow, was already part of the evening. Only Brunelleschi's great dome of Santa Maria Fiore, and Giotto's Campanile were distinct above the huddle of tiled roofs and enclosing walls, as if they sought the light while its source hung in the heavens.

Cicadas filled the lonely place with their incessant scraping. Above her, swallows wheeled and chattered, full of the feverish activity with which they greeted oncoming night. Against dry grass their shadows were myriad whirling leaves . . . a portent of autumn.

The tall cypresses were black on the golden hills surrounding Fiesole, and the distant buildings bathed in russet light. The world was a still, warm place. The deep shadows cast by the trees were as soft and comfortable as bed on a cold, dark morning.

For miles around, vineyards, orchards, streams, farms, wayside inns—their produce, animals, and game—belonged to the Narnis of Castelfiore. They were among the oldest Florentine families, descended from the *magnati*, who had been deprived of their oligarchical rule in the city when all the nobles' proud and advantageous towers had been truncated to no more than fifty *bracchia* as a reminder that no one could rule over his fellows merely by virtue of an old title.

Franca threw open her arms to embrace the sweet air, perfumed with an abundance of wild thyme—the drowsy haunt of murmuring bees. She licked her lips, savouring the taste of herbs implanted by the caressing breeze. That summer, around her thirteenth birthday, Franca had grown almost agonizingly aware of her senses: of colour, of texture, of smell, of sound.

She was glad to have the beauty all to herself. Who could tell how she would feel after the betrothal? With the registering of her dowry, and the exchange of rings, the future would be prescribed, and no longer full of infinite mysteries like an unexplored continent. Now, she must imbibe the glowing ripeness as the final draught of wine. Indeed, Franca felt as lightheaded as if she had drunk too freely of undiluted Trebbiano.

At least the marriage itself was five years off. "Thank all the saints for that," she breathed. Something exciting must happen in all those days and months.

She stroked her smooth golden cheeks. Surely one day a beard would sprout, her voice become manlike, and she would not have to turn into a helpless female, forced to submit to her husband's will, condemned to sit by the hearth, quiet the children, and watch over the servants, while the men explored the world's wonders.

Franca had prayed ardently at the Badia Fiesolane that the baby growing inside her mother would be a girl. It was impossible being the only daughter in a household of men. Like some curse. If the new baby should be a girl then some of the burden of unwanted femininity could be temporarily shed. Someone else would be forbidden to roam the country-side, sit astride the spirited Narni horses, climb trees or the backs of oxen. Oh yes, the child must be a girl. That too would prove the validity of prayer.

Yet, living on the farm had taught her without subtlety the respective male and female roles. She knew there was no escaping her womanhood no matter how much she might fume at its limitations. Her mother and her nurse, Gostanza, had warned her she could not avoid destiny: to become a woman, a wife, and bear children.

"It is the duty allotted by God Himself," Madonna Ginevra explained, "And if the Holy Virgin did not protest at such a life, then my daughter must not complain."

"Aye," Gostanza muttered out of her mistress's hearing, "and sometimes motherhood precedes a marriage which then does not take place. May the blessed Virgin intercede for all female weaknesses in the face of soft-talking rogues of men."

Franca had a notion her words had something to do with the unhappy cripple, Taddeo. The stable boys threw stones at him, while all other people crossed themselves whenever he appeared . . . especially pregnant women. He was said to be half-witted because he mumbled to himself. Like some grisly carnival mask, a livid purple mark stained his upper face.

Berto Spenozzi hated him. Whenever Taddeo glanced at Franca, he would drag her away. "It's a vile sin," he declared passionately, "that such a fiend should be allowed to look on beauty . . . as if the inmates of hell peeped through the windows of Paradise."

Franca was not quite sure how she knew Taddeo was Gostanza's son, but it never surprised her to see the nurse creep out to give the stunted creature scraps from her own platter. Although Madonna Ginevra was pious and kind, she did not encourage beggars to crowd her doors: that would mean she was a wasteful housekeeper. Besides she was appalled by her maidservant's lapse and doubted whether Franca should be cared for by such a woman. Yet Gostanza had begged so hard to stay with the Narnis' beautiful baby girl, swearing by all that was sacred never to go with another man, nor have anything further to do with her miserable sin-made-flesh, that Madonna Ginevra had relented.

Gostanza did not know Franca often talked with Taddeo. He showed her the first wild strawberries, the hares dancing on spring mornings; he let her hold the fox cubs he reared because their own mother had been slain. His home was a cave near the charcoal burners' clearing deep in the upper forest. They paid him little attention, fearing intruders from the outside world more than winter wolves or outcasts seeking refuge in their trackless territory.

Franca rolled back on the ground, relishing her freedom, pointing her narrow feet towards the sun. There was no Madonna Ginevra to scold on the folly of idleness, and lolling with her skirts anyhow. "If only you would train yourself, Francesca, then in time to behave like a perfect lady, the future wife of an important man, would be no effort, but second nature . . ."

"One day," Franca vowed, yawning luxuriously and scratching flea bites, "I'll do it, but not just yet. Life is too sweet to waste sitting upright, sewing, praying, and learning."

There was no grumbling Gostanza either to warn her that acting like a hoyden could never tempt a fine rich gentleman to be a husband. Certainly not if she spent time in the company of Giovanni Spenozzi's boy.

"And getting up to Lord knows what," her nurse added darkly. "Though the blessed saints know you're but a child, yet there's plenty of strange men who prefer their fruit unripe. Berto may be only fifteen but the Spenozzi were always a curious secret lot. His grandmother was a witch

from Norcia—they're all witches there—and the boy has an
evil name. Just keep out of his way."

Franca had ignored Gostanza's warning for at least six
years and knew Berto as well as any of her own brothers.
If he had not been among the crowds bringing in the harvest, he would have insisted they spend this last golden hour
in their spasmodic pursuit of a wily carp that lived deep in
the dark lake.

Berto was the only son of a tenant farmer who worked a
few fields on the Narni estate. The one-roomed stone hovel
had smoke-blackened walls, and housed the family, an
emaciated goat, and some scraggy chickens. They ate plain
pasta unless Berto snared some wild creature in the woods,
or caught a fish. Franca never considered the differences in
their lives, only bemoaning the fact she was a girl and
couldn't run as fast as Berto. Maria Spenozzi's hands were
rough and red, but she was always mutely amiable to the
lord of Castelfiore's daughter, even allowing her to help roll
out the greyish dough for macaroni. Giovanni hardly ever
spoke to anyone. It was impossible to tell if he minded
Franca's occasional visits.

All the women around Castelfiore considered the Spenozzi
undesirable, and Berto the worst of the lot. A by-blow of
Satan, for surely his mother had danced naked with the
witches, and then copulated with the devil's cold, scaly horn.
One fine day Berto would end on the gallows, so they warned
their sons, but more particularly their daughters to keep
away from him.

He was tall, dark, and well made. The forbidden reputation
made his unsmiling features attractive to the girls, who gave
him soft, sideways glances with their liquid, knowing eyes.
The boys thought him a great lad: always ready with his
fists, strong enough to knock down a grown man, and with
enough manhood in his loins to father a legion of sons.

Slow-thinking and taciturn, Berto did not deny the tales

spread about him, so they grew. He was indifferent to the rumours. This increased his notoriety as a vicious, godless creature, who would violate any woman he encountered, be she nun or grandmother.

Franca de' Narni was the one member of the female species he had any time for. The others were good for only one thing, though naturally they feigned unwillingness, even when their eyes said "yes," so that, afterwards, he suspected, they could declare themselves ravished virgins, even if their maidenhead had vanished years before.

Not that he had been with any woman. All he knew was from listening to wineshop and stable gossip, and from what he'd seen in the woods when the couples thought they had the secret places to themselves. He knew just how the giggling, sighs, and foolery ended: ailing babes; the pretty wench suddenly an old nagging drab; and the man tied all the stronger to his master's land, out of necessity of feeding a new mouth every year. Freedom lost because spring had entered the blood, and a man acted out of instinct with an eager girl.

Surely there was another life for a man: else a peasant was no more than one of the beasts he tended. Yet, when the awakening of masculinity set his body afire, he feared one day, he too would be caught in that sweet brief snare which led to eternal captivity and turned the dreams of youth into the sterile dust of discontented age.

Franca had inspired his restlessness: She was entirely outside his knowledge of females. Unlike the rest of 'em, she didn't weep all the time, not even when she cut her knee. She didn't make sheep's eyes, or chatter about love, or run to her mother with false tales of how he had pulled her hair, tried to lift her skirts, or used a bad word. She did not look for miracles behind each bush, as his sisters had done before they were pinned down to reality with babes in their bellies and unwilling husbands to wait on.

"So now folks are saying it wasn't religion Tessa and

Gina found in the forest," Berto growled to Franca one day in disgust and shame.

According to Gostanza the Spenozzi sisters were harlots: They lay with any man for the joy of it and a crust of bread, so it was no miracle how their bellies had been filled.

Franca demanded in her usual direct manner, "If they are so poor and hungry, how can we blame them seeking pleasure?"

"Don't ever let me hear you say that." Gostanza's own fall made her unforgiving. "Death is better than to lie with a man without a wedding ring."

"So the giving of a ring makes the same thing good that was bad without it," her small charge added thoughtfully.

"It is a sacrament." Gostanza crossed herself, thanked God that Madonna Ginevra was not around, and wished she hadn't plunged into such deep waters.

Berto loved to hear Franca talk in her strange husky voice that did not quite belong to childhood. It could crackle like crisp autumn leaves, and then slide away as dreamy as the sweep of birds' wings on still air. It was none of your usual girls' daft chatter. She told him all she knew of the places beyond Florence, even across the seas: of the dread and godless Turk who had wrested Constantinople from the Christians twenty-four years before, of ivory, gems, monkeys, ginger, and cloves that the merchants brought back from the east. Strange words described goods unlike anything the itinerant peddlers displayed in the villages on feast days.

She told him all she read in her father's famed collection of manuscripts and new printed books: the sad and bawdy tales from Boccaccio's *Decameron*, the dread images of hell in Dante's own words, Petrarch's Italian poetry, and the wonders from Ptolemy's *Geographia*. The more tantalized he was by these fragments from an unattainable world the more he brooded about his own lot.

Sometimes Franca spoke of her dream to sail far away

and discover some uncharted world which she and Berto could rule. His unimaginative, hungry soul believed it would happen. He sat with mouth open, and hands idle, as she recounted the preparations for her brother's great journey in the russet-sailed carrack, *San Miniato*, from Maremma. Her father had poured a fortune into Raffaello's expedition to find trade with Naples, Sicily, Greece, and Spain. The youngest son was more practical than the others, and longed for travel.

He had departed before the storms. It would be a year till his return. If the voyage proved a success then Raffaello would bring back fifty to a hundred times what had been invested. Besides the lure of wealth, the Florentine spirit of gambling found this kind of risky venture irresistible. As well as the natural hazard of storm and shipwreck, there were the pirates working for their own gain or in the pay of rival kingdoms, and of course the Moors with their fast, light craft whose fight against the Christians was holy.

Raffaello might be murdered, or tortured, or sold into slavery, or forced to abjure his faith. Franca spun a great story about his adventures until sometimes her tears flowed at the privations her mind imagined he was enduring. Then she would laugh at her fancies, like sunlight bursting through a storm. The sudden change of mood reminded Berto of the kingfisher on his brilliant flight among the reeds, flashing with colour, alighting in tremulous beauty, until the watcher cannot believe his eyes—only that he must be dreaming of this swift lovely vision.

There was another talent Franca possessed that only Berto had really noticed. With her thin child's hands she could fashion out of mud or clay dogs, birds, soldiers, and ships. With a twig or a feather dipped in dye from petals, or juice from berries, Franca made pictures from her mind: battles, castles, streets, ugly and beautiful faces on some smooth white stones. She could not explain how she did these things, except they seemed to spring from her fingertips as the brain visualized them.

Berto marvelled that such magic could be wrought, and feared it. Yet when he was with Franca he believed she could do anything she chose. She was a fairy child who wove an enchanted ring around them, and in which he could forget the outside world, its indignities and injustices.

Franca did not believe there could ever come a time when the two of them would not wander the countryside.

"And when I'm bigger," she said confidently, "we shall walk further. Over the hills to Pistoia, where they make those fine daggers."

She did not understand the impotent misery and anger in Berto's black eyes.

Neither talked of their friendship. Franca was forbidden the company of boys, or even to play outdoors without the attendance of nurse or tutor: a rule which had proved unenforceable. Berto knew this relationship would have been the subject of coarse jests. He didn't want Franca's name linked with his. Other people would not understand, only besmirch everything with their foul lies.

It just wasn't fair that soon she would grow up. Then their disparity of rank would be irrevocably apparent to her. He could no longer be the playmate who took out splinters and stings, buttoned her gown, or tidied her hair so that her appearance would not provoke too much curiosity when she arrived home late. As a man he would merely be a boorish, unlettered peasant, to whom she would not even care to bid good day. His little Franca would be an exquisite gifted lady, the finest in the whole of Florence or anywhere else he didn't doubt, and wife to some knight, worthy of a king.

When Berto thought of that inevitable marriage he was consumed by such fury he battered his fists against a tree trunk until blood ran down his arms, but pain did not drown the knowledge the future must lead them along divergent roads and the slowly developing body could not become woman in his arms. He would no more have touched her carnally than he would have spat on a statue of the Virgin. It would have profaned his deepest faith.

Franca knew nothing of his torment and found him neither wicked nor fierce, only superstitious and silent compared with the voluble, questioning Narnis. But then she saw a side to his character no one dreamed existed. Anyhow she preferred to do all the talking.

Her education owed as much to Berto's rough influence as to Ser Agnolo, who had been her brothers' tutor, and was now, in his own opinion, working off days in Purgatory, by attempting to teach the Narni girl.

Franca squinted up through the interlacing of leafy boughs and began to giggle at the memory of poor Ser Agnolo's scandalized face when she told him her own forthright views on Paradise. The pale features seemed to grow even narrower, until she thought his face would disappear, and the long unhappy nose glowed red with indignation.

". . . and if it's not like endless summer, singing among our lovely hills with fegatèlli for dinner," she was stung to insist, "then I don't intend going there. I shall seek out those ancient gods, whom the Greeks wrote about as having a very good time."

"My little pagan!" Vincenzo de' Narni exclaimed with amused affection, avoiding his wife's horrified gaze. "Our ancestors' crusades to the Holy Land did nothing to erase the blood left by Etruscan forefathers."

Madonna Ginevra crossed herself and automatically began to tell her beads. Of course, Franca was a foolish child. Yet, she had spoken heresy and blasphemy. The sin could not go unpunished on earth in case a higher authority demanded greater punishment. In order to drive these unholy concepts out of her daughter's rebellious head she had forced her to kneel in prayer in the musty chapel one glorious afternoon when Franca and Berto had planned to catch trout. That evening, a wooden bucket appeared containing three fat fish. Franca understood Berto didn't blame her for not keeping their appointment, something that troubled her all afternoon and caused the penitent expression.

Madonna Ginevra also hung a great topaz set in a golden claw on a gold chain about the girl's slender neck. The stone ensured its wearer's chastity. Franca loved jewellery: her mother could not really be so angry if she gave her such a pretty trinket—one she had worn as a girl.

She reached inside the wool-embroidered bodice of her linen gown and drew out the jewel. Against the light it was a mass of crystallized sunshine. Flashes of gold radiated from the many surfaces. Her eyes fixed on it until she felt drawn into its yellow depths. . . .

The golden trance broke as the advent of evening was emphasized by vespers chiming out from San Francesco. Almost immediately the call was taken up by bells pealing throughout the valley. Then came the sonorous tones of the great bell in Castelfiore's tower, summoning the household to the evening meal. The labourers in the fields knew the long working day was over.

Carts, loaded with hay like plaited gold, and huge panniers spilling forth masses of jade and amethyst grapes, trundled along the rough tracks, churning up clouds of pale dust which inflamed the eyes and further whetted the thirsts of harvesters trudging behind. Pairs of snowy oxen swung heavily towards the farms, as dignified as the white-haired grand-sires in the market place. From every side came the plaintive lowing of heavy-uddered cows going home to be milked. The cooling air was full of chatter, laughter and snatches of song, as if the whole world was suddenly happy to be released from its toil. Franca blithely joined in the refrain of a ballad.

"An hundred, and yet one, are we;
In heart and will we're all united,
Let every dancer jump for glee,
And he who will not be blighted! . . ."

Hunger drove Franca homeward like a spiked goad . . . although part of her longed to stay out among the deepening shadows to watch the new sickle of golden moon drift over the city, and the sparkling stars peer down through the olive trees like jewels mislaid amid the branches.

The memory of Tullia's words made her race down the steep hill towards Castelfiore. That morning while Madonna Ginevra was at Mass, Franca had crept down to the vast kitchen. It was hot, steaming and dark but for the glare of the enormous enclosed cooking range. Always full of noise and movement, it was affectionately named by Tullia "Maestro Dante's Inferno."

She whacked maids, kitchen lads and flies with a wooden ladle used for tasting everything from broth to sweet batter . . . and screamed like a wounded boar if anyone annoyed her, or too many rats scampered in her territory.

Only the sight of Franca softened the woman's glowering expression. To the girl it seemed incredible this mammoth creature had once been the most popular strumpet in the San Spirito quarter of the city. Madonna Ginevra had taken Tullia into the Narni household to reform her, and the slender temptress became the largest and best cook for miles around: sacrificing one fleshly pleasure for another.

Tullia had beamed greasily and crowed like a furious cockerel: "For my little darling I've made fegatèlli in case none of the special dishes are to your liking." She smacked her lips resoundingly, "Such beautiful calves' liver, so tender so tasty, they deserve a sonnet in their honour. They will make a dish fit for my princess, although"—Tullia frowned terribly and reminded Franca of an angry red moon— "there's some fools who consider fegatèlli only belongs on peasants' tables.

"As for the rest," the cook began counting on her bulbous fingers, "there's the sweetest melon cooling in the well, and my finest berlingòzza, as light as a virgin's first kiss."

This large cake of flour, sugar, and eggs was a speciality at wealthy men's tables, but the Narni version was regarded as supreme. In Franca's honest opinion, it didn't compare with everyday pasta fried and flavoured with garlic and cheese, but she would certainly have a large slice of it after the melon.

". . . and my famous sausages, and plump capons, and tender veal stewed with rosemary, raisins, wine, and spices, and young kid with almonds, and delicious lampreys . . . oh, and a few trout—" Tullia continued her litany to the belly, "They're for the finicky, or those whose heads are overcome from too much Trebbiano. There's some fine ripe cheeses, and fruit . . . and those saffron jellies you love, shaped into fishes. Just you wait till you see the palace of marzipan. No one will go to bed hungry tonight. I, Tullia, swear that."

She thumped her massive bosom as if it were a drum. Madonna Ginevra left the task of upholding the reputation of Castelfiore's table to her cook, whenever there were guests: for she was more taken up with praying and fasting for the good of her soul than eating for the pleasure of her life on earth. Tullia considered this a blasphemy, but it did give her the opportunity to be munificent with ingredients.

"You, my little beauty, like to eat. God be praised. That's on the side of life. One day you will be ripe for love and bear fine sons. And your brother Andrea, that wicked scamp . . ." She rocked with laughter so that all her fat chins quivered like a dish of saffron jellies. "Holy Mother, how he likes to eat and needs it to pursue his amorous sport . . ."

The appearance of Madonna Ginevra curtailed Tullia's rich remarks about Andrea's flagrant pursuit of Lucrezia Donati, Lorenzo de' Medici's titular and virtuous mistress.

Poor Mamma, Franca thought kindly. She believes I don't know what dearest Andrea does with the lovely ladies in the city.

Castelfiore

THE FARM BUILDINGS were grouped around the ancient castle to form a great square. Granaries, stables, and cow byres occupied the lower story. Above dwelt labourers and their families, who tended the home farm.

Franca ran through the archway into the inner court. A flock of doves rose from the cote—white feathers gold-tipped, their soft voices as much part of Castelfiore as each one of its worn stones. The birds drifted down to mingle with the painted frescoes on the inner curves of the colonnades, or range themselves like sentries on the four outside stairways which led to the upper floors of the great house.

She pressed her face against a golden stone wall, feeling and smelling the warmth it had absorbed from a long summer. Castelfiore's unhurried seasonal life was as secure as sunrise and sunset, and Franca loved it wholeheartedly.

She gazed at the brilliant frescoes which never failed to entrance her. How proud she had been the day her father had allowed her to help mix the colours when he refurbished them. Then she had understood just how complicated it was to produce the new damp "buon fresco" which lasted so well and couldn't scale, because the colours seeped right into the walls. Both Gostanza and Madonna Ginevra had been appalled by her stained fingers and insisted she'd be better occupied at real lessons. Painting could never be the province of women, but Franca had remained in silent disagreement.

These frescoes lived in her mind. She had studied them minutely since her eyes first grew aware of sight. The lion, who miraculously failed to devour Daniel, had a friendly, doggish face like old Cassio. The Red Sea that Moses divided for the Israelites contained some dumpy cross-eyed fishes. The "Wedding at Cena" was lightened by an old man asleep in a corner unaware of the great miracle.

More than anything Franca preferred the tournament scenes—so vivid and brave that sometimes she listened for the crash of arms, the snort of horses, the cheers, the screams. All the sounds she could remember from that glorious tournament held two years before in honour of the exquisite Simonetta, Guiliano de' Medici's mistress. Her flame of beauty had already been extinguished by consumption, but Sandro Botticelli's miraculous art had made her and himself immortal with the painting of the "Primavera."

It was then Andrea, looking like Apollo, all gold and white, and wearing some unnamed lady's favour, overcame the eldest sons of the Pitti, Salviati, and Pazzi clans in chivalrous combat. The delighted crowds had been swift to note that the sweet Lucrezia Donati had bestowed her gentle smile on Andrea de' Narni, so that many wondered if hers was the glove pinned to the handsome youth's sleeve, and it was said that Lorenzo's eyes were narrow with resentment. The family had little time to enjoy Andrea's popularity, for Umberto had contracted the plague while watching the tilting, and the sunlit glory of a battle game became entwined with the reality of death. Vincenzo de' Narni had nursed his youngest boy without fear of catching the disease, but the plague reaped its unripe harvest. To Franca it seemed Umberto had gone on a long visit; when she thought of him it was to wonder if he would return grown taller. Death had not yet proved itself to be any great tragedy. It was, after all, as normal as birth.

The light in the empty court was red and made the intricate patterns on the flagstones appear freshly painted. Like some beacon the rounded time tower was wreathed in fiery creeper. Vermilion leaves nodded about the sundial and the clockface and whispered that they did not care for time.

The place was deserted. Even the dogs were at their food. There was no chance to make herself tidy. Gostanza would be cross, for she had laid out the new green-and-yellow-shot taffeta. Hastily Franca smoothed down the rough skirt, recalling the blissful softness of that other gown, but the tantalizing aromas of food chased out vanity.

She did not bother to look into the familiar white chamber, with its dark wooden supports making elegant patterns on walls and ceiling, where the family generally ate, talked, and played games and music in summer. Tonight they were dining in the great hall so the guests could admire the costly new wainscotting. Each time she saw it, Franca marvelled that wood could be carved to make flat surfaces appear like chairs, a desk, and cupboards full of books and musical instruments.

She pushed her way among the serving men and women. Candles had not yet been lit in the vast chamber. The long table was illuminated by the last soft light of day. The high ceiling and distant corners were already in darkness; the company grouped about the table seemed to be under a golden halo. Through the open shutters, the outside world was tranquil beneath the new moon.

The place was warm with the throb of chatter and bursts of masculine laughter. The best of the Narni silver and gold chinked musically against the majolica dishes. The few rare pieces of Venetian glass sparkled like rubies. The air smelled of good food and wine. The berlingòzza rapidly disappeared amid enthusiastic praise.

Despite his wife's unspoken disapproval Vincenzo de' Narni never allowed mealtimes to be formal, and insisted children, dogs, and their tame goose, Bicci, were part of the company. Those who wished could talk. Those who desired could make music and sing. All he required—and Franca had learned this as a baby—was that anyone who spoke, or played, or sang should do his best. He was not content with prattle or false notes. Talk should be witty or informative, music tuneful.

Beside the empty hearth, with the Castelfiore emblem of two towers set inside a ring of lilies carved on the immense triangular chimneypiece, the newest member of the family, Franca's nephew, Christofero de' Domenico Narni, aged five months, gurgled in his basket, a splash of milk on his fat chin. Madonna Isabetta smiled down at him, while she laced her tawny velvet bodice. Her cheeks were plump and glowing, her round blue eyes were proud and content.

Domenico led her to the table. He looked upon his wife and firstborn with extreme tenderness and the same keen interest he gave to all life on the estate. Domenico was happy to have married his childhood sweetheart, although she came from a very ordinary family who owned only two farms and had no business connections in the city. Other girls had been offered him, with greater dowries and noble relatives, but he had been obdurate. Isabetta came from good stock and would produce lusty children without any finely bred airs, and he wanted to wed young. Now she had proved herself to them by bearing his son. This new mantle of motherhood gave the plain, good-tempered girl the assurance and dignity of more than seventeen years and an uneducated background.

Franca loved Isabetta, who uncritically mended her gowns

to prevent Gostanza's wrath. She was as predictable and stolid as her husband, and neither of them minded being teased about their rustic life. They waited comfortably for the next baby, secure in the knowledge that harvest must follow seed time—and they intended to live out their days as part of that great cycle.

Franca missed Raffaello, so conspicuous by his absence, since wherever he was arguments and fights abounded: Castelfiore had never known such peace as the past two months. He was as sharp and questioning as the other Narnis, but without the sweetening of his mother's nature, or his father's lazy good humour: the dash of pepper in the Narni dish. Raffaello reminded Franca of an aggressive little bull: shorter and stockier than his brothers, but with hair just as red, his face forever irascibly flushed, and eyes a scorching blue like the core of a candle flame.

Standing in the shadows Franca was a spectator on this vivid tableau, enjoying the few seconds before stepping into the scene to take up her role. She was safe, content, hungry, and close to nearly all her dear ones. It was truly raining caresses, to use one of her father's favourite quotations. Paradoxically, she felt cheated that such a perfect moment could not be held forever.

Even now as I think, she mused, time is passing. With bewildering clarity the girl perceived everything was in a state of perpetual change. There could be no finite except death . . . or to transcribe the scene into words, or paint, or bronze. Yet the most perfect representation by the most skilled hand could be no more than an approximation to the reality as felt.

So there was no forever. It was a momentous recognition. Soon, she was to thank her mind for revealing this truth ahead of maturity. At present, she mourned for the happiness which like some delicious sweetmeat melted away even as she relished it.

Is that what always troubles my mother, she wondered, studying the woman who sat on the left of Vincenzo de' Narni and in the old-fashioned manner shared his platter? The quiet brown eyes were so often glazed with unshed tears, the hands always folded in a beseeching attitude as if begging life to treat her gently. The bronze velvet houppelande trimmed with sable, the heavy golden necklace, shoulder ornaments, bracelets and earrings, studded with large amethysts, seemed a burden rather than a decoration. Beneath the golden gauze butterfly, Madonna Ginevra's face was drawn and weary. The sockets round her eyes were full of shadow, and the lines at the corner of her mouth gave it a sad droop.

She reminded Franca of the Mother in a Pietà. The girl felt guilty. What right had she to feel such compassion for her own mother? Yet, it always seemed that Madonna Ginevra was never at ease in the rambling castle, with her noisy children and smiling, thoughtful husband. She seemed an alien, a visitor to her own family, who would prefer to live in their elegant palazzo down in the White Lion district of the Santa Maria Novella quarter. Unlike the heads of other prominent families, Vincenzo de' Narni preferred to reside in the country for most of the year, instead of merely during the hottest, disease-ridden months.

Ginevra de' Narni glanced down at her be-ringed hands clasped over her swelling belly. This was her fifteenth pregnancy. She had done her duty to Vincenzo, and borne him four living sons, and a daughter who promised to be a great beauty. She thanked the Virgin for blessing her so much more than many women. Though she could not understand her children's tempestuous natures, at least they were healthy and well formed. Thus, it did not seem a sin to pray in the darkness of the great marriage bed that this would be her last confinement. She was very tired, and her head and back ached. It would be bad to miscarry now. How the men

talked . . . but it was their world, and had always been so
. . . she could barely understand one word in ten.

Her upbringing had been founded on extreme piety and
modesty. She had been taught to converse only with other
women. To express an opinion on anything beyond house-
keeping and children still seemed to Ginevra, even after
twenty-three years of marriage, indelicate and unchaste.

Vincenzo considered such ideas archaic. She had reluctantly
yielded to him on the matter of Franca's education and
knew her daughter would grow into one of the sophisticated
breed of Florentine women who were intellectually equal
to their husbands, could converse widely and wisely, and
draw the great thinkers and artists to their tables. Yet, what
did it profit them? Still their role was to conceive, bear, and
rear a child. All the Latin, Greek, logic, and geometry in the
world could not alter that fact, or make nine months but
five minutes.

The learning had only enabled Franca to read her father's
manuscripts, all of which, except the religious writings, were
unsuitable.

If the girl had to be educated beyond housewifely duties,
Ginevra would have preferred to send her to a convent where
all knowledge would have true Christian foundations and
not be tainted with this Humanism her husband so admired,
which impiously questioned all that had been accepted for
centuries.

Then she noticed her daughter. Franca's gown was creased
and stained from moss. Blackberry juice had turned her lips
dark crimson. Wilting honeysuckle was tangled among her
thick curls, for she had woven a chaplet of the sweet-scented
blooms, and then admired the effect so much in the surface
of a pool she had quite forgotten to throw it away.

"Francesca Lauretta de' Narni, where have you been?"
Madonna Ginevra shook her head so that the gauze butterfly
fluttered like a shimmering cloud. "You're so late, and how

untidy! What would Botticelli say? To think his miniature depicted you as one of the graces! Pay your respects to your father's guests, and sit down."

All heads turned to the girl. Carlotta Corbizzi—a distant cousin—blew her a kiss. Isabetta removed the tired honeysuckle. Franca turned laughing eyes to the company, made a graceful curtsy, and then grinned unrepentantly at her father.

Madonna Ginevra bit her lips crossly, but her husband held out his arms to their daughter. The girl would never learn discipline from him. He was always saying childhood endured so briefly that he wanted his children to be free to enjoy it.

Franca threw her arms around him and kissed his mouth. She loved to see his face close, with its strange tawny eyebrows which seemed to leap about above pale green eyes that lived in deep lines forged by constant good humour. His unruly russet hair had a streak of gray, and he, too, had failed to change into the fine clothes his wife preferred him to wear. The ragged sleeves of his green, everyday robe were stained and spotted with paint and powders: evidence of his two overmastering pursuits—painting and chemistry.

"My bad girl," he said affectionately, "what will our guests think of me for allowing you to be so wild?"

Franca peeped at the stranger next to her father, and saw wise black eyes studying her with unwavering attention.

"Eat." Vincenzo patted her shoulder. "You must be hungry."

She slid into her chair, and with more zeal than grace dipped grimy hands into the bowl of lavender-scented water her father's page, cousin Lionello, handed her. They eyed each other without comment, as if they had not fought that morning, after he'd pulled her hair and said that girls should not be running and jumping as they were so bad at it. They should sit and sew and pray for a husband, like his

sister Nannina. Franca had immediately challenged him to a
race, and then beaten him by a whole *bracchia*, so he had
to swallow his words.

She dried her hands vigorously and handed him the
fringed towel. As he took it, Franca made a face, crossing
her eyes and screwing up her nose. Lionello hurried away
in case he was drawn into another scene that would damage
his reputation. Franca noticed the handsome stranger observed these actions. To cover her faint confusion she
winked at Nofri across a wedge of yellow melon.

"You look very fine and learned, Maestro brother."

His serious features were parchment compared with the
sun-touched skins of his relatives. Yet when he grinned, his
greenish eyes were gay with Narni laughter, and the thin,
straight hair was bright red though it already receded from
his high forehead. The deep purple gown was costly and
trimmed with lustrous fox, a heavy gold chain hung about
his neck, and many rings adorned the thin, nervous fingers.

"While you, little sister, resemble a shepherdess in one
of Lorenzo de' Medici's poems in praise of rusticity. Don't
you remember any of our guests?"

Franca smiled in recognition at an elderly man with a full
grey beard and deeply set brown eyes. "It is the gentleman
of the sweet spices!" she exclaimed.

The company laughed. Paolo del Toscanelli could often
be found in the spice merchant's warehouse of the San
Spirito quarter, which belonged to his nephews, but he was
famed near and far as physician and astronomer. The
doughty navigator, Christopher Columbus, had sought his
sea charts and advice to seek out routes to new lands full
of wonders and riches. Toscanelli also owned a magnificent
library of scientific works, where scholars came to browse.
Franca had heard he was among those who considered the
world to be round like a China orange. She had spent some
time trying to convince Berto without being too sure of her

facts. "But if it is," she'd declared triumphantly, "we can sail round it!"

"And I recall," Toscanelli said gravely, "a certain little lady who came into the warehouse with her father, and whose pretty but inquisitive nose could not be kept out of sacks and bins. One deep sniff ended in a fit of sneezing that shook the bats out of the rafters and sent the 'prentices running as if the earth quaked!"

Franca laughed. She had not realized how strong pepper-corns were.

"Because you like to breathe sweet aromas I have brought you a gift." He dug into the pouch suspended from a jewelled belt and produced a fine gold chain on which hung a tiny pierced orb.

Franca inhaled deeply, closed her eyes, and murmured: "Ah, so sweet. What is it, Maestro Paolo?"

"Cloves, cardamon, coriander, and nutmeg." The words had a magical ring to them. "When you visit the city use this pomander against the foul odours rising from the river and the narrow streets.

"Thank you, my doctor of spice." She kissed him and called to her mother, "Would you like to smell this pretty thing?"

Madonna Ginevra held out her hand, but Isabetta inter-vened. "Nay, Franca, your mother must not inhale anything which might irritate her nose. To sneeze is bad when you are carrying. God!" she added merrily, "what trouble we had to stop me sneezing while Christo was on the way."

"And do you advocate such beliefs, Nofri?" Vincenzo demanded. "I'm for destroying old myths and letting new ideas take their place. Yet, the ladies, bless them"—he smiled indulgently at his wife—"cling to their grandmothers' advice."

Nofri said gravely: "I think the ladies are right in this instance, sir. A sudden jolt disturbs the child and might pro-

duce a miscarriage, or misplacement which would make the
birth hazardous. This is woman's province though, kept near
as secret as the ancient Bacchic rites. Mainly we are forbidden to attend confinements and still don't know enough
to help mothers and save babies."

Toscanelli nodded. "Your son is right. The Church prevents genuine doctors from discovering so much, although
I realize many of our profession are naught but mountebanks
and rogues, doctoring with simples concocted of cabbage
leaves."

There was laughter. It was the current city joke that any
cabbage patch contained all the nostrums . . . and a cuckold's
garden held a deal of parsley!

"We are gradually gaining respect," Nofri added. "Sometimes I wonder whether we should follow ancient Galen's
teachings quite so blindly. It is almost medical blasphemy to
ask this: But are his discoveries made some twelve hundred
years ago really the final words on anatomy and medicine?
We have borrowed much valuable knowledge from the
Arabs . . ."

"Surely," Madonna Ginevra interrupted timidly, "the infidel knows nothing of value, and I believe our doctors
must work best in conjunction with holy relics."

Franca stared openly at the man with the glittering black
eyes whose soft tones seemed to make the shadows leap
with astonishment. His pointed beard was unusual on so
young a man. Above the amused mouth a fine dark mous-
tache gave him a sardonic air. "Madonna Ginevra, during
my travels through Europe and to Jerusalem, I have seen
wondrous things, and also many foolish ones. The Moslem
has plenty of wise notions that have not been constrained
by the Holy Father in Rome and can follow paths of
thought, which are not open to our savants on grounds of
heresy and the terror of being accused of witchcraft. Knowledge should not wear blinkers, even if it sometimes confounds

all we have held true and sacred for centuries. Let us question everything afresh, and learn to be wise."

Madonna Ginevra's gasp of horror made Franca start. What
right has this man to disturb my mother, she thought furiously?

"The churches all over Christendom are full of relics," he
continued ruthlessly. "How many phials of the Virgin's milk,
how many heads of saint this or that, and so many splinters
of the true cross I verily believe our Lord was crucified in
a whole forest! Nay, madonna, I tell you truly—and though
you may doubt I am a Catholic—sometimes I am ashamed
our religion can be so ridiculed, and that the priests will buy
up such relics often knowing themselves to be duped in
order to have glory attached to their churches . . ."

Vincenzo nodded vigorously. "I am sure Messer Ridolfo
speaks sense."

Franca stole a glance at her mother and saw the brown
eyes were glowing with angry tears and that she twisted the
crucifix hanging on a finger ring. Meekness did not permit
her to argue with any man.

"You only underline what I have always thought of
priests," Vincenzo went on, glad to have such a well-
informed ally. "I would not let any of my children enter
religious orders which have become so corrupt. I believe it
is the greater evil to take vows and forswear them with
rich clothes and every kind of fleshly indulgence than to be
a sinner in the world outside. I would not have my girl
taught by the nuns either," he added with unusual vehemence, "for I am all in favour of worldly education, but
not when it is given with sly winks and nods. I would not
have Narnis sin against the light they have sworn to keep
burning . . ."

The arrival of platters of meat halted conversation. The
fegatèlli dish beside Franca emptied rapidly. Now and then
she found the bearded stranger watching her with amuse-

ment, but she threw back her hair and continued eating. I do not like that man, she thought; he makes everyone feel uncomfortable and enjoys it. Yet her eyes often returned to his compelling figure.

One guest ate more ravenously than anybody, and as usual his untidy beard was scorched. Between great mouthfuls of stewed kid he explained: "I am working on new designs, but though I badly need the florins that work pays me, it uses up so much valuable time . . ."

"My friend Cosimo"—Nofri spoke with mock severity—"you are foolish to spend your talented time on alchemy. You are nearly ruined."

Franca's eyes opened wide. They said Cosimo Rosselli was a magician. "I don't think Maestro Cosimo has found the Philosopher's Stone yet," she piped.

"Little Franca has a sharp eye." He grinned. "You're noticing my garments, eh?"

His velvet gown was worn and rubbed, and the stockings so often darned they seemed patterned. He was bereft of jewellery except for one thin silver ring, and his gaunt restless hands were stained and burned from his experiments.

"We artists have our weaknesses," he murmured, smiling dreamily at Franca. "Perhaps that is the way our God forces us to realize we're merely human beings when our fellow men tell us we have the divine spark at our fingertips. Sandro Botticelli dotes on his wine and girl friends. The sweet Filippino's late father, Fra Filippo Lippi, adored lovely ladies to the point of idiocy. Your brilliant friend Leonardo, Maestro Paolo, is always bursting with marvellous and impossible schemes, but fresh ideas frequently force him to leave old ones incomplete. My own weakness might at least bring me a fortune.

"Last week I vow I was so close. I had just reached the Yellow, the stage of Separation. It is not easy to get thus far . . ."

Franca's father leaned forward, nodding expectantly.

"At any moment the final step would be in my grasp, I am sure I should have created the Stone that would give me gold, and the secret of life . . ."

The company ceased eating, held by the artist's words. "Then my neighbour's flea-bitten mongrel ran in. Seeing the steaming pot, he overturned everything and ruined the experiment—all because I had once been foolish enough to feed him a mutton bone. He thought I must be preparing one for him again . . ."

Even Madonna Ginevra laughed at this, and cups of wine were raised in tribute to Rosselli's sweet humour. He did not seem embittered, even though he'd lost an eyebrow in the explosion.

"Did you know, Vincenzo, that San Ambrogiano is being renovated at long last?" Rosselli's voice was distorted by the leg of capon he gnawed. "Mino da Fiesole is producing the tabernacle, and the della Robbias the two angels. It's decided I shall paint the transubstantiation, and a picture of Our Lady with the saints. How I should love to use your wife's head"—he smiled kindly at his hostess—"she has just the features I bear in mind when I paint God's Mother."

Ginevra coloured. Her eyes smiled. Franca was happy that the ill-clad, comic figure had soothed the hurt the elegant worldly stranger had caused.

"Tell me, Rosselli," his authoritative voice demanded, "do you also use astrology . . ."

Franca knew Rosselli like her father consulted the planets' movements to discover propitious times for his experiments.

"Who is he?" she whispered to Domenico, who was stolidly chewing his way through a mountain of sausages and taking no part in the conversation. Mealtimes, he insisted, were for eating. I open my mouth to put in food. There's too much idle talk.

He swallowed a whole sausage and murmured behind

greasy fingers. "He's someone important from Milan. Supposed to be in the service of Duchess Bona. She's the French king's sister-in-law. Nofri told me privately that this Ridolfo clandestinely visited Pisa where . . ." Domenico looked round. "His close friend, Lodovico Sforza, lives in exile. He's the brother of the late Duke Galeazzo. Note how Ridolfo wears only mulberry-coloured clothes—a subtle announcement of his real allegiance since it's a pun on Lodovico's nickname Il Moro, which derives from one of his names, Mauro. The widow Bona is reputedly stupid and obstinate, but she won't have Cardinal Ascanio or Lodovico in Milan in case her wily brothers-in-law seize the power she ineffectually holds in trust for her young son, Duke Gian Galeazzo.

"Ridolfo is very rich, and a great patron of the arts. Those with little sense claim he's a magician. Our Nofri met him at Padua where he was studying law and medicine. Besides all this learning, he's said to be a first-rate soldier. Looks a shrewd devil, doesn't he?"

Gostanza and Lionello brought in the candles. Their winking flames made Ridolfo di Salvestro's slim figure glow like the interior of a goldsmith's shop on the Ponte Vecchio. His clothes were of the richest material, heavy with gold thread. Around his neck was a collar of rubies. Several precious rings embraced each finger. The cabochon ruby on his right thumb was engraved with a lion grasping a man in its jaws. Messer Ridolfo gave the impression of darkest night with his smooth sable hair and swarthy skin. The strong white teeth reminded Franca of some ferocious animal devouring its prey. He ate his food with one of those new forks—the first she had ever seen. It seemed a strangely graceful action for such a man, as if he attempted to conceal his power under delicate trappings.

It was the first time Franca feared someone without any apparent reason. Whenever Messer Ridolfo looked at her,

she longed to stretch out two fingers in "cornu" to ward
off the evil eye. Catching her glance, he smiled and bowed,
then whispered something to Vincenzo de' Narni.

Vincenzo laughed heartily. "Franca, my love, come here.
Our illustrious guest has asked me if you are already betrothed."

"For if you are not, Madonna Francesca," the soft voice
contained intensity, "I shall wait until you are of an age to
marry. My eyes tell me of your beauty. Your father and
brothers tell me of your wisdom, and I have observed you
have wit. In five years I shall be under thirty, which is not
old. I promise you a fascinating life and unquenchable love.
What do you say?"

Franca could not decide if he jested, but she would not be
discomfited and run away like a silly giggling child. His
mention of love made her skin feel strange as if it replied
to some question she neither heard nor understood.

She curtsied. "May I thank you for your offer, Messer. I
am indeed honoured, but unable to consider it, for I am to
be betrothed to Messer Lambarda della Sera's son, Daniello."

"The Medici's favourites, eh?"—he chewed his lip—"I
can't yet compete with such an influential family. To show
you bear me no grudge for putting such a bold question in
public, will you share this peach?" He cut the juicy globe
in two and handed her half on the little golden fork.

Franca recalled Berto's warning about witchcraft: if he
is indeed a stregone, as he seems, and I accept something from
him he will gain power over me. Then she gave a soft laugh
and bit into the fruit, watching him eat the other half. There
can be no bond, her mind said, unless I agree to it. The black
eyes regarded her fixedly.

"Your daughter is born under the sun, in the house of the
Lion," he said quietly.

"How do you know?" Vincenzo was delighted.

"Can you read the future?" Franca burst in excitedly.

"Ser Agnolo cast my horoscope, but it describes more my nature than my destiny."

"And she is as willful as good Ser Agnolo predicted," her mother remarked.

The tutor bowed his head in Madonna Ginevra's direction, and Franca noted that the whey cheeks had turned a sore red. He loves her, she thought, like the knights in old tales—a faithful lover seeking nothing but the right sometimes to speak with her. Franca knew her mother could not be aware of this, for then Ser Agnolo would have been sent away. The thought of a man's love would not quicken Madonna Ginevra's heart. Its shadow would endanger all she held sacred. Franca noticed her father's eyes smile roguishly towards the tutor, and she understood he shared this intuitive knowledge and was amused and compassionate.

Poor Ser Agnolo, she thought. If I were married, and a man other than my husband loved me, I should be proud. She smiled at the idea. The smile was returned by Messer Ridolfo. Franca had the uncanny sensation that this stranger knew her thoughts. Her large eyes regarded him fearlessly. "What can you tell me of the future?"

He took the small sunburned, right hand and traced the lines on the palm with his flashing fingers. Franca tried to conceal the tremor his touch provoked. The others at the table leaned forward. Isabetta muttered to her husband: "I fear that man. He has the power."

"Governed by the sun, fire cannot burn you, but others will be scorched by your bright flame . . ." he murmured, and then passed a hand across his eyes as if to obliterate whatever his wisdom showed. "Nay, Franca, I shall not tease you with lies of the future. There is too much shadow in our own times even to know the present with any certainty. Be happy while you may . . ."

Then, as if she were a great lady, Ridolfo raised her food-stained fingers to his lips and kissed them.

Franca was uneasy. This dark godlike man had cast a cloud over her own sun, and she knew foreboding, as if summer could be ended. Her hand felt inflamed as if it had been too close to the fire. No one spoke for a long minute.

Gazing at his daughter, Vincenzo momentarily glimpsed how she would look when grown: a beautiful, alluring woman, but what deadly clarity sparkled in those eyes . . . eyes that usually reminded him of the new violets found in the deepest part of spring woods, dew-glossed, peeping from under dark green leaves. For the span of a breath Franca's gaze held what he would have her ignorant of: complete knowledge of the world. Vincenzo wanted to throw up his arms and plead with fate, or the saints, or whatever power controlled their future: His little girl must not be corrupted or suffer. It was written she was to be wed, the mistress of a vast household, and know only beauty and peace. Whatever unhappiness Messer Ridolfo had read in her palm he would prevent. . . .

The tension around the table was broken by the barking of dogs outside. Old Cassio, Vincenzo's greyhound, rose to his feet, yawned and growled. Bicci strutted crossly in the shadows, honking warningly . . .

Storm Clouds

THE DOOR WAS FLUNG OPEN. Candle flames trembled and almost dissolved into darkness. The intruder was clad in the coarse, sleeveless garb of a humble labourer belted close about his tall figure. A hood concealed his hair and shadowed his face.

Without hesitation, Franca ran straight to the stranger. He

threw her high in the air. The hood fell back to reveal long, curling, red hair.

"Andrea! My sweet brother!" She clung to him, kissing his lips. "What has happened to your poor face?"

He smiled, but one eyelid was puffy and bruised, nearly concealing the eye beneath, although the other was as green and merry as ever. A wide gash on his smooth forehead was crusted with dried blood.

Ignoring all questions and greetings, Andrea moved to his mother and knelt at her side. He took one of her frail hands in both of his and kissed it with genuine devotion and love. "Madonna, Mother mine, forgive me for my unkempt appearance and tardiness . . ."

Ginevra placed her free hand on the thick hair so bright it seemed to emanate warmth. The Narni torch casting gaiety and light, friends said. With cunning to match a fox's brush, muttered others. She loved her firstborn intensely, yet he troubled her. How could this wild and sensual man have once been the tiny baby who had sucked the milk from her breasts so that she knew fierce joy and pain? She still recalled the pride of giving her husband a strong son as their first child . . .

She sighed as if in travail: "Andrea, why must it always be so? Fights and secrets. Why not settle with a good and sweet girl?" Her glance strayed to Carlotta, who was watching Andrea with anguished, adoring eyes. "Then there will be no need for brawls and disguises."

Andrea looked up at his mother with the same rapt expression he gave to the elevation of the Host. "Madonna, I am not good enough to be your son."

"Go and eat."

As she spoke, a tear fell on his forehead. For a second it pained Andrea more than the cuts and bruises. He rose to his feet, blinking as if dazzled by candlelight.

"You need food, Andrea," Vincenzo called, smiling and

understanding. "Afterwards you might care to give some account of how you earned your wounds, and why you are wearing such plain garb when I know, to my cost, just how much you spend on finery."

Andrea grinned and bowed to the guests. He began to eat with ravenous concentration, and Franca, sitting beside him, kept adding more food to his plate. She adored her eldest brother, who saw life as an unending sunny day . . . and loved his sister as much as that life.

"My little sweetheart," he whispered. "Surely there is no lady in Florence as beautiful and kind."

"You would know, eh, brother?" Domenico asked with sly good humour. "How you eat!" He closed one eye in a slow wink and then asked seriously: "Nofri, don't you think Andrea resembles Papa's horse, Scipio?"

Nofri considered, then gave a staccato burst of laughter. Andrea joined in, and the three brothers, alike in colouring, yet so different in temperament and interests, were linked. Franca also laughed, although the jest was not meant for her understanding.

As all the farm hands knew, the stallion liked nothing better than serving mares. Afterwards he would eat and eat. Many times Franca had witnessed Scipio's prowess, even joining in the burst of ribald cheering which the horse seemed to accept as his due.

She looked around the table. A great love welled within her embracing everyone from unborn babe to aged dog: To be a member of the Narni of Castelfiore was the most blessed fate in the world.

Despite teasing and entreaty, Andrea would say no more about his disguise than that it had been part of a wager to go around without friends recognizing him near the Mercato Vecchio.

"As for these wounds, they're nothing." He jerked his head as Nofri's fingers probed the cuts and applied a honey-based salve. "That stings worse than a dagger thrust. I was thirsty so I went to the Snail. The vernaccia is always good there, although the inn is in a cursed dark alley. When I came out some ruffians took exception to my face."

"Weren't those ruffians wearing some distinguishing badge?" Ridolfo di Salvestro demanded.

Andrea looked astonished and held the dark gaze. "They say you have magical powers of acquiring knowledge, Messer Ridolfo. You know as much about our city as you do of Milan," and he added significantly, "or Pisa. What are you suggesting?"

Ridolfo's smile made Franca uneasy, but his voice remained as gentle as the brush of taffeta. "And you, Andrea, appear to know a lot about my business. Yet, I do not fear your tongue, because the name Narni carries honour and no deceit."

Andrea bowed his head as if accepting a rebuke, and the guest continued: "Their clothes bore the Palle device."

The company stirred, for Messer Ridolfo had mentioned the proud and unmistakable emblem of the Medici's.

"How did you know?" Andrea whispered.

"Better pursue some other treasure than one already publicly prized by so noble and powerful a being."

Andrea's tanned skin darkened as the blood surged near its surface. "It's all rumour."

"Rumours provoke daggers as much as plain truth," Toscanelli remarked. "Be advised, Andrea. Admire the lady from a good distance."

"Both ladies," Ridolfo breathed.

Andrea reacted sharply. "You are the very devil with knowledge, Messer." Then he laughed. Sunlight poured over dark clouds. Franca's tension dissolved. "I broke at least three heads. They were forced to retreat. All because I wrote some pleasant verses in honour of a fair lady."

Vincenzo shook his head ruefully. He knew that at least two golden-haired toddlers on the estate owed their existence to his son's charming audacity. Girls just melted before his warmth. Andrea was kind and generous to the mothers of his love children and never avoided his responsibility, even if lately he rarely visited them. Lucrezia Donati, if that was really the quarry, was not a simple wench to be pursued, wooed, and won away from another man . . . not when the other man was Lorenzo de' Medici.

Gazing at Andrea, Franca was convinced that any woman must prefer him to the ruler of Florence.

At last, only flagons of wine, dishes of fruit and nuts, and Tullia's exquisite marzipan confection remained on the table. The men pushed back their chairs, and some loosened their belts. The ladies brought forward the embroidery frames to work at the altar cloth Madonna Ginevra had promised to the convent of San Francesco. Blushing at the enthusiastic masculine praise of their intricate and fine sewing, the three ladies started to sew, only stopping to compare threads or stitches in faint whispers.

From the safety of her father's feet, Franca prayed Gostanza would not suddenly appear with that wretched piece of needlework she was always endeavouring to mislay. "Your grandchildren will finish it for you at the rate you sew," Gostanza used to chide. "And those butterflies will turn back into caterpillars . . ."

Domenico began to mend a saddle. Nofri and Ser Agnolo returned to the chess board to continue the game they had started before the meal. While Rosselli sketched the sleeping Christo, Toscanelli and di Salvestro examined their host's latest acquisition from Vespiano Bisticci's bookshop, a handsomely illuminated copy of the *Aeneid*. They took it in turns to declaim their favourite passages. Franca found it difficult not to join in. It was her father's fond boast that she knew this work by heart. It wasn't surprising: Ser Agnolo's choice punishment was to set her to learn screeds of Latin and translate them into everyday Italian.

She noted with contemptuous amusement that Lionello was ostentatiously reading from the *Dialogue* of Santa Caterina of Siena, slyly looking up to see if anyone observed his piety in the midst of so much irreligious entertainment. Just like his awful father, the boy was always trying to win the attention of any important personage who might recall him favourably at some later date.

Andrea had said, "Uncle Weasel"—they all called Maximo di Aquia that for obvious reasons—"would crawl on his belly to any man's tune. He's afraid to fart in case it's against the wishes of some potential patron. It seems a shame that at fourteen Lionello has acquired a similar trait!"

Uncle Weasel volubly disapproved of the Narni attitude towards life and politics. He had only married into the family for the generous dowry but was never adverse to using their name when his own more meager one failed to open the right doors.

"Your father must have choked swallowing such a lump of pride," Andrea had observed when Lionello arrived, "actually sending his beloved son to act as page at Castelfiore, but I suppose he can bend his *antimagnati* principles as the Narnis often entertain renowned folk!"

Although Ginevra complained about her children's recklessness, she was dismayed by her nephew's constant displays of piety. Though practised silently they seemed to be accompanied by a fanfare of trumpets blaring: "Look at the good Lionello di Maximo Aquia! . . ."

"It's not normal in a child," she confided to her husband in their bed.

Vincenzo patted the soft face close to his own. "That young scamp is as two-faced as Janus. He doesn't fight, but he's always sneaking about bearing tales and causing other people to fall out. I don't like him now. Can you imagine how he'll be when he's a man? Poor Riccarda is too weak to have any influence over him."

He sighed, remembering his sister's plight. She had never seemed more than a chattel to be disposed of by their autocratic father, Messer Riccardo de' Narni, and she had never known how to do anything but bow down to the rule of all men. Vincenzo could not bear to visit the di Aquia residence in the city, for he was sickened by the sight of his sister—a pale shadow constantly in terror that her slightest glance, because of its Narni origins, might bring disgrace to her husband's noble profession as lawyer.

Vincenzo despised only lack of nobility of soul. "It is better to be a pauper with dignity and honour," he instructed his children, "than cast in the mould of that Maximo, who cannot even be loyal to himself." And he quoted Petrarch to remind them that they must not rely on their ancient name: " 'One is not born noble, one becomes noble.' "

"What do you think of the Medici?" Messer Ridolfo asked, putting aside the book, and breaking off a piece of marzipan. "I am to visit him soon and would know the manner of man I'm to deal with."

Vincenzo cracked walnuts and fed them to Franca. "A noble patron of the arts, always surrounded by poets and philosophers. A lover of beauty and gaiety, and much liked by ordinary folk for the wonderful spectacles he arranges on feast days. Truly he is not called the Magnificent without reason . . ." He added guardedly, "I have no quarrel with the Medici family, but it pays to be among their close friends especially in times of rigorous taxation—which is ever—but to be favoured by Lorenzo often means total tax exemption . . ."

"He is assiduous in scotching the faintest of plots against him," Toscanelli interposed. "Exile, assassination, or execution takes care of any potential rivals. Thankfully, he is not among those blood-crazed rulers who employ cruelty for the love of it.

"With subtle, almost invisible power, Lorenzo controls Florence by withholding offices from the *magnati* unless he personally trusts any particular family. He ensures the *Signoria*—our governing body—is composed of men without great names, or wealth, and whose loyalty is secure because they dread the return of the ancient families . . ."

Vincenzo glanced at Andrea who stood staring into the evening, uninterested in the conversation, and sighed: "Personally, Messer Ridolfo, I should advise every citizen to be loyal to the Medici, and try not to provoke his enmity."

He stroked Franca's cheek, and said soberly: "We shouldn't complain. The Medici keep their enormous banking concerns safe by controlling our state, and they wish to make Florence rich rather than embroil her in costly wars which only damage trade. Prosperity cannot flourish in the midst of turmoil. Alas, past attempts at so-called democracy lead to nothing but squabbling factions in the commune. Perhaps men will never be able to rule themselves. The increasing gulf in learning standards ensures that a favoured, highly educated minority must always gain control, because only they can understand the world and its complexities."

"Philosophers for rulers," Ridolfo said bitterly, "with hired soldiers to put right errors of thinking by the sword!"

Vincenzo frowned. "Each state wishes to be superior, and so all rulers fight and scheme for advantage." Soldiers, swords, and politics seemed to Franca an unfriendly intrusion in the familiar comfort and affection of home.

"None more so than His Holiness." Ridolfo spoke out sharply. "Examine most plots these days, and the villain is that bad-tempered, one-time fisherman from Savona, Pope Sixtus. His desire to increase papal domains is only exceeded by his incredible nepotism."

Madonna Ginevra's eyes were sad but she could not dispute this fact. Rumours of the life at the papal court sounded very like the debaucheries of ancient Rome. She had been shocked when the extravagant, carnal and cruel Pietro Riario had been made a cardinal. Nominally he was Sixtus' nephew, but everyone knew he was the Pope's son. Still, dissipation, or God's judgment, had killed the young cardinal within three years of his receiving his hat!

"Our present unrest is the fault of that ex-customs clerk, who used to sell oranges in the streets of Genoa." Vincenzo's voice contained venom. "Another of the Pope's favourite *nephews:* Giralomo Riario."

His sons laughed. Vincenzo and half Florence blamed young Riario, and his Holy Father, when anything went wrong . . . even if it rained for the *palio.*

"He's come a long way, that one," Vincenzo continued, "Captain General of the Church, and Commander of Castel Sant' Angelo. Serve His Holiness right the day dear Giralomo has to do any serious fighting. They say he's the biggest coward and military fool in Christendom. He's also Count of Bosco, and the Pope giving him control of Forli and Imola caused all our problems."

"Giralomo is loathed in Rome," Ridolfo commented. "He's fat, lazy, and cruel, and dare not walk abroad without a guard because of the many murders he's said to have committed. I attended the celebrations when he wedded our Caterina Sforza, the late duke's natural daughter. She's rich, lovely, and brilliant . . . and now pregnant. How she endures her boorish husband I don't know, but his new titles probably compensate for his character. The young Lady of Forli is an arrogant and forthright girl . . ."

She's only two years older than I, Franca mused, and Ser Agnolo claims, when he's in a good mood, I almost rival her in learning. Yet she has had to marry a vile and despised creature for political reasons. She shivered and thought of her own betrothal.

"My darling girl is cold," Vincenzo said with gentle concern.

Andrea lit a heap of pine cones in the grate. Soon the evening chill was banished by a soft warmth and the scent of woodlands. The flickering light made Franca sleepy, yet she did not wish to go to bed. It was pleasant to dwell in this circle and listen to the men talk of events which could not affect her life.

"Yet Florentine problems go back further than young Riario, my friend." Messer Ridolfo spoke earnestly, and Franca leaned forward to watch him. "Just look at the geography of politics."

With the point of a splendid jewelled dagger, he drew a rough map in the dust of the hearth. "Your territory"— he marked it with circles to emphasize the Medici's control —"is bounded on three sides by petty states, nominally papal in allegiance." He marked these with crosses. "But they look to the city of the Red Lily because of its greater trading power . . .

"Besides, your rulers have always been clever in taking their sides in disputes against other petty states, just so long as they were far away from your borders. It's easy to look brave by sending out a band of *condottieri*. Rome could equally claim such actions were subtle attempts to extend Florentine influence.

"We are all agreed that Sixtus is desirous of expanding his territory . . . not in a necessarily holy manner. It was no wonder he thought to secure Imola and Forli by making Riario their ruler. Look at their position in the plain of Romagna, just at the foot of the Tuscan Apennines . . ."

"Messer Ridolfo, you must allow that Lorenzo could not permit the little upstart to control these towns without some struggle," Andrea interrupted. "No one with half an eye would look away from Sixtus extending his power. Where will it end? None of us is safe. Milan and Venice are just as anxious as Florence about Rome's ambitions."

Nofri spoke quietly: "All the same, Lorenzo went about matters badly. The pact made in November, 1474, with Venice and Milan nominally to safeguard the peace of the peninsula, but actually to curb Sixtus' spreading power, has proved a great error."

"Why so?" Narrow dark eyes studied the speaker.

"It's simple, Ridolfo. In the past, Milan, Florence, and Naples were allies. Only after everything was arranged with this new pact did Lorenzo invite Naples . . . oh and of course the Papal States, merely for the look of the thing, to join the alliance. Even a child would take offense at such a piece of trickery. Would any of us join a pact after three other people had secretly conspired to form it, especially if we'd always considered we were all friends? That old treaty with Naples had existed since the Magnificent's grandfather's days. Poor old Cosimo must be turning in his grave. So now we have pushed cunning King Ferrante of Naples into the eager arms of Rome. Lorenzo sometimes spoils his game with speed."

"It's a matter of personalities," Toscanelli remarked shrewdly. "Sixtus and Lorenzo are both strong men. When either makes a mistake he knows it, but pride does not allow retraction. Each only gets deeper entrenched, determined to prove himself right."

Domenico, who hardly spoke unless it was about the price of maize or pigs, astonished his father by saying: "The final straw for Sixtus came when Lorenzo sided with the Vitelli family when they took Città di Castella. Then onwards the Pope was obviously determined to hit out openly and secretly at our state. It has become like some mad game of tennis. Can anyone know what or where His Holiness will strike next?"

"And what a hornets' nest the Pope stirred up," Rosselli observed, accepting the hot spiced wine Lionello offered round, "when he appointed Francesco Salviati as Archbishop of Pisa in place of a Medici. The Salviati clan are Lorenzo's archenemies in Florence, and they have ever hated the Medici upstairs as they think of the ruling family."

"It's not only that the Pope nominated a Salviati," Toscanelli said wisely. "Remember, His Holiness had given the Medici a solemn undertaking not to appoint bishops or archbishops in Tuscany without consulting the *Signoria*. Lorenzo could not be other than furious at this slight."

Andrea gave a shout of laughter. "Angry that he is! So's Salviati and his entire family. The Medici has them looking like fools. For the past three years Lorenzo has used *condottieri* to prevent the archbishop from entering Pisa . . ."

"It's not funny except in a comic poem." Ridolfo spoke cold reality. "These are not petty farmers squabbling over a prize sow. I am to talk with Lorenzo very soon because he wants to know Milan's exact strength in any alliance. Alas, we are greatly weakened after the murder of Duke Galeazzo by the wretched Lampugnano . . ."

"That was a dread business," Vincenzo said fearfully, "to kill a man on Santo Stefano at High Mass in the Duomo. I hear the assassins were only prevented from fleeing by the ladies' skirts. Galeazzo was in some respects a bad man, but . . ."

A bad man, Vincenzo mused silently. He could not say how wicked before the ladies. Galeazzo had relished the refinements of murder and torture . . . he had delighted in raping the ladies of his court, and even forced some victims into prostitution. Could an assassin's dagger really be an instrument of divine justice?

"Is it true that Duchess Bona asked Sixtus to ensure her husband escaped Purgatory?" Madonna Ginevra asked curiously.

Messer Ridolfo bit his lips to hide amusement. "Aye, for a deal of money Sixtus agreed. The only endearing streak in Bona's crass stupidity is that she did love Galeazzo while acknowledging his gruesome sins. I imagine the Medici fears

our weak and foolish administration, but let me speak bluntly
. . . as I shall to him. In our turn we fear that Florence,
despite her tremendous wealth, is being undermined by the
enemies Lorenzo has made, either by imperious action, or
through the violent hatred of the *magnati* . . ."

"Who hates the Magnificent besides the Salviati?" Carlotta
ventured, and her face was a blush rose. She rarely spoke
to any man outside the family, but gradually her needle
travelled slowly until it remained poised in her fingers, and
she listened openly to the conversation.

Ridolfo, looking at the smooth oval of Carlotta's face,
thought her beauty belonged to a purer world: a gentle,
unearthly being who made men remember virtue and attempt
a better life.

"You, madonna, are of an old honourable family," he
said gently, "who share the Narni view of the world. They
do not crave power simply because of their noble past. Yet
there are others who believe that a glorious family tree en-
titles them to great things in the present. After the Imola
business Sixtus found a practical way of attacking the Medici.
He took away the hefty papal account from their bank and
placed it with the Roman branch of the Pazzi bank. The
Pazzi are *magnati*, but in Cosimo's time they were removed
from that damning list that prevents nobles from rising to
high office. Therefore quite legally the family can look for
greater power, but not while Lorenzo holds the reins."

Ginevra pursed her lips. "You are saying in a somewhat
oblique way, Messer Ridolfo, that the Medici should beware
because the Pazzi family might attempt to usurp the Magnificent's rule. Don't you realize Lorenzo's sister, Bianca, is
married to Guglielmo Pazzi? She's a fine girl . . ." she added,
"not just at her books, for she manages her household very
well . . ."

Ridolfo raised his wine cup to his hostess. "Madonna, I
bow to your superior knowledge on womanly matters. You

may be right that the Pazzi do love the Medici because of this family connection. However, I shall urge Lorenzo, and his advisers, to study that rival banking firm . . ."

"I, too, fear things are coming to some climax," Nofri murmured. "From a distance Florence is not the calm trading city that we Florentines insist it must be. There are enemies inside and out. If real trouble arose it is not easy to guess which way the people would turn. Then I think . . ." and his wise eyes sought his father. "We shall be asked to state our true colours. There will be no place for those who try to remain outside the argument."

"May heaven forbid that your beautiful city become as Milan," Ridolfo said quietly. "Pray for the long rule of Lorenzo whatever his faults. Where there is weakness too many men seek to seize power. In their fight so many perish. The order and peace painfully won are easily lost, and it takes a long time to rebuild a strong state . . ."

Franca's soul stirred apprehensively: it was silly to fear fireside gossip, yet the words suggested a threat to her own future . . . as if the outside world could thrust its violence into their orderly midst . . .

"Enough of this gloomy talk," Isabetta cried, as the men's faces settled into grim and thoughtful lines. "Thank God, we live in the country away from all these problems." She smiled tenderly at her mother-in-law, then picked up her own child and clasped him to her breast. "Cannot one of you learned gentlemen cheer us with a song?" She stood close to her husband, who slipped his arm around her waist until a big callused hand lightly caressed their baby's golden head.

Still leaning against her father's knee, Franca let her eyes wander around the company. Their faces seemed unreal in the firelight. Ser Agnolo picked up a viol, while Andrea plucked at the lute strings. All the Narnis loved music, and were gifted in this art, but Andrea had the greatest talent.

More white than mother's milk are you
More red than dragon's blood your hue.
When at your casement you appear,
The sun is risen we declare.

The sun is rising, the moon sinks lower
Say good morn to your lover.
The sun is risen, the moonlight goes.
Say good even to your rose . . .

There was something intensely moving about the handsome man with the bruised face singing so passionately. Nobody could doubt he was in love. Carlotta's heart throbbed. Messer Ridolfo read her expression and shook his head.

Gostanza invaded Franca's haven. Her rough hands and scolding voice dragged the child to the normality of bedtime. She scarcely had time to make a faint curtsy to the company. Messer Ridolfo kissed his sparkling fingers towards her.

"I hope, little lady," he called out, and his voice seemed to follow her from the room into the shadows of her own chamber, "that we shall meet quite soon. It is already written that the great magician must bring us together . . ."

Her last glimpse of that stranger whose wise words and eyes disturbed her was a face etched against fire, which caught at the gems on his person.

Gostanza grumbled and questioned while she undressed the child, but Franca was too tired to reply. She was asleep by the time the woman climbed into their high curtained bed, still scolding the darkness and life in general . . .

Betrothal

FRANCA HAD vehemently objected to her hair's being washed. After all it wasn't a Saturday, the customary time for women to wash their heads in preparation for Sunday's blessed joy. Saturdays always saw meatless fare—you couldn't rely on any complicated dishes with most of the womenfolk washing, drying, curling, or colouring their tresses.

"If only the sun weren't shining I shouldn't mind staying indoors," Franca moaned, kneeling on a cushion-covered chest in the deep window embrazure. Warm gold countryside beckoned her through the open shutters.

"I never met a maid so unwilling to face her betrothal unless of course she was set on becoming a nun, which you show little signs of," Gostanza retorted. "Think, how fortunate you are. Many a girl is forced into a convent because her family don't want to find a suitable dowry. What's the world coming to? In the city, marriages are going out of fashion. Men and women actually live together without sharing a bed. They call it spiritual marriage. I call it plain stupid. At this rate human beings will come to an end."

She held up the soft curling skeins on the teeth of a double-sided carved ivory comb so that the morning sun glowed through a rippling brazen veil, and then let the hair drift back to envelop the child's nakedness.

The chamber was full of the sweet-scented warmth of the walled herb garden. Chamomile flowers and verbena had been steeped overnight in rainwater to rinse Franca's hair thirty times to keep it bright and perfumed. The unemptied bath still smelled wonderfully of roses, even though the water was cooling and cloudy.

Bathing and clean underlinen were daily rituals enforced by Madonna Ginevra's gentle rule. She insisted that a real lady was always fresh and sweet, no matter how she felt, and Franca looked on the customs as a pleasure rather than a chore . . . though Gostanza kept muttering that all this washing was unhealthy and only fit for dirty folk.

"Come then, my love," the nurse coaxed, kissing the girl's cheek. She slipped a new silk *camicia* over Franca's head, which temporarily stifled the protests, and then lifted the gown from the bed. Myriad Castelfiore emblems embroidered in golden threads and tiny pearls decorated the filmy white robe that peeped through the opening of the violet silk overskirts and at the top of the low square bodice.

Franca found it impossible to maintain a mutinous expression as soft cloth caressed her flesh, and perfume teased her nose. Whenever she moved silks whispered, jewels rang like distant church bells. Her lips relaxed, and her eyes dreamed, as Gostanza plaited a lock of hair with a string of pearls to form a bandeau which held back the cascade of curls.

The woman's harsh face softened. Her eyes misted. "Thank the sweet Virgin I have been spared to see you this day. May I live to dress you on your wedding day and help put you to bed beside your own dear lord. Look on your beauty, my little madonna."

She held out a Venetian mirror in a frame of golden seashells. Franca could not associate the reflection with herself. A dainty creature of gold, violet, and snow, glinting whenever a mote of light caught the jewels at ears, throat, or on wrists impossibly fragile beneath the trailing sleeves lined with white lawn. The flame of hair tamed, the perfect face painted with a serene smile and faint flush; the long sweep of dark lashes gold-tipped shadowing eyes that exactly matched the silk's hue; the hair-fine brows arched against a broad creamy brow. All this belonged not to wild little Franca de' Narni but to a miniature Florentine beauty.

"Perhaps it will not be hard to behave like a lady," she murmured, kissing her fingertips at the reflection who returned the homage. "Dearest Gostanza," she entreated, "let me go down into the court to dry my hair completely."

Franca turned her face upwards, and the nurse scrubbed at her own eyes. "When you look so I can't refuse you anything. I vow when you are full grown all men will give way before such magic."

Franca walked out into the pillared upper loggia and descended the staircase, demurely holding her skirts to display the dainty white and gold slippers, embroidered with pearls, that scarcely pinched toes so unusually constrained. Ordinarily she went barefoot, loving the soft moss or damp earth under her feet. Consciously, she ignored the admiring whispers of serving women and the approving catcalls of the stableboys. Then, the old and familiar Gostanza reached her ears.

"You listen to me, Franca," she screamed. "Don't go getting your gown soiled, or your hair untidy, or running like a wild thing. Remember that young lady betrothed to a duke: she danced so boisterously she broke her leg. Then of course her noble suitor wouldn't marry her. Think of the shame . . ."

Franca's laughter mingled with the calling doves. Life was as usual despite the day and her finery. Since her first unsteady steps Madonna Ginevra and Gostanza had cautioned her with that story . . . no doubt they would be saying the identical thing on her wedding day.

She managed to escape from the inner court. In the distance Berto's familiar figure shambled along, a heavy sack on his shoulders. Franca picked up her skirts and ran towards him.

"Berto! Look at me!"

There was no recognition in his eyes. "Madonna." He touched his forehead.

Franca began laughing. "Fine clothes don't alter me that much, you melon head! You know who I am? Shall we go fishing tomorrow?"

His gaze was hostile. "That gown tells me who you are indeed," he agreed slowly. "Good day, Madonna Francesca Lauretta de' Vincenzo Narni. Pray excuse me from coming out fishing with you. I have to help bring in the harvest which buys you some fine name as a bedfellow."

She caught his arm. Coarse cloth burned fingers suddenly accustomed to silks. "Don't you like my gown?" she demanded. "Today is my betrothal day. I must look fine. Tomorrow will be different."

"Tomorrow will be very different. So you're to be wed to some young lord without his wits, and a strange taste for embracing boys . . . or to an old man with rotten teeth, stinking breath, and limbs twisted from gout, who only needs your warmth in his bed against the winter chill. You will turn to heat yourself against the loins of some worthless gallant decked in pretty ribbons, while your old husband mutely wears horns gilded with your dowry. Be happy, Madonna, for that is what tomorrow brings."

Berto swung away. She started after him, understanding his words, but not the change in attitude. She wished for her old gown. Then she'd chase and punch some good sense into that Berto. "Just you wait," she muttered, looking down at the purple silk which had become a burden.

Franca began walking back to the house with unwilling feet. It was colder. Clouds massed between her and the sun. Summer was waning swiftly. A bevy of unfamiliar servants in the distinctive della Sera dark blue and gold livery crowded the court.

Franca sought the chapel and lit one taper before the Virgin. She sank down and buried her face in her hands. "Holy Mother, let fate be kind . . . please."

Yet, a mature streak in her mind could say: it is already completed. No prayer can alter the age or disposition of Daniello della Lambarda Sera . . .

The carved and gilded cassone was decorated with a lordly hunting scene. It stood open in the wainscotted hall, overflowing with the rich items which were the smallest part of the dowry, for the bridal chest could never contain all that Vincenzo de' Narni would be giving by putting his name and seal to the marriage contract.

The cloud-decked sky poured pewter light on the pearls, the ropes of jewels, the rings, the bracelets, the pins . . . the rare porcelain, the crystal and golden goblets and plates, the majolica tableware, the gem-studded *Book of Hours*, the collection of gold medallions and engraved jewels, the exotic bolts of silks, velvets, and brocades, heavily encrusted with pure silver and gold thread, and turquoises, emeralds, and diamonds . . .

With the eager eyes of a hunting dog, Roberto di Bini, the *sensale*, read aloud the details of the dowry and tried to keep the excitement out of his dry lawyer's voice. It had been interesting acting as the go-between in these marriage arrangements. Certainly, the owner of Castelfiore was a generous father, but then his ambition for his daughter was as high flying as any Gothic steeple and could only be attained at extravagant cost.

The dowry was worthy of a foreign princess, but how else could anyone marry into a family elevated by the Magnificent's affection? Eighty thousand golden florins in cash: none of the customary practice with Florentine dowries which meant waiting for the official Monte to pay out part, or all, the amount from interest accrued on an investment made fifteen years before any actual wedding. The scheme was a good one to ensure a bride brought a suitable dowry, but lately the Monte was getting more than a little backward in its repayments. Fortunately—from the point of view of Florentine revenues—many a girl died or decided to become a nun before her wedding day, so the original investment became the rightful property of the State.

Besides the lengthy inventory of small but valuable items similar to those displayed in the cassone, the girl was to receive a country house on the edge of Castelfiore which had been designed by Michelozzi; two farms, vineyards, and olive groves; a prosperous inn, "The Golden Grasshopper" just outside Fiesole; a goodly share of the annual profits from the Freddiano Lucca silk business in the city; and naturally part of the riches from young Raffaello de' Narni's expedition.

For once Vincenzo looked a wealthy man, arrayed in splendid velvet and dark ermine, gold and jewelled collar about his neck, and each finger seemed to droop under the weight of many costly rings. His smile was ironic but he kept silent. Franca was fit for a king with her beauty, education, and noble ancestry, but he knew it was the abundance of the dowry that had tempted the extravagant della Seras into marriage with any family so undistinguished as the Narnis.

With the completion of the contract a great piece of life would be settled. Every day the times seemed more hazardous, but whatever happened Franca would be secure under the Medici aegis. Vincenzo knew he was right to tie up so much wealth in this match. His sons would have plenty anyway and might yet make the name Narni famous and respected in modern Florence. He doubted it though: they were too learned, too bold, or too contented. His certain stake in the future was the beautiful girl who would become Madonna Francesca della Scra.

With reasoned detachment Vincenzo saw this alliance

might cause the name Narni to be struck off that all-prohibiting *magnati* list, so one of his sons could become eligible for the *Signoria*.

For once sweet Ginevra need not be disappointed with her husband's planning. They had never really loved or understood each other, and yet the marriage had been quite happy . . . in fact better than most. He had reason to be grateful to her as a virtuous wife, a good mother, and an excellent housekeeper. He had never loved another woman —the pursuit of ever elusive wisdom was his true mistress.

Vincenzo smiled at her. The brown eyes were not sad. Their gleam of triumph inspired by Franca's prospects competed with her jewels, and she resembled her shrewd father, the late Paolo di Freddiano Lucca. Despite wealth, high position in the Arte de Sette, and frequent offices in the *Signoria*, that merchant had longed to link his self-made fortune with the name of a noble family. For him that was the secret accolade of success.

Messer Riccardo de' Narni had permitted Vincenzo to wed Ginevra because of the enormous dowry, and in the hope that marriage into the merchant class would outweigh the *magnati* stigma, so that his only son could aspire to high position in the city.

Both fathers and the gentle Ginevra had been frustrated in their ambitions, because they had misjudged Vincenzo's character. He was content to emulate the ideal life as set down by his Humanist hero, Alberti. What else did a man need if he had a home filled with beautiful treasures, the love and laughter of his children, conversation with wise and witty friends, good music, books, and frequent opportunities to sit in the sun and drink the wine of his own estate?

He scorned all those who connived to gain power in the city. "Like maggots crawling over a carcass!" he'd declared, when Ginevra timidly suggested he try to become one of

the four gonfaloniers who represented the Santa Maria Novella quarter for a period of two months. It only needed a
word here, some money paid there, and these things could
be arranged. "What do they do but sit and argue through
day and night, and never decide, while the Medici controls
everything. Being in the public eye is liable to win you as
much enmity as honour. I don't want to end up exiled for
some concocted misdemeanour because I spoke out of turn,
nor do I want to have to reside in the Palazzo della Signoria
for two whole months with a pack of argumentative Florentines . . . No, my dear love, let us be content with our rustic
tranquillity, and leave power to those who hunger for it . . ."

He signed his name, and then looked towards the man
beside the window. There was a satisfied smile on the
heavy lip, and he nodded: "My dear Vincenzo, welcome
into our family."

Vincenzo de' Narni bowed and poured Trebbiano into
four silver cups.

"Now, it's all settled." The *sensale* rubbed his hands and
accepted the wine. "Legal work is thirsty business. Let's
drink to the young people's health. Can we meet the little
lady?"

"I shall bring her." Madonna Ginevra prayed Franca
would still be tidy.

The sun emerged from behind a swollen cloud as the
door opened to re-admit mother and daughter. The three
men blinked at the sight of the figure standing in the blind-
ing light, for Franca sparkled like one of the ornaments in
her dowry. She curtsied and then smiled up at her father
who kissed her brow.

"Allow us to congratulate you, Franca. You and Daniello
are now betrothed."

Roberto di Bini forgot about money and property and remembered his own granddaughter, and smiled kindly.

"Where are the della Seras?" Franca demanded.

She gazed round the chamber. The smile on her lips stiffened. The man who had risen to his feet wore magnificent clothes and jewels. He had heavy blond hair, but was only a little taller than herself, and appeared ill-balanced because of his massive shoulders. Fine crimson and gold brocade did not disguise his slightly hunched back. Prayer had not altered anything.

She looked accusingly at her father, but he said in a level voice: "Franca, this gentleman is Matteo della Sera, Daniello's uncle."

Her smile was bright with relief. The curtsy deep and grateful for it was directed towards the Virgin. The low-statured man raised her and kissed her cheek.

"Had you thought your beauty was to be mated with my ugliness, little Madonna?" His question contained amused bitterness. "Remember this one day when you are old enough to understand: a man is still a man even if his body is not fit for Adonis. Sometimes a handsome face and figure offer no real manhood."

"It's not that!" Franca cried, anxious to soothe the hurt she understood her expression had caused. "You are much older than I had imagined Daniello. I feared I had nothing wise to say, and I shouldn't like to bore my husband."

"Bravely said." Matteo glanced at her father. "She has a swift mind and the rarest beauty. Allow me to explain, Francesca: I represent the della Seras, who alas are unable to come here for this greatest of all days. They ask me to beg the Narnis' forgiveness, but the Medici brothers are hunting close to our Buonventura estate, and the family must be at home to receive them."

Vincenzo avoided his wife's hurt eyes and did not speak his thoughts aloud: they had secured the dowry. What else mattered? This uncle was saying as much. The Narni wealth was required to entertain the Medicis.

She knew disappointment. The *sensale* beckoned her towards his chair.

"They tell me you can recite whole works in Greek and Latin; that you know logic and geometry; that you converse learnedly on Plato and Socrates; that you compose sonnets, and play the lute, the viol, and the flute; that you sing like a choir of nightingales; that you dance like a summer butterfly; that you sew and cipher and cook and weave. But, Francesca, don't you ever play ball like other little girls?"

To her mother's chagrin and her father's amusement, Franca launched herself onto the old man's knee. "I'm not always this good," she confided with a sideways glance at Madonna Ginevra. "Sometimes I climb trees, and I adore riding and hunting . . . only"—and she put a finger to her lips and eyed Matteo della Sera with some doubt—"perhaps you should not mention those things to Daniello. He might not want such an unruly wife."

"If he saw you now," Roberto di Bini spoke with doting admiration, "I believe it wouldn't matter if you chose to ride in the *palio*."

The uncle shook his head. "No, Francesca, our Daniello worships beauty, so you would be permitted to do what you chose." He drew a tiny silk purse out of the pouch at his belt and emptied a small ring into his palm. "This is called a gimmal ring, and always worn by the young lady betrothed to the eldest della Sera."

Franca examined the slender gold ring that ended in a delicately formed hand; each fingernail a perfect diamond.

"From this day onwards," Matteo della Sera explained, "Daniello wears its twin. The two hands clasp to form a single ring which after your marriage you will wear to show you are a wife." He glanced expectantly towards her father.

"Franca, my dove, you must give Daniello a ring." Vincenzo handed her a thick gold band heavy with intaglio work and set with one fine bluish diamond.

She watched Matteo della Sera smile as he weighed it on his hand. "Daniello will treasure this token of your affection. Come, allow me to put his ring on your finger."

Franca held out her hand, and admired the glinting stranger. "See, Mamma," she called. "I am a betrothed lady."

"Only if you behave like one," Madonna Ginevra replied promptly. "Remember this, Francesca, you must not put your future husband's ring to shame by playing the hoyden."

Franca lowered rebellious eyes. Vincenzo read her expression and stifled his laughter in an orange sleeve.

"Would you like to see your husband?" the *sensale* asked.

She looked hesitantly toward the door.

"No," said Roberto di Bini. "You will not meet him until you are grown up, but here is something for you from Maestro Verrocchio's workshop."

He produced a small painting of a golden youth in exquisite clothes and jewels. He was tall and well formed. Long curls gathered about his beautiful face as if they wanted to kiss the soft flesh. A cheetah with a jewelled collar looked up at him, but the man's blue eyes only saw the rose marking the page of the book he was holding. Behind him the Tuscan hills reached towards a morning sky.

"Ah, sweet Virgin," Franca gasped, enchanted. "What a glorious youth."

"That is Daniello della Lambarda Sera," Matteo said simply. "Your reaction speaks of your pleasure, and I am glad for you."

"Then I am to wed a man even more handsome than Andrea," she breathed. "How good the saints are to me." Abruptly her eyes narrowed with suspicion and she demanded: "Is he truly like this, or did Maestro Verrocchio make a pretty picture for many florins to please Messer Lambarda della Sera rather than describe the truth? It would not be difficult for an artist of his worth to transform Vulcan into Apollo."

Vincenzo swallowed some wine. Ginevra's voice was shocked: "Franca, apologize. What a wicked thought!"

The *sensale* laughed, and kissed her cheek. Matteo della Sera's worldly eyes creased with merriment.

"Franca, you have a wise head, which is better than being beautiful, and rare in one so young. Many a maid has been duped into marrying some fellow . . . like my ugly self . . . with a pretty painting. Just as Sandro Botticelli painted your likeness for us to marvel at, so this is a true representation of Daniello. Neither artist has painted as truthfully as he should . . . but they haven't that much talent: for you are more beautiful than your painting and Daniello handsomer than this portrait. He loves to ride, to run, to play tennis, but best of all he prefers music, dancing, and to sit in a lovely garden and tell stories. His many friends are a proof of his pleasant disposition. I don't believe I've heard him utter an angry word."

Franca could almost see the future. She stroked the betrothal ring with a gentle finger. They would have a blissful life . . . like the fair men and maidens in the *Decameron* who escaped the plague-ridden city to dwell in idyllic surroundings and recount tales, sing, dance, and talk of love . . .

"Now I shall not mind when the years have passed. I shall welcome my wedding day," Franca said softly. "Marriage to such a glorious youth must bring happiness."

Madonna Ginevra's lips smiled, but her eyes were forlorn. Pray God, she entreated silently, that it will be as she sees it.

The *sensale* was delighted to join the boisterous Narnis at their table and admired everything from the food to the baby. Matteo della Sera was silent and obviously ill at ease. He slipped away before he had sampled more than one of Tullia's festive dishes. The family sat in uncomfortable and unusual silence as the company of horsemen faded into the evening.

In an effort to dispel the grief in Madonna Ginevra's features, Ser Agnolo began to tell a story:

"A foolish young man who had sampled too much Chianti fell into a drunken sleep. When he awoke, this melon head could not remember anything. He stumbled to the closet, opened the doors, and seeing it was so dark, went back to bed." The tutor stared in red-faced triumph at the astonished Narnis. "You see, he thought he was opening the shutters!"

It was so unusual for Ser Agnolo to relate a comic tale that the brothers and sister laughed more than the joke deserved. He was well rewarded with one of Madonna Ginevra's gentle smiles, and Vincenzo poured him another cupful of wine.

When their mirth had subsided a little, Andrea gasped: "Perhaps Matteo della Sera was scared we'd poison him. These great families are brought up on such terrors. Probably their cooks are bad."

"Andrea!" his mother reproved, trying to hide her smile. "He is most likely a busy man."

"No," Franca said, smiling at Isabetta and Carlotta, who were trying to mask their sympathetic concern with merry looks, "he has what he came for. If he hurries he'll be in time to sit down and eat with the Medicis. You wouldn't expect him to miss that."

She glanced at the gimmal ring and grinned wickedly.

"But, they're bound to come to the actual wedding. I don't think they can avoid it."

Franca's wry humour caused further mirth, but the women wept as they laughed. Vincenzo looked tenderly at his beautiful child, whose glowing hair had come unbound, so that she resembled a wood nymph. Naturally his sons were wild —that was how it should be—but his girl had a streak of more than wildness: fine, burning, and devilish. God help and bless the man who loves her, he breathed, and then said aloud:

"For my part I'm not too worried. Let Daniello see our Franca but once, and he is bound to love her as we do. The Narnis are all here, save one, who I know would share our feelings, so it doesn't matter who else is absent. We can drink to the betrothed's happiness."

The cups were raised in Franca's direction. Outside voices sang lustily, for Vincenzo de' Narni had supplied all his workers with good wine so they could pledge his daughter's health.

Everyone was smiling. Even Ser Agnolo. Gostanza, Tullia, and the other house servants crowded at the open doors laughing, crying and calling out God's blessing on their little madonna.

Franca felt the great love which enfolded her . . . but also knew doubts. The betrothal had shown the world outside to be a complicated place . . .

Nativity

THE WEEK BEFORE CHRISTMAS a flurry of snow brushed the hills. Rain soon washed away the frosting. Damp mist concealed the city and the river. The dun-coloured land was sodden. A chill wind keened through trees bowed in grief. The world was a flat dull place. Days disappeared in the blink of an eye. Morning was always dark, and evening seemed to chase away noon . . .

Franca wondered if she would ever be warm again. Her hands were red and itchy from crouching by the fire, which made writing, sewing, and playing music painful. Even indoors breath condensed in clouds of vapour. Food was as monotonous as the weather. Summer seemed to have departed, taking with her everything that made life pleasant. Winter was worse than Lent. The Christmas feast would make an ambrosial change, but Tullia was always furious while she prepared the special delights; not even Franca dared approach the kitchen.

It seemed lonely in the great house with her father and Andrea down in Florence and Nofri back at Padua. Domenico had taken Isabetta and Christo to visit her family in the Mugnone. A despondent Carlotta had returned to her parents, praying that Andrea might pay her more attention in the city, for both families hoped for such a union. The repellent Lionello had been banished—to everyone's pleasure —only he, Franca, Berto and Vincenzo knew why. He had attempted to force his loathsome tensile state on his furious young cousin, and Berto had tossed the lecherous dog into a cattle trough . . .

Franca knew something was wrong when she found Ser Agnolo missing from the winter parlour where he gave her lessons. Papers, pens, and books were scattered. The great house was ominously quiet for that time of morning. Her mother's women hurried about the upper floor with chalk-grim faces which had not known sleep. Gostanza passed carrying a bundle of coarse linen, and Franca caught her skirt.

"What's wrong?" she demanded.

"Your mother's pains started in the night, and there's a show of blood," she muttered. Beneath the brown hood her face was grey and the whites of her eyes threaded with red. She looked twenty years older than usual. "The baby is coming much earlier than expected. I've sent a man for the midwife. Pray God, they are quick in this weather. Normally, she would come to live here three weeks before Madonna Ginevra is brought to bed."

"Did you send Ser Agnolo?"

"Him!" Gostanza's lips pinched with contempt. "I told

him our lady was in labour and that this time it would be difficult. All he did was begin to tremble. His eyes filled with tears as if he were having her pains. That Agnolo is only fit for mooning around with his music and books. No doubt he's praying for your mother's soul, the poor fool. He's not a real man. Carlo from the stables has taken the master's fastest horse, Fulmine. They're both good enough for the *palio*, and God knows this is a more important race. How I wish the master was at home."

Franca wandered down to the chapel. It was cold and damp, and smelled of mice, candlewax, and stale incense. Fresh candles had been lit on the altar, and the stars of winter jasmine were clustered in a silver vase before the statue. The mother and baby had always been Franca's favourites: They resembled Isabetta and Christo—so plump and happy.

Before the brightly painted and gilded figures knelt her tutor in an attitude of abject despair, his face buried on his arms. Grief seemed incongruous beside those carved smiling figures.

"Why must she suffer so? My poor lady. She has had enough pain in her life." Agnolo's voice contained infinite sorrow.

Franca sensed he would hate her for witnessing his agony. She curtsied briefly before the altar and slipped away.

The wind blew shining diagonal needles of rain across the sullen sky, and the courtyard was filled with cold emptiness. She crept up an outside stairway, uneasy in the troubled atmosphere pervading Castelfiore.

Generally, her mother's quiet rule kept the place running smoothly. Each servant knew his or her duty according to the hours of the day. No maid dared stand in idle chatter, or call down to the men working outdoors. To earn Madonna Ginevra's calm rebuke was far worse than facing Tullia in one of her volcanic rages. Now, the women clustered together, talking in whispers. At intervals, a farmhand would run upstairs—something totally forbidden—to ask if there was any news. All eyes strained to skim the mist from the distance and see if the midwife was approaching.

Franca ran along the terrace, dodging between the painted pillars, towards her parents' chamber, but no one heeded her. She felt utterly useless.

Despite its enormous size the bedroom was stifling hot. The closed shutters were covered by tapestries. A fire roared in the vast grate. Gusts of wind wailed down the chimney and sent the flames sparking. There were only six women in attendance, yet the chamber seemed crowded, for each draught sent the shadows cast by candle flames pursuing each other across the hangings which had been among Madonna Ginevra's dowry.

Whenever Franca had been ill she was put to sleep in her parents' bed, which novelty relieved the dismal imprisonment . . . so the designs on the tapestries were old friends. Each marvellously worked panel depicted the story of the Creation—the last one being the expulsion from the Garden of Eden. In the shadows the serpent appeared to sway, as if preparing itself to descend into the world and lead her into temptation. The first time Franca saw it she had screamed in horror, and her father had sketched an angel with a fiery sword so his little daughter could use it to frighten away the snake!

Madonna Ginevra lay propped up in that great curtained bed. Her face, as tiny as a child's, was yellow and sheened with sweat. It seemed impossible that the ungainly bump under the fur-trimmed coverlid was any part of the frail figure. The long, brown hair was loose and flowed heavily over the thin shoulders and small breasts. The coral necklace Gostanza had fastened about her mistress's neck to facilitate the labour was a touch of bright colour.

Franca expected to be sent away, but Ginevra managed a smile and beckoned her to the bedside. As she approached, the child saw the calm, familiar face contort and heard the faint cry. Teeth clenched on the lower lip. Small garnets of blood gleamed in the light. Franca took her mother's cold, moist hand and did not pull away as the fingernails bit into her own flesh. Tenderly, Gostanza wiped away the blood and sweat with a linen cloth steeped in vinegar.

The tide of pain receded, and Madonna Ginevra said unsteadily, "You should not be here, Franca, but it does me good to see you. If only Vincenzo were at home. I'm so lonely."

It was the first time Franca had heard an adult admit to a feeling she imagined only belonged to the uncertain realms of childhood.

"I shan't leave you, Mamma," she said calmly, but was deeply afraid, understanding that at this time she had to be stronger than her mother by pretending to have no fears.

"Sit by the fire where your mother can see you," Gostanza commanded. "And keep quiet. Now, madonna"—her voice pretended a brisk cheerfulness—"do not be as brave as when this little maid was born. It is no sin to cry aloud. If only you would scream whenever the pangs come, I swear it would ease the birth."

Ginevra shook her head and Franca thought: She will never cry out even if the pain kills her.

Afterwards she only remembered a procession of unconnected memories, like a wall painting with faded indistinct patches where the paint has worn away.

The stifling heat . . . the smoky atmosphere . . . the dull haze of damp covering the unreal world outside whenever she peeped through the shutters . . . the faint moans from the bed interspersed with long, empty silences when her mother lay so still, with her eyes closed, and Franca feared to put her dread into thoughts . . . the serving women's rising and descending murmurs like the ebb and flow of a troubled sea . . . the soft opening and closing of doors . . . running feet outside in the gallery . . . the hiss of rain falling down into the hearth . . . Cassio, his old eyes partly filmed with blindness, prowling about the room or sprawling at her feet.

Now and then Gostanza moistened her mistress's lips with hippocras from the *desco da parto*. The birth tray, laden with sweetmeats and spices, awaited the time when the ordeal would be over, and the mother could be plied with every delicacy to restore her strength and spirits.

Down in the kitchen Tullia lovingly prepared stewed breasts of capon larded with almonds and truffles. As she worked she cursed the anatomy and appetite of men who caused suffering even to the most gentle and virtuous of ladies.

No one thought of Franca. She forgot herself, not even remembering to eat or drink. Every part of her mind and body attuned itself to this vigil.

It was evening when the midwife arrived. Many more hours elapsed before Madonna Ginevra's women supported her to the birthstool.

The aroma of almond oil the midwife used on her hands and Madonna Ginevra's parts filled the room for a few minutes. Then Franca's most distinct memory that shocked her from a bout of drowsiness was of the pig.

That was the first time she had inhaled the rank hot smell of blood. When they killed the pig. Some of the thick dark clots had splashed on her skirts. Berto had regretted agreeing to take her along. Afterwards he had to hold her head while she vomited. Then he'd washed away the stains and bathed her face in cold, clear stream water. Franca had known self-contempt.

She couldn't even look at the sausages and puddings that resulted from that pig's slaughter. Tullia had been heartbroken and feared her darling to be sickening from the plague. No one knew Franca had been at the kill. It would only get Berto a beating, and herself a lecture, and another page of Plato to translate.

Now her mother's chamber, with its smoke-shrouded ceiling, was full of that stench . . . her mother who was always so clean and fragrant . . . who kept her own and the household's clothes and linens fresh and sweet by strewing linen bags of dried lavender and rosemary in the cypress wood chests . . .

Madonna Ginevra squatted upon the birthstool. Gostanza and Violante grasped her shoulders, while the black-garbed midwife crouched before the spread legs, hands reaching beneath the voluminous linen shift. A knife gleamed red from the fire. Women were sobbing around Castelfiore's mistress, their covered heads like massed clouds in the hazy light.

Franca wanted to scream to prevent their slaughtering her mother. Her lips opened, but she never knew whether the cry came from her own mouth. Then there was a different sound: a thin wail that broke the spell.

The women at the doorway ran forward with linen strips and ewers of hot water, their faces smiling and relaxed because at last there was something practical they could do. The long waiting was at an end.

A tiny mottled creature with wisps of red hair on its head squirmed in Gostanza's hands, screaming furiously. Cassio wandered close, sniffed at this protesting newcomer, and then loped away as if he had satisfactorily completed the inspection on his master's behalf.

"A real Narni. God be praised," Gostanza exclaimed joyfully. "Red-haired and bawling for food. Come, Franca, look on this miracle."

With a sense of wonderment, the girl watched the child being bathed in a silver basin. Gostanza's face was wet with tears, but she was laughing.

"See, it's another fine man for Castelfiore," she pointed

between the fat, waving legs and gave a bawdy wink. "Oh, it's not much now, but given the years he'll show the girls some pleasure. Domenico started out with one no bigger than this, and look at his fine son."

To Franca the baby's minute sex seemed a sweet and ridiculous proof of her new brother's manhood. Expertly, the nurse began to swaddle him in linen bands.

"So, it's a boy," the girl's voice contained relief and a strange respect for some invisible force.

Chattering like happy sparrows, the women put her mother back in the bed, which had been warmed with hot bricks, and removed the bundles of blood-stained linen. Violante, the youngest maid, whose berry-red cheeks and round white neck had won all the farm men's appraising glances, held a silver cup of dark wine to Madonna Ginevra's lips.

"Come, madonna," she encouraged. "Drink it all. Then you will take a little of Tullia's special dish. Your struggle has earned you the right to eat and rest. The wet nurse is here to feed the babe so think of yourself and getting strong."

Beside the hearth, a plump peasant girl was already giving the baby her breast. Monna's soft eyes fixed on the minute red head nuzzling against the heavy curves of white flesh. Her own firstborn had died ten days before in the freezing weather. This flow of milk had been a constant reminder of his loss, now she was content that it could be put to such use. During the cruellest winter months she would live and eat amid comfort. It would be an affliction not to be allowed even to see Ercole all the time she fed this Narni, but at least the money she was being paid might ensure that their second baby survived. Meanwhile she had as much love as milk to give this young starveling.

"It is the first time I have no milk." Madonna Ginevra

patted her empty breasts with regret and sighed to herself. "I'm getting old, I suppose."

Franca took her hand, and the woman smiled and smoothed her daughter's tresses. The mother's face was tranquil, but the eyes were set deep in dark circles as if they peered through tunnels.

"Oh Mamma, it is so wonderful, and so terrible." Franca's tears flowed for the first time that day.

"No, you must not cry, my little daughter. The pain goes, and think what joy follows. One day you will know."

It was to share a secret, Franca thought, that only women could know. Oh yes, it took a man to father a child, but the rest was all woman's work. What a miracle it was! Someone so frail, so gentle, so calm as her mother could in great torment bring forth a lusty little boy.

"I'm sorry it's a boy," Madonna Ginevra whispered sleepily, and Franca realized that all these years of secret grudge had been known to her mother.

"It does not matter," she smiled. "Suddenly I am glad to be a girl, Mamma. Think how proud Papa and the boys will be. Will he be a doctor, a lawyer, or perhaps as great a merchant prince as the Magnificent . . ."

The mother's eyes closed, and Franca looked with swift fear towards Violante. The young woman shook her head. "Don't you fret, Franca. She is very tired now, and will sleep."

It was a perfect Christmas at Castelfiore.

The closely knit family adored little Benvenuto as if he were the Holy Child, and lavished upon him a love as precious as the gifts brought by the Three Kings.

Franca was much closer to her mother, and the brothers smiled at this change. She was quite happy to sit rocking Benvenuto in his carved cradle, which had lulled them all in turn, and sing to him in her sweetest voice.

"Do you realize," Franca said to her sister-in-law, as they watched Christo and Benvenuto sleep side by side, "they are uncle and nephew?"

Isabetta put a finger to her mouth, which wore a contented smile, to show she shared a secret. "In six months, Benvenuto will have another nephew, fittingly younger."

Franca smiled and kissed her. "Perhaps it will be a niece."

"Oh no!" Isabetta shook her head, "Narnis do not have girls."

"Then despite my hair," Franca laughed, "I am a changeling."

Vincenzo treated his wife with even more tenderness, and let her talk to him for hours about their baby's progress, without showing any signs of boredom, or wanting to leave her bedside to find a book. The streak of grey in his hair had widened.

He waited until the Epiphany festivities were ended to tell his family:

"While I was in the city, I received news of the *San Miniato*," he pressed Ginevra's shoulder. It was the first day she had been allowed downstairs. Wife and children looked towards Vincenzo with sudden fear. "The ship was attacked by Moors off the Spanish coast. The crew were slain or captured."

He sat down heavily. The deep laughter lines in his unsmiling face made him look old. Ginevra put her arm around his shoulders and seemed curiously stronger than her husband. "Let us pray that our dear Raffaello has only been taken captive," she whispered. "I would not have Benvenuto born to replace another son."

Andrea smiled sadly. He was thicker with Raffaello than the others, and they had enjoyed many a swaggering, carousing time together in the city. "You always said that scamp would set the saints at each other's throats up in Paradise, Papa. If Raffaello is alive, and pray God he is, then the Moor will send him back, just for the sake of a peaceful life . . ."

It was a noble attempt at a jest. His father's glance thanked him.

The fortune lost in this tragedy was not remembered. All eyes rested on Raffaello's empty chair, which always had a place set before it in case of his return.

Franca found the lump of grief in her throat unbearable, and she was forced to speak aloud with a savage conviction: "I have a feeling he is not dead. He cannot be. Indeed I know I shall see him again."

"We can only hope your words are predictive, my dove." Vincenzo sounded weary. He held his last-born in the crook of his right arm. "There is nothing more precious in life than my children . . ." and he bent and kissed the baby's puckered face to hide his tears . . .

The Lovers

No FURTHER NEWS of the *San Miniato*'s precise fate reached Castelfiore. Shred by shred hopes for Raffaello's survival were picked away by the passing weeks, leaving a carcass of grief.

When the first buds broke to deck the distance in a mantle of faint green gauze, Andrea took his sister riding. He had spent a rare week at Castelfiore. His ill-concealed impatience and sadness were replaced by quickening excitement.

The countryside was alive with the sounds of rebirth. Franca believed she could hear spring waking . . . like a beautiful maiden opening her eyes, stretching her pale limbs, and murmuring to herself before rising to run through the land scattering blossom and the promise of fruitfulness. The lilting music of streams in full spate, and the chorus of birds which increased each dawn were her heralds. Franca felt that if she put her ear to the damp ground she would hear the soil stirring as new shoots sought the returning sun.

She was grateful to Andrea for this outing. The twenty-fifth of March was after all a significant date—the first day of a new year. To spend it uneventfully suggested the next twelve months would pass without anything exciting happening. Lately everything had become uninspiring . . . a long yawn of monotony. The others had a nearer boundary to their expectations: Benvenuto's first tooth, Isabetta's new baby. The men were free to ride out to claim their own lives. Her own future seemed too far away. Often she woke with a secret prayer: that her betrothed, overcome with curiosity about his future wife, would make an unexpected visit. She went to bed angry with herself for being disappointed.

It was obvious this ride served a definite purpose. Andrea had dressed himself very finely indeed. The new green doublet with yellow embroidery, violet hose, soft yellow leather boots, and the sparkling multitude of jewels seemed more suitable for visiting a king than a gallop in the hills with a little sister. There was an earnestness about his beautiful mouth that made her feel he was praying.

Franca was not surprised when they rode through the gates of a large estate, with a squat red stone castle at its center.

"Casa Cuono." Andrea said.

"Ugly!" she commented. "It looks like a prison."

"It guards the most precious treasure."

"What is *her* name?"

"Madonna Cosima di Vanozzo Cuono."

"So you did not really pay court to the Donati all these months?" Franca said shrewdly.

"Of course not. She has eyes only for Lorenzo. That just served as a device so no one would know where my true feelings belonged. Cosima had been betrothed since her childhood to a knight from Rome. He has died lately. Now we are thinking of some way to persuade her father to permit her to become my wife. She is uncertain of his intentions, so we meet secretly in the city. Sometimes I have to go about disguised as a labourer just to bid her good day. We can't exist without each other." His voice broke with passion. "Since her father brought the family here for a few weeks we have been apart. My Cosima sent me word that today so many people are visiting Casa Cuono my presence would be unnoticed. I thank the Blessed Virgin, for I swear, if I had to spend another week without seeing my beloved I should have gone stark mad."

"Poor Carlotta," Franca remarked sadly, at the same time feeling honoured by her brother's confidences.

Andrea looked astonished. "What has our cousin to do with this? When you meet Cosima you will understand why I am a captive of love."

"Was hers the favour you wore two years ago?"

He smiled remembering. "Aye. She was fifteen, and bold even then. No one knew but she and I."

"Couldn't Papa arrange matters so you two may be betrothed, and put an end to all this secrecy?" Franca suggested. "He will not object if Cosima is neither rich nor well connected. He is only concerned for our happiness."

"Her family are also *magnati*," Andrea said proudly, "distantly related to the Salviatis. They are wealthy enough to judge by Cosima's and her brother, Guido's, finery, and their palazzo lies close to the Medici's. My darling fears we shall not get permission from her father, or the Magnificent —you know how he scrutinizes *magnati* alliances—if we reveal our feelings too soon."

"You could run away." Franca's eyes shone.

"But I want to live and be happy with my Cosima. She is to be the mother of my sons. I am not going to be a character in one of your sad ballads or tales, who ends up murdered, or castrated . . . or with his head planted in a pot of basil for his bereaved darling to weep over until she too dies . . ."

The stableyard was crowded. Servants in different liveries showed there were many other people about besides the di Cuono family. A young groom took their horses without question.

"If anyone asks your business—though I'm sure they won't inquire such a thing of a little girl in humble attire," Andrea instructed, "say you came with someone who is delivering a message."

"So I am to serve instead of Madonna Lucrezia Donati in the country," Franca said slyly. "No man would go a-courting his true love accompanied by a grubby young sister, eh? If you had warned me we were visiting somewhere fine I should have dressed more suitably . . . but perhaps that would not have fitted your purposes."

Andrea became contrite. He put his arms around her. "Are you angry, my little love? But I have to see her, Franca. I adore her. Can you understand? We have to guard her fair name. She says her father and brother have murderous rages, so . . ."

She looked into the anguished eyes and smiled kindly. "Save your kisses and protestations for Cosima."

"I won't be long," he promised. "Keep to the courtyards and the gardens."

Franca lingered among the horses for a while, but since no one questioned her presence, she began to wander among the walled courts and gardens surrounding Casa Cuono, each linked to the other by archways. The sun emerged. Its warmth tempted her to loll on a stone seat supported on carved lion's paws, beside a small artificial lake.

She admired the bronze fountain at its center, and guessed it came from Maestro Verrocchio's workshop. A naked youth struggled to hold a dolphin spewing jets of water. The gentle breeze stirred this sequinned cascade. It wavered from side to side, catching the sunlight that created rainbow strands like hovering dragonflies.

A boy with a flushed face and flour dusting his Cuono livery came from the kitchens and crossed the water garden. He held a huge tray on his head. A spicy aroma made Franca's nostrils quiver greedily. She fixed the lad with her most beguiling smile.

He looked round hastily before grinning. "I have here cakes for the fine folk who are out riding with Guido di Cuono. The steward has the wine, but they allowed me to carry our cook's famous delicacy."

He winked. "Now if you were to give me a kiss, sweetheart, in return I'd give you a piece of this beautiful pie, which is never tasted by the likes of us."

Franca considered the bargain, smiling all the while. If Andrea had been around he would have thrashed the imp, but how could this scullion know she was anything other than a peasant's child in her rust woollen hood and gown.

"Very well," she agreed, "but to show you are a true gentleman you must first give me the cake."

He handed her a large slice with crumbling edges. Franca's teeth crunched ecstatically on almond paste, juicy raisins, and Madeira sugar. She darted to the far side of the lake, knowing he wouldn't follow in case he dropped his precious burden.

"What about our bargain, you little witch?" he shouted, half in anger, half in jest.

"I forgot," she mocked, and with a dainty gesture kissed her hand towards him.

"Next time I see you, my fine lady," he threatened, "I'll take that kiss. You watch out for Gianni."

But Franca had slipped through another archway out of his sight. Gianni reminded her of the kitchen boys at Castelfiore. Though naturally whenever she appeared they ceased their tease-and-kiss games with the maids in case she reported them to Madonna Ginevra.

She picked the last crumbs from her gown and sucked her fingers, anxious not to lose the least delicious morsel, and then regretfully scrubbed the stickiness from her face and hands.

A narrow stairway entwined with ivy wound up the back of the house. Below, the formal walled garden, with its many bushes cut to resemble strange birds and beasts, was quite deserted, except for one timid chamois. Every time Franca approached the creature it fled. At last, with nothing left to do, she began to wonder just where those twisting stairs led.

At the top a long window opened onto a chamber furnished with greater luxury than she had ever seen or imagined. It belonged to a fine lady . . . if not a queen.

An inlaid table was scattered with alabaster boxes and pots of unguents and cosmetics, vials of perfume, ivory implements for paring and shaping fingernails, carved combs, a mirror in a gold frame set with alexandrites. A tangle of jewels spilled from a silver casket surmounted by a gold and enamel bay tree. The silk wall-and-bed hangings were thick with golden threads. On a small marquetry table rested Venetian goblets and an elegant silver wine jug with a great topaz set in its lid.

In the center of the room stood a large bed of inlaid wood. Its open curtains showed embroidered linen sheets and a coverlid of stranded fur hung with small silver medallions. Beautiful soft rugs made bright pools of colour on the floor. Over the back of a marquetry chair hung a crimson gown trimmed with dyed-red fur. The gold and jet embroidery on the sleeves formed designs of trailing flambeaux. An open cassone overflowed with other costly vivid gowns.

Franca absorbed all the details with envious wonder: a wolf's head fashioned in gold and crystal to hold candles in its snout and ears . . . a carved jasper lion . . . the heavily jewelled crucifix above the bed . . . a Carrara marble bathtub half concealed behind silk curtains . . .

When I am wed, she promised herself, I shall have a bedchamber just like this.

The sound of voices made her dart to the side of the window, so that she could observe without being seen by the occupants of that wonderful room.

A girl stepped close to the window. In daylight her pale nakedness was almost translucent. The ebony shadows of hair on loins and underarms emphasized the whiteness of the flesh with its tracery of faint blue veins. Franca was reminded of full moonlight spilling onto a dark woodland.

The young woman was tall and full-bosomed. Her narrow waist flared to a firm belly. Soft, rounded hips tapered into long, shapely legs, with slim ankles and small feet.

With each movement the dark fall of hair swirled to reveal a lovely arrogant face. Its finely boned features had strength and a completeness rare to find on a young girl. The cheeks were softly pink and shadowed by a long feather of eyelashes. The red mouth was wider than perfect beauty demanded. A sultry lower lip suggested its owner was difficult to please and accustomed to being obeyed by people who longed to make her smile. Indeed when her mouth relaxed, Franca understood that any man might ruin himself to receive such a smile. Beneath finely plucked black brows the enormous brown eyes contained golden specks as if they reflected two distant lamps.

Franca regretted her own bright hair and thin body, and was jealous of the exquisite naked girl so openly enraptured with her own beauty. She circled the room, laughing and singing, her rounded arms gracefully spread as if between invisible partners. Occasionally with slow caressing movements she ran her narrow hands over the jutting breasts, whose small dark nipples were tight rosebuds.

An elderly serving woman, puffing with the exertion of following her young mistress, tried in vain to comb the tendrils of hair.

"Madonna, be still," she begged.

"Have done, old nurse." The high-pitched imperious voice sounded breathless as if its owner could scarce contain her excitement. "Am I not beautiful enough?"

"You are too perfect for your own good, but I always knew you would be, right from the day you were born, and I laid you in your lady mother's arms . . . God rest her soul."

The girl laughed and threw her arms about the woman, so that her breasts were crushed against the dull woollen gown. "Who else could I trust to share my wonderful secret?"

"A secret that will cost my life if anyone discovers it," the woman spoke with genuine terror.

"But nobody will. We have been very careful."

Franca grew aware of a man's voice singing within that room, and then understood that the lovely creature had been displaying herself for this man's eyes.

"Now, my good Bianca, pour us the wine, and then go, so I can lock the door. If anyone asks, I am indisposed . . . tell them I have the colic and can't leave my room. Run away. We have so many things to do, eh, my love?" she called towards the shadows.

The woman did as she was bid, curtsied to the unseen man, and then scurried from the chamber. The girl turned the ornate key in the lock, and then flung herself on to the bed, extending her arms as if beseeching an embrace.

From the shadows bounded a naked man. The lean, muscled body was as tall and ideally proportioned as any classical statue, and the perfect partner for that female figure. The locks that curled towards his broad shoulders were the same hue as Franca's own.

So that's the message he had to deliver, she thought, and this lady is his Cosima. Pray heaven she is as kind as she is beautiful for he has a soft heart and is near-foolish in this passion.

The couple drained the wine goblet . . . green and brown eyes laughing across gilded rims. Andrea stood before the bed, gazing down at the girl whose provocative position contained no modesty, and showed that this was not the first occasion they had been together in such intimacy. He knelt and buried his face against the apex of her spread legs.

Cosima laughed: a high, mocking note, and stretched her hand to cover the intumescent passion of his loins. He seized the pale, voluptuous body. She struggled, but only to tantalize him. With fierce hunger, he began to kiss her mouth and breasts, tears coursing from his eyes, although his mouth was laughing. Their breathless utterances of each other's names drifted to Franca's ears. Then Andrea's body covered Cosima.

Franca turned away. The air felt chill on her burning face. She climbed down the stairs leaving the couple to their loving. Although curiosity surged within her, she knew this was a secret thing . . . and that she had already witnessed too much even to try to forget it. I should not like to be spied upon, she reflected, when I am grown old enough for such pleasures. People are not animals. It is not like watching Scipio with the mares.

"Oh Andrea," she whispered, frightened for her brother. "Where will this folly lead? You are reckless to love your mistress while she is under her father's roof, and your Cosima is crazy to yield her virtue so carelessly . . . even to you . . ."

Franca perceived love was a madness which swept human

beings into a maelstrom without allowing them time to reason. Even if it destroyed its victims, there was no controlling this force. She feared and longed to be caught in the flood.

Lest her presence in that secluded garden provoke someone else to mount the stairs to a personal paradise, Franca hastened back to the main court. A group of men, still on horseback, were drinking wine, and eating the famous cake, while grooms held the reins of restless, sweating horses. Sunlight struck harnesses, spurs, jewels, and swords with touches of fire.

One young man seemed to be the center of attention. The others edged their horses close to his chestnut gelding . . . as if he were a flame and they merely moths entranced by the light he shed. He was clad in pale blue and gold, and his short blond hair resembled silk. Now and then he bent to soothe a young cheetah with a jewelled collar attached to his wrist by a strong leash. In order to eat a sweetmeat, he removed one blue kid glove decorated with a golden acorn.

Franca's heart began to palpitate. For among the many rings that practically hid his fingers was the twin to the gimmal ring on her own hand. The painting had lied. The reality of Daniello was far more beautiful. Beside him in grim contrast sat a humpbacked dwarf, who made her remember Matteo della Sera as quite a handsome being. Close to the golden angel this swarthy pockmarked face seemed to belong to a demon.

Daniello's voice reached her ears above the laughter and speech. It was clear and gentle and suggested an equable nature. "Thank you, Guido, for a pleasant day. Now I must ride back. We have guests."

Guido di Cuono inclined his head. Even in the saddle he was tall and curiously like his sister with fine pale features and shining, dark hair. Whereas her colouring suggested vibrant, sensual beauty, his had the detached austerity of an aesthete . . . as if he could control all emotion to suit action. While other men and women gesticulated to accentuate their mood and words, Guido's white hands remained calmly clasped. Even in the parti-coloured flame and blue finery, Franca found it easy to picture him in the drab robes of some hermit, because of his appearance of immense spirituality.

"Is your little bride visiting you?" the dwarf demanded.

Daniello shook his head, and the blue ostrich plumes on the beaver hat stroked his flushed cheek. He glanced at the betrothal ring before drawing on his glove. "Not for many a year, Altoviti, thank the Lord. She is only a child, not ripe for any act of consummation."

"Our Daniello seeks more immediate pleasures, eh?" Guido said.

Daniello smiled, and Franca's heart leapt so hard it hurt her faintly swelling chest.

"Would you have me wait? She brings a vast dowry. Not that it will be so hard for me to accept. Little Francesca Lauretta is damnably lovely. Look—like the dutiful lover I'm supposed to be, I carry her likeness."

He drew the small picture from a pouch, and Franca crept into the shadows cast by the house. "In fact the dowry will be very welcome . . ." he added, laughing and touching the diamond crucifix on his chest. "The way our family spends gold. They say Vincenzo de' Narni dabbles in alchemy. The family's so rich I'm inclined to believe he's successful at the art."

The other men examined the picture but Franca did not heed their doubtful jests. Even to hear him speak of the Narni wealth as the sole inducement for their marriage did not diminish his splendour. She recalled Andrea and Cosima. Was it possible that one day she and that remote godlike creature would cling together in naked embrace? She could visualize it as a picture but not infuse the scene with feelings that had not yet been aroused.

"Then stay and dine," Guido urged, "if you haven't the wealthy Narnis to entertain."

"Really I cannot. Madonna Clarice has been staying at Buonventura with my mother, and Lorenzo and Guiliano are joining her, so we can celebrate this blessed first day of the year together."

He spoke without any particular pride of his intimacy with the Medici, but the other men's eyes held mingled respect and envy.

"Then I will not attempt to detain one who basks in the warmth of the Magnificent's love," Guido di Cuono said civilly. "I wish you pleasure, dear Daniello, and that this year of the Incarnation 1478 brings you and your family God's Grace." They clasped hands affectionately.

Surrounded by a retinue of servants in the della Sera livery, Daniello rode towards the gates, the lithe cheetah loping alongside. Once he reined in his horse, and turned in the saddle to smile at the group of friends who were still watching in silent admiration. He raised his hand in salute. Franca found herself waving at that glorious figure, which was finally lost among the dark evergreens ringing the estate.

A cloud obscured the sun.

The men dismounted and went into the house. Franca felt sleepy and cold. She trailed indoors. Nobody paid any attention to the solitary child. Servants hurried back and forth with trays of food and flagons of wine. Everywhere gentlemen were eating, discussing the merits of their falcons, horses, and dogs. The hounds prowled about picking up scraps. Gradually the atmosphere reverberated with raucous laughter and ribald song, and the air became stuffy with the smells of food, sweat, and leather.

Franca mounted a steep, wooden staircase. It led to a gallery. Here in the evenings, concealed by ornamental wooden latticework, musicians played for the entertainment of the company dining below. At the back of this gallery was a bower for the ladies who wished to retire from male company while continuing to listen to the music.

A worn ledge concealed from all eyes by a wooden pillar made an ideal nook. Franca curled up like a puppy and tried to sleep. She dozed uneasily on this hard couch and woke with the sensation of falling from some great height. I must have been dreaming, she thought sleepily, as her heartbeats subsided to their normal rhythm. She stretched her cramped legs and then became aware of men's voices in the bower.

Franca listened without really comprehending, blinking at the particles of dust which drifted in the long shafts of light shed by the high windows opposite the gallery.

"You are quite sure we are safe to talk up here, Cuono?"

"Of course, Archbishop. We purposely arranged to have the house full of Guido's friends. No one with any sense would think we were discussing such a plan in the midst of the young men's roistering."

"And your son is with us?" a choleric voice demanded.

"Naturally, my dear Francesco. Your idea is much to Guido's taste. We, Cuonos, just like you, Pazzi, would sleep easier if the tyrant were removed. Then our hopes for the future will not be impeded: power will be where it rightfully belongs—in noble hands—and the rabble won't be able to dictate to us any longer. What I require to know is, Archbishop Salviati, do we really have His Holiness's blessing for our venture?"

Franca stirred. She recollected these names.

The modulated priestly tones contained amusement.

"Blessing . . . ahem, old Sixtus is too cunning for that, Cuono. As the being closest to God on this earth, he approves that the present order should be changed . . . just so long as no one is killed . . ."

"But that's impossible!" Vanozzo di Cuono interrupted.

Salviati laughed gently. "Quite. I told His Holiness he

must permit us to steer the boat . . . my very words . . . that way his papal conscience will be clear. That I was accompanied by Giralomo Riario naturally helped convince the Holy Father. The new lord of Imola and Forli is very anxious for our plan to succeed. At present I am not actually Archbishop of Pisa, but if Sixtus died, then Riario would probably lose his newly acquired territories. They lie right between Venice and Florence, so he would be crushed by the two allies . . . therefore he wants to strike first and remove the chief enemy."

"We all have good reasons." Cosima's father's voice made Franca tremble. "But I want to be sure that I do not commit my family to a band of hotheads who are unlikely to succeed, so I must know their names."

Franca judged the man who answered was old and accustomed to being obeyed. In a dry tone he said: "My dear Vanozzo, I would not approach you until I was sure of our numbers. Last week they swore their fealty to this cause at my Villa Montughi. As head of the Pazzis, I, Jacopo, guarantee my relatives' help. In fact, Francesco here was the first person to be approached by the lord of Imola, and Salviati the second.

"Giralomo can hardly come here himself. He found us the gallant soldier, Gianbatista Montesecco, who went to the Pope with him and Salviati. Gianbatista is to be our instrument of justice. Then my priestly secretary, Stefano, will die for our cause if need be. Another priest, Antonio, is also one of us. He hails from Volterra and wants revenge for what the Medici's *condottieri* did to his city when they put down that uprising. There are two daredevils below with your son: Bandini and Francesi . . . and Bracciolini too: He'll do anything for gold in his impoverished state. Do you want me to continue, Vanozzo? The list of noble names pledged to help is very lengthy indeed."

"An odd assortment," Cuono commented.

"What the devil's the matter with it?" shouted the irascible Francesco Pazzi.

"Hush, Francesco," the eldest Pazzi soothed. "Cuono is right to consider carefully. You know we can rely on his loyalty."

"This is how we'll proceed then," Francesco said belligerently, "unless of course Vanozzo di Cuono has some objections: a detachment of soldiers will be placed at strategic points outside the city to secure our power once we are in control and the brothers are removed."

"Brothers?" Cuono questioned.

"Both must die at one time," Jacopo Pazzi replied gently. "To leave one alive even for an hour might give him a chance to rally support against us . . . a clean kill is what we want."

"Surely that'll be very difficult," Cuono said meditatively. "How do you intend to get them together at a suitable time?"

"There we have His Holiness's help," the Archbishop explained. "He has provided us with the perfect opportunity. The new young Cardinal Raffaello Riario is to be made Legate of Perugia. He must pass through Florence. Naturally he will be entertained as befits his station, and he must return his noble host's hospitality. Very graciously Messer Jacopo has offered to lend the Cardinal one of the Pazzis' splendid villas so that he can give a dinner in honour of the Medici brothers. Then we will have them both in our hands."

Franca pressed her fist against her mouth to prevent herself crying out. What had she overheard? That those four urbane gentlemen were planning to kill Lorenzo and Guiliano and seize the state? Did Andrea know, she wondered suddenly . . . was he involved in this plot . . . and what about her own father . . . after all they too were *magnati*.

Terror held her in a manacle so she could not move. If they discovered her presence, it would be easy to dispose of one small girl without even asking her name. Franca cowered there, sweating with her fear.

"I must depart," Salviati said. "My men are waiting for me in the small wood to the north of the estate."

"Francesco and I must leave separately," Jacopo Pazzi added. "No one would suspect me of anything, but it is well known Francesco is no friend to the Magnificent, and people may already be wondering why he's not in Rome."

"You'll inform your son," Francesco said irritably.

Vanozzo di Cuono spoke calmly: "Why are you always so bad-tempered? You'll make yourself ill. Of course I shall tell Guido, and we'll hold ourselves in readiness. As soon as you know the day for the dinner party, I'll expect an invitation for my whole family." He gave a soft laugh. "The presence of my beautiful Cosima will ensure that the Magnificent attends even Riario's invitation. He has not been exactly subtle in his attentions to my daughter . . . and she, the minx, encourages him . . ."

One by one the men left the bower. Franca counted the pairs of feet. At last, shaking uncontrollably, she crept downstairs, sidling along the wall . . . and then ran out into the courtyard to the horses. Andrea was waiting, but failed to notice her agitation.

They rode away from Casa Cuono. Andrea's tired eyes and smiling lips spoke that his mind was still in Cosima's warm embrace. Franca found herself wondering if the beauty would make him a good wife. Somehow she could not imagine her visiting Castelfiore to discuss babies and servants with Isabetta and Madonna Ginevra. Yet, Andrea certainly deserved to marry a princess . . . and princesses could not be expected to lead mundane lives.

"Andrea," she said insistently. "I have overheard a dread plan. Please hear me."

He listened abstractedly, and then waved his hand as if to dismiss a mayfly. "Forget it, Franca. You've heard Papa say there are always intrigues. He's often been approached to join plots to overthrow the Medici. Nothing will come of this. It's just winecup talk."

"Couldn't you warn the Magnificent?" she persisted.

"That would only involve our family for no purpose. Let's leave well alone, and not draw Lorenzo's attention on ourselves. Besides we mustn't do anything that might harm my dear love."

Fontelucente

IT WAS THE FIRST TIME she had visited Fontelucente that year and the only time she'd been there without Berto. Even before her betrothal he had suddenly refused to go swimming, and would not listen to threats or cajolery.

Of course, it had always been a forbidden thing; yet so long as nobody knew they threw off their clothes to plunge into the deep pool, there was no harm in it. No one ever came to the place, for it was widely claimed that male and female witches visited the spot to practise their diabolical arts.

Franca was disappointed that up till now she had never glimpsed one of those dreadful beings . . . but Berto had explained they only came there on moonless nights. Yet she had witnessed magic at Fontelucente—when Berto taught her to swim.

How magnificent to cut through icy water that made her gasp, and turned the cape of hair into fronds of dark red weed and her pale body into an arrow of quicksilver as it flashed among the green depths.

"You're just like a fish. I don't believe any girl can swim like that," Berto had muttered doubtfully, crossing himself and staring down at the girl splashing beneath the tumbling waterfall that fed the pool.

His grudging approbation always made her shriek with glee. He was just like Ser Agnolo really, though neither would have been flattered by the comparison. Both were always complaining she didn't listen to instruction and then discovering with mortification that she did in fact know her lessons.

Under the canopy of new green leaves the pool was a stretch of chrysolite, fringed with tender ferns. In its depths pebbles shone like a hoard of precious gems. Franca had often dived for them, only to discover they were ordinary stones beyond the water's enchantment. Violets scented the fresh warm air. Ripples spread over the pool's surface as the fish rose. A blackbird trilled winsomely to his mate.

Franca's heart knew loneliness. The unsought-for knowledge isolated her from her loved ones. Since it would mean betraying Andrea's secret she dared not confide to her father the fragments she'd overheard. The burden made her unusually solemn, and she slept badly, awaking unrefreshed. Vincenzo insisted Franca needed fresh air to restore her good spirits, so this expedition into the countryside was donated rather than filched.

Each day she waited in trepidation for dire news from the city. The young Cardinal's visit had begun, and tales of the splendid entertainments given in his honour were widely discussed. Yet the Medici brothers continued to flourish . . . so much so that Florence had a new piece of gossip to relish: the lovesome Guiliano had got with child one of his mistresses: Gorini's young daughter. Sometimes it occurred to Franca she might have dreamed those voices, whose names and intentions could have been spun out of threads from her own memory.

To plunge once again into the clear green water would be to slough off winter for good and perhaps rid herself of these terrors. Impulsively, Franca unhooked her gown, stretching her arms towards the warmth which stroked her skin. She sighed, looking down at her body. She would never have those luxurious curves of Cosima di Cuono . . . like spoonfuls of thick cream.

She slid into the deep and splashed boisterously in an attempt to get warm . . . and laughed at the joy of the year's first swim. That was what she always relished: the year's turning, and the chance to be able to do and eat all the summer things for the first time. As she swam, she knew winter was really fled. The promise of summer stretched before her: an infinite golden road.

The sun climbing towards noon shone warm on bare shoulders and tangled wet curls, and Franca began to sing:

> A youngling maid am I and full of glee,
> Am fain to carol in the new-blown May,
> Love and sweet thoughts-a-mercy, blithe and free . . .

She did not hear the soft whinny of a horse being tethered, nor see the bushes parted by a stranger who came upon the pool, induced there by a sweet voice singing an old ballad. The man was unable to wrench his glance from the singing creature, as she hoisted herself out of the water by an over-hanging willow branch . . . a shower of tiny drops put a rainbow halo around her slight form.

Like a deep echo another voice picked up her song:

> I go about the meads, considering,
> The vermeil flowers and golden and the white,
> Roses thorn-set and lilies snowy-bright . . .

Franca's eyes grew large with terror. She turned, but was dazzled by sunlight and could only distinguish the dark outline of a tall man against the pale greenery as if he had been fashioned out of night and crept insidiously into the day. So one of the devil's creatures had come to claim her soul for trespassing in the magic pool.

"Good day, little madonna." The voice was gentle and human.

Franca slithered back into the water, remembering Gostanza's grim warnings that she must not walk alone in solitary places or talk with strangers. Now she was doing both and naked as the day she was born.

"I do believe," he continued, "that last time we met you were clad, though somewhat simply. You still wear the topaz, I see . . . a great protection against amorous advances in lonely groves!"

Franca had not forgotten that soft voice, and he was wearing dark mulberry again, slashed with black and silver. "Good day, Messer Ridolfo," she said breathlessly. "If you will kindly turn your back I may dress myself."

"If I don't?" he spoke seriously, but his eyes were merry.

"Then I must stay here until I turn blue, but"—her eyes grew dark as sea beneath rolling storm clouds—"when I manage to tell my papa and brothers of your unchivalrous behaviour, you will have no eyes left to spy upon swimming maidens . . ."

Messer Ridolfo began to laugh gently. He drew aside his cloak and fingered the hilt of a sword decorated with his lion emblem. "Madonna Franca, did you never think that a man might chance upon you here, force you to accept his body's pleasure, then cut your throat and leave a young corpse for the crows to pick clean?"

Franca shuddered. "Is that your intention?"

He held out her gown. "Madonna, I hope I am always a man of honour. I assure you I have no need to force ladies; besides, my taste is not for the bud but for the flower in full bloom."

She climbed out of the pool and reached for the gown, then held it before her, flushing brightly under eyes which refused to look away.

"One day though, madonna, you will be in full and beautiful bloom. Already your breasts are burgeoning like the earliest spring buds, and the first golden hairs of modesty have grown on your body."

Franca could not find a way to cover her chest and sex as she scrambled into her dress. She tried to pull away as the man hooked it together, and straightened her hair, but his hands were too strong. He turned her round to face him and bent his head so that the black eyes were close to hers.

"Yes, one day, little Franca, you will be a woman, and then you will belong to me."

She said defiantly, "You seem to forget that I am betrothed."

"Oh, of course." His eyes mocked the ring on her finger. "You will find Daniello cares more for his beauty than yours . . ."

"And for my dowry more than anything," she retorted with heat. "I know, but he is to be my husband, and I shall love him and bear his children."

"No, Franca, I vow that when you are a woman you will belong to me and bear my children."

Franca began to laugh. "What makes you believe these things?"

"It is written we cannot escape our destinies. Our paths are to run the same course, Franca. No matter what your intentions are now . . . or how far you wander from them, one day you will lie close to this heart. These lips and hands will teach you about love."

She began to tremble. His words disturbed her thoughts and stirred her untried senses. They stared at each other. Finally Ridolfo smiled, and offered the girl his arm.

"May I escort you back to Castelfiore, just in case you encounter some less gallant fellow?"

Franca asked: "What are you doing so far from Milan?"

"Attending the festivities in honour of Cardinal Riario."

"You see Lorenzo de' Medici often?" she questioned.

"Obviously. He is Riario's host, even though he detests both Cardinal and Pope. Rulers have to obey these tongue-in-cheek politenesses."

"Messer Ridolfo, can I trust you with my secret?"

He looked amused. "Have you another sweetheart beside your betrothed?"

Franca snatched her hand from his arm. Her eyes filled with angry tears. She would not weep before this prince of darkness who derided everything and disrupted her hopes. "Yet I am so perplexed." Her voice broke with agitation. "I have to tell someone I can trust."

"Come then, Franca," he said gravely, and kissed his ring with its carved ruby. "This is my family crest, and I swear by it to take your secret seriously."

When she had finished telling him about the fatal dinner party intended for the Medici brothers, Franca could not help realizing it did sound improbable, and began to feel foolish before this dignitary from Milan.

"Where did you hear these details?"

"At Casa Cuono."

He looked baffled, then his eyes lightened with understanding. "You went there with Andrea?"

Franca bit her lips.

"You are not betraying his secret," Ridolfo said gently. "He is love-blinded if he thinks sharp eyes don't detect his feelings for the lovely Cosima."

"So you know her?" Franca felt unaccountably jealous.

"All Florence sits at the feet of this beautiful creature."

"But she loves Andrea," Franca insisted proudly.

He gave a secret smile. "Perhaps, but others may yet win her even from your glorious brother. Like a spoiled pet cat, Cosima tangles up men's hearts as if they were mere skeins of wool. Now for your plot, Franca—the dinner has already taken place without misadventure. Guiliano was unwell and could not attend, but Lorenzo enjoyed himself mightily in

Cosima's company, and scarcely spoke to Cardinal Riario."

She began to perspire with relief. "Then there is nothing to worry about. Andrea was right as usual. It was just wild talk."

"Probably. I shall make some inquiries in the city and attempt to warn the Medici without revealing where I heard about this business. The Cardinal leaves Florence soon."

"Don't ever tell Andrea," Franca begged.

"You love him so very much?"

The smile that flooded her face spoke of complete adoration.

"Then don't fret anymore."

He lifted her into his saddle, and, as if he were her groom, took the reins and led the great black horse down the hillside towards Castelfiore. He left her near the house. "I must ride on to the city, Franca. Remember all my words."

"Thank you for your reassurance," she said gratefully, and then in mocking tones which belied the doubts he had aroused, added: "As for the other, Messer Ridolfo, you had best find yourself a wife before you grow too old, for my future is already sealed."

Eastertide

ALL FLORENCE REJOICED in Easter. Who could wear a dismal countenance when the sun shone on pretty ladies, carrying nosegays as bright as their faces and gowns. Multitudes decked in new finery made their way to the churches. Afterwards they would embrace family and friends with the joyful greeting, "Christ is risen," and then go home to break their fast on good food and wine, amid song and laughter. People would feel, and celebrate, the Resurrection in their hearts and bodies after weeks of Lenten fare, and the agony of Friday's Tenebrae.

The route between the cathedral and the Palazzo Medici was lined with crowds waiting to see Cardinal Riario pass by. The young Eminence had requested to hear High Mass in the beautiful Santa Maria Fiore. General opinion had it that not even in the Eternal City had he prayed in such perfect surroundings. Afterwards the Medici brothers would bring him to their house to dine with important members of Florentine society.

Noon lacked little more than an hour as Giuliano de' Medici neared the cathedral. Men and women called blessings on his handsome face. He was a universal favourite, the acknowledged leader of fashion, admired for his prowess in sport and love. The gods truly loved Giuliano and had given him a trusting heart and guileless nature. Whenever he smiled Florentines felt rewarded as if with gold. He and Lorenzo were their darlings.

"Thank Heaven," he said with endearing frankness to the men at each side of him, "that you two were kind enough to call by and bring me to the service. The canon must already have begun. As usual I overslept. Lorenzo frequently tells me I'll be late for my own funeral, which isn't as impolite as being tardy for High Mass in the Cardinal's presence."

His companions, Francesco Pazzi and Bernardo Bandini, displayed affection and friendship by embracing him whenever one of their sallies provoked too much laughter for them to continue walking. People were amazed to note that for once Pazzi's ill-temper had evaporated: The spirit of Easter must have softened his nature, for his squat figure rocked with mirth instead of paroxysms of rage.

Fragments of these jests made maidens hide their blushes behind gloved hands, but men and matrons openly giggled. Nearly all featured the popular theme of tired old men marrying hot young girls, and brisk lovers escaping through bedroom windows without their hose.

"And he knew all the time?" Giuliano demanded, wiping his eyes with a fringed silk handkerchief.

"Naturally"—Francesco's face shone red with glee—"it saved him a job he really hadn't been able to complete for years. He just used to roll to the far side of their bed, and when he thought there'd been enough sport for one night and wanted to get some sleep, he'd snore and snort as if about to wake up. Then, the young man would depart. There's no denying the old boy achieved more satisfaction as the silent audience than by being in the performance . . ."

"We must compose ourselves," Giuliano gasped. "We can't burst upon a pious congregation sniggering as if our drawers were lined with feathers . . ."

A vast crowd packed the cool interior of the cathedral. Incense and fresh flowers suffused the atmosphere with intoxicating fragrance. The murmur of prayer, behind-the-hand gossip, and the whisper of silks and taffetas played a soft background harmony to the melodious choir and the celebrant's reverent chanting.

Greenish gloom filled the soaring dome and resembled an evening sky. Against it hosts of candle flames and lilies formed constellations of stars. The vivid-hued garments of the congregation completely hid the fine marble floor.

Lorenzo de' Medici noticed Giuliano standing on the opposite side of the choir between Bandini and Francesco Pazzi. He smiled warmly, then raised expressive dark brows in the direction of the Cardinal apparently wrapped in devout prayer. Giuliano understood. It would be a relief when this particular Papal Legate went to Perugia. Were they always to be inconvenienced by some Riario or other?

What a gaggle of Pazzi and Salviati, Lorenzo thought, and wondered why old Jacopo Pazzi was absent from their numbers. His thin lips twisted ironically. We're all such good friends on the surface. We smile and dine together, while I watch their movements as sharply as my peregrine falcon searches for heron. Messer Ridolfo told me nothing new when he suggested I beware of their desire for power, but he's wrong in imagining they'd usurp our rule with violent methods. They're too subtle for that. They'll try to outwit me through some political maneuver among the *Signoria* . . . so I must take care none of their sympathy gets office in the Palazzo.

He noticed Ridolfo di Salvestro dressed in his usual colour. A wily fellow, Lorenzo considered. I'm looking forward to seeing if the future brings his real patron into power—that would be of some help to Florence. Duchess Bona and her father-in-law's one-time secretary, Cecco Simonetta, are unreliable. Milan is a burden, not an ally.

Messer Ridolfo's eyes scanned the brilliantly clad young ladies, like so many exotic plumed birds . . . and Lorenzo's own gaze slid covertly among them too, guessing they both sought the same proud, dark head. He sighed. The Cuono family must have chosen to attend High Mass elsewhere.

The recital of the canon ended. The celebrant spread his hands over the bread and wine. The air moved expectantly. Lorenzo's mind returned from contemplating politics and beauty to the Mass. He noted close by two priests—their pallid faces seemed to burn with the white fire of religious fervour.

Giuliano, who had been wondering about the sex of his unborn child, and just which political marriage his brother might inflict upon him, crossed himself devoutly and smiled with genuine joy. His fine eyes embraced the men at his side. It was good to celebrate the Mass among friends—just what the Last Supper had been about.

Audible surprise stirred among people close to the main doors as Archbishop Salviati hurried from the cathedral with his brother, Jacopo, and a group of followers. He was overheard to whisper, "Our mother is unwell . . ."

The priest recited reverently: ". . . *accipite et manducate ex hoc omnes . . . Hoc est enim corpus meum . . .*" He genuflected, then took the Host in both hands and elevated it to show the waiting worshipers.

The bell rang.

Those who had previously agreed that this most solemn moment should serve as a signal began to carry out their plan.

Giuliano de' Medici's features did not even have time to register shock. Bandini, standing so close, suddenly thrust the blade of a short dagger into his chest. Their demonstrations of affection had ascertained the younger Medici carried no weapons. The savage blow sent Giuliano tottering a few paces. He fell to the ground, his lips parted in an attempt to say a Paternoster. Men and women screamed in alarm. The Mass came to an abrupt horrified halt . . .

Francesco Pazzi flung himself onto the dying youth. He struck again and again at the convulsed figure and once-beautiful face. The sight of spurting blood seemed to increase his frenzy . . . and he failed to feel the dagger plunge into his own thigh . . . the blood of attacker and victim mingled.

Lorenzo had no opportunity to see what had befallen his brother, for when Bandini attacked, the two priests produced daggers from their sleeves and started towards him. One of the Medici's closest friends, Francesco Nofri, sprang forward, giving Lorenzo a chance to unsheath his sword.

The dagger thrusts stuck the human shield. Francesco Nofri fell dead. Only one blow penetrated Lorenzo's neck. Blood poured onto his jewelled shoulders, as he fought off the priests with desperate strength. Poliziano and Cavalcanti, their swords drawn, strove to reach his side, cursing and yelling. The two priests fled, their daggers clattering on the marble.

Panic ravaged the congregation. Surging shadows suggested the cathedral walls were collapsing. Wailing in terror, people rushed to escape, colliding with others fighting their way forward to see what was happening.

Cardinal Riario, his eyes wild as an unbroken pony's, clutched a crucifix and threw himself towards the altar, where the celebrant, deacon, and archdeacon defended him against the incoming tide of fury.

Noting the priests had left their task undone, Bandini and Pazzi launched themselves at Lorenzo. He leapt over the choir and across the cathedral, accompanied by Cavalcanti and Poliziano. They dashed into the sacristy. With the clangor of a giant gong, the enormous bronze doors slammed shut in the faces of their pursuers.

For the first time Lorenzo failed to admire Luca della Robbia's twenty exquisite panels framed in a damascene of gold and silver, and only thanked God for the strength of the bronze that stood between himself and his assassins. Screams of terror, anger, and pain echoed horribly from without.

"My sweet Lorenzo"—Poliziano was pale and trembling —"I must suck that wound in case they used poison on their daggers."

"I have loyal friends indeed." Lorenzo's hoarse voice contained a sob. "One has already died for me, and you do this. Mother of God, what have they done to my brother?"

Afterwards they bound his neck with a silken scarf.

"What can be happening out there?" Poliziano asked.

Lorenzo leaned on his sword, his face ashen with fury and pain. "We shall not know until we leave here. At present we dare not open those doors. We are caught like snared rabbits."

After an hour, the sounds of turmoil subsided, and voices began chanting: "Come out, Lorenzo. All is well."

Through the bronze barrier, the calls were sepulchral and menacing.

"But who wants me?" Lorenzo turned to his companions. "How can we know if this is also part of their accursed plot?"

"There is a way to find out." Cavalcanti stripped off his crimson doublet with its ballooning upper sleeves that narrowed into tight cuffs, and began climbing upwards to the cantoria.

All Florence considered the singing gallery of carved marble to be Luca della Robbia's finest achievement. Below it the tympanum was also his work. The enamelled terracotta reliefs depicting the Resurrection were a tragic reminder of this Sunday's true meaning.

"I can see them," Cavalcanti yelled. "Friends, God be praised. Let's open those doors, and get out and kill the treacherous bastards!"

"Lorenzo must be tended by his physician Leoni," Poliziano insisted, and the shabbily clad writer supported his friend and patron through the doorway.

Lorenzo looked at the Cardinal cowering beside the altar, and commanded: "Escort His Eminence to the palazzo, and keep him safe. We must discover just what role he played in this piece of bloody theater."

"Believe me . . ." Riario pleaded as armed men led him away.

The Medici ignore him and knelt beside the body of his brother, his hands and knees stippled by the pool of gore. He kissed the cold lips and closed the unseeing eyes that would never charm the world again. When Lorenzo looked up, the flat features had become a mask of vengeance. No tears flowed.

"Fifteen wounds. Giuliano never harmed any man, may Heaven accept his sweet soul. No punishment is too terrible for those involved in this bloody deed. Our city will not fall into their inhuman hands . . ."

Somehow Francesco Pazzi managed to return to Messer Jacopo's mansion. He stumbled indoors, threw off his sticky, gore-soaked garments, and sank onto a bed, grinding his teeth with pain and fury.

Old Jacopo Pazzi's eyes were distraught, but Francesco ignored his questions and commanded, "You must rally the citizens to arms. They will follow you. Bandini, curse him, has fled with his usual swiftness. Part of our plan has gone awry. The tyrant still lives and is safe within his palazzo. I would call the people myself, but for this accursed wound. Where are Vanozzo and Guido di Cuono? They should be here now to help gather our supporters. For the honour of our name, and the freedom of this city, Jacopo, you must take my place. Salviati will by now have control of the Palazzo della Signoria. With the seat of government in our hands the people will flock to us, and Lorenzo's power will be at an end . . ."

Old age had unfitted Messer Jacopo for sudden desperate action, but he mounted Francesco's horse and galloped towards the Piazza della Signoria at the head of a hundred armed men. Waving a sword above his head, he roared out the rallying cry: "Liberty and the people!"

His followers took up the call but were dismayed to realize that Salviati had not succeeded with his part of the plan. Their own attack on the Palazzo's massive walls was beaten off by a savage hail of stones thrown down by the *Signoria* under the command of Cesar Petrucci, the Gonfalionere della Giustizia. The members of government flourished spits and larding pins from their kitchens in case the supply of rocks did not fulfill the need.

"Liberty and the people!" drowned under another chant which swelled through the narrow streets to burst upon the piazza. The people summoned by the urgent ringing of the Parlemento bell, in the palazzo's tower, demonstrated their loyalty and fury with the Medici's own emblem as their rallying call.

"*Palle! Palle! Palle!*" rang out from all quarters. The Medici's personal followers galloped into the packed square, and the city seemed about to explode with the screams, the clanging bells, and the crash of arms.

Jacopo Pazzi understood their cause was lost. They had underestimated the Medici's popularity among the common herd. From the upper windows of the Palazzo della Signoria the bodies of the Archbishop of Pisa, his brother, and Bracciolini appeared hanging by ropes. Gradually their legs ceased to twitch. They swung back and forth like sides of butcher's meat in the Mercato Vecchio. The archbishop's costly robes were kirtled about his loins, and the purple silk stockings made a touch of macabre gaiety.

Messer Jacopo turned his horse and, crouching in the saddle, galloped from the city through the Porto alla Croce, in the direction of the Romagna.

As the news of Giuliano's murder spread, a frenzy of blood lust and revenge siezed the populace. Men and youths, armed with every sort of weapon, hacked at the corpses of the archbishop's followers, which lay in a grisly tangled heap on the piazza's paving stones. They carried the bloody relics on staves through the streets, screaming: "Death to the traitors!" while the *Signoria*'s men-at-arms diced for the dead men's clothing.

Crowds milled before the Palazzo Medici to protest their allegiance. Lorenzo, his face gaunt above a swathe of bandages, showed himself to the citizens, acknowledging and encouraging their loyalty. His own followers ransacked each of the Pazzi mansions to bring to justice all holders of that name, and their minions. Many had already fled. Guglielmo Pazzi only survived because of the Magnificent's perfect knowledge of his brother-in-law's innocence.

The mob discovered Francesco Pazzi and dragged him naked through the streets, spitting on him and throwing ordure. His round, ugly head remained unbowed, and his eyes glowed malevolently. In the Palazzo della Signoria fire and iron were agonizingly employed to wrest the names of the fellow-conspirators from his lips, but Francesco shrieked nothing save: "Death to the Medici!"

They hung his mutilated body from the window beside the Archbishop. As Salviati and Pazzi knocked together the crowds below hurled obscenities. They returned again and again to disembowel the stiffening corpses . . . like children never tiring of a new game. The air reeked with the excreted terror of the executed, their blood and guts.

When night spread across the city, torches flickered crimson on the increasing necklace of human pendants strung across the palazzo. All gates were closed to prevent the guilty from escaping.

The joy and flowers of Easter were stamped upon by fear and hatred . . .

Blood and Fire

FRANCA TRUDGED down the path from the woods, whistling against the eeriness of thickening dusk. Somehow she'd failed to hear Castelfiore's bell. The family had all gathered for Easter in an effort to cheer Vincenzo de' Narni who brooded too much on Raffaello's absence. It had been a happy day though. The adults' sleepiness after their sumptuous feast had enabled her to sneak away on a pilgrimage to the shrine of San Christofero at the lonely crossing south of Fiesole. There Franca had placed fresh flowers before the tremulous little light, and prayed for Raffaello's miraculous return, trusting that this holiest of Sundays would make her prayers favoured by the saint who had a fine reputation for aiding travellers in peril.

The breeze carried a faint acridity of smoke. They must

have become anxious, she thought, and sent out searchers. That's the smell of torches.

Franca topped the rise from where she always surveyed Castelfiore on her way homeward. No torches, like a swarm of fireflies, starred the darkness, but pale smoke plumed from the farm buildings; yet she could not hear the shouts of men who must be beating out the fire. A sudden eruption of flame sent her running down the hillside.

Unreasoning terror blotted out the ability to think. She tripped over her skirts, unaware of the stones and brambles that tore at her hands and feet. The nearer Franca came to home, the emptier seemed the surrounding dark. Now she could hear the flames, and the fiery glow through a barn's open door threw the buildings into black relief.

Not even a dog barked.

Franca stumbled into the courtyard, her mouth dry, her eyes streaming, and her rasping breaths interspersed with attacks of coughing from the stinging smoke. A pain nagged in her side.

Then she saw the dog. Cassio lay before the open door, as he often did on sunny days. Franca bent over him, then recoiled. The animal had been clubbed to death.

Beyond, the silent unlit interior astonished rather than frightened. Familiarity allowed her to feel the way into the wainscotted chamber where the family must be awaiting her at the end of this feast day.

Once she called out: "Andrea!"

There was no answer.

The big room was lit by that orange glow slowly encircling the house and also by the last red ashes in the hearth. Overturned chairs . . . fallen hangings . . . a never-before-seen confusion . . . suggested the family had fled away.

Then Franca saw them. Her beloved ones. Vincenzo de' Narni stared across the room at his daughter. She ran towards him, and stopped. He was transfixed to the wainscotting by his own sword. Franca backed away. Her foot touched something soft and heavy. She looked down. Nofri lay there, his head almost severed from his neck. Her bare feet knew a moist stickiness.

She did not cry out or move. Her eyes roamed the scene like a sleeper unable to waken from a nightmare.

Domenico sprawled across the long table among the debris of broken china, scattered food, and spilled wine. His hands had been lopped from the wrists, and his head was an unrecognizable bloody mass. On the ground beside him lay his young wife. The matted long hair half concealed her face, and the plump throat garotted by the gold chain from which hung the pearl crucifix—Domenico's gift on the birth of their first son. Isabetta was quite naked, and the white flesh tinged orange from the fire's light. Blood smeared the heavy breasts, the inner sides of the obscenely flung apart legs. The swollen stomach had been ripped open.

Franca understood what had happened to Isabetta before she was slain. She knew it with a primitive female instinct rather than the certainty of any taught knowledge, and her hand involuntarily pressed through her gown against the top of her own thighs.

"Mamma . . ." Franca kept repeating the first word she had ever learned in a flat, monotonous wail.

Madonna Ginevra, her heavy skirts covering her face, had been as brutally assaulted as her daughter-in-law. This wasn't her mother . . . for Franca could not associate the sweet, virtuous lady with that grotesquely spread-eagled, blood-stained horror. Beside her, Gostanza had shared a similar fate.

Close to them lay the pathetic nakedness of Ser Agnolo. He had been obscenely mutilated, and the skin on the soles of his feet was charred away in strips like meat which has been grilled overlong. Beside one stiffening hand rested the knife he used to sharpen pens—a last futile and gallant attempt to protect his dear lady.

Both babes were dead, their small rounded bodies hopelessly twisted like discarded toys from being flung against a wall . . .

Jewels and precious ornaments were gone. The new clavichord Franca was just learning to play had been hacked into firewood. Torn leaves of the prized illuminated manuscripts littered the floor with autumnal profligacy.

Someone was missing from this carnage.

Franca searched, dreading to find him. Andrea was nowhere to be seen. A tiny flame ignited in her heart. He would seek out the killers and bring them to justice even if this could not wipe out the hideous sin.

She did not cry. Grief could not encompass the feelings. She clasped and unclasped her hands, and could not understand. Her gentle, often mundane world had come to an abrupt end . . . erased with steel, fire, and violence. No one had ever suggested such a thing could happen. Franca shut her eyes, reopened them, believing it was all the enchantment within an evil dream . . . but the ghastly setting remained. An etching in darkness and blood filled with the odour of the shambles and burned flesh.

Footsteps slapped against the darkness. Terror and shock did not allow Franca to move. A fitting apparition for this red and black hell, Taddeo resembled a misshapen demon that had come to claim the souls for the devil's kingdom of agony.

He wandered the room, stopping before each corpse. At last he stood over his mother, and with unsure fingers—in case she suddenly sprang up and started to berate him as was her wont—he pulled the skirts down over her belly and legs to reveal Gostanza's face curiously tranquil even above the gashed throat.

Taddeo stared for a long while at the girl frozen in the center of that room. Then he tugged at her cold, clammy hand. She did not react. He peered into the transparent face and listened to the shallow rapid breathing. The staring eyes conveyed a great void as if they could see nothing. The soul had flown, and the shell awaited its return or the entrance of another. Taddeo pulled at her arm fiercely and began to drag her from that human abattoir.

Once Franca screamed: the hopeless cry of a small animal swooped upon by a night-hallowed owl.

"You cannot stay," he mumbled, the words as usual tumbling over his too-large tongue. "You will be killed too."

The fire had increased. Despite the cool of night, the air held the intense heat of an August noon sun. The roar of flames belonged to an overhead thunderstorm. Now and then a violent crash sounded as a barn wall collapsed. Stinging smoke filled their lungs and made breathing a painful, tearful process.

On the paving stones lay a limp silken banner: a scarlet ground with a trailing black flambeau woven into it. Some distant memory echoed that pattern. Franca picked it up as Taddeo dragged her across the painted court.

Once the girl looked back from the hilltop. The flames had encroached upon the house now. Sparks cascaded into the darkness. An enormous funeral pyre that reduced to dust not only the beloved characters in her life, but also all the beauty, comfort, and civilization she had ever known. With it went the greater part of her own self, for that belonged to Castelfiore.

It was dark and stale within the cave, but untouched by the heavy dew. Franca crept to the very back and cowered against the rock face. Taddeo handed her his one comfort: a stinking goat's skin peeled from some beast that had died of exposure. The girl ignored it, remaining crouched, staring and trembling.

He left her, to return shortly with a rough wooden bowl of fresh milk. The young goatherd was easy to scare from his duty. Whenever Taddeo's terrible head peered at him over some bush, the boy would flee with the agility of one of his own creatures, as if the hounds of hell were snuffling at his heels.

"Drink," Taddeo ordered, and pushed the rim against her mouth. Dutifully she sucked at the thick, sweetish milk, but he had to wipe away the creamy outline from her lips with the back of his hand.

Vision seemed to return to her eyes and concentrated itself upon Taddeo's belt. Before he could gauge her intentions, Franca darted forward and seized the knife.

"No . . . no . . ." he protested, and tried to force her to drop the blade. She fought like an animal, and he did not want to hurt her. He licked his scratched arms, and blinked as she seized fistfuls of her own hair, and hacked at it until she had a shorn head as ragged as Taddeo's. A wealth of soft red gold carpeted the cave.

He picked up a strand and stroked it.

"Beautiful," he grunted. "Why?"

She gave a wild laugh. "Now I'm a boy. You must call me Franco. Do you understand? I'm Franco," she insisted. "Then they cannot do those things to me. I shall not have a baby to be destroyed . . ."

The mirth became sobbing. She cried without tears, rocking back and forth in an agony of memory, which stayed fresh-painted on the canvas of her mind.

For four days Taddeo kept her in that cave. He gave her milk, but she would not touch the flesh of rabbits he snared and cooked. During daylight she sat holding the stained silken pennant. At night she curled up on the floor and stared into the darkness until sleep claimed her.

Taddeo was woken by terrible screams. He could not know what she saw in her dreams but vaguely recalled that when he was smaller he too used to waken in the lonely places, crying and trembling, from encountering some horror that prowled the avenues of his sleep. Taddeo did not dare touch her and knew no ways to soothe . . . for gentleness was something he had never experienced. When he lay down to sleep he closed his fist on a tress of that wonderful silken fire as if it were a talisman.

Sometimes Franca would question him with a wild intensity, and he tried to tell her his jumbled memories of the destruction of Castelfiore.

"A man," Taddeo mumbled thickly, wary of Franca's spurts of rage. "A prince of night from afar, but when I crawled closer to the track I saw his clothes were of that dark red, like the fruit silkworms feed upon. He had many sparkling stones, even in his hat, and he rode a great black horse."

From the pointed beard and long, dark eyes Franca determined the man was Messer Ridolfo di Salvestro. Yet whether he had come to Castelfiore before or after the company of horsemen that had dropped the banner, Taddeo could not recollect.

She sat rubbing her hands in pitiful triumph. "I know my enemy now. Andrea will find him out, and we will destroy him . . ."

Then she commanded: "Fetch Berto to me. He will take us down to the city. My brother must be awaiting my news."

The voice was wild with hysteria . . . as if the mind that proposed this plan was about to split asunder under unbearable strain. Though Taddeo was unwilling to seek out a youth who tormented him, he could not ignore Franca's order. He left her alone for the whole day, but Franca had ceased to notice time.

Taddeo returned alone.

"Berto?"

He sank down, tired and puzzled. Suddenly his familiar grim world had turned a somersault, and he seemed to be the one person who had not altered.

"The night the house burned," he grunted. "Berto hit his father and ran away. In the village they are saying he hurt a woman very badly so that she almost died."

Taddeo's explanatory gesture was crudely direct.

"Berto too . . ." Franca shuddered.

She was not to know he had visited Castelfiore that night of violence and seen enough to be convinced his playmate had suffered the same brutalities as the Narni ladies and all their maidservants. When Berto returned to his father's hovel he had demanded they seek out the killers of their master's family.

"What, and get ourselves butchered!" his father shouted. "Listen to me, you idle lout, let the noble folk slay each other just so long as they leave us alone. We have no rights. Why should we look out for others?"

"You know what they did?"

Giovanni Spenozzi shrugged. "They do as much to our women and children for sport, and we are not allowed to defend ourselves. You've just had your head filled with madness by their fine daughter. All you wish is that you could have had your chance with the strumpet . . ."

It was then Berto struck his father.

Franca was defiled and dead. Therefore life had tricked him monstrously. No such things existed as goodness and beauty . . . The devil ruled. The rest was just a sweet fantasy to incense man and then leave him arid and empty. From now on he was free to be as wicked as he chose. He would take what he wanted. That would be his revenge on a world that had duped him.

So the middle-aged countrywoman he encountered on the road, knocked senseless, and raped was his first act of rebellion . . . by which he hoped to banish Franca's magic memory.

Franca curled up on the floor like one of the fox cubs which had long since departed for the woods. Lassitude enmeshed her. Taddeo, ignorant in the ways of the artificial world, but cunning in the laws of nature, thought only of discovering some protection for the foundling he succoured. In the night he listened to her calling desperately: "Andrea . . . Andrea . . ."

She awoke, feeling Taddeo's hand shaking her shoulder, and her voice contained accusation: "You're not Andrea! You're a fiend!"

He ignored her harsh words just the way he ignored the bites and scratches of wounded wild creatures.

"We must go now."

Her eyes dilated in terror. He was quick to reassure. "There is no danger. You must come to them. They are waiting for you."

He could not answer any questions as to who the "They" were, and almost carried her out into the cold night. The air smelled thin and pure. It hurt her nostrils after the stuffiness of the cave.

Night was total, for it was that phase of the month when the moon presented her dark face to the earth, so that the oldest mysteries might be practised away from the eyes of men who wished to eradicate those deepest beliefs engraved upon the night before May's first day . . .

The chuckle of a waterfall told Franca they had reached Fontelucente. She longed to be clean. Taddeo's rough attempts at washing her face, hands, and feet had only been to remove the blood. Her skin itched from countless bites, and reeked as if it belonged to a stranger. She felt permeated to the marrow with the odour of the frowsy cave and the goat pelt.

Fully clothed, Franca waded into the icy pool, heedless of Taddeo's urgent call. She did not even flinch from the numbing cold, as if her senses were already frozen, and her nerve ends failed to respond to normal feelings. At last, she clambered onto the bank, where Taddeo grumbled: "You'll die of cold."

Her fierce, bright look penetrated even the dark and spoke of a total indifference for life, and he was scared. In the thicker darkness of the grove above the pool, Franca saw the figures and tried to pull free, but Taddeo held her fast.

At first, she thought they were beasts standing on their hind legs, but then realized they were men and women, their bodies half concealed by animal pelts with swinging tails.

A woman with wild grey locks approached. Pale eyes stared at Franca. She was conscious of her own lack of fear. Once she would have automatically recited the prayers that had become part of herself. Since that night she had not even thought to say a *Paternoster*.

The woman put thin, knotted hands on the girl's shoulders. "Not afeared then," she muttered, reading the unwavering expression. "They who have been through the fire and known the worst either madden or die . . . or else they are made new. You are reborn and so can be one of us. Take off that wet dress. Put on this cloak and get warm."

Franca did not stir. The woman pulled off the soaking gown and bundled the frail body into rough wool which smelled of fresh air and grass.

"Who are you?" Franca demanded, gazing at the figures outlined in the flickering light of the fire behind them.

"We are members of *La Vecchia*—the oldest faith."

"So you are streghe then." Franca did not shy away. She had found the witches of Fontelucente . . . or rather they had sought her out.

The different voices proclaimed their stations in the daylight world. Some accents were of peasant folk: the wise women who supplied villagers with philters that procured love, abortion, the easing of labour, or fertiilty. When all went well, their arts were secretly and gladly solicited . . .

but if folk died, crops failed, or cattle sickened the blame was located on these streghe, who paid with their lives. Other accents belonged to the educated and priestly. These were the wizards of the city who tried to understand the universe, pored over the Cabala, and the Clavicle of Solomon . . . attempted to conjure up spirits to unlock the secret wisdoms. Their powers as astrologers, alchemists, and necromancers were consulted by popes, princes, and kings. Yet their experiments and beliefs could lead to torture and execution on the grounds of heresy and witchcraft.

"The world only knows what the Church tells it about us. To gain power the Christians have garlanded our faith with every abominable deed," the wise woman explained. "We do not pay homage to the Devil, for those who do merely practice the converse of Christianity, seeing rebellion against their baptized faith as a means to gain power. We worship the dark queen, Diana Aradia, who rides with us through the skies, and whose domain over men's minds belongs to the womb of time. Tonight is hallowed, and we hold a feast in honour of our lady. Sometimes she sends us a special envoy to take her place in our revels. All hail to you, child, for you are sent by our lady."

She drew Franca into the circle of thirteen. They did not touch her but bowed their heads in welcome.

"We shall invoke the spirits to guard you, little lady," said a man's educated voice.

"I'm a boy," Franca insisted wildly.

"Our goddess permits you to be both," a pretty wench explained softly in the accents of the Mugello. "You may serve her in whatever guise you choose. Whoever you are, little creature, you have nought to fear from us, who know what it is to be hunted down in the name of the god of love, or by the vagaries of power-greedy laws."

They removed the cloak and sat Franca upon a stone slab.

It formed a natural throne in the midst of a dark clearing studded with the pale stars of Jack-by-the-hedge, which by day tempted butterflies of a similar appearance to linger on its stems. Sometimes Franca had brushed this garlic-scented plant and laughed to see what looked like flowers flying up into the blue. Beside her was a lock of her own hair, and a small silver ax with a dark bone handle. Upon her head they placed a crown of herbs and flowers interwoven with dried poppy heads.

"These are the flowers of forgetfulness," the old woman said. "You will learn life is but a dark dream."

Franca did not fear them . . . even when one of the men, an old and silvery-haired being, took the ax and gently touched the ten orifices of her body, and her left breast with its blade. He recited words in a tongue she did not understand, and placed the hair in a small box, which he buried at the base of the throne.

They danced around her in a solemn circle. Their complete nudity did not repel her, for in that flickering firelight they were not creatures of the world. Then each knelt and kissed the child's hand, laying their heads for a moment upon her knees in homage.

"Tonight we do you honour," the man said. "For you will sit in the place of our queen at this love feast. Ever after you will be among the elect, although you may not recall this ceremony until many years pass. It is written in your hands that this event will come to pass.

"You cannot but accept a strange destiny. Our powers will be transmitted into your own blood, for you have been brought to us, newborn, neither man nor woman, without name or place, cut off from the world of men. You will never betray our secrets, and we shall not reveal yours until the death."

Even as he spoke a star shot against the black heavens in

a stream of silver spray, and its reflection touched the ax blade. Franca understood this was a special omen as if the queen of night welcomed her to La Vecchia.

"You must be marked with our sign," the old woman said. "It will not pain very much. By it, the chosen will always know you are one of us, for we all bear such a sign. Our enemies call it the devil's mark, claiming that it is inflicted by the devil's kiss when a worshiper forfeits his Christian soul. We are not creatures of hell."

Franca smiled. "No, I have been to hell," she said, and the low voice was not a child's.

They anointed her upper left buttock with a herbal salve that deadened the flesh, and then marked her with fire. She felt the slightest discomfort. Later, the burn healed to leave a tiny star-shaped scar that could almost have been part of her flesh since birth.

They placed her at the head of their company and gave her to eat and drink. A silver beaker was passed among them. Franca swallowed the liquid slowly. It was heady and sweet and made her feel warm for the first time since the fire. "What is it?" she asked.

"Our enemies would say it contained all the vilest ingredients . . . like human blood, fat of a murdered babe, our own excrement, and naturally the ashes of a toad which has been fed on the Host," a girl replied cheerfully. "It is just good vernaccia laced with honey."

They ate new white bread, fresh cheese, green herbs, and honey cakes. Taddeo sat in the deepest shadows, and partook wolfishly of the fine food they offered him. He played no part in the gathering and was completely uninterested in their doings. He was content, for he believed that whatever transpired in the future now the child would be protected.

They sang songs Franca had never heard, in an old tongue: strange, joyful chants which seemed to be echoed by the whispering springtime leaves . . . as if the grove were impregnated with such music from the birth of all time.

Afterwards the women rubbed her body with a pungent-smelling ointment, which stung a little when it touched broken skin; then they all anointed their flesh in a similar manner.

"As the leader of our revels," they said, taking her hands, "you must dance with us. You will learn how to fly and begin to understand your own powers."

The steps of La Volta were not difficult. Franca found herself laughing, but it was not her old carefree laughter: this was the sharp-edged mirth of the defiant, who have lost everything, yet dare all. She felt as light as a sycamore butterfly caught in a gust of wind.

They formed a chain that danced among the trees. At its head leapt the figure they called the child of Aradia . . . She felt safe, and that she belonged to those who were cast out from society by secret and forbidden beliefs, or through cruelty and ignorance.

So many stars shone in the heavens it seemed the dark backcloth had worn thin and begun revealing its glittering hidden kingdom. Each leaping step carried Franca up towards the eyes of night, until she was flying amongst them . . . right above the trees. Even outcasts and vagrants could enjoy miracles impossible for ordinary safe-abed mortals if they performed the mysteries.

They set her reverently on the ancient throne. No one attempted to molest the child who witnessed their rites in a grove which was dedicated to such deeds. Firelight painted the flailing limbs red against the black shadows. Franca stared impassively, without once shutting her eyes or ears to the sight and sound of the witches slaking their unhallowed passions . . .

BOOK II

"*The Red Lily*"

The Outcast

No ONE PAID ATTENTION to the two beggar children who entered the city by the Porta della Ficsole. One was too repugnant to look upon, for his hood failed to conceal the purple birthmark. His smaller companion was almost lost under a drab, hooded jacket. The tiny, pale face, so hollow and pointed, held none of the roundness of childhood . . . nor the onset of premature age as often seen among the derelict poor . . . but belonged to some new remote age, which, having been forged with the cleansing fire, stepped purified into the everyday world. The enormous amethyst eyes did not smile or weep. They had learned to mask thought so that an observer might conclude the pitiful creature did not feel.

A group of urchins ran, yelling and laughing, through the streets, dragging something on a long rope. A terrible stench of putrescence emanated from this plaything. The boys fixed one rope end to the doorbell of an elegant palazzo, which bore the *Signoria*'s seal forbidding anyone to enter. Each time they jerked the rope their grisly burden rose up as if to ring the bell. Convulsed with laughter, the boys kept screaming: "Knock on the door, Messer Jacopo! Knock on the door!"

The beggars watched silently. At last the smaller demanded of one of the urchins: "What are you doing?"

"Don't you know anything?" he retorted. "You two must come from well outside the city. We dug him up this morning—old Messer Jacopo Pazzi—the bloody traitor. The soldiers captured him escaping, so he joined his relations and pals hanging in the piazza . . . and everyone had the sport of sticking him in the guts . . ."

"What did he do?" the small, husky voice asked.

"The Pazzis, the Salviatis, and a host of other accursed *magnati* killed our marvellous Giuliano, attempted to murder the Magnificent, and seize our city. The Medici forced young Cardinal Riario to write to his uncle, the Pope, and inform him about the conspiracy. That's a real joke, for Count Montesecco has blurted out the whole truth. He was supposed to kill the brothers but refused to perform such a deed during Mass, and he revealed that old Sixtus was at the bottom of all this villainy. For his confession Lorenzo allowed him to be honourably beheaded. The Pope keeps demanding Riario's release, but our Magnificent is making uncle and nephew sweat for their impudence. Wish they'd string up the Cardinal and the Pope . . . That'd be worth watching . . ."

He returned to his game. When the boys tired of their sport, they threw the toy from the Rubaconte Bridge. The swollen, dreadful carcass floated on the surface of the Arno towards Pisa.

The Aquias' house stood behind the Mercato Nuovo. Franco and Taddeo threaded their way among the bankers sitting at green-covered tables with purses and ledgers ready for transactions. They halted briefly to watch a bankrupt obtain discharge . . . by publicly striking his bare buttocks three times on a black and white marble circle—the site of the symbolic chariot of the city.

"My father's sister is bound to help me," the smaller child muttered and tugged at the bell rope. "Perhaps Andrea is already here."

It was a long time before a maidservant peered through the grille in the outside door.

"Go away!" she cried. "My master won't have beggars hanging round his gates."

"We aren't beggars."

The maid laughed. "Who are you then—princes? Clear off!"

Reaching into the neck of a filthy ragged shirt, the smaller child drew out a glistening yellow jewel. "Show this topaz to Madonna Riccarda. Go on. It's not stolen and won't bite off your nose. It belonged to someone who is dead."

Reluctantly, the maid took it, and disappeared. They waited a long interval before Tommaso di Aquia appeared, his sour features like a streak of rancid fat.

"You've no business here. Get away before I summon the Eight."

Mention of the body of law enforcers did not send them packing. Instead the pale child pushed back its hood. "Can't you see—I'm a Narni?"

"You!" his eyes slid fearfully along the street to make sure no one was watching. "I'll not be linked to anyone who bears that name. I've had to bar my door for days because I'm married to one of them. The shame of it. The mother of my children. I'll never live it down. I always knew that alliance would ruin me. You get away from here, or I'll set my dogs on you."

"Don't you know that the family have been slaughtered?"

"They deserved worse than death. Joining with the vicious Pazzi and Salviati to murder our sweet Medici, and overthrow this wonderful state. They were traitors."

"That's a lie."

His mirth had never been pleasant; now it was the raucous call of a carrion crow. "Is it? We have to be grateful to Messer Vanozzo di Cuono and his brave son, who overheard part of the foul plot. When they learned that the villains had almost succeeded in the city, they went and exacted vengeance at Castelfiore. The law is that all who bear the name Narni are to be hunted down and destroyed like the vermin they are. Their name is to be erased totally from all records. Their estates and possessions are forfeit. Do you understand? The Narnis, like the Pazzis, do not exist."

"We are innocent," the child stormed. "We have been traduced by those who wish to conceal their own complicity. I shall go to my betrothed. His family will help me."

"They would merely turn you over to the Eight," he jeered. "It is forbidden to marry with a Narni on pain of losing all rights and possessions. Luckily, the della Seras are such intimates of the Medici, else suspicion might have fallen on them too, and"—he gave a narrow unpleasant smile— "despite my accursed wife, everyone knows how loyal I am."

"To whoever comes into power," the child retorted. "What will become of me?"

"You'll die on the streets of plague or hunger, and your body will be tossed into the river. Or else you can play the whore. I've already heard how you tried to corrupt my innocent Lionello. Your presence is as contaminating as a plague spot."

The door slammed in their faces. Franco picked up a handful of dirt and flung it. "Weasel!" she shouted. Taddeo looked at the ground and shuffled his feet. He was accustomed to such treatment and knew that in order to survive his companion would have to learn a similar lesson. Slowly they walked away, but the sound of hurrying footsteps made them halt.

Riccarda di Aquia, her face ghastly with grief and fatigue, red eyes set within enormous violet shadows, ran after them. Her grey hair contained a few rusty streaks: the only sign of her Narni heritage.

"Francesca," she sobbed.

"Franco," the child countered.

"Whoever you are, may God protect you. Here, I dare not give you more. He would beat me for this if he knew." She thrust some hard, dark bread and the topaz into the child's hand and began retracing her steps, her shoulders heaving pitifully.

"Stop," Franco called.

The woman half turned, hunched and fearful.

"Where is Andrea?"

"In the piazza, but you must not . . ."

Franco refused to listen further. "Her lot is worse than ours," she commented, and threw the bread into a refuse channel. "It's better to die than live imprisoned with the Weasel."

Pained and hungry, Taddeo stared at the discarded crusts.

"It would choke us to eat something so unwillingly given." Franco's tired voice could still ring with pride.

They wandered along the Calimala, which was unnaturally quiet for the center of the thriving wool industry; but the city, fearing new conspiracies and Papal reprisals, had not settled back into its normal trading rhythm. Each day fresh conspirators were rounded up and joined to ranks of corpses. By day and night guards patrolled streets. No citizen was permitted to carry weapons, or be outdoors after dark. The air smelled of treachery.

In the Piazza della Signoria, Taddeo gazed wonderingly at the soaring tower and crenellated roof of the palazzo and at the graceful Loggia dei Lanzi, where on fine days government matters were debated in full view of the citizens. He had never thought to visit the city. The loud noise, strange odours, and sense of being enclosed terrified him, but Taddeo was also filled with awe at the spectacle of so many fine folks and beautiful objects. Occasionally he trembled to hear the lions roaring in the palazzo's menagerie.

Franco was blind and deaf to all these wonders, although not very long ago every aspect of Florentine life entranced her. Now she only saw the festoons of remains hanging from the civic buildings. The air reeked of decomposing flesh and hummed with innumerable flies, while packs of stray dogs chased about the square, snapping hopefully each time a corpse swayed on its rope. Now and then irate citizens stopped to shake their fists and shout abuse . . . publicly demonstrating their loyalty.

Only the brilliant hair made what had once been a lovesome young man distinguishable as Andrea de' Narni. Swarming flies gave the limbless trunk an indistinct outline.

Franco swayed, and Taddeo grabbed the thin arm. Yet, like someone who believes there is some solution to an impossible problem, she purposefully entered the Santa Maria Novella area.

The Narni palazzo and the great silk warehouse bore the *Signoria*'s forbidding seal. All the emblems of Castelfiore—even Niccolo Grosso's elegant iron torch-holders and door-knockers, cunningly fashioned into the Narni crest—had been smashed. There was no longer any sign to show that the building had till recently belonged to a gay, handsome, and noble family.

Franco led Taddeo down to the malodourous river. While he blinked at the goldsmiths' shops along the Ponte Vecchio and the boats being unloaded beside the grain wharves, she gazed into the waters.

In the greasy depths Franco seemed to see a procession of faces of her father's and brothers' influential friends. No one would risk lives, reputations, safety, and wealth to help the insignificant child of a treacherous family . . . whether or not they believed in the Narnis' guilt. This was the law of the world. God's own Son had fared no better among his own friends.

Franco perceived that without name, possessions or rights, she did not really exist. Only death remained.

She pointed to the river and said simply, "That is my only destination."

Taddeo thumped his stained forehead with an angry fist. "No, there is another way. Your nurse once told me that if anything ever happened to your family Frate Sandro would be the one person for you to turn to . . . only I had forgot. Forgive me." He pawed at her hand like a dog that fears a whipping, but Franco managed a brief smile.

"I have not heard of Frate Sandro. Who is he?" she asked, at the same time thinking: How strange he never calls Gostanza mother and accepts that she belonged to me rather than to him.

It seemed that Paulo di Freddiano Lucca had begotten a bastard on a young peasant girl 'Sandra. She had died giving birth, and Franco's maternal grandfather, ashamed of his brief amour, had sent the boy to San Marco to become a Dominican.

Darkness filled the alleys as they limped towards the monastery. Franco was exhausted and faint, for they had not eaten since the crust of bread they had begged and shared at daybreak just outside the city. Her feet bled, and her head ached and contained a dull buzzing.

"If he will not help us," she murmured, "the guard will throw us into the dread Stinche prison. Taddeo, you must leave me. You heard what my uncle said: No one will help me, but you could manage alone. If they discover who I am you might suffer. Here . . ." she held out the topaz. "Try to buy yourself food and comfort with the money it fetches. But go now . . ."

"I shall never leave you," he said.

And if this Frate Sandro spurns me, what then, Franco kept asking herself?

As if in reply, life displayed the alternatives in the alleyways and courts. Among the piles of stinking rubbish, flung out by housewives and merchants, emaciated beggar brats rummaged for scraps, fighting for subsistence among the slinking rats, curs, and shrieking cats. In the darkest corners girls of no more than Franco's age sold their immature bodies for the smallest coin to any sort of man. The briefly heaving and panting couples against the walls suggested a grotesque sideshow at a carnival.

It was the first time Franco had visited the city to find it anything but fair. The architecture of Michelozzi and Alberti, Ghiberti's heavenly doors to the Baptistry, gateways showing palatial courtyards with pretty fountains and graceful statues . . . these meant nothing. All that counted were the immediacies of life and death. Beauty dwelt on another plane: To reach it there had to be time to pause in the midst of the struggle for existence.

The gaunt-visaged Dominican, who opened the grille in the gate, examined the beggars without hostility. "Who wants Fra Sandro?"

"Franco," the smaller child answered wearily.

Fra Sandro unlocked the monastery gate without question. He sent Taddeo to the kitchens with a young novice to ensure the cripple was given food and a straw mattress. Though starving, Taddeo left his companion with reluctance, fearing to lose what was familiar in this curious new country.

With a gentle hand Sandro piloted Franco among Michelozzi's cloisters and into his own cell. Momentarily, the child forgot weariness. The heavy eyes flared with pleasure at the devotional picture of the Annunciation.

"How beautiful. So light and airy, like the first morning of the world."

"So, you appreciate beauty. It is the work of the blessed Fra Angelico. God be praised for giving one man such talent and sending him to San Marco. He has gone to his Heavenly Father but left behind a touch of paradise . . ."

The child recognized Madonna Ginevra's features set in

masculine mold: melancholy brown eyes with heavy lids, the gentle smile, the sallow, tight-pulled skin, but there was an aura of peace about Fra Sandro. He fetched some thin beer, bread, olives, and cheese.

"Sit down. You are famished and can hardly stand."

Despite hunger, Franco could only sip the beer under the monk's solemn gaze. Staring round the tiny, sparsely furnished chamber, she thought: It seems a lifetime since I sat on a chair inside any house and saw food on a plate. I had almost forgotten these things.

"Do you know who I am?" It was a struggle for her to ask this question.

He nodded. "An innocent caught up in events beyond any individual's control . . . like the majority of mankind, alas, my child. Rest now. We shall decide what is to be done with you."

"Then you won't help me," Franco protested bitterly. "I am truly cursed."

"Hush. Be still. I must go to Compline, and then confer with our good prior. I fear you cannot remain here simply because you are a female."

"No!" the anguished cry drowned that soothing voice. "Look, my clothes and my hair. I am a boy. I won't be a girl."

He flinched before the terror in her eyes as if it contained the dark images of all she had witnessed, then placed a tender hand on the ragged head. "You have seen too much of man's inhumanity. Sleep now. Do not fear betrayal or hurt."

The distant murmur of plainsong lulled her into sleep as deep as any swoon. Franco awoke to see Fra Sandro kneeling in thoughtful prayer. Without turning, he said: "I have been asking that I might be shown the right way to help you. Will you pray with me?"

Franco shook her head vehemently. "Never! There is no

God! Not since that night. If He really knows everything and allows such evil to happen then He is not good . . . and if He could not save the innocents then He is not all-powerful. Man and the Devil rule this world. So what is the point in asking for God's help?"

Sandro did not chide her. "God sent his Son to share our worst suffering and to show whatever our earthly fate we shall be redeemed to a greater joy. If we dismiss all that is good because of man's wickedness, child, I should say we despair and allow the Devil his triumph. I have been praying for the souls of our dead in the complete faith that they will dwell in the company of saints. Tell me, if you could pray, what would you require?"

"That I may have vengeance on my enemies." The torrent of words gushed with desperation. "On the Medici who believed in the Narnis' treachery, and allowed my good brother to be hanged like a common felon . . . On Messer Ridolfo di Salvestro who betrayed my confidence and warned the Cuono family . . . On *that* family who silenced my own dear ones to protect themselves. Perhaps Messer Ridolfo was jealous of their daughter's love for Andrea and saw an opportunity to rid himself of so perfect a rival. I have reasoned it all out and blame myself for ever admitting what I overheard. I, too, have blood upon me." She spread the thin, dirty hands and looked at them with anguish.

"Have you reasoned rightly?"

"Yes, and it seems to me I was appointed to be the instrument of revenge," Franco insisted.

"You must shed these thoughts." Fra Sandro's stern words sounded odd in that cell, which seemed a whole world away from violence and horror, and where the dark was just held at bay by the flickering glow of a rushlight. "They will embitter your soul and stunt your mind. Hatred is a canker. Eventually it destroys the hater. You must learn to love mankind and God. He alone knows what purpose your life will serve . . ."

He held the pointed, white chin in a firm hand so that the blazing eyes were forced to look up at him.

"Think, Franco, what can a nameless pauper do against the mighty of this world? It would be best if you could resign yourself to fate. Why not seek out the solace of a convent? Your cousin Carlotta has entered the Carmelite order at Santa Maddalena."

"Carlotta is too good for our world," Franca said miserably. "Andrea's death must have broken her sweet heart. Another lady suffers such torment too . . . a worse one if she realizes the full truth. But I don't want to hide for the rest of my days. Is that all I was spared for? To triumph over my enemies I shall live. That, Fra Sandro, will be my revenge if I can have no other."

"Then you must be very careful, for the Eight are more assiduous than ever in carrying out their policing duties. There are spies in all sorts of guises seeking the Medici's enemies."

An adult smile hovered on the fair young lips. "This is a good moment for any ruler to investigate all those who have been against him in the past and also to tighten his own control on the city."

Fra Sandro was torn between admiring the world-wise head on the slight body and wishing the child had no need to be tainted by such knowledge.

He sighed: "Very well, you may stay here until we discover what is best for you. To remain in this monastery you had better continue with your pretense as a boy . . ."

The Apprentice

DOMENICO GHIRLANDAJO had just begun a great painting of the Last Supper in the small refectory. He was anxious to find some way to make his picture different from those executed by fellow artists. Not just another Last Supper, the heavy features sagged in obstinate thought, but Ghirlandajo's Last Supper.

The monks irritated him too, always slipping in some pious suggestion about how they thought the apostles should look. Of course he contained his temper, but then shouted twice as loudly at his apprentices, who winked and nudged each other: "Old Domenico hasn't his fine high society manners today . . . what would some of the noble patrons he likes to flatter say to that language!"

It was not long before the artist espied the silent red-curled lad with the beautiful, almost unearthly, pale face, who watched each movement and listened to every command given to the apprentices.

Ghirlandajo's own smile lightened his face, and he became what he was: a young, enthusiastic, and highly professional artist who could wonderfully fulfill any commission. "Do you want to learn to paint?" he asked.

"I want to learn everything," the child declared passionately.

The artist laughed. "All of us die ignorant but striving after perfection. What can you do? Have you any spark to be fanned into genuine artistry?"

The child beckoned him to follow. On a worn white patch of a corner pillar was a sketch of a man with dark eyes . . . even the rough drawing suggested that these were eyes not too ready to meet another man's gaze. The expression battened down some dread secret knowledge.

Ghirlandajo stared, openly astounded by the skill shown in such a rough drawing. "You did that? Who taught you?"

"No one." Franco backed away like a dog that expects to be kicked.

"Who is this fellow meant to be?"

"Judas," she said with conviction. "It is the likeness of a man I once saw who deserved the name. Behind him I think there should lurk some creature . . . yes, a cat. A fiend in disguise." The thin, capable fingers drew in the animal, as the husky voice described the thought.

"A strange idea," Ghirlandajo commented. "If you will allow me to use it I shall take you as a pupil and try to teach you all I know . . . which of course is not everything."

From that moment onwards the workshop in the cloisters saw little of Franco. The monks had been quick to notice her wild defiance and lack of religious vocation, but also the natural talent for sculpture . . . she enjoyed learning to copy the draperies and muscles on antique statues, but was more interested in painting or sketching designs than chipping them out of stone. It had already been widely remarked and regretted that the powerful innate artistry leaned towards classical pagan subjects and not the conventional religious ones.

Franco was so hungry for knowledge that she scarcely found time to eat. She could not learn enough, as if it were fresh air and sunlight after being long incarcerated in some stifling, dark dungeon. The technicalities of the craft never ceased to intrigue her.

She rapidly became adept in mixing colours, laying on gold, sizing canvas, and painting on fabrics in such a way that the tints did not run. The optics of perspective enchanted her . . . so much so that the other pupils were often infuriated when this thin, intense child examined their handiwork to declare that the perspective was quite wrong. "You've merely copied what you see," she would say, "which doesn't convey that sight to another spectator."

"Franco!" Ghirlandajo would shout in exasperation. "You'll end up like poor old Paulo Uccello—he can't pay his taxes because he never makes enough money . . . he's so taken up with his love of perspective!"

He was furious too when this brightest of all apprentices started to pursue the revolutionary invention of Leonardo. "That dabbler, da Vinci!" Ghirlandajo cried. "He's not your master. You'd never learn anything from him. He spends all day looking at something without once applying his brush, and some of his ideas, God save us! You, Franco, can execute beautiful clear outlines. Why go for this, what's it called, 'sfumato'—blurred mellow stuff which merges together?"

"To stir the imagination and make people see even greater depth in any picture," Franco replied calmly, "but no one will ever outmatch Leonardo's use of this technique."

Franco's own small areas of work on the master's large paintings could soon be distinguished from all other apprentices' attempts by its soft and airy contouring. As a baby's bone structure is the foundation for a man's body, so the deepest memories of sun, shade, texture and colour among the Tuscan hills of childhood became the essence of Franco's painting.

Light and shadow were not just skillfully applied. The canvas seemed to radiate light from somewhere within, while the shadows held a disturbing depth that seemed to draw the onlooker down into their murk.

The master almost feared this fountain of talent had some divine or diabolical origin. Certainly, Franco was a troublesome pupil, but the others showed grudging respect rather than jealousy, which grew into rough comradeship. For the child was always up to some wild prank.

It had been Franco's idea to tie a mountebank's tame she-bear to the bell rope inside a small church. Bells chiming in the still of night had brought the priest out of bed, but he had been too scared to examine this nocturnal bell ringer; for in the darkness he was convinced it was a demon . . . and sent for another priest to join him in a ceremony of exorcism!

The story had circulated widely and provoked the mirth Florentines always enjoyed . . . and also shamed the congregation into spending money on locks for their church door.

Yes, Franco had a growing reputation, but Ghirlandajo felt only a little envious of his pupil's talent: The child's charm and beauty erased the irritation that impudence inspired.

"This is an even rarer talent," Domenico confided to his old friend Bernardo Gozzoli, over a jug of wine in the *Buco*. "Sometimes I lift my hand to wallop him for his sauce, then those great eyes mock me, and I begin to laugh at my own fury. God knows what will happen to a lad endowed with such craft and that smile. He thinks I'm holding him back out of jealousy, but it's for his own sake. He must learn some discipline and patience. He always gives you the feeling he's gobbling up life, as if frightened it'll be wrested from him . . ."

So Franco lived in a newfound haven. It smelled, sounded, and felt so different from the violent tunnel through which she had been thrust to be reborn. In these complicated acts of creation and self-expression, beauty and happiness could be grasped however briefly. The grimmest memory could be incorporated into paintings and so oust some of the personal terror and grief.

To create was to comprehend God just a little. But this God was wholly pagan: Dionysius and Apollo warred in Franco's spirit.

At night Franco dreamed only of the intricacies of the art she pursued in daylight, and the paintings she longed to start. Taddeo, who curled up on the palliasse at her feet in the novices' cold and cheerless dormitory, was no longer woken by shrieks of horror.

By day he sat in the darkest corner of the refectory or Ghirlandajo's studio and watched Franco's efforts and marvelled. He was content with the new order. He ate regularly, dwelt indoors, and had a reason to live: to watch over this magical changeling he would have followed into the mouth of Hell, and who allowed no one to torment him for his deformities.

The apprentices and urchins they consorted with in the squares and streets quickly learned this lesson, for Franco had acquired a reputation as the most reckless fighter. She fought with an audacity that undermined far bigger opponents . . . anyway some had glimpsed the small dagger concealed in the shabby sleeve . . .

Even the excommunication slapped on the city by the Pope in retaliation for the execution of Archbishop Salviati did not turn the people against the Medici as had been intended. The Florentines openly mocked Sixtus and his interdict and considered he was fortunate to get wretched Cardinal Riario back alive.

The Pope's threat that he, Ferrante, king of Naples, and their allies would make war on Florence unless they rid themselves of the Medici tyrant, provoked only the citizens' contempt. The *Signoria* promptly announced that Lorenzo's life was bound up with the well-being of the state and allowed him a large bodyguard and so many prerogatives that he was prince in all but name, and acted accordingly.

Anyway among humble folk, who cared if Lorenzo's power had somewhat altered the concept of government, so long as he continued to provide such clever, lavish entertainments on public holidays . . . and the sculptors, writers, and artists warmed themselves under the interest of this keen and sympathetic Maecenas.

Because of the aftermath of the Pazzi conspiracy the cele-

brations for the feast of San Giovanni—the city's patron—
had been postponed until early July. Pent-up gaiety after so
much fear and tension exploded in the streets with the force
and colour of the countless rockets and firewheels, constantly
igniting to form brilliant brief pictures of houses, palaces,
ships, and animals.

Apprentices shoved their way in and out of the holiday-
attired crowds, screaming, whistling, and throwing melon
rinds to incite the cat in the cage. Accompanying this wild
beast was a shaven, half-naked man, whose task it was to
kill the near-demented cat with only his teeth.

The Cat and the Knight was one among many popular
spectacles arranged to delight the revellers. Above their heads
ruddy-faced, enormous giants and thin spectral figures moved
as if by magic, so that people forgot they were merely men
borne on stilts. Their up-gazing wonder gave the cut-purses
a happy day too.

The palazzi were hung with fine tapestries. Equally decorative were their crowded balconies. On velvet-upholstered
chairs sat throngs of ladies throwing down flowers and smiles
to gentlemen admirers. Sun caught on gems, rich brocades,
and ostrich plumes, so that the scene seemed a Gozzoli fresco
inspired with breath.

In the Piazza della Signoria a hundred golden towers ro-
tated on wagons to show the crowds every aspect of their
relief designs . . . beautifully fashioned dancing girls, soldiers,
fruit, or flowers. These represented the tributary cities. On
the *ringhiera* of the palazzo multi-hued flags fluttered a proud
echo of their allegiance to the city of the Red Lily.

All morning, processions made their colourful and cheerfully solemn way to San Giovanni with offerings. Members
of guilds marched in twos under the banners of their crafts,
and each citizen under one or other of the sixteen gonfalons
—a subtle demonstration of the State's requirement for an
individual to play some stipulated role. Franco could read

the underlying message: find a way to belong here, or else forfeit rights and happiness.

"Come on, Taddeo!" She dragged him away from the Cat and the Knight, each now spattered with the other's blood. It was not the barbarity that affrighted Franco but she recognized the bulging-muscled Knight. Berto Spenozzi had also come to the city.

"If he's that desperate to make some money," she muttered, "he'd be glad of the reward for selling my identity to the Eight."

"He wouldn't know you now," Taddeo mumbled.

"I'm not going to give him the chance. Oh Berto, I never believed you would turn into such a savage beast." She shuddered. "How little I knew of human beings."

Rather like a wizard who enchants people to follow in his wake, as soon as Franco moved off, the apprentices chased after, yelling: "Hey, wait for us. We're coming with you."

Franco took full advantage of the situation to lead her wild cohort to the Aquia residence. It wasn't long before they were chanting: "Tommaso di Aquia is a stinking old weasel . . ." and hurling every kind of missile, except flowers, at his house. Other boys attracted by such an enjoyable chorus swelled the numbers. Franco slipped outside the crowd.

From a discreet distance she saw Lionello emerge and with pompous indignation order the gathering to "Be off!" All he succeeded in securing was a bloody nose and a torn doublet.

Franco's mocking joy merged with the apprentices' shrill hoots of triumph as they chased back into the piazza which overflowed with a deafening pandemonium of screams, songs, and laughter. The air was rich with the sulfurous fumes of fireworks and the sweet or savory aromas of food, temptingly displayed on street vendors' trays. The whole scene was a pageant of beauty and savagery . . .

Franco ate it all up as greedily as she munched a fresh

crumbling pie filled with curd cheese . . . desiring to absorb the very ethos of Florence into her blood.

In the late afternoon the buildings glowed a soft rose like the cheeks of the citizens overreplete from too much food and wine. Sleepily gay after the siesta, they staggered into the streets to see the *palio* run from the Porta alla Croce to the Porta al Prato.

Franco, Taddeo, and some other boys stationed themselves near the finishing post close to the magistrates who judged the race. Fat, belching merchants, their frisky flirting wives and daughters and apprentices all held similar conversations: the horses' past performances, bets laid, and tips given.

Speculation ended as the bell in the palazzo's tower rang three times. The *palio* began . . .

The city began to swell with the murmur of mounting tension. The powerful horses decorated with their owners' emblems galloped through the streets. The moving roar of the crowds punctuated their progress.

A crescendo of applause, cheers, shouts, and laughter clearly showed the Florentines' delight when the *palle* just beat the Golden Acorn, and the Dark Torch. So the *palio* —that highly prized length of crimson silk, trimmed with gold and fur—went to the Medici. Afterwards it was paraded through the city on a four-wheeled wagon, decorated with a carved, gilded lion at each corner.

Franco did not listen to the moans of the losers or the gloats of the winners. She barely noticed the Medici. Her attention was concentrated on the golden smiling youth by his side. Daniello della Sera did not seem at all vexed that his own Arab horse had been beaten by less than a flick of its ears.

The hungry, violet eyes softened. Her lips parted. Under her shirt the gimmal ring knocked against the topaz. It did not matter that now Daniello's own hand was bereft of that particular token . . . though he still wore the Narnis' magnificent diamond. Just to gaze on his beauty inspired the frozen heart with hope. One day, she vowed, he will clear my name of all stigma.

As ever Daniello was surrounded by the dark nimbus, that group of young men who demonstrated their fidelity to the Medici by loving his handsome companion. They were finely dressed and elegantly educated: the brightest flowers of young Florentine society—yet a sharp eye might detect the faint pollen of the effete and vicious. Despite his ugliness Altoviti was a permanent member of this glittering retinue.

Franco wondered if Daniello knew of his friends' notoriety: sadly, she concluded that his natural goodness made him their dupe, ignorant of their defects.

Her gentle expression vanished as she saw Guido di Cuono. The Medici placed his hands on Guido's and Daniello's shoulders. Onlookers gossiped that Lorenzo had found two brothers to replace sweet Giuliano and were glad for him.

To Franco it was a symbol. She laughed unmusically at her own romantic notions of revenge and restoration. The di Cuonos were now as secure as the della Seras; any dream that the Medici's favourite would jeopardize such a position by fighting for her rights was beyond the bounds of fairy tales.

The gentlemen's attention shifted from the panting, steaming horses to a young woman who drifted gracefully into their midst. Her loose gown, so heavily embroidered with precious stones, seemed fashioned from a sunlit waterfall rather than from any textile. Curls of black hair trailed over the gently vibrating, upper globes of white breasts like a blackamoor's caressing fingers.

Guido's fine lips twisted in amusement at the effect his sister had on Lorenzo and Daniello. Cosima seemed plumper than Franco recalled and even more beautiful. The Medici's gaze never left her face, but her great dark eyes smiled at Daniello who seemed almost ill at ease.

They made a perfect couple—Adonis and Venus. The way Cosima turned her neck suggested a flower that bloomed in the sunshine of male adulation. It would be unreasonable to imagine her retiring to any convent, Franco reflected. Perhaps there was now even a scheme for her to wed Daniello. That way the Narnis' wealth, possessions, and future plans would be neatly resettled. Although some small items were sold when all the Pazzi conspirators' possessions were publicly auctioned, the Medici had permitted the della Seras to receive most of what had been promised in the Narni girl's dowry . . . and the di Cuonos had been rewarded for their zealous loyalty from the same source.

With a bitter mouth Franco smiled. Probably Messer Ridolfo received some political favour for his valuable services. The Medici's helping arm could stretch as far as Milan . . . or Pisa . . .

A cloud had shifted for an instant to reveal Olympus, and Franco knew that mere mortals could not topple the gods . . .

The Magnificent

THE THREATENING STORM of turmoil broke in chaos and suffering. Rome, Naples, and Siena declared war on Florence, Milan, and Venice. It soon became obvious, however, that Pope Sixtus and King Ferrante—like skillful puppeteers with long wires attached to their marionettes—had cunningly contrived to stage this bloody performance well away from their own territories. While Siena and Florence shouldered the burden of war, both armies reaped its spoils.

Refugees from Florentine subject cities, toting bundles that contained all their worldly possessions, flocked to the security within the city's walls.

There were other grim sights too . . . Men, women, and children of every degree might be seen falling dead in churches, markets, and streets. For the increase in population helped produce ripe conditions for a virulent outbreak of the *moria*, which was ever simmering in the humid atmosphere and frequently bubbled over into an epidemic whose hunger was appeased only by gorging itself upon countless citizens.

As many were decimated by plague in Florence as by violence in the battle areas. Franco grew almost accustomed to losing familiar faces among her apprentice acquaintances. The comfortable folk who owned country retreats fled to escape the disease, but no one could avoid the steep rise in taxes needed to finance the ever-increasing hostilities.

War ruined trade. The Florentines cursed their enemies and their own commander with equal fervour. The law required the *capitano*—who received a generous remuneration for his services—to be a noble nonresident. Ercole d'Este, duke of Ferrara, had a fine military reputation. Despite this and all the Florentine gold he rarely gained a victory or pressed home an advantage.

With ironic humour, the Florentines concluded his curious failures might be traced to his marriage: after all, he was the son-in-law of the king of Naples. Meanwhile all soldiers relished a continual looting spree, and it was claimed with some truth that both armies went to considerable pains to avoid conflict!

One other ludicrous aspect of this war was the French king's personal intervention. It did no good whatsoever, except cause the Florentines to slap their sides in bitter mirth. Louis, the Spider King, sent ambassadors to all rulers concerned in the fight with the hasty suggestion that they join forces in a crusade against Constantinople. Christian leaders, he claimed, and especially the head of their faith, should not be seen squabbling amongst themselves. Citizens even contributed funds to this cause which never came to anything . . .

To forget death Franco chose to lose herself in a painting. When voices of strangers could be heard approaching along the cloisters, she hunched over the canvas, determined to be left in peace.

"One interruption after another," she muttered, "if it isn't Maestro Ghirlandajo sending me on some fool's errand then it's visitors coming to admire his handiwork . . ."

Of course, this was the best way of securing wealthy men's patronage; whether they were prominent members of the major guilds—wool, silk, bankers, and furriers—wanting their churches, warehouses, or halls beautified, or noble gentlemen interested in decorating their palaces and chapels, and seeking to be tastefully represented for the eyes of posterity as a character in some religious or historical fresco.

Sometimes it was irksome to listen politely to uninformed criticism or praise, although Maestro Ghirlandajo could be relied upon to be charming to any noble patron. Like the other apprentices Franco found it difficult not to laugh as their master suddenly oozed amiability to those who came a-visiting his workshop. He had many satisfied clients though, for he always managed to depict their wives, daughters, or selves as handsome and hallowed!

The sudden shadow darkening the ground at her feet roused Franco from the painting—at this rate she would never complete it while the vision was fresh in her mind. She glanced up unsmiling. The man who leaned over the incomplete canvas was simply dressed, and the way he screwed up his eyes suggested he was very shortsighted. The dark, flattish features seemed vaguely familiar. She noticed a crowd of other men, all finely clad, who stayed at a respectful distance.

"Do you know who it is you paint with so much care?" His harsh accents contrasted oddly with the gentle smile.

"A face in the crowd," Franco said brusquely, "beautiful but dangerous."

There was a low murmur of consternation, but one or two men stifled their laughter in kid-gloved fingers.

"If I say she is a dear friend to me and my wife, won't you then change your remark, and describe her as beautiful as an angel with the features of the Virgin?"

"No," Franco replied coldly. "Why should I? Lovely certainly, but she would serve as a model for one of the maenads, or Leda, or even Helen who caused the Trojan war. Hers is hardly saintly beauty."

Domenico Ghirlandajo rushed forward, his fat cheeks flaming with embarrassed fury. "Sir, I implore you to ignore my pupil's churlish manners. He's always this rude and only cares for what he's doing. He regards any interruption as an intrusion upon his muse."

"That's not bad manners"—the hoarse voice contained humour—"rather honesty and dedication. He doesn't believe in flattery, yet recognizes beauty. Maestro Verrocchio and others have described this lad to me. He's the one who's forever running in and out of their workshops like a bee in a honeycomb. They say he can be devastating in his criticism for one so young. Therefore I sought an opportunity to see if his own talent merited such self-confidence . . . and, of course," he added hastily, reading Ghirlandajo's injured expression, "I longed to examine your own great work, which is as superb as ever. Yet, this boy's painting though unfinished has captured the radiance of Madonna Cosima di Cuono. Tell me, boy, what's your name?"

"Franco . . . of Florence."

"You have no kin then?"

Franco shook her head ferociously.

"Then you are right to adopt the city of the Red Lily

as your family. I am also of Florence." The man spoke simply. "My name is Lorenzo de' Medici. I like this painting."

Rare colour stained the pale face, but the purplish eyes boldly examined the Magnificent's undistinguished features. He gazed down at Franco in puzzlement, creasing his forehead thoughtfully. "You recall someone I've known," he murmured at last. "Yet you are no one I've ever seen, I swear that. Tell me, Domenico, is he a good pupil?"

Ghirlandajo nodded grudgingly. "He thinks there's little more I can teach him . . ."

"That's a lie!" Franco flashed. "You just won't show me all I want to know. You prefer to send me back to fetch paints or sketches you've forgotten . . ."

"Franco, be silent!"—the cloisters had rarely heard Fra Sandro's rebuke. "Remember before whom you speak. Learn a little humility."

Lorenzo grinned down at the indignant, small face. "I like your spirit, Franco of Florence. In the future, I vow your master will allow you to learn all you can, while I invite you to my palazzo in the Via Larga. Bring me this painting when it's finished." He produced a handful of golden florins. "Here's payment in advance. I want to give your picture to a friend."

The monks and Ghirlandajo's helpers clustered between the carved pillars to stare at the child, the painting, and the Magnificent. Only Fra Sandro shook his head doubtfully.

Domenico Ghirlandajo's face expressed mingled fury and delight, as he roared: "The sooner you know all you need, you rascal, the sooner I can rid myself of your presence. I can't believe I'll ever have such a troublesome apprentice. If I do I swear I'll send him to another master. Remember though, Franco, you've begun to acquire a reputation. You'd better live up to it. Or I shall put these hands to more forceful work than painting . . . I'll enjoy turning your scrawny backside the very fashionable shade of scarlatto d'oricello!"

Lorenzo's large, dark eyes, ever eloquent ahead of his tongue, were highly amused by the excitement he'd caused and also by the impassive child who had returned to the painting.

"Come, gentlemen," he sighed and turned to his friends. "We mustn't spend all day in pleasure. We can never forget we're at war . . ."

"And your revenge?" Fra Sandro asked, when later that evening Franco sketched his gentle features.

She did not look up. "The Medici has given me my chance to live as a Florentine, and I must seize it. Perhaps through this I'll find a way to clear the dear name that can never be uttered." Her voice became somber. "Yet I shall never forget that he can have me removed as simply as I wipe out this charcoal line which displeases my eye . . ."

The finished painting met with enthusiasm when Franco presented it at the Palazzo Medici, especially since the fair subject had denied the city her presence because of the plague.

"Now at least you can see her whenever you wish," Lorenzo chaffed when he presented the likeness to Daniello della Sera. "You can even take that face into your bed-chamber and set it on your pillow without risking a dagger thrust from brother Guido."

Daniello sincerely admired the painting and bestowed one of his golden smiles on the artist whose own expression transfigured a silent, skinny boy, growing out of ill-fitting rags, into an ethereal and beautiful creature of fire and ice. That the picture pleased him erased Franco's jealousy of his interest in Cosima.

"If only you and she would wed," the Medici continued.

"Why so? You know I have no mind to marry at present."

Franco's heart surged with relief, yet her mind mocked the ridiculous dreams for stirring once again.

"Then I could see her every day," Lorenzo explained merrily.

"And crown me with horns, which I'd have to wear in silence, or else look a fool, as is the custom with complaisant Florentine husbands, eh?"

Lorenzo winked. "That's not my style with friends."

Franco thought: yet he is only half jesting.

Guido too was delighted with his sister's picture and took special pains to be pleasant to the silent young painter who had earned the Medici's interest, but his smile shed cold winter light and made Franco shudder.

"Perhaps you will visit us soon"—Guido's voice sounded as sharp as thin ice cracking underfoot—"and paint Cosima from life."

Fierce emotions racked Franco and she was unable to cope with the strange paradoxes. The sight of Daniello still inspired a mixture of hero worship and girlish adoration, while Guido's presence induced unreasoning terror more than thoughts of revenge. Now that she was actually within the Medici's magic circle, her overwhelming desire to become an artist with a place in Florentine society superseded the wish to destroy her enemies: for she could see with perfect logic this would involve self-annihilation . . .

So Franco was permitted to enter that glittering company, who met to talk, to sing, to feast in one or other of the Medici palazzi in Florence or the countryside. Her talent alone ensured membership to the most select Florentine guild, and she rapidly became one of those to be pointed at, whispered about, even fawned upon for her friendship with the powerful and famous.

The Magnificent quickly perceived Franco's wide education and encouraged her to use his superb library. He permitted her to begin a study of his little daughters, Maddalena and Lucrezia, holding Giuliano's natural baby son.

It was a joyous relief to escape the rigid monastic routine

of San Marco to stroll among the palazzo arcades studded with Donatello's best plaques . . . almost to visit another world . . . or return to the memory of Castelfiore.

Lorenzo's intimates—the poets, philosophers, and artists—who formed an informal Platonic academy, welcomed Franco's sharp questioning brain and quick wit. They would discuss for hours anything from the nature of the soul to the current war. Ideas were merry and serious but never solemn or constrained by doctrinal rules. The teachings of Christ, Plato, and Socrates were argued with equal vigour, and nothing was too sacred to be probed or ridiculed by the skeptical minds.

With sad and reminiscent amusement Franco noted that Lorenzo's wife, Madonna Clarice, was openly shocked by her husband's frivolous friends. Pious and haughty, this daughter of the Orsinis, an aristocratic Roman family, disapproved in vain of her children's classical education. None of her stern glances could quell the turbulent happy river of concepts, jokes, and songs that flowed unceasingly from the Magnificent's brilliant coterie.

Franco's own life glowed with a set of bright new tints from this palette of fresh experiences. She listened with delight to Gigi Pulci recite his fascinating *Morgante Maggiore* about the absurd exploits of a dwarf and a giant . . . and the ever-shabby Angelo Poliziano discourse upon St. Augustine, or relate stories from Herodotus as if they were his own . . . and Marsilio Ficino stammer: "My very dear ones in Plato . . ." before expounding Platonic teachings . . . and the Medici himself display his craft as a poet in bawdy, humorous, and delicate verses.

The Magnificent's hospitality, easygoing manners, and simplicity of dress sustained the idea of equality among men, but Franco was swift to realize that this gave him superiority over them. Yet it spoke much for the belief in such equality that a nameless young painter could join the Medici and his friends when they rode through the evening streets in vivid masks and costumes. They all carried torches or musical instruments and sang to the delight of the citizens leaning from their windows to listen.

Lorenzo's own unmusical tones ceased, and he motioned to his more tuneful companions to be silent, so that the youth with the red-gold locks and violet eyes could sing alone those verses the Magnificent had written for Lucrezia Donati.

> Was the sky bright or clouded when we met?
> No matter, summer dwells beneath those eyes
> And that fair face creates a paradise . . .

Franco accompanied her melodious voice upon a lute. The full moon shed soft light on the city and the pale lovely face . . . and the eyes of Guido di Cuono and Daniello della Sera rested almost spellbound upon the perfect features of the singer who rode between them . . .

Across this newly won horizon drifted a cloud. Despondency settled on Franco's heart. Her head often ached, and she found concentration difficult. Maestro Ghirlandajo had frequent cause to scold this unusual absentmindedness.

"Losing your great talent, eh?" he yelled, "and wasting my paints into the bargain! Pull yourself together, Franco . . . or is all that nighttime revelling with the Magnificent's fine friends going to your head? Perhaps you're deep in love with some little wench who is sapping your brain by draining your spindly loins with her hungry white thighs. When I asked you to dip your brush, I meant . . ." and he roared with laughter.

The coarse suggestiveness appealed to the other apprentices but Franco could ignore it.

Taddeo watched with anxiety. Only the day before they had passed the cathedral, and a woman had dropped down dead of plague within a few paces of them. It was now impossible to disregard the *moria* that visited rich and poor, palazzo and hovel.

Even Ghirlandajo showed real concern when this brilliant and mercurial apprentice fainted in the refectory while they were clearing up after the light had grown too dim for painting.

Taddeo leapt forward and would permit no one to touch Franco. "No, no," he grunted, pushing them all away with his elbows. He lifted the slight figure and carried Franco into Fra Sandro's cell.

"Can it be the plague?" the monk demanded anxiously. "Shall I call for a doctor. . . ?"

Taddeo shook his head and pointed at Franco's shrunken working clothes, which always made the slender wrists and ankles appear long and awkward. Fra Sandro flushed deeply, and he clasped his hands in agitation.

"Dear Mother of God, I had forgot this. But it is woman's business." He spoke with horror. "What can we do? We have ignored nature, but nature will have its way. No doubt, terror postponed this event . . ."

When Franco swam back to consciousness, she could smell the sharp vinegar on the damp cloth Taddeo had placed on her forehead.

"What has happened?" she demanded, staring up at the monk.

"You must go into a convent," Fra Sandro murmured, and then added with acute embarrassment, "you are now a woman, my child. You cannot deny it any longer."

When Franco realized the truth, a terrible rage engulfed her. The frail body shuddered with fury, nausea, and self-disgust.

"This cannot be," she kept repeating. "I shall not let it happen again," and she pressed flat the small breasts her jacket concealed.

Fra Sandro took hold of the strong, fine fingers that had lost their childishness. "I cannot talk about these matters to you, Franco . . . you see that is the name I know you by . . . but whatever you are called your body now belongs to womanhood and is subject to that same cycle which rules all femalekind. This is not something to resent, but rather welcome . . . and once . . ." He sighed and shook his head. "If life had only run its proper course, you would have been glad, for it means that your body is prepared for child-bearing.

"My daughter, I have seen enough outside these walls to know what the world expects of a lone woman without family or fortune. In the simplest female raiment you would be an incomparable beauty. If you sought honest menial work you would be pursued by men and forced to play the harlot. Whatever you did . . . wherever you went . . . your very beauty would ensnare you and most men. That must not happen to one of your name, even if that name no longer exists. For your honour and happiness I beg you to enter a convent. There, your secret will be forever safe."

"And my hope for vengeance?"

"Can a woman seek revenge? It is against her very nature."

"And my painting?"

"Women do not paint . . ." Fra Sandro suddenly laughed and seemed young and foolish. "No, you have proved they can. But, Franco, nobody would accept a female artist . . . you would not be allowed to work in churches or mona-steries or be safe in this world of men. I doubt if there will ever be women artists . . . it seems shamefully unfeminine."

Franco began to chuckle and ignored the pains raking her stomach. "Then I must stay as I am."

The priest thumped his high, yellow forehead with a bony fist. "You cannot. You know that. You are dominated by all that women must feel and can never deny this."

"I shall not deny it," Franco returned quietly. "I recognize it, but no man will ever discover my true nature unless I choose to reveal it."

"Child . . . child," Fra Sandro remonstrated. "What will befall such arrogance? Surely it is a sin to deceive mankind."

"As to that," she retorted, "I am the one who was deceived about life."

Fiametta

FRANCO DEVELOPED a boldness and self-assurance to disguise the seal of femininity and bound her small hard breasts with linen strips. She wore the fine clothes purchased with money earned with the air of a prince. Men and women turned in the streets to admire the tall, slim youth whose swaggering walk and fearless eyes epitomized the ideal young Florentine.

"You're becoming a handsome devil, Franco," Lorenzo remarked to his protégé, and put a hand briefly on the green velvet-encased shoulder. Franco shook it away, and the Magnificent smiled. It had been widely remarked that this youth aggressively disliked physical contact, so much so that people dared not slap him on the back in case it was greeted with a swordcut.

"Daniello will have to look out," the Medici continued, "for long he's been the most perfect man in our city. Beware the ladies who will cast languishing eyes on your bold beauty and try to steal your freedom with their sweetest wiles. By the time I return I suppose you will have lost your heart and any gold you've been paid to some scheming little goddess, who is in reality a fat merchant's philandering young wife."

Lorenzo left for Naples accompanied by the prayers of the Florentines for his safe return. It was an act of personal bravery . . . and clever gambling . . . in an attempt to bring the protracted pointless war to some conclusion by cajoling or bribing the crafty Ferrante to sever his alliance with Sixtus. It meant that the Magnificent must walk right into the enemy's camp though, and no one could trust the king of Naples . . .

"And if he never comes back?" Taddeo asked after Franco had explained Lorenzo's departure.

"I do not know," she said soberly, "chaos most likely leading to the Pope's triumph."

They were passing the small house in which Dante's Beatrice had dwelt long ago, and making for the Duomo when a single rose fell at Franco's feet. She picked it up, smelled the faint perfume, and then looked around. On a narrow wrought-iron balcony sat a young girl wrapped in a deep red woollen cloak against winter's chill. She had soft brown hair and eyes that contained a gentle wistfulness. When Franco bowed and smiled, the pale cheeks took on the wool's tint, and the eyes glazed with swift happiness.

"Thank you, madonna," Franco called, and kissed a gloved hand towards her.

Each time they passed that house, the girl was sitting up there.

"Do you sing, little lady?" Franco demanded one day with a merry turn of heart.

"Sometimes," the voice was sweetly pitched. "Why?"

"You remind me of a caged songbird that Leonardo likes to buy in order to set free. How I wish I knew a way to let you fly from your little prison." Franco feigned a lover's sigh: for it was a game that all young gallants and maidens enjoyed playing.

"Leonardo who?" came the serious question.

"Da Vinci of course. Don't you know what wonders our city possesses, madonna? He is more than an artist. I swear he is a god among men. His brilliance confounds us all, and there is nothing that doesn't excite his interest." Franco spoke with reverent enthusiasm. "He is also the handsomest of men."

"No. He can't be," the high voice rose in confusion. "You are."

Franco laughed gaily. "Oh, you've been taking lessons in how to flatter your future husband," she teased, "so that he will never deny you a new gown or pearl necklace just like his neighbour's wife wears. What's your name, honey-tongued madonna?"

"Fiametta."

"I am Franco, a poor wretch of a painter. Won't you walk with me, Madonna Fiametta?"

"No," the girl replied sharply, and her eyes brightened with tears.

"Even though I am so handsome," Franco laughed. "Perhaps your sweetheart will be jealous, eh?"

"I have no sweetheart," she sighed.

"I don't believe you. If this is the way you reward one who treasures the rose you threw him I shall away and drown my sorrows . . ."

Franco went off to attend a meeting of the Company of the Cauldron—a group of artists who met regularly to eat, drink, sing, and jest. The centerpiece of the entertainment was the dishes of food fashioned to represent scenes from Dante: capon legs and tripe became marvellous buildings . . . marzipan horrifically depicted the gates of Hell. As they demolished these models, they declaimed their favourite lines from Purgatoria or Paradiso. Franco chose: "There is no greater sorrow than to be mindful of the happy time in misery . . ."

She enjoyed these evenings, achieving sly pleasure that this all-male province had been penetrated by a mere girl . . . and that if any of them had known they would have been utterly mortified. It was an accolade of some success to sit down with Botticelli, Gozzoli, Ghirlandajo, Cosimo

Rosselli, and the rest . . . and it was also amusing to realize that none of them who had visited Castelfiore in the old days associated young Franco's appearance with the daughter of the unmentionable Vincenzo de' Narni . . .

Franco never drank as much as the others and always held herself aloof in the midst of horseplay. Afterwards, when many of them rolled into the evening to pursue further pleasures with compliant ladies—their own personal property or merely borrowed from someone else for a few hours— Franco left them to return to San Marco.

"Spending your substance on boys then?" Ghirlandajo jeered. "You beware, Franco, you don't want to be accused publicly of sodomy like Leonardo. Did him a lot of harm. Many still cast accusing eyes. You don't want to be thrown into the Stinche as a reward for your Italian appetite . . ."

Botticelli encouraged the young artist to go along with him to a mammazuole. "You can play cards, read, write letters, talk, and drink in humble but fair comfort, Franco. The little ladies are supposed to be available for hire as serving wenches. To perform their particular sweet services many of them never leave the house.

"Sometimes though one of 'em takes your fancy as a model, and you bring her home for your very own. I'm not suggesting you smuggle one of these pets into San Marco, Franco . . . though it's probably been done . . . but just pay a quick visit. It's not like visiting the great courtesans. After all, such as they are not for the likes of us . . . they're frequently our patrons, and the friends of great men rather than bed partners. We don't want to rise to such dizzy intellectual heights for a bit of fun . . ."

"From the way you're always out of funds," Franco retorted, laughing, "it'd be cheaper for you to get married. You spend so much on that particular pastime."

She felt a secret sense of relief that at least she had escaped life in a mammazuole.

Rosselli urged with earnest argument: "Franco, you must

join your fair body to a woman's sometime. I swear it's only a brief arrangement. Do you want to keep what you've got brand-new until your wedding day? Your bride won't thank you for bringing to bed an enormous appetite and no manners. It's like going to table after starving for years. You can't be an artist only in paint and not in bed. You've learned one craft. Come on, learn another. It doesn't take so long, and it's easier to get pleasurable results from a moist bit of flesh than a bad canvas . . ."

But Franco was always deaf to these suggestions . . .

At her balcony little Fiametta was pale and listless.

"You've not come by for two days," she complained when Franco and Taddeo passed that way.

"I thought you had no wish to see me," Franco said lightly.

"No, you forgot all about me," Fiametta reproached. "I know about you young men . . . you've been enjoying yourself in the company of lots of laughing girls."

"Of course," Franco agreed nonchalantly. "Tell me, Fiametta, what does your papa do to leave you all alone like this forever sitting at your window?"

"He's a wool stapler. I'm his only child. My mother died when I was born." She smiled dolefully. "So I sit at home and wait for Papa to return for his meals . . ." and added with pride, "I take charge of the household, and my pleasure is to watch the world pass by."

"Would your papa allow me to take you for a walk around the piazza with a maidservant, so that you may join the world at least for a brief while?" Franco asked, feeling sorry for the practically imprisoned girl.

"No, I can't do that." The anguished cry pierced Franco's mind and heart.

"What is wrong?"

"You have a gentle voice, Franco," Fiametta whispered, "but you would not talk with me if you knew. I am a cripple." Tears poured down her pale cheeks like rain on snow and began to thaw the ice in Franco's own heart. "I can't walk or dance with light steps. I stumble and limp like your servant. Now you will leave me, won't you?"

"No, Fiametta, I shall ask your papa if I may visit you to paint your portrait."

When Matteo Panetti learned that the strange young fellow with the gentle manners was one of the Medici's favoured companions he made no objection.

"Indeed if you can cheer Fiametta," he confided to Franco, "I shall pay handsomely for this painting. She should be away from infection at this time," he sighed, "but my poor little girl hates to be out of the familiar world she knows . . . and I would miss her so."

It became the custom for Franco to sit each afternoon for a few hours with Fiametta. The servants left the young people together, and Panetti seeing his child flushed and laughing praised God for the young man's kindness. It would be worth half his fortune at least to see her happy, and he had dreams of an artist becoming his son-in-law, even though it wasn't what he called a steady trade . . . but if this Franco would love and care for Fiametta then a grateful father could provide the rest.

"Do you still keep my rose, Franco?" Fiametta asked. "You may have a fresh one."

Beside her chair a small potted rose tree bloomed unseasonally in its indoor surroundings.

"However many you give me," Franco said, "I shall hold the first one dear, because you gave it with spontaneous affection. That is something no one has shown me for a long while."

"Do you need affection, Franco?" Fiametta asked shyly. "I'd have thought you were pelted with love tokens."

Franco grew serious. "I had hoped to live without feeling, Fiametta. You are crippled in your legs yet can offer affection, but I am deformed in my heart yet can run and jump. I have learned it costs too dear when you lose what you love, so I'm determined not to suffer again."

Fiametta thought for a while and then said: "Why are you always accompanied by that hideous servant?"

"We with fair faces must remember that those who are disfigured carry a terrible burden in this world which worships beauty to the extent of being cruel to those without it . . ."

Her eyes filled. "You are wise to chide me, Franco. If Taddeo is loyal to you then he is good. I'm sure he loves you . . . oh Franco . . . from the first moment I saw you smile I fell in love."

Fiametta hid her face, and the blush flowed over her long white neck. Franco looked at the soft bloom on the innocent profile and put a paint-stained hand on the frail, pale one. Fiametta trembled like a captive bird, but she did not pull away.

"I feel so safe with you, Franco."

"You are quite safe, I vow."

"You're laughing." Fiametta pulled away her hand.

"Only at myself, dear Fiametta."

"Can't you ever love me, Franco?" the voice was muffled, and the bright brown eyes beseeched affection above the tumble of white fingers covering her mouth.

"I love you as if you were my dear sister."

"Because I'm plain and crippled," Fiametta stormed. "You will paint beautiful amorous ladies with shapely, dancing legs and slender feet, and you will love them in ways other than you would a sister."

She stumbled from her chair, and defiantly and inexpertly flung herself into Franco's arms and kissed the laughing lips.

It is the first time, Franco thought with shock, that I have been embraced these two years.

They gazed at each other in surprise and embarrassment,

and then Franco kissed the smooth forehead. "No, Fiametta, you must not play at love with your painter."

"I am not playing," she whispered, as Franco helped her back to the chair. "My heart seems about to burst whenever I hear your voice."

"Your father would send me away," Franco said. "I cannot ever love you other than as a sister, believe me."

"Because you love someone else?"

Franco sighed. It was a rare, cruel joke. The kind the boys of the Cauldron would relish, but it could never be recounted. Oh yes, playwrights might enjoy the comedy of their situation but living it was to share a tragedy. "No, Fiametta, my dove, I have sworn never to love a woman."

Before Franco left, she kissed the girl's cheek, and felt the young full bosom heave against her own bound breasts.

When she came to the Panetti house two days later, Franco found one distraught serving woman.

"What is wrong, Nencia?"

"The master left for Fiesole yesterday, but this morning our little lady became sick. We fear it is the plague . . ."

Franco ran upstairs. Fiametta lay on the bed, her hair wet and tangled, her eyes and cheeks bright with fever, her white limbs knotted around the sheets, her lips frothed with vomit.

"Get me cloths and vinegar and cold water," Franco cried.

"But the infection?" Nencia began. "And a man should not see a maid in such a state . . ."

The violet eyes scorned her protests.

Franco bathed Fiametta's face and body, and then tucked her between clean sheets.

"Oh Franco, I'm glad to see you once more before I die," the girl whimpered. "Alas we shall have no more lovely afternoons together . . ."

"No. No," Franco insisted. "We shall make you well."

Fiametta lapsed into another wave of delirium, and Franco stood helplessly watching the fever ravage the fragile young body it had captured.

At last she wrapped Fiametta in blankets and her own cloak and carried her downstairs.

"If Maestro Panetti returns tell him I have taken his daughter to La Scala Hospital. Pray God he will come quickly, but I cannot leave the child to die without seeking some help."

Franco held the light little figure as reverently as if it were the Grail. Taddeo followed, mumbling to himself, anxious about Franco's own health. Groups of citizens fanned away from their progress. It was no unusual event to see a plague victim borne to a hospital by a bravely obstinate relative.

Once Fiametta opened her eyes and smiled. "So you are taking me for a walk, dearest Franco."

"Yes, my dove, and the beauty of the city smiles on your sweet face."

"I love you very much, Franco, and am not afraid, if only you care for me."

"I love you, my dearest Fiametta," Franco's voice broke.

"Oh I knew you would," she smiled at the unsteady husky voice and closed her eyes. Franco felt the soul fly from her like a bird . . . winging away from disease, pain, and misshapen limbs.

Franco stumbled but did not let the burden fall. Dear God, it cost dear to love. She shed her first tears for many months . . .

Benedetto

LORENZO DE' MEDICI RETURNED in triumph from the kingdom of Naples. Not only had Ferrante permitted his departure but also signed a peace treaty with Florence. Without his chief ally Sixtus found it impossible to continue the war. The interdict was lifted, and the papal account returned to the Medici bank. Praise to God—if not Lorenzo—the plague too began to abate. Once more the sun of fortune shone on the city of the Red Lily.

The Magnificent's personal popularity had never stood so high, and he ruthlessly capitalized on it. Florentines looked the other way when he raised taxes to subsidize the Medici banking concerns . . . and grumbled quietly when the *Signoria* devalued the currency thus leading to a further increase in taxation . . . although the crafty government valued its receipts at the old rate!

Lorenzo's bold astuteness virtually gave him a mandate to rule. The pretty glove that concealed his power was fashioned from the finest Florentine silk, but the hand beneath had the cruel sureness of the keenest dagger. No suspicion of a plot against his rule escaped violent reprisal. Yet, most citizens preferred to live in a secure state and so were prepared to pay the price the Medici exacted.

He was quick to notice the change in Franco when the leaders of Florentine art, learning, and pleasure assembled in the Via Larga palazzo.

"There's a suffering and a gladness on your handsome face," Lorenzo remarked. "You are suddenly adult. Can you have fallen in love, young Franco?"

The company crowded close, curious as ever about their chaste Franco, who shook her head smiling.

Guido di Cuono spoke with cold amusement. "Lorenzo, the lad's still a virgin. Can't you read it in those eyes? None of our citizens' wives appeal to his fastidious taste; no smiling slut tempts him to her bed; and no brother artist's model inspires a lickerish desire. Yet now he has left the monastery, perhaps he'll shed his monkish ways and begin the hot chase. Whoever knows that body first will be fortunate indeed."

"You follow my movements closely, Guido," Franco observed.

"Naturally. We don't want another city to tempt your talent from us, eh, Daniello?"

Della Sera nodded. "We do want you to be happy among us, Franco."

It was pleasant to know Daniello looked so kindly on her, but as ever Franco felt the brush of fear at having attracted Guido's attention.

She had not wanted to accept Matteo Panetti's payment for Fiametta's unfinished portrait, yet it would have been churlish, even unkind, to refuse.

"Pray God you are not infected, Franco," Panetti examined the pale face.

"Pray God I am infected with her gentleness." Franco spoke fervently.

The solid merchant voice contained shyness: "Franco, would you not alter your life to become my son? You have no family. Now, nor have I. If things had been otherwise I should have welcomed you for a son."

"It's impossible, dear friend," Franco found it hard to disguise the emotion this offer inspired. "Let me thank you with a full heart. Circumstances have made it so that I can belong to no one but myself."

"Then, promise me that if ever you are in dire trouble, you won't hesitate to ask for my help. For Fiametta's sake, and also yours, I shall do everything I can."

With this money, Franco took humble lodgings above a candlemaker's shop in the Camaldoli near Porto San Freddiano. It was a poor district, and a strange address: for such rooms were usually taken by a *cortigiana di candela*. The candlemaker and his slatternly wife found it an amusing change to have a young artist and his servant as tenants.

Taddeo was delighted by the different surroundings. He capered about like an excited dog and set to cleaning the shabby apartment with great zest. One room served as a studio where they took their meals, and he would sleep. The other was for Franco, and she revelled in this new luxury of possessing a whole room to herself. A magnificent vista across the rooftops and the Arno compensated for the sparse furnishings, and the flood of light through the open shutters was ideal for Franco's purposes.

"It was bound to happen," Fra Sandro sighed, "but you will visit us sometimes? Thank God for that creature Taddeo. Guardian angels come in strange guises. I need not be overanxious about your safety while he lives."

"I'll visit you . . . my dear uncle," she whispered. The monk's thin face glowed. "And I'll never cease to thank you for my life."

"The other brothers will miss you, despite your wild ways." He smiled. "They've grown fond of their changeling artist. One day perhaps you will eschew pagan subjects and use your art to add beauty to our monastery."

"I doubt Fra Giralamo will miss me," Franco grinned. "He's certainly a holy man, but those black eyes like burning coals, and that great eagle nose projecting from haggard features the colour of a shroud speak that the Day of Judgment is already here . . . and I'm to be cast into the pit!"

"He's a good man. One day his voice will awaken the Florentines' faith. At present we are almost a pagan people. The merchants spend vast sums beautifying the churches, but if a voice in the pulpit speaks out against their doubtful business ethics they begin to grumble, and say religion has no right to meddle in trade. Everyone sees holy days as occasions for new clothes, feast, and merriment. The young men and maidens attend church to flirt, the older ones to gossip. If we do not mend our ways, then we must expect God's wrath . . ."

Giralamo Savanarola's eyes took on fanatical fire whenever he encountered Franco singing in the cloisters, and wearing some bright new raiment.

"Vanity!" the monk mocked. "Don't you know that all fleshly things end in dust. It is your soul you should clothe: in the fierce white light of godliness. You are only concerned with life here and now. One day you will repent for your idle, lascivious life. You care only for what feeds and clothes your body, you waste your talent by not putting it to the glory of God, and you spill your manhood on those lumps of flesh with eyes . . ."

An echo of the Pazzi plot sounded in the city when the Sultan of Constantinople returned the murderer Bandini who had sought refuge among the Turks.

How long ago it seems now, Franco mused, mingling with the crowds which had turned out to see Giuliano's murderer hanging from the Palazzo del Capitano . . . a whole lifetime of learning to live again and discovering that some things are still sweet to savour despite the agony of memory.

"I don't envy you your commission," Franco remarked to the handsome man in deep rose silks, who stood sketching Bandini, and making notes about the hanged man's clothes in curious mirror-writing.

". . . tan coloured cap . . . a black-lined tunic . . . a blue cloak . . ." Leonardo muttered as he wrote. "Good day, sweet Franco. I too shall be glad when the task is over, for I have been commissioned by the monks of San Donato Scopeto to paint an altar piece, and I am not allowed more than thirty months for it." He sighed thoughtfully. "Do you

think our art is ever great enough to describe the evil mankind perpetrates? Yet what can we expect: We worship
beauty but live from cradle to grave in the midst of filth
and degradation . . ."

Franco accompanied him to his frugal lodgings for supper.
"I am sorry," Leonardo apologized. "This will be a scant
meal, for I believe it a sin to kill a living creature so cannot
offer you meat."

"Dearest Hermes"—Franco addressed da Vinci by his
nickname—"it does not matter what we eat so long as I
can hear you talk."

Indeed, she thought with wonder, his lips must either be
touched by God or madness. For idea jostled idea until her
head spun from listening, and there was no possibility of
ever understanding more than a fraction. Da Vinci was
forever rising from table to find sketches to illustrate his
theories.

There were water pumps . . . devices for repelling scaling
ladders . . . for breathing under water . . . a canal with
locks and weirs . . . a portable bridge to use in warfare . . .
and also a fantastic machine in which he insisted a man
could fly through the air.

"I cannot argue with your wisdom," Franco said impa-
tiently, "though some of the ideas sound demented, but I
do wish you would cease all this experimenting, dreaming,
and drawing . . . and only complete some of your wonder
ful works. Just look at all those unfinished sketches. If you
dissipate your talent, dear friend, nobody will know what
to take you for. Are you an anatomist, magician, or artist . . ."

"I dream of one great patron," Leonardo explained, "who
will give me freedom to put some of my ideas into practice.
Don't tell anyone yet, Franco, but I'm about to write to
Lodovico Sforza and offer my services. God alone knows
how he managed to seize the reins of power. He's exiled
Duchess Bona, had Cecco Simonetta executed, and sent away

his own brother Cardinal Ascanio—the sensible action of a man who knows he can't trust a relative of similar caliber . . . Although Il Moro is regent for young Duke Gian Galeazzo, I have the feeling he may yet prove to be one of the greatest princes of our age. As such he might find a use for my talents in his own court . . ."

Franco's heart leapt into her throat. She did not doubt that Milan's new ruler must owe his change of fortune partly to the secret machinations of Messer Ridolfo, who would now stand high in the new order . . .

"Yet you are right, Franco," da Vinci continued gravely. "Sometimes I fear I'm doomed to die without creating anything. I am like a grasshopper, leaping here, there, and everywhere." Even as he spoke he began to sketch Franco's face, and suddenly added: "You are one of the mysteries that beguile Florentine gossips. Being seen in my company won't enhance your name with the narrow-minded, but one thing I do realize that others seem to miss is that you haven't a man's face . . ."

Franco tried to control the flush that surged into her cheeks. "Because I grow no beard," she jested. "I'm fair-skinned, and many young men of my complexion have hairless faces."

Leonardo observed the sudden agitation and spoke reassuringly. "I keep my thoughts to myself, and though I don't know who or what you are, Franco of Florence, I recognize that you are the most beautiful living creature in a city which abounds with inanimate beauty . . ."

Sometimes the city suffocated Franco. Then she and Taddeo would hire horses and ride out through the Porta al Prato, past the boys and young men playing football, running races, and testing their agility in jumps of great distance. Thence to the fresh fields and woodlands where the only sounds were the splash of streams, birdsong, the trill of shepherds piping to their flocks, and cattle lowing on the breeze.

During these expeditions, Franco would send Taddeo away with their horses, so she could seek out an isolated pool and plunge into its chill flow and bathe herself. It was not possible for her to visit the public baths, and washing in the cramped lodgings was possible and necessary but hardly pleasurable. To swim naked in the open air brought back snatches of childhood . . . which had begun to seem a dream in someone else's existence.

Franco never looked at her reflection in glass or water . . . even when she trimmed or combed her hair into a burnished helmet. Someone who minutely observed people, objects, and nature had chosen to remain blind to the reality of herself.

On one such drowsy afternoon, Taddeo wandered off to find fruit for their journey back to the city. Franco lay on the grass, drying her body in the sunlight, listening to the hum of insects, and planning the painting commissioned by a furrier acquaintance of Matteo Panetti, who obviously wanted to be depicted as wealthy, worldly, proud, but also saintly and wise . . . and could see no contradictions in his demands. She had not dared to suggest "Saint Croesus," although the Cauldron members had roared at her sly wit when she explained the problem of the furrier!

Suddenly aware of the crackle of twigs underfoot, Franco reached for the cloak but was too late to prevent the young man glimpsing her body as he stepped from among the trees.

He was dressed as a priest and asked in a hushed voice: "Are you real, or are you a nymph? I have never seen such a beautiful girl."

Franco held the cloak tight against herself, and drew out the small dagger.

"I shan't harm you," he said earnestly. "You have no need of that weapon. What is your name?"

"I am no one," she insisted. "I am not even beautiful."

"But you are," he declared ardently, and dropped to his knees in an attitude of adoration. "You are the very spirit of love. I believe I have discovered Venus in this little forest. Madonna, I vow I love you."

"Fine words," Franco retorted acidly, "and easily spoken, but ill-suited to someone of your cloth."

"Until today I never minded being a monk. It was all arranged long ago by my parents who are dead. I was content with my fate until I saw you." He rose and came towards her, smiling.

"No. No . . ." Franco recoiled. Her face contorted with horror.

The young man stopped. "I swear I shall not harm you," he held up the crucifix at his belt. "By the blessed Corpus, you have nothing to fear. My name is Benedetto, lady. Promise me that you will return here sometime and let me talk with you, and I will go away now. I shall come to this same place every day."

"My servant will be here in one minute," Franco whispered. "Perhaps I will come back, but don't depend upon it . . . Benedetto." Even as she spoke, Franco wondered why she chose to part-promise anything so foolish.

That night before she went to bed, Franco examined her nakedness by rushlight.

"Too slender for the present fashion," she murmured, as if talking to someone else, "but still a woman."

She ran her hands over the small firm breasts, and down the long waist and curved but tight-muscled hips. The skin was milk-white and silk-fine, and the hair of modesty a blaze of gold. Without male attire beneath it, the face in the small mirror did belong to a very beautiful girl, although the thick curling hair was worn too short for women's styles.

Franco knew a pride in herself, and a fear.

She chose to ride out to the trysting place alone, and Taddeo stayed behind, puzzled. There was a sudden gentleness in Franco, and she seemed to be concealing some elation . . . like someone who wants to laugh but dare not.

Within the screen of foliage, Franco slipped off the male garments and donned a plain pale gown she had borrowed from one of Botticelli's models on the pretext that she required it for one of her own.

Benedetto appeared and stared at the girl.

"I have come here every day since I saw you," he reproached.

"It is hard for me to get away."

"Where do you live?"

"In the city."

"You are a . . ." He examined the simple gown. "No, not a servant. Your voice and manners belong to a lady."

"Perhaps I am a nun." Franco smiled, and the man's eyes filled with tears.

"When you smile," he whispered, "my heart breaks. Have you taken your vows already?"

"Perhaps I am about to," she countered. "And sometimes to escape the restrictions of my life I flee into the greenwood . . ."

"How could your family let you become a nun?"

"I have no family."

"And you are to hide that beauty behind a veil?" he said sadly. "It should be crowned with jewels brighter than your hair or eyes. You should be the wife of a prince . . . or do you shun love?"

"I don't know," Franco said simply.

"What a terrible thing to say." Benedetto stepped towards her, and Franco tried to flee, but his restraining hands were so gentle that she understood she was imprisoned by her own feelings.

"I have never thought of love until now," he said.

Franco tensed, but the young man clasped her to him until she ceased to feel fear. They remained thus until her own arms stole around him. Benedetto kissed her forehead, her eyes, and her cheeks . . . and then very softly her lips.

Franco could not respond, but the heart stirred, and when the young man looked down into her face, she pressed her head against his shoulder . . . suddenly content and safe in his gentle affection.

"You really must learn how to kiss, little nun," he said with mock severity. "Perhaps the lesson will make you forget your vows."

He pressed her mouth tenderly with his own, and Franco's cold lips grew warm and moist until at last they opened. His arms tightened about her, and though she tried to pull away when first she felt his tongue caress her own, Franco slowly grew accustomed to his touch and sweet breath. They stood linked by their mouths for a long while, and above them the leafy boughs whispered endearments.

"This is the first time I have ever kissed a man."

"And will it be the last?"

"Who can say?"

"Oh, lady, lady without a name, let me call you Venus . . . Venus and Madonna, flee with me and we could be wed. I shall take care of you, and you will never wear that wild frightened look in your great eyes."

Franco remembered many things. "I would bring you misfortune," she said. "Besides we must not snatch each other from our vows. Let us be to each other a dear dream, so that there will be nothing to regret, and much beauty to remember if our world grows dark . . ."

She asked him to call her Lauretta, and that name seemed to belong to some other person.

They met every afternoon. Though Benedetto pleaded, she would never permit him to accompany her to the city. When she was sure he'd ridden away Franco donned her man's clothing. Taddeo watched her broodingly in the evenings, blinking without understanding. Franco spoke but little, for she was engrossed with a new painting that no one was allowed to glimpse. It was kept covered with a cloth, and Taddeo knew better than to pry.

Franco's love was a little flower. It opened and bloomed, and soon she was the first to offer kisses. Benedetto grew delighted that her shyness had vanished, and she could show such trust in him.

They lay beneath the trees on the warm grass, tightly embraced.

"Lauretta . . . Lauretta . . ." Benedetto spoke the words as religiously as any *Ave*. "I love you . . . I love you . . ." He kissed her face with a gentle passion, always frightened of scaring her . . . and also frightened of the feelings surging within himself.

His fingers stroked her throat just where the pulse fluttered and then slipped down into the bodice. Although Franco's eyes widened with a tiny fear and she protested a little, his hand found her left breast. His soft sigh of ecstasy was echoed by her own, as he gently squeezed the perfect globe he had discovered.

Benedetto unbuttoned the gown and buried his face against the soft breasts, closing his mouth on the hardening pink nipples with almost reverent passion.

Franco looked down at the dark head with wonder. He was so gentle and loving, and the stolen adventure so idyllic.

"I must strew your lovely breasts with flowers," he breathed, and garnered bunches of orchis and wild iris to garland Franco's pale flesh.

Benedetto gazed for a long time at the girl lying before him in artless disarray. At last, he sighed and began to re-button the gown.

"Ah, my Lauretta, I long to kiss every one of your secrets, but if we explore all the beauty in one day," he whispered, "we shall have nothing left for the morrow."

"Tomorrow is something else," Franco returned gently.

He touched the chain at her throat. "You wear a betrothal ring, but you did not tell me you were already promised."

"Dearest Benedetto, there is no betrothal, but I still keep this ring as a memento of another time."

And Franco thought of lying beneath the trees in Daniello's arms, yet could not imagine sharing embraces with him. Benedetto made her feel girlish . . . while Daniello was very much the companion of her pretended manhood.

"I am sure you will marry me," Benedetto insisted, kissing her lips with determination, "even if I first get you with child . . ."

Franco's face flamed, and she pulled herself from his embrace. "No . . . No . . ."

"Hush, Madonna mine," he whispered. "It was but a coarse jest, and I am ashamed. Is that what you fear: to be seduced and deserted? My dear one, I would leave you no more than I would leave life itself. And I am sure you would love a little babe to dandle on your knee, to suck at those sweet breasts . . ."

But the terror stayed in her eyes, and he could not understand its fountainhead.

"Is it the act you fear?" Benedetto persisted. "They say all modest maidens have such fears, and yet most take to it as happily as birds to flying. I am sure it is not so bad"—it was his turn to blush—"not that I know, for you will be my first and only lady, and we shall explore this great mystery together."

"No . . . No . . ."

"Not now, of course." He was disturbed by her vehement terror. "When we are wed, and I shall be so gentle, my Lauretta, and never leave you . . ."

Franco rode back to the city in starlight. The dreams that Benedetto stirred were impossible, she would break his gentle heart if she allowed him to hope.

Why not run away with him, her mind prompted?

"Because it would blight his life," she whispered, "and I could not . . . could not . . ." Her cheeks burned in the cool night, but she was unable to put into exact thoughts what it was she feared . . .

Venus Revealed

WHEN FRANCO REACHED the lodgings, Taddeo seemed unusually glum. He had prepared her favourite broth of beans and pasta. Only after they had eaten did she discover that the painting was no longer beneath its covering.

"Where is it?" Franco shouted. She seized Taddeo by the arms and shook him violently.

He had never seen her in an uncontrolled rage. The huge eyes turned almost black, and the white teeth grinding against the lower lip belonged to a wild creature. For once Franco could not show patience as Taddeo stuttered over the words, and she raised her hands in fury, so that he crouched behind his arms to shield himself from the torrent of blows. Franco was immediately horrified by her loss of self-control. She put her arms about the stunted youth.

"Oh, dear Taddeo, what have I done? Can you ever forgive me for striking you, my poor friend?"

He could not bear to see her so upset and kept mumbling: "It's all right."

At last she heard the story. Sandro Botticelli and Leonardo da Vinci had dropped by to wait for her. They had sent Taddeo for some wine, helped themselves to cheese, and begun in their usual inquisitive way to explore the contents of the studio.

"Then they uncovered the beautiful painting," Taddeo explained, "and asked me who it was."

"What did you say?"

"Nothing." In the stained flesh the small eyes grew cunning. "But I know. It's you, Franco."

Her face set in a cold mask as if it had been chipped from a glacier. "Why do you say that?"

"I have watched you bathing," Taddeo replied slyly, "before you chose to go out alone. This lady's hair is long and curling. That's the only difference."

"And they took it?"

He nodded. "They want to show it to someone."

"It's not for show." Franco clutched her hair as if she would tear it out.

She had to wait until morning to seek out the culprits. Sandro Botticelli was in his studio, as usual roaring furious insults at the weaver who lived below.

"He shakes everything with his accursed loom, so I can't concentrate," he explained when Franco burst in.

"Where's my canvas?" she demanded without preamble.

Botticelli had never seen the young artist so distraught. "My dear Franco, calm yourself. First let me tell you we've never seen anything to equal your painting. My 'Primavera' and 'Venus' do not have that magic . . ." He smacked his lips with appreciative relish. "But who's the glorious female?"

Franco dismissed the compliments. "I want my painting back, Sandro. If I don't get it, I swear you and Leonardo won't live to hold a brush."

Botticelli's full mouth slackened, and his round eyes opened so wide they looked as if they might fall out. "We took it to the Magnificent. We wanted to help you . . ."

Franco dashed downstairs, and the weaver yelled up to Botticelli: "As for you, you fornicating, wine-bibbing paint-splasher, I've had enough of your rowdy visitors . . ."

At the Via Larga palazzo they told Franco that the

Medici could not be disturbed as he was in conference with an important personage. She pushed through the aghast bodyguard to enter the long gallery exquisitely ornamented with the Magnificent's collection of *pietra dura* vases and cups in lapis and jasper.

The Medici's dark eyes registered anger at the noisy intrusion, but when he recognized Franco, he began to laugh and slapped his knee.

"By San Giovanni, this is wonderful! Here is the artist, my friend. Franco, I always knew you could paint, but this surpasses anything I thought you capable of creating . . ."

"I want it back." Franco did not attempt polite phrases. "They had no right to bring it here."

"Yes they had," Lorenzo interrupted. "Such a thing of beauty must not be hidden away. Of course you have to finish it, but . . ."

"It's not for sale. Not for any money," Franco said defiantly. "That painting is for me."

"The lady is your mistress, or your sister?" a soft voice asked.

Franco's eyes moved from the Medici to examine his visitor. She did not listen to the introduction, but recognized Messer Ridolfo di Salvestro as ever debonair in darkest mulberry.

"I have no sister."

"Then you have fallen in love with someone of your own colouring," the Medici returned gaily. "As you are a prince among handsome young men, Franco, this lady is the queen of women. Who is she?"

Messer Ridolfo's expression put the same question. "Once I knew a young girl," he explained gravely, "who I believed would grow into such a beauty, but she is dead, and . . ."

"So he seeks a replacement," Lorenzo quipped. "Come, my dear Franco, we shall not compete—and probably could not do so—for your mistress's favours, but at least sell your completed painting to beautify some gentleman's palazzo . . ."

"Lodovico would desire it," Messer Ridolfo stated. "But I fear in this matter I cannot be loyal, for I want that painting for myself."

"And so do I," Lorenzo exclaimed. "Daniello della Sera also wants it, and Guido di Cuono has wagered that he will buy the picture for his own collection.

"Don't you understand what this clamour means, Franco? From it will spring commissions from all the most influential patrons, not just in Florence, but wherever beauty is feted . . ."

Franco anxiously examined her canvas to ensure it had received no hurt. Venus reclined unclothed beneath some trees and held a red lily against her fair breasts. In the shadows beyond a silvery stream stood the dark, bearded goat god. The painting palpitated with desire and the promise of fulfillment. Although the subject was classical, the figures appeared alive, and the Tuscan landscape was recorded in faithful and minute detail.

"You have won Leonardo's praise," the Medici remarked softly. "You know he always says that merely to copy other artists produces but mediocre work. Only a painter who studies nature and transmits what he sees and feels onto the canvas has the divine creative spark. You, Franco, have that.

"I would call this painting 'The Red Lily.'" His harsh voice softened. "It is the symbol of our beautiful city . . . perfection amid the Tuscan hills, yet overshadowed by external dark desires. Franco, your work personifies Florence. That alone means it cannot be hidden away."

"And I should like to meet the Red Lily," Ridolfo appeared much older than she remembered. The lines had deepened.

Lorenzo grinned. "Franco, you really must introduce your lady to Messer Ridolfo. He has come here to ascertain that we are allies now Lodovico Sforza is Regent of Milan. To prove we love this new arrangement we should at least let him see the Red Lily."

"Is that something you desire so much, Messer Ridolfo?" Franco asked quietly.

"More than anything now."

Franco smiled without opening her mouth. I have no power to destroy any of them, she thought, only to withhold what they all want.

"It's impossible," she said. "This lady will show herself to no man."

Rumours concerning the identity of the Red Lily ran wild throughout Florence. Since no one knew very much about the painting they were free to speculate . . . until Franco began to see the funny side of all these incredible tales. For some whispered the model was a Carmelite abbess, while others insisted she was Lorenzo de' Medici's own wife.

Franco had suddenly acquired a reputation as a secret rakehell, her name was firmly established in the Florentine calendar of painters by this curious throw of fate . . .

From every quarter of the city dogs began to bay. Their chorus grew until night itself seemed to be howling. Franco awoke. Her nerve ends responded to the animal fear. She lay shivering. The latch lifted. Taddeo stumbled in.

"The end of the world," he mumbled, his eyes showing much white in terror. "The dogs are all fleeing from the city . . ."

"Go to bed," Franco commanded. "We are quite safe."

He obeyed instantly, reassured by her tone. Franco wished she could convince herself, and began to recite a Paternoster.

The darkness became ominously silent. Then a murmur of thunder expanded into a dull roar. It rolled about her until she felt contained within a rapidly beaten drum. It was not the air that moved, but the earth.

For a few seconds the room rocked and tilted. Franco

leapt from bed to prevent paints, knives, and brushes from sliding off the table. Next door Taddeo rescued plates and dishes and straightened tumbled chairs. Shutters rattled. Doors banged . . . the night was full of invisible intruders. From the squeeze of dwellings came screams, curses, prayers, and children crying.

The shock subsided. In the moment of silence the city held its breath awaiting the tremor that did not come. The slight quake did little damage but seemed an omen of impending change. Florentines rushed into the open to gaze up at the heavens, expecting some imminent supernatural event. Tomorrow the churches would be full of penitent worshipers.

Franco's flesh crept against her spine. She lit the rushlight and examined the completed painting. "The Red Lily" was unharmed. In the faltering light the pearly body seemed as vibrant as the artist standing before it.

"Until I created you," she whispered, "I had felt in control of my new life."

It was to ride forth on a powerful horse which needed skillful handling, yet she had understood how to master the animal and follow the winding road. Suddenly the horse had broken into a crazed gallop. It veered from the path into a strange perilous country. The familiar reins flew from the rider's grasp. She felt bound to crouch, cling to the trailing mane, and grip the heaving sweating flanks with her knees. Whip and spurs were pretty toys for which the wild steed cared nothing.

Franco pushed open the shutters. The oppressive warmth slid into the room and touched her nakedness with moist hands. It brought with it the foul stench of the alleys and the river. Now and then a torch flared in its iron bracket on some outside wall, and the shadows of people wandering the maze of courts and turnings resembled an army of phantoms. Across the river a misty red glare showed where a group of buildings had caught fire.

The candlemaker's wife began screaming: "The end of the world is upon us . . ." Franco hardly blamed the drunken husband who hurled abuse to quell that monotonous dirge. A child cried out in unhappiness. The night was a sad, fearful time. Those terrors held at bay during daylight returned to stalk in men's minds.

If the city survived then she would have to show Messer Ridolfo the completed "Red Lily" in the morning. Half of her dreaded the confrontation; half warmed to its challenge: the gamble of outwitting this powerfully wise enemy, who no doubt felt he had an unknown painter upon the hip because the Medici would wish to secure Il Moro's friendship by all possible means.

She leaned on the window ledge and watched the storm rip open the belly of night bulging low over the city as if about to flatten all the proud buildings. Under sheet lightning the river glowed blue-white. Against this swift fading curtain of light, towers and cupolas were unreal marzipan confections.

Then the rain poured from the wounded dark. It lashed the Arno into a boiling serpent. The alleys streamed and refuse poured down to the river. Raindrops pelted roofs with the fury of an attacking army.

The heavy air began to sweeten. Franco's body was sheened with a refreshing coolness. People running through the heavy mud, scarcely bothered to look up at the faintly lit room. Only one man noticed the pale shoulders and breasts, and copper hair of a girl at the window. He stopped among the shadows, oblivious of the rain and watched until the little light drowned in darkness, and the white form closed the shutters . . .

"You seducing dog!" Insults rang through the court where

puddles reflected the pale morning light. Franco spun round.
Standing in the shelter of a doorway was a young man
with a worn face, and eyes reddened from weeping and lack
of sleep. In an unsteady hand he held an unsheathed sword.

Franco's voice was as chill as the mist rising above the
river. "How have I offended you?"

Then she recognized Benedetto. It took all her self-control
not to laugh and doff her elegant hat, with its fall of purple
silk that folded about her throat and concealed the brilliant
hair.

"Your rage hardly becomes your garb."

"And you are the artist called Franco: a fawning beard-
less demon, the Medici's favourite, and the creator of 'The
Red Lily.' Now there are three of us who know her name.
You, she and myself . . ." Tears stood out in his eyes, and
Franco felt sorry for him.

"What's her name then?" she inquired, keeping her voice
even lower than usual.

"Lauretta, my Lauretta." It was an anguished cry. "By
ill-chance I have found out about you and her. The first
time I saw her . . . that sweet day is engraved upon my
memory with sunlight and green leaves, I chanced to glimpse
the misshapen creature who I thought to be her servant . . .
Now I know he's a ruffiano—her pimp. Yesterday in the
Mercato Vecchio I saw him buying eggs and followed him
to see where my Lauretta lived. How happy I was: I had
discovered my treasure's hiding place. It meant I could come
here each day and wait to see her fair face. Last night when
I feared the city would be destroyed, I came to die with
my Lauretta.

"When I saw her at the window, I feared to go up. It
was so late, and I had no wish to harm her sweet reputation.
This morning I asked the candlemaker the name of the lady
living above. He told me the rooms belonged to Franco . . .
and the lady I'd glimpsed was probably his elusive mistress.

Lauretta is well placed beneath a candlemaker's roof . . . the strumpet! Is she still up there?"

"No, she left at daybreak." It was the time Franco always dressed.

"Why didn't God destroy us all?" Benedetto cried. "This wicked city corrupts the pure and beautiful. All last night you kept her in your bed and took pleasure in what she would never yield to me . . . or perhaps"—and his face was ashen with pain—"she only feigned virtue to play my foolishness. I did not offer the bawd money. That's what is required to prime their passions, isn't it?"

"She is not a whore," Franco insisted, knowing it foolish to feel indignant.

Benedetto snatched at the canvas she carried for Messer Ridolfo's inspection, uncovered it, and then cried out as if he'd fallen on his own blade. "Not a whore? When she has unclothed her very beauty for you to display to all the lewdest men in the city. This way she and you will receive much gold from their dissolute desires."

He flung the painting on the ground and lunged desperately and inexpertly at Franco's throat. Hers was a reflex action: She loosed the dagger concealed in her right sleeve, and deflected the sword blade. The force of this deft pass caused Benedetto to stumble. His sword slid away and he looked up blankly when Franco did not bother to take advantage of the reversed situation.

"Come on, kill me," he begged, leaning against the damp-stained wall, panting wtih fear, anger, and misery.

"Let's stop brawling," she urged. "We don't want to be thrown in the Stinche for causing an affray, and the Eight are ever patrolling this area for thieves. Believe me, your Lauretta met no hurt in my bed . . ." A smile darted to her lips. "Indeed she seemed as comfortable there as in her own."

Franco suddenly remembered Andrea. It was a long time since she dared think of him for the pain memory brought.

God, how he would have loved this ridiculous tragic scene.

Benedetto slumped forward, the skin on his face sagged as if he'd lived many years in one short night. "Mother of God, then she is a harlot. Tell me, at least, that you love her, Franco."

"No." She replaced the dagger. "But I shall guard her, good priest. She'll always have food to eat and a place to sleep so long as I live."

"But I offered her love. Did she never mention me?"

"You're Benedetto. In her own words: the sweetest fool. She could never be your wife any more than she can be mine."

"One dark night I shall slit your liver with that sword," Benedetto threatened with greater bitterness than conviction. "And gouge out those mocking eyes to give as a gift to faithless Lauretta."

Franco retrieved the painting and asked seriously: "Would you like this in memory?"

"And have half the gentlemen of Florence seeking my blood? No, you sell it and Lauretta for gold."

He slunk away, bent as if carrying some unbearable burden. Franco sighed and straightened the short purple cloak, edged with silver fox. It was better to let him believe what he chose, rather than risk betraying her own secret with the truth. She had needed his love: it had been to bask in brief summer sunshine and learn she was truly feminine. She understood she did not love Benedetto. Even if she played again at Lauretta and fled with him, it was too late for her to be the sweet amenable maiden he dreamed of. To have ever been such a creature, Franco understood clearly, would have meant she died long ago . . . in fact Franco could never have come into existence . . .

"You did not need my help then?" A low voice chased her from thought. Ridolfo di Salvestro emerged from the gloom at the end of the courtyard. "You were late," he explained his presence, "so I sought your address from da

Vinci, who had a letter for me to give Lodovico Sforza. I came to ensure you had not forgotten our appointment. I waited to see if you needed my aid, but Franco is evidently as adroit with a weapon as a brush."

"He was but a poor priest who knows more about good than evil," Franco said soberly. "He would not be much of an opponent, but, Messer, you should not walk these alleys. You are a glittering temptation."

Di Salvestro shook back his cloak to reveal even more splendid gems. He said nothing, only smiled with thin amusement and stroked the sword hilt with the hands of a lover.

"Perhaps you had best come up," she said. "We cannot talk here."

Indeed the overhanging walls had sprouted sudden live gargoyles. Nothing could occur in this neighbourhood without countless curious eyes watching.

She sent Taddeo out of the studio, for his terrified expression showed he recalled their visitor from another time. Franco poured wine.

"I hope you will excuse these humble lodgings," she apologized, and felt the warm red power set her blood racing and begin to inspire her with a mad courage. This morning had turned into a dangerous game . . . as if she played at dice with the Devil and so had to win every throw. Once more with gentle pain she recalled Andrea.

"You have been accustomed to better surroundings." Ridolfo looked round the cluttered room and wrinkled his nose against the odours rising from the alley. The rainstorm's good work was fading under the stinking onslaught of daily life.

Franco's sharp mirth drew those dark, watchful eyes to her face. "What! A nameless youth know better than this! You jest indeed."

"Then why are you so unwilling to sell your painting? Think of all you could buy with the gold."

"It is not for sale."

"Because Lauretta is your mistress?"

Franco shivered. This man was not a love-blinded, unworldly priest. How much might his observant eye discover and his clever mind discern? She became very calm.

"Why do you want to purchase 'The Red Lily' so much?"

Ridolfo looked through the windows at the clouds that dissolved and re-formed as they sped across the city. "I lost the maid I should have loved. My own belief in the astrology, which showed we should belong to each other, has foundered. Since then I have little faith in what the stars and planets foretell . . . although my noble friend, Lodovico, does not share this skepticism. His own astrologer and I read that he would return to Milan . . . even greater triumphs await him."

"What was the name of this girl you lost?"

"It no longer exists," Ridolfo said harshly. "Her family was involved in a conspiracy against the Medici, as far as popular opinion and the law are concerned. One does not meddle in the political intrigues of another city, unless one is armed with great power."

Franco poured more wine and handed the pewter beaker to the man. As he received it, his fingers inadvertently brushed her cold hand. His dark eyes flared. "Who in the Devil's name are you, Franco?"

The blood withdrew from her face, but she replied: "You have answered your own question by naming me."

Ridolfo looked from his hand to hers, and Franco felt the unease which heralds a storm. They continued to stare at each other for a long moment. At last, Ridolfo re-examined the painting.

"I must seek out this Lauretta," he announced flatly, "for she is the mirror image of my fate."

"She would have nought to do with you, Messer, so you would be wasting your dreams." Franco's lips lifted in a grim smile.

"As you don't wish to sell me the painting it would be ill-mannered of me to bargain further. I shall watch with the keenest attention the future career of the young Florentine, Franco."

Messer Ridolfo's words suggested a threat, and Franco thought: He suspects something about me without knowing precisely what it is. I must endeavour to guard the past, present, and future from his eyes . . .

Cosima

How STRANGE TO RIDE again into the courtyard of Casa Cuono on a spring afternoon. Franco tried to banish memory. This time her companions were Guido di Cuono and Daniello della Sera, and they were followed by mounted servants in the two distinctive liveries, with Taddeo riding a mule in their brilliant midst.

"It's a hideous place," Guido apologized. "One day, Franco, you must visit my charming villa at Poggio, a more fitting environment for your artistic taste."

"And you have never seen Buonventura." Daniello's reproach was accompanied by such a sincere smile that Franco felt he really regretted this omission.

"My sweet friends, what would the city merchants say if I was forever leaving commissions to visit you?"

"You will attend Daniello's wedding," Guido said, "and you can paint the newlyweds."

"You are to be married!" Franco exclaimed. Her heart grew heavy. It was to lose something she could never have, but the loss was nonetheless painful.

"It is still secret," Daniello explained diffidently, "but you are our confidant. The Medici approves. Now I have only to ask the lady's consent."

"Of course she'll marry you," Guido insisted.

"Any lady would," Franco said. "The golden god of our city smiles, and the maidens tremble and pale. Who is this fortunate lady?"

"My sister, Cosima," Guido replied.

"May I wish you all happiness and many children." Franco spoke somberly.

Daniello sighed. "Even in front of Guido I must admit I don't relish this marriage . . . not that Cosima isn't the finest girl in Florence—saving your mistress, the Red Lily— but women are such unaccountable creatures. Though the della Sera name must be continued, I don't enjoy the sight of babies. They're worse than fountains . . . squirting and spewing from every aperture, and not caring who they dampen."

"I thought you were already betrothed," Franco ventured.

"That was long ago, and the maid's dead."

She had heard him use a less unconcerned tone about a missing glove.

Franco entered the great house like someone visiting a place for the first time . . . yet feeling all the while she had been there in some distant dream or other life. Certain objects were shockingly familiar: the large golden dish supported by Tritons . . . a small painting of the "Judgement of Paris" by an unnamed Tuscan artist . . . a splendid ivory and silver crucifix . . . they had once graced the interior of Castelfiore.

The closer I am with my enemies, Franco mused, the less power I feel. This must be the frailty of my sex. A man would not hesitate to accomplish his vengeance. I require something other than destruction: that the past could be unwritten. Revenge now seems strangely pointless.

When Cosima appeared time ebbed away. Franco was a child again, gazing in wonder at Madonna Ginevra on feast days: Around Guido's sister's throat, and in the cascades of dark hair, were the amethysts set in gold her mother had been so proud of, for Vincenzo de' Narni had given her them on Andrea's birth.

The present returned. Franco saw only Cosima. She had altered to slender maturity and grown even lovelier. The dark eyes seemed troubled, and the soft colour faded to leave a lily paleness as she gazed on the young artist. Guido caught her arm.

"We were just saying Daniello sets all the ladies a-swooning . . . and now you demonstrate that truth, sister."

"Who is this youth?" Cosima asked tremulously without looking at Daniello.

Guido laughed. "This is Franco of Florence come to paint your beauty."

Cosima became gay to the point of wildness. Franco had only seen little cocottes in the taverns tease and smile with such abandon to attract customers.

"So Maestro Franco, you are the faithful lover who will not sell his mistress's likeness to Lorenzo, or the Regent of Milan's special emissary. My brother will buy it yet, for he can be very convincing when he sets his mind on some desire. Now, tell me true, am I less beautiful than your Red Lily?"

"No," Franco spoke emphatically. "You are the loveliest woman I have ever seen."

Cosima clapped her hands with delight. "He speaks so ardently. I must believe him. That is the kind of man I most admire." She smiled at Daniello who failed to respond, and Franco knew a swift, secret pleasure.

Franco found it difficult to sleep in that house, although the chamber, with its curtained bed, tapestries and carpet, carved chest and chairs, was the most luxurious she had

ever stayed in. Despite Guido's and Daniello's expostula-
tions she insisted on Taddeo's sharing it.

"How can you have that abortion of nature near your
couch?" di Cuono demanded. He loathed Taddeo, and delighted in striking the ground with a riding whip so that
the poor creature leapt and snarled with terror.

"Because neither of us is accustomed to living in such
palatial splendour," Franco explained humbly. "He is used
to my ways. Your servants might find me uncouth."

Taddeo slept fully clothed before the door, waking and
snuffing the darkness at the faintest footfall.

To be a guest in her enemy's house seemed to Franco
a crazed dream, but it was amusing to be waited upon by
Gianni who had grown into a stout, solemn fellow, and
offered the cook's famous cake with deference and a silver
goblet of the house's finest wine.

Franco took a long draught of Orvieto to steady herself,
for this cup with the large beryl set in its base had belonged
to Andrea. She could still recall his holding it to her baby
lips so that she might taste his wine. Gianni stared at the
artist in some perplexity.

"You stir a memory, maestro, but I can't pin it to a
time."

It proved difficult to wrest some daylight to work, for
Daniello and Guido constantly required her company on
hunting expeditions. Cosima chose to be painted in her bedchamber. "Otherwise my brother and Daniello will keep
distracting your attention," she pouted. "You are a target of
much admiration, Franco."

"I expect, madonna, it is rather like having a new hawk
or greyhound . . . after the novelty wears thin I shall cease
to seem interesting."

Entering Cosima's room, Franco's heart twisted with a
scimitar of memory. She could not look at the bed . . . the
ornaments . . . or the lovely woman whose nurse, Bianca, was
as ever fussing over the unbound tresses.

Franco's eyes sought the window. A chamois still curvetted among the clipped bushes in the garden below. She half expected to glimpse a girl with a shabby dress and cape of red hair peering into the room. But she wasn't there . . . or anywhere else anymore.

The angry wail of a child drew Franco close to the window. Lying in a wicker basket was a boy child of about two or three . . . plump and pink, his fine hair a field of corn at sunset.

She knelt down and tickled the necklaces of fat. The eyelids flew open. The eyes were green. Franco understood. This was the reason Cosima had not visited the city during a long interval. Andrea was not quite dead. She picked up the damp child who smelled of warm sleep and soured milk. It was the first baby she had held in an age, and he was a Narni.

Oh Andrea, Andrea, Franco said silently, you should have lived to know your son.

He began to squall, punching the green taffeta doublet with little crumpled fists. Tears that had started in her own eyes became laughter. She had almost expected this love child to sense their kinship and be content in her arms. The nurse took charge of him, and the howl became a dimpled roguish smile.

"He's a real boy," Bianca explained. "A man's hands anger him, but he smiles at a woman's touch."

Spirit of Andrea—Franco looked ruefully at her own hands—you can't tell I'm your aunt.

"What a beautiful child, Madonna Cosima, what is his name?"

"Mario. He belonged to the Caucasian slave my father purchased for me. Anna was young and foolish. Some unknown gentleman got her with child, as is the way of this wicked world, and then deserted her without paying us the customary fine for such an offense. Anna died when the boy was born. He was so beautiful it seemed heartless to send him to the foundling hospital, so I keep him by me instead of a pet. Each day he grows more adorable. When he is of an age to learn, Guido will send him to a monastery to be a priest. It is the best way with bastards. Perhaps he will rise high enough for a cardinal's hat and bring glory on our family."

"Wouldn't his father acknowledge him? Many a marriage bed does not beget such a fine son."

"No. Mario is very well as he is. Besides he keeps Bianca occupied, and she stops treating me as if I were five years old . . ."

"You are a gentle lady, Madonna Cosima. I had intended to depict you as a proud pagan goddess, but now you shall be Our Lady with the Blessed Babe . . ."

Franco knelt to drape the gown against Cosima's feet and felt the knees quiver as if in fear.

"Don't be alarmed, madonna. Here is Mario. Give him . . ." She saw a dish of fruit, and handed a golden-rinded pomegranate to Cosima.

The baby crawled at his mother's feet and then reached for the fruit. The bright curls and dimpled profile etched against the dark blue drapery of the skirt made an irresistible picture, and Cosima's own attitude suggested gentleness as she leaned towards the child . . .

The painting grew, and Franco began to know Cosima: know her for her beauty, vanity, and foolishness. She had a babbling tongue that any clear mind could trip into revealing closely kept secrets. Franco was not surprised when she said: "Do you know why I nearly fainted when I first saw you? You recall someone else, though your eyes are different. His were as green as sea water."

Or as Mario's, Franco amended silently. "Who was he?"

"Someone I thought I loved."

"Alas, poor man. To be loved by you is Paradise upon earth," Franco complimented. "But that you only thought you loved him must have cast him into Purgatory. If you should begin to hate him then he will be thrown into the fires of Hell . . ."

"He is already there," Cosima said, and her eyes were grieved and baffled.

Guido rarely visited his sister while Franco worked. He loathed Mario, who began to scream immediately whenever he appeared. Franco noticed that Cosima, who paid scant attention to the child when they were alone, would hold him to her breast and smother him with kisses in a frenzy of defiance as soon as her brother entered.

Daniello never came near the chamber. Although Franco missed his company, it delighted her that he found Cosima so irksome. As soon as the lovely creature appeared his handsome face dulled, and he withdrew into strained and polite monosyllables. Yet in Franco's presence Daniello waxed merry and talkative, delighting to exchange anecdotes, sing songs, and play chess or dice. He does not like her, Franco thought, and marries merely to please the Medici.

It appeared that Daniello disliked physical contact with women, and Franco began to fashion an impossible dream of one day being united with him in a spiritual marriage . . .

When the painting was all but complete, she discovered Bianca and Mario absent from the bedchamber. Cosima reclined on her couch, wearing a white *camicia,* trimmed with spangled ribbons and fine lace, but the material was so filmy that the voluptuous body might just as well have been naked. She lay as one unable to sleep on a sweltering summer's night . . . her cheeks flushed . . . her hair tangled . . . and her ankles and calves uncovered. Each time her full breasts heaved their dark nipples peeped over the lace

"Are you unwell, madonna?" Franco inquired politely. "You seem feverish. Shall I call your nurse?"

"No." The beautiful mouth wore swollen discontent. "Do stay with me. Tell me, Franco, why are you so distressingly faithful to your Red Lily? You never treat me as anything except the model for your wretched painting."

"Why do you berate me, madonna? That is the reason I was brought to your house."

"I thought you found me beautiful"—Cosima's voice was warm and sweet as fruit plucked in sunshine—"and I find you a most lovesome youth . . ."

Franco tried to stifle mirth, but it bubbled forth. The wench certainly had a taste for Narnis.

"Only because I resemble a man you thought you loved," she returned gaily.

"Don't mock me," Cosima reproved. "I like you because you are Franco. Feel how hot my head is." She caught the strong, slender hand and held it against her temples. "Can't you feel the pulse throbbing?"

"Indeed, madonna, I think your nurse might make some herbal infusion to soothe this fever."

"There is no infusion that will do that," Cosima whispered. She dragged the hand against her left breast. "How my heart beats because of your proximity." The dark eyes examined Franco's burning cheeks. "I do believe Guido is right, and you have never lain with a woman."

"That is true." Franco's husky voice contained an indignant edge.

With supple arms Cosima reached out and pulled the slim figure onto her bed. Franco fell forward, aware of the scents of orris root, bergamot, and warm armpits. Cosima drew the red head towards her and began to kiss Franco's mouth.

Benedetto's kisses had not prepared her for this embrace. Cosima's hands and mouth contained a terrible hunger, as if she wanted to draw the breath and blood from whoever she held captive in her arms.

I have heard men speak of such females, Franco thought fearfully. They are ever hot for a man's body, yet cannot be satisfied, so must go from lover to lover without care for their honour or modesty in the pursuit of some unattainable pleasure. It is a sickness, not a loving spirit. She is merely inflamed by the belief that I possess an instrument of a magnitude to satisfy her.

"How cold you are." Cosima stroked the red hair, and passed the tip of her tongue over the white neck. With alarm Franco realized that very soon this amorous creature would discover the total absence of the instrument she so desired.

"You should learn about love," Cosima urged breathlessly, and she took Franco's hand and pressed it between her moist thighs.

Franco pulled away and cried out, "Nay, madonna, your brother would slay me . . . and rightly so . . . if he found a worthless artist touching his sister's body."

She felt sick. The disguise was no defense against certain situations she had not even envisaged. She knew such practices existed betwen women in convents . . . many preferred to satisfy their appetites that way rather than endure some brutish fellow in their beds. Although she feared the complete embraces of any man, Franco spurned the idea of carnal games with another female.

Cosima entwined her legs around Franco's thigh, and her body shuddered with desperate spasms. Franco sprang free. Horror and disgust were written across her eyes and mouth.

Cosima's own eyes grew wild and furious. "Shall I tell Guido you forced your attentions upon me?" she hissed. "I can tear off this shift and swear you raped me. He and Daniello would castrate you like the worthless animal you are. Then, see if your Red Lily wants the body you refuse to cede to me . . ."

The more fear Franco knew the more controlled she became. It had always seemed that when other men's eyes clouded with hot blood the one who saw with cold clarity must outwit their fury.

"Would your brother believe your accusation?" she asked.

"What do you mean?" Cosima reared up, and her face and eyes belonged to the ferocious tigress in the *Signoria*'s menagerie.

Franco threw the reckless statement like dice. "Because I know the name of Mario's father and also his real mother. Would the gentle Daniello della Sera agree to, or Lorenzo de' Medici countenance, a marriage with Cosima di Cuono, however fair, if they knew that the so-called traitor, Andrea de' Vincenzo Narni, had given her a child?"

Cosima's feverish brightness faded, and the lamps in her eyes dimmed. "How do you know?" she whispered. "You must be possessed with the devil's own knowledge."

Franco smiled. The power was with her, and she felt it. "Why did you keep the babe?"

"I tried to lose it, God knows!" Cosima muttered, and her face took on lines of pain at the recollection. "No matter what vile potions I drank, or what my nurse did to me, I could not miscarry. When my brother discovered it he wanted to kill me . . ." She clutched at her throat in agitation. "They say the shock killed our father: he worked himself into one of his rages and then died. But, Guido is cold reasoning man. To slay me or lock me away from the world would have provoked curiosity and the Medici's disfavour. I kept to these apartments for many months so that no one could observe my condition. When my time came I was tended by my nurse and Anna. I made Bianca take the child away as soon as he was born: he was so pretty even at birth, and my very own. Guido would have strangled him then. I think he vented his fury on my slave."

"And she is dead?"

"I don't know. For all his passionless appearance my brother has a temper more violent than a volcano . . . yet he can be so kind . . ." Cosima smiled at some reminiscence, and softly fingered her own bare breasts. Franco looked away and detested her imaginings.

"When I grew stronger I made a bargain with him: I should keep my Mario, or else enter a convent—then I would not be available to charm the Medici and foster our family's fortune. Guido surrendered . . ."

Cosima's voice faltered. She twisted her fingers; "I did love the child's father. You are like him somehow, but much harder . . . a diamond, whereas my sweet, loving Andrea was soft gold. Yet he and his whole family were traitors and my brother said I had endangered our safety and reputation by allowing him to visit me. I didn't understand . . ."

It would be easy for Guido to weave the threads of intrigue to enmesh this sensual sister who wanted nothing but admiration and gratification, Franco thought dispassionately, and she must have been terrified, and no older than I am now . . .

"Are you going to tell your brother I ravished you?"

The soft, dark eyes Andrea had worshiped flinched before that implacable gaze. "No."

For the first time Franco was glad her brother was dead. Better that than he should have discovered his goddess's true value . . .

The Medici brought a crowd of friends, including Ridolfo di Salvestro, to admire the completed painting at Casa Cuono. No one failed to notice that Madonna Cosima's eyes followed the young artist everywhere with a beseeching expression . . . even while the Magnificent announced her betrothal to Daniello della Sera . . .

The Bride

In the Panico the Company of the Cauldron caroused until late. So much wine was consumed no one could recall whose saint's day they had gathered to celebrate. There was nothing to do but to toast each of the members again to round off a jolly evening. With arms linked they swung through the streets, singing lustily:

> How fat you are, my girl!
> May Heaven blast you, churl! . . .

Now and then they would stop to yell abuse at the linen-capped merchants who opened their shutters to hurl imprecations and nightsoil upon the disturbers of rest. Franco dubbed these would-be-abeds "the companions of the piss-pot," which added to the merriment and encouraged further catcalls.

Gradually the party broke up as individuals sought their lodgings. Taddeo was not in his usual spot behind the Duomo, where he always waited to light Franco back to the Camaldoli when she was out at night.

"Lazy vagabond must have drunk himself to sleep!" she grumbled. "I'll give him such a drubbing . . ."

Franco whistled as she stepped out. Her head began to clear from wine fumes. This was an odd life for any father's daughter, she mused, but better than that rich unwholesome existence within Casa Cuono.

For a few minutes she relished her precarious freedom, then a gradual awareness of being followed in the darkness quickened her senses. Franco did not increase her pace or glance back. It might only be another nocturnal reveller . . .

The small court some way ahead with two alleys leading from it would give her an opportunity to ascertain innocent or malign intent.

A sliver of moon was emerging above the roofs. By its uncertain glimmer Franco saw that both narrow passages were blocked by men, and the passage she had entered through would at any second frame her pursuer. Moonlight caught on drawn swords.

She grasped her dagger, aware of its coldness in her hot palm. "Do you want my purse?" she called. "I've but two florins in it."

"You're Franco the artist?" one of the men demanded. His face was concealed by the shadow of a hood.

"What of it?"

"I have to deliver a message from a noble gentleman who regrets your interest in a certain fair lady. Here it is."

Franco had no time to ask the identity of man or lady, for a sword point pierced her padded sleeve. She began to fight for her life, but it was to duel with shadows where only eyes and blades gleamed.

This is the finish, she thought, dodging their lunges. I cannot hope to defend myself against two, even if darkness gives us the same disadvantage and protection.

Franco noticed the third blade.

It was useless to fight any longer. The noble gentleman would get his wish.

Then the new sword flickered against her two attackers. They had not expected this second opponent and fled through an alleyway, leaving Franco alone with the swordsman. She had never known sweat could feel so chill, as she leaned panting against a wall. "Who is my protector?" she gasped.

The tall figure did not reply. He turned and walked away in the direction from which they had come. There were sudden shouts, running feet, and the flare of distant lanterns.

Franco knew better than to tarry. The Eight were on the prowl. She dashed into the warren of alleys.

In the studio, Taddeo was curled up on the palliasse. Franco kicked him in the side.

"What in the name of Creation are you doing here?" she raged. "I've just missed being murdered, not that you'd have proved much protection."

Taddeo began to stammer: "But you sent me a message. You are to stay overnight with Maestro Botticelli . . ."

"I sent no such message," Franco shouted scornfully. "Sandro's room's so packed with drabs there'd be nowhere to stand, let alone sleep. Who told you this nonsense? Or is it a figment of the wine barrel?"

"No, Franco," Taddeo insisted. "The messenger was a lad in dark red with gold embroidery on his sleeves . . . a great beast holding a man in its jaws . . ."

She smiled bitterly. So Messer Ridolfo wanted her dead. Whether to secure "The Red Lily" or because he suspected the artist of being a Narni who would accuse him of being involved in that never-forgotten plot did not matter . . .

The rumour that Franco had escaped murder travelled through the city and fellow artists advised her to leave Florence.

"I may as well suspect one of you," she retorted when Leonardo, Sandro, and Domenico visited her studio. "What, isn't there enough work for us all?"

Ghirlandajo put a restraining hand on Franco's arm, and said earnestly: "Listen, just this once. It would appear you have offended a noble patron, either by your stiff-necked refusal to sell him 'The Red Lily,' or mayhap you've been creeping into the scented bed of his wife. Such things are always happening to us. Go away, and let the air clear. When you return the matter will be forgotten, or some new problem will occupy your enemy's mind."

"I refuse to be driven from my home," Franco cried defiantly.

At the Palazzo Medici, Lorenzo's close friends and family gathered around the artist, inquiring who the attacker could be. The Magnificent's eyes showed concern, as he drew Franco into the shade of the arcade.

"Thank God, you are quite safe. It would appear that the climate outside Florence might be healthier for you at this time," and his voice brooked no alternative.

Ridolfo di Salvestro joined them, followed at a discreet distance by a page. Franco did not need to examine the embroidery design on the mulberry livery.

"An excellent idea, Lorenzo," he interposed swiftly, "I'm to return to Milan. Franco can come with me. Lodovico would welcome his talent."

"I have no thought to visit Milan," Franco said coldly. She was scared . . . trapped between these two powerful men, both apparently determined to send her from the city.

"Of course not," Lorenzo agreed, and his dark gaze triumphed over di Salvestro. "I had thought of dispatching you to Rome," he added confidentially, and Franco knew this was no rash decision. The ruler of Florence planned each move well in advance. "Here is a letter to His Holiness, recommending your talent, of which I'm sure he will avail himself. By going there, you will be rendering me a great service. I should like you to discover in subtle fashion what is in Sixtus' mind regarding our State now he's started this new war with Ferrara. That would give us useful information, my dear Ridolfo. No one would suspect our charming Franco of gathering such snippets."

Franco took the letter reluctantly. She understood this was a command and could not fathom the real reason behind it. Yet to disobey the Medici would be to forfeit his patronage . . .

"I must finish Guido di Cuono's portrait," she said unhappily. "Then I shall go to Rome. Messer Ridolfo," she added, "your page gets into odd company . . ."

Di Salvestro's eyes were narrow bars of jet as he answered.

"Sometimes a lad with willing manners does services for those other than his master."

Lorenzo looked at them in turn but said nothing. For once Franco found his eyes inscrutable . . .

Completing Guido's portrait was not an unpleasant task, and it was very well paid. His palazzo on the Via Larga held no agonizing memories, and Cosima rarely intruded on her brother's apartments. Daniello often dropped by to watch the picture's progress, gossip, and drink wine . . . and where he was Franco knew soft contentment.

Guido never ceased to ask what the artist would accept for "The Red Lily."

"It's not for sale," she insisted.

"Take my advice and give it to Lorenzo. It might sweeten his attitude towards you. I fear he finds certain acts of yours disloyal . . ."

Franco laid down a brush to stare at the sitter with astonishment. "You jest. He is sending me to Rome on a special mission."

"Of course, that will take you far away from Cosima." Her smooth brow lined in puzzlement.

Guido smiled. "Deny all you will, but I fear Cosima tried to seduce you from your virtue. I realize you are immune to such dalliance. However, Lorenzo could never believe that any man my sister looks upon so ardently as she does on you would not immediately fall into her bed. . . . To win her interest is an act of disloyalty to our ruler."

"Surely, Daniello warrants the Medici's displeasure more than an unimportant painter?"

Guido shrugged. "As a loyal citizen, he would not hinder his ruler's desires. To share your wife with the Magnificent is not to be cuckolded by a groom . . ."

Franco looked appalled. "We are not discussing a courtesan. How can you speak thus of your own sister?"

"Your solicitude speaks of rare good breeding—strange

in a vagabond artist—but you already know Cosima quite well enough to be aware my words are not misplaced."

"What has she said?"

"That you have a well-informed and beautiful head." Guido still smiled. "Be careful not to lose it. Knowledge can be very dangerous."

"Is that a threat?"

"I have no need to threaten," he replied reasonably. "I can crush you as easily as this." Guido tore a petal from a crimson carnation and squeezed it until colour, texture, and clove scent were lost. "Besides, Messer Ridolfo may well remove you from this world for reasons of his own. I hear he shows a keen interest in all your doings. Perhaps he has some personal grudge, or merely wants the original Red Lily for his bed. He has the devil's own temper, they say, when he is roused . . ."

"Why did you commission me to paint your picture?"

"Because you do my features much justice, and I like to have you under my eye so I can determine the amount of your knowledge. What do you really know about my family, Franco?"

She gathered together the brushes and palette to show the day's sitting was at an end. "Enough to turn the Magnificent's friendship into suspicion and hatred."

"I doubt he would believe *you*, for that would mean he had to forgo Cosima's passionate charms. Besides I can silence you before you begin to chatter. See this ring I always wear . . ."

He held up a finger with a golden orb set in a jewelled shank. "I can press a minute pin, which releases perfume into the atmosphere . . . or poison in a wine cup. I admire your courage, Franco. You're like fire and steel. Because of that very boldness I offer you my personal protection."

Guido rose and placed a hand on her arm. "You're a curious youth and damnably handsome. Are you as cold as you pretend?" He put an arm around her shoulders and casually kissed the soft cheek.

Franco pushed him away. "That is a sin," she cried in horror.

"A pleasant one," he countered levelly. "Do you know Daniello and I have made a wager that I shall melt your ice? He says you are too pure, and I contend that all purity can be corrupted. I am tired of vicious, knowing boys who perform their tricks for anyone who gives them fine gifts." Intensity filled his voice. "I want someone with a mind and a soul as well as a beautiful face and body for my intimate."

He smiled at her disgust. "Why are you so shocked, Franco? Half the men who are married have a boy they can turn to when women's wiles and temperaments become too much . . . even if it is both sin and crime . . . Men can have much pleasure with each other, and there is no chance of begetting a bastard to maintain . . ."

Franco produced the dagger. Guido began to laugh. It was not an unpleasant sound. "My dear boy, I can summon my servants immediately. They will drag you before the Podesta, and I shall swear you tried to rob and murder me. And my word would be accepted. Put away that little toy."

He drew near. Franco's terror overwhelmed and weakened her. Casually Guido pushed the dagger from her inert fingers. Their eyes looked down to where it rested on the ground between them. He had gentle hands, and his lips were cold and hard on her closed mouth.

"There," he exclaimed gaily. "That was not so terrible. We have sealed our friendship. You may count on my protection against men like di Salvestro, and I can rely on your not revealing whatever trifling secret you believe you possess that could ruin my family."

"And Cosima's bastard?" Franco spat the words with contempt and repugnance for herself and her companion.

His hands tightened on her shoulders. "One person who

dared taunt me with that still bears the scars and can no longer speak. It would be a pity, Franco, for me to mark your beauty in a similar fashion, or . . ."—and he smiled—"maim those clever hands so that you would have to put your body to a calling you eschew to earn your bread. As for the child, I can destroy all trace of him . . ."

"No! Not that!" Franco's plea pierced the shadows.

Guido stared at her. "There is some mystery. Before either of us are much older I shall know the truth."

He drew Franco hard against him, and then gasped. "By Christ's Passion, you're no male." Guido pressed one hand to her doublet, and muttered, "Women's breasts by Heaven." She tried to struggle free as his hands travelled down her body. Tears overbrimmed the cold, dark eyes in an extravagance of laughter. "My sweet friend, you have been gelded, or else are indeed a girl. This makes rarer sport. Either way it is a pleasure to embrace you."

He began to kiss her mouth with growing passion. Franco broke free. She was less frightened by his insolent touch than the fact he had discovered her secret.

"Do you know who I am, Guido di Cuono?" she panted.

He raised his shoulders to express unconcern.

"I am a Narni," she whispered.

"They are all dead."

"Your butchers did not find the girl who overheard the Pazzi plot brewed at Casa Cuono."

Guido grew still. His dark eyes took on understanding. "Della Sera's betrothed: Francesca Lauretta. So you came to our house with your seducing brother." He examined her face minutely. "By all the saints, you are the Red Lily . . ." He began to laugh again. "So the men who desire her must turn sodomite to discover her hiding place. Now I have the Red Lily in my palm."

"I am going to destroy the di Cuono family," she whispered, backing from him.

"You have too much spirit and talent for a mere woman not to realize your words are folly. By doing as you threaten you will reveal your own identity and be forced to flee to the sanctuary of some nunnery. After your accustomed liberty life would seem unbearably restricted. Besides, I seriously doubt the Medici will take notice of your accusations . . ."

"Your father was . . ."

"He is dead. Lorenzo will not want to pick scabs from old sores without excellent reason, if that means relinquishing Cosima." Guido smiled gently. "Life is not as simple as you wish: self-interest governs most things. You should understand something, Franco: I was not involved in that plot and had no particular wish to bring down the Medici. I won't deny I wanted your brother's blood for dishonouring my sister.

"When my father had wrung from her that the day the conspirators gathered at Casa Cuono she had Andrea de' Narni in her bed, he swore to have the whole family silenced, lest Cosima's seducer speak out against him. I don't dispute our sire was a vicious man, or that his servants were overzealous in their acts of slaughter and plunder. He claimed that since Vincenzo de' Narni had acquired his riches through alchemy it was not stealing to bring part of them away . . ."

Franco shuddered. With sudden vehemence Guido demanded: "Do you suppose I enjoy this blood guilt on my own head? Perhaps that is why I allowed Cosima to keep her brat. And would you have betrayed your own father in my position . . . I doubt that."

She was shaken by this confession. "Are you going to reveal who I am?"

"If I do," he said quietly, "your career will be ended. As it is your life is in hazard. You cannot always rely on a saviour with a sword. You need permanent protection and comfort . . ."

"They were snatched from me on a certain Easter Sunday," she retorted, "so I have to shift for myself."

"I offer you a bargain, Red Lily," Guido's eyes shone with a strange hunger. "To atone for my father's misdeeds I shall marry a nameless girl without fortune. As my wife you will be safe and able to take your proper place in our golden society. Surely that is to be preferred to a convent . . ."

"Don't be ridiculous," Franco cried.

"Your sacrifice is far less than mine. The Medici wants me to marry into his own family . . ."

"Then you fear my knowledge?"

Guido's smile held no warmth. "No, but I am a collector and should like to withhold the Red Lily from all others . . ." His tone was grimly detached. "If you don't accept my generous offer I vow you will not escape me: one day I shall be tempted to rid myself of the slight anxiety of your disclosures. Death will snatch you in some alley . . . or a wine cup . . ."

Franco perceived she had little chance to avoid agreeing. "Guido . . ." she stammered: "I am unused to a woman's role . . . and I fear . . ."

He took her hand and kissed it formally. "You will be the most exquisite lady in the whole of Florence. People will say Guido di Cuono found the Red Lily, and Franco the painter fled brokenhearted. So what is there to fear?"

She held her head very high but could not prevent the colour flooding her cheeks. "I dread the embraces of a husband."

Franco expected some lewd jest, but instead Guido nodded gravely. "Very well, I shall not treat you like a woman until you give me leave. I daresay you will change your mind." He smiled. "I am not as handsome as Daniello, but ladies have never found my attentions displeasing."

Franco wandered by the river, followed at a troubled distance by Taddeo. It was an impossible decision to make.

"Either marriage," she muttered, "or destruction . . . and life is sweet sometimes. I can't bear to yield it to death . . ." Then Franco remembered that there was an alternative. "Very well, I shall go to Rome and not return. It means remaking my life, but that is better than losing it . . ."

When they reached their lodgings, the candlemaker called out: "Oy, Franco, there's a young priest awaiting you." He winked. "Think he's after your mistress."

When she opened the door of the studio, Franco uttered a faint cry. Slumped across the table was the slight figure of Benedetto. A dagger very like the one she had left at Guido's . . . or similar to most carried by ordinary folk . . . protruded from his back. A splash of his blood had touched "The Red Lily." She rubbed it off with her sleeve and rolled up the painting, the perfect sample of her skill.

"Come on, Taddeo," Franco called. "We must leave . . ."

Taddeo eyed the unmoving body.

"If I stay . . . I shall be executed for a murder I did not commit. Whoever attacked sweet Benedetto must have intended that . . ."

They had not ridden a league beyond the Porta al Croce before a mounted company of armed men surrounded them.

"You are to come with us, Maestro Franco," the leader commanded.

"No." Her clear cry rang with defiance, and she drew her sword. "I shall kill anyone who impedes my journey, for I ride to Rome with the Magnificent's permission."

"You will accompany us to Milan," and Franco noted the mulberry livery beneath the riding cloaks. "We have orders not to use force, but if you resist, we must . . ."

The thunder of other riders attracted their notice. Franco recognized the scarlet and black of the di Cuonos' banner.

The two factions milled around her. Franco strove desperately but could not prevent Messer Ridolfo's men from carrying off Taddeo, who was knocked unconscious and flung across a saddle. A Milanese grabbed her horse's bridle and had his hand hacked off by a di Cuono servitor.

"Ride with me now, Maestro Franco," he urged. "It reached my master's ear that these villains intend to abduct and murder you. Let us leave them to fight. For Christ's own sake, come . . ."

She could not recall much of the journey. The insistent pounding of galloping hooves drove out all thought except a faint memory of a crumpled pennant lying in a burning courtyard . . . now she rode under its protection. They came to Guido's house near Poggio: Villa Hermes so called because an antique figure of the gods' messenger had been unearthed in the grounds. The charming retreat was set amid gardens and trees, and Franco felt calmed by the scent of flowers, the murmur of water, and the evening song of a nightingale.

An unspeaking woman with a coronet of flaxen braids above a hideously disfigured face led her to a moonlit bedchamber. Franco drank deeply from the proffered wine cup and fell into immediate sleep on a soft couch . . .

She was woken by a man's hand. "Taddeo," she mumbled, and opened her eyes to see Guido marvellously attired in night-blue and silver.

"For your safety's sake," he smiled calmly, "I have arranged our marriage for today. It is given out that Franco the artist was attacked on the road to Rome and has either been abducted or slain."

"The authorities will soon be seeking my blood for a murder I did not do," she remembered fearfully.

"I know nothing about that. I left the city as soon as I learned of Ridolfo's intention. Once you are my wife you will have nothing to fear. Allow me to thank you for bringing me a priceless dowry: 'The Red Lily' painting."

"Is there any way to rescue my dear Taddeo?"

Guido's expression showed revulsion. "If di Salvestro has

him I wish them joy of each other. I cannot have my bride tended by a monster. A woman will help you dress. It is to be a secret ceremony; no one will suspect the transformation of Franco into my wife."

"If there is no other way," she said heavily, "then I must accept your offer."

The silent maidservant remained impassive when the youth was transformed into a girl. She helped Franco bathe, and with the aid of pearled nets skillfully concealed the shortness of her curls.

The cloth of gold gown was beautiful but old-fashioned: It had belonged to Guido's mother, and the maid stitched the seams to fit Franco's slenderness. Only when a casket was set before her did she begin to feel, for she recognized this jewellery: the pearl ornaments her mother had worn and which had been lent to Isabetta on her wedding.

Franco threw them aside. "They are blood tainted . . ."

The servant left the room and returned with Guido, who stared amazed at Franco's appearance.

"Madonna, you are the most ravishing creature I have ever seen . . . you put the very stars to flight," he whispered. "I mean you no insult with these jewels. I am merely returning what is yours."

With shaking fingers Franco fastened them about her throat and wrists. She felt as if she had entered some dream. How strange to walk in that heavy trailing gown . . . the swaggering stride had to be replaced by small gliding footsteps . . .

The ceremony was brief and lonely and performed by a palsy-ridden priest.

"What day is this?" Franco asked her husband when he had given her his ring.

"The tenth of August in the year of the incarnation 1482."

She sighed. "I am eighteen this day, and it was destined to be the date of my marriage."

They dined alone in great splendour. Guido drank glass

after glass of red wine and never took his eyes from the girl opposite him. It began to grow dark, and the servants lit many candles.

Franco ate nothing. She felt like a wild animal suddenly put into a cage and stared around the fine room, twisting the unfamiliar ornaments at her wrists. Her dream was all awry. If only the man sitting there could be Daniello, everything would seem right.

Guido spoke at last. "Now I must show you to our chamber." He laughed at Franco's alarmed eyes. "Come, Madonna Francesca, I have given you my word."

The silent woman helped Franco to disrobe. When her husband entered she was clad in a white silken shift.

"No," he said to the woman. "That is wrong. Get out!"

She fled, and Guido drew from a chest a young man's raiment of gold and white.

"Come, Franco," he said with amusement. "You must wear these."

She could not understand but allowed him to help her re-dress and tie the points of her hose. At last, Franco was arrayed as a gilded youth, and all trace of femininity had vanished. Guido's eyes shone.

"That is how I know you, Franco," he murmured. "That is what I want," and he pinioned her against the tapestried wall and began to kiss her face with monstrous passion.

Franco tried to pull away. Once her mouth was free, and she screamed until she thought her lungs must burst.

"There is no point," Guido's pale face was unusually flushed with laughter. "The servants have heard far worse sounds coming from this room and would be more frightened to enter and disturb me at my play than to journey into hell. This whole villa is dedicated to my pleasure . . ."

The mystery of men's and women's embraces was not as secret as this. Franco's disgust and horror were boundless. Her husband ignored all the femaleness of her body and forced her to play the catamite.

Afterwards Franco lay weeping with shame and pain. Guido's voice came from a smiling mouth in the darkness. "Why mourn? You are still a virgin, sweet bride."

"Why did you marry me?" she pleaded, stifling the frenzy of sobs with the heel of her hand.

"It's a rare joke," he explained. "I wanted 'The Red Lily.' Now I have painting, artist, and model . . . and know a secret that no one else does. You wanted revenge, Franco, and so did I. You will personally pay each day of your life for what Andrea de' Narni did to my sister."

"He only wanted to wed her. They loved each other."

"At that time my father and I did not want Cosima to marry."

"Why not?"

Guido laughed, and Franco closed her ears to his abominable explanation.

"Aren't you afraid I shall betray all these ungodly secrets?" she whispered.

"You are my wife, Franco, and I have complete power over you. I can lock you away as a mad or wanton creature, or kill you if you prove more problem than delight.

"At present though it satisfies me to have you at my side . . ." He touched her nakedness, and did not withdraw his fingers when she winced. "When you have suitable finery, we shall ride to Florence and be feted as the most lovesome young couple. Now I have nothing to fear from you, and Franco has nothing to fear from the outside world."

While Guido slept, her mind searched for an escape from this terrible gilded trap. Occasionally in the past she had daydreamed of how pleasant it might be to live as a woman dependent upon some powerful man . . . now she only sought for a way back to the free life as Franco of Florence . . . and to unknow the vileness her husband had inflicted upon her . . .

BOOK III
"*Metamorphosis*"

The Fabulous Cage

A HAWK DRIFTED lazily across that high blue which is the ceiling of the earth and may also be the pavement of heaven. It plummeted as if falling . . . then abruptly wheeled upwards and away to become a dark speck on the distance. Two vultures, hideously efficient, had been circling the hillside of olive trees all afternoon. Their patience was rewarded. They swooped. Death was always somewhere close at hand.

A warm zephyr cavorted freely about the colonnaded inner court. It shook the bright geranium heads until the single petals, like tiny gules of blood, fluttered onto the decorative tiles. The spiralling waterfall, emitted from the sex bud of a plump marble child, oscillated and shimmered above the lily pond. The moisture stippling the ground quickly dried in the warmth. The breeze brought with it minims of sound from the outside world: cows lowing as they waited to be relieved of their swollen milky burdens . . . a shepherd's lilting reed pipe . . . the distant pealing of a monastery bell . . . only to snatch them all away and leave behind vibrating silence.

The air stirred the green silken hem to reveal a gossamer of lace. It tugged bronze curls so that they kissed the sun-gilded cheeks. It made the gems suspended by fine golden chains tinkle and dance beneath the ear lobes.

Then the breeze dropped. There was no movement save for the silently lengthening shadows, as the glowing grains of daylight ran out to make space for the void of evening.

Francesca was mewed up. Within her the spirit raged and roamed and strove to be free, but outwardly she was as immobile and serene as the marble figures decorating the villa's pediment. Her hands were folded on a volume of Catullus' love poetry, and her eyes sought the canopy of sky.

She kept forcing herself to recall what befell those wild bright birds when they were snared and caged. How often she and Leonardo had stood watching the street vendors offer these fragments of feather and song in the market . . . six wicker prisons strung on a long pole. Sometimes the sweetest singer grew silent and banged its downy head against the imprisoning bars until it fell dead in its own lifeblood. Heaven-hearted da Vinci never failed to buy scores of these fluttering creatures in order to give them their freedom. She knew she must try to control her spirit lest it struggle too much and extinguish itself. That must not be. She would conserve her immanence in case it was ever needed.

As matters stood there was no hope of liberty. There was nobody to unlock her marriage so that she might regain her old existence. Yet life had taught her that everything was in a state of perpetual flux and changed too rapidly to be comprehended by a mankind which had been forced to accept a supernatural agency as the prime manipulator of all those factors outside its control. There had to be some purpose—or else life was a cruel farce, and man's arrogance could not allow him to be nothing more than a beast of the earth. Thus the complete obscurity of this purpose was described as Divine since it could not be perceived by mortal men. Only the Creator knew where all paths led and would see the ending as He had seen the beginning. God's advantage over man was to be transcendent and immortal: No matter how wise individuals might be no one could escape mortality.

Francesca had long since shed any belief in an omnipotent scheme being worked out in terms of man. Twice now a whole pattern of life had been erased, so she was unable to see it as more than a senseless tangle. If you could pull from it one bright thread and start to weave a tapestry of your own, you were fortunate. It was certain that the thread would be wrested from you: But in time you might seek another . . . and with each fresh seeking you grew a little wiser. But at the end of it—and who could foretell the when and how of that?—you would die, and your body would rot and be eaten by worms.

What did it profit her at times of profound misery that the Church insisted she possessed an immortal soul which might rise from Purgatory to Paradise on the wings of prayer where it would know infinite joy, and that divine justice would cast the souls of her oppressors into the everlasting fires of torment? Life was here and now. Eternal bliss compensated nothing for an empty belly, nowhere to sleep, or physical agony, while the enemy prospered and was also promised redemption through gold-purchased prayers.

Holding tight to her philosophy of change she would bide still and try to prevent the seed of utter despair from germinating into a dark blossom within her mind . . . a flower which as it grew wrapped its stem around all other emotions and sapped their essence until they withered, and it was fat and full and solitary—mistress of the soul's wasteland.

The daylight colours faded, and the atmosphere lost its warmth. The soft brilliant silks that draped day had been exchanged for the chill crispness of indigo taffeta from which was fashioned the curtains of evening.

Francesca continued to sit. Only when the slave's fingers

tugged at her sleeve did she move and show that she was a living creature.

Across one arm Anna held another rich garment. She pointed at it and then motioned her mistress towards the house. As if burdened with leaden weights the girl slowly rose and preceded the servant until they came to the bed-chamber where the candles were already lit. The huge bed loomed among the shadows . . . a damask-curtained monu-ment from which she averted her gaze.

Francesca stood passively while Anna removed the gown and unclasped the jewellery and then fitted her into new finery, starting with a fresh silk *camicia*.

"It seems utterly pointless to be forever decked out like some bedizened image," she murmured, "just like a life-size figure the goldsmith's guild carry in a carnival procession. I am nought but a plaything, forced to serve his pleasure . . . part of his collection of precious, exotic, or . . ." and she shrugged, trying to shake off the memory of the small antique statues he'd shown her, ". . . obscene treasures to be fingered and gloated over . . . because possessing means withholding from other people, which soothes his overween-ing pride and avarice . . ."

Anna showed no sign of hearing this soliloquy, and Francesca could not fear her talebearing. She had ceased even to attempt to befriend the woman. Kind words elicited no response. The light grey eyes remained remote and blank. She treated her young mistress with excessive humility and tended her as if she were bereft of strength . . . and was quite unlike any of the garrulous, inquisitive, or tempera-mental servants Francesca had once known. But, then the Narnis had never owned slaves. Anna seemed to have no will of her own or expect any more attention than a piece of furniture. She existed only to serve her master, like anyone in the di Cuono power.

What do you really feel about me, Francesca pondered,

looking down at the turban of pale plaited hair, as Anna knelt to place soft leather slippers on the narrow, high-arched feet? Certainly if you had any idea of my true identity then you must hate me: the sister of the man whose passionate folly indirectly ruined your appearance and robbed you of speech.

Obviously Anna feared Guido, and Francesca guessed she must once have lain in his bed subject to his hard white body. Any being who came within Guido's power would be forced or charmed into satisfying his lusts and curiosity.

Do you envy me? A creature without family or fortune, who suddenly became your master's consort. Or, do you pity me? No, not that: if she knows what he inflicts on me, then she is probably content his cruelty has found another outlet.

Francesca concluded Anna was indifferent to almost everything . . . as if her infirmity had turned her into a gelded animal that lives only to work and eat.

The sudden commotion below was rare: running feet, banging doors, barking stable dogs. There were shouts for torches . . . and much masculine laughter.

Francesca's eyes did not question Anna. In this household she was mistress only in name and was not permitted any control over the comings and goings or the ordering of the servants who waited upon her with silent incuriosity. Guido had never even offered her the bunch of keys that opened the store and linen cupboards.

She smoothed her shimmering bodice. "My lord is a generous man," she observed. Anna smiled, or, rather, the hideous scarring turned what might have been a smile into a grimace as the skin puckered away from the large yellow teeth and gave the slave a wolfish inhuman look . . . so that she seemed to be sneering at words her affliction prevented her from answering.

This new gown was of thick peacock silk over golden

tissue. It became Francesca's rare colouring to perfection. Anna adorned her mistress's wrists, throat, fingers, and ears with turquoises set in patterned gold. She combed the fiery cascade of hair and used gold-headed bodkins to secure some tresses into a coronet of curls and let the rest fall in rippling tendrils in front of Francesca's small ears. A small headdress of golden mesh covered the arrangement. This suggested much more hair than she in fact possessed. It had grown since the wedding but was still far from the spreading mantle she had hacked off to play the boy.

Francesca studied her reflection in the burnished hand mirror. Nowadays she recognized her own beauty but knew such loveliness was as much its owner's prison as a trap for the beholder. Often she earnestly wished she had been born without this allure which had always marked her out for special attention in whatever guise.

The door opened. The sudden draught made the candle flames sway. Anna darted into the gloom as she always did when her master appeared, for ugliness provoked his abuse or chastisement. Guido stood in the wedge of shadow watching the glittering figure in the center of his room.

By his cold smile Francesca knew she pleased him . . . this man who had the power of life and death over her . . . her jailer . . . her corrupter . . . the man who had deepened her knowledge of pain, fear, shame, and evil. And yet, she could still see with detachment that he was a handsome creature: pallor and darkness. She had learned too that he had turned to unnatural vice for a chosen sin, not because of any unfortunate reason of birth. He had set himself up like Lucifer, thrilling to do only his own will and daring any power to contradict him.

"Each day you grow in loveliness, madonna," he said. "Soon you will lose all trace of that other Ganymede creature."

The violet eyes mocked him but she did not say aloud: "Then what purpose will you have for me, since I shall never willingly yield myself to you as woman?" She had learned too painfully that chastising her gave him a perverse pleasure: an ecstatic climax she had once falsely assumed to be associated only with love and passion, and so she tried to avoid giving him cause for inflicting punishment with the small knotted thong he used for disciplining his dogs and horses.

Instead she dropped a formal curtsy. Guido came forward and placed one cool hand beneath her elbow.

"Madonna, this evening we are honoured. We have the most illustrious of guests, who have ridden all this way in answer to the letter I sent to Florence."

"What did your letter contain?" Francesca asked warily.

"Why, what else, but I had married the Red Lily, and begged the Magnificent's forgiveness for my rash action which was caused by an overpowering passion for a beautiful lady and not through any desire to displease him."

"He has come here in reply?" she whispered, and began to twist the rings on her fingers. "But, he must surely recognize me by my mien or voice."

"Whatever he recognizes, my little sweetheart"—Guido's fingers held her chin so that she had to look up into his cold dark eyes—"he will not be able to explain. For how can a swaggering young painter turn into a lovely girl? If he called his physician to examine you, suspecting I was living in disguised sodomy—and so flouting Florentine law and polite society—they'd find nought but woman's attributes," he laughed and kissed her cheek, "and those in virgin condition."

"I wonder when you will crave for me to consummate your womanhood and our alliance . . ." Francesca tried to pull free, and her eyes flared with anguish.

"No matter," Guido continued. "One day, you'll change your mind, if not from longing then out of desire to bear a babe."

She could think of no more loathsome a fate than to carry

this man's child in the womb she had tried to deny, and one of her innate fears was that Guido might suddenly want an heir and force such a situation upon her.

"No, my Francesca," he added. "The Medici will have to believe you are the sister of a vagabond artist, and I have thrown up the honour and advantage of waiting to marry his own daughter by preferring a model whose nakedness has been captured and displayed. No doubt he will warn me that I will soon be a cuckold, or that you will foist another man's brat onto my name . . . or may even be already with child. But, you and I know the truth of your ancestry, don't we, lady? Yet, hear me: For your own sake, be circumspect. Remember now you are a girl and act accordingly. Be not too clever, too forward, or too free. Should shrewd suspicious eyes discover your true heritage I would not save you. In fact I would disclaim all knowledge . . . and to show allegiance to the ruler of Florence I'd yield up my wife to whatever justice the state chose to mete out to a survivor of an accursed family."

"Still threats, Guido?"

He shook his head. "No, my Francesca, I merely show you a lesson. You are wise . . . too wise for a woman, so you understand all that you have at stake, and why to remain my wife is your sole protection."

With her hand resting lightly on her husband's left arm Francesca descended the shallow polished stairs. She appeared very calm, and though Guido's eyes examined her face he could not determine whether fear or resignation was her uppermost feeling.

Only Francesca knew that her emotions were a strange mixture. She relished this confrontation as a rare gamble, although at the same time she understood that the stakes were higher than anything: her safety and her life.

In the hallway the group of men in Medici livery sprawled on benches, their belts unbuckled, drinking wine. Lorenzo's bodyguards, clubs and swords laid aside, but eyes ever vigilant even in a friend's home. Hadn't an innocent-looking priest once infiltrated a Medici villa probably with murder on his mind? They'd taught him a lethal lesson: forced him to dance on burning coals, and then rubbed salt onto his charred flesh. So he died, screaming innocence and agony . . . as should perish all enemies of the state! Their talk ebbed to a murmur like dogs grumbling over bones, and all eyes hungrily marked the slender girl at Guido di Cuono's side.

The door of the long salon was flung wide and the couple entered. Within, five men dressed in riding clothes and mud-crusted boots were lounging before the fire. Sweet-smelling cedar logs mingled with the sour and salt scents of sweat and leather. They were drinking vernaccia from the di Cuonos' finest silver goblets, and their faces were reddened from wine and the gallop in the brisk evening air, but their attention was riveted upon a painting. Guido had hung "The Red Lily" in this room, and since the windows gave out onto a backdrop of the Tuscan hills the solar seemed devoted to the goddess.

"My sweet friends"—Guido's voice was soft and amused —"see, I also possess the original."

The company turned. Laughter died. Eyes leeched onto the exquisite creature who seemed to have stepped down from the canvas: Venus had attired herself in the current finery of the city.

Francesca kept her own eyes lowered and dropped a deep, graceful curtsy in the direction of the plainest clad figure. Lorenzo had but lately lost his mother, and the genuine bereavement he felt in his heart was echoed by the dark clothes and the deepening of those somber lines first etched by Giuliano's murder. The sallow flat features did not conceal amazement. He screwed up his nearsighted eyes and stepped forward.

"By Christ's Passion, madonna, you are even more ravishing than your picture." He took both her hands and raised her so that she stood before him—prisoner of his attention.

Francesca pitched her voice a little higher than was her wont, which gave it a sweet uncertain lilt, "Thank you, sir."

Then, her lips ventured a capricious smile, which revealed small, white upper teeth, and for a second the long, gold-tipped lashes swept apart to reveal eyes that reflected the candle glow as brilliantly as two myriad faceted amethysts. Anna's herbcraft included knowledge to enhance her mistress's perfection, and the eye-rinse made from a decoction of belladonna in rainwater certainly increased the eyes' natural beauty.

The men's reaction could almost be heard like a wave sighing against a sandbar. Pico della Mirandola, whose own glorious hair was several shades paler than Francesca's, stifled an oath and exclaimed in a voice which mingled astonishment with delight: "The lady is the very twin of that runaway rogue painter, Franco, who stabbed the priest . . ."

There was a murmur of assent, and Francesca looked covertly at the young scholar. Was Pico wise enough to prize open her secret? They had after all been roistering companions along with these other gentlemen of the city. True, he could speak twenty-odd languages and had attended four universities before he was her own age and claimed to be absorbing all there was to know in the different spheres of knowledge . . . but his impetuosity—especially with regard to female beauty—precipitated him into more scrapes than many a foolish fellow. Francesca could only rely upon Pico's eyes being dazzled by her femininity to prevent that subtle brain from realizing the truth.

His own beauty was a shade haggard from his last amorous skirmish. However, to judge by the soft curve on his lips, he was set to begin another lovesome intrigue . . . this time with his host's and friend's new wife.

The Medici grinned and shook a warning finger at Pico. "No, my boy! This time I can't save you, or blame your secretary, who's presently forced to accept the somewhat dubious hospitality of Arezzo's constables. Guido would have the blood spurting from your throat before I had time to think up some bold-faced excuse for your behaviour!"

The men gave shouts of laughter, and Francesca concealed her own knowledge behind a puzzled expression. So, she mused, Lorenzo slyly admits his own duplicity . . . at least, before close friends.

In the guise of Franco she had of course been acquainted with Pico's lunatic scheme to capture his young mistress, who, after the death of her grocer husband, had been married off to some dull and distant member of the Medici clan. Accompanied by his secretary, Pico had abducted the lovely, willing victim. Alas, the Arezzo constables overtook the lovers. In the ensuing melee fifteen of their men were killed, and poor Pico landed up in jail.

Only Lorenzo's cool intervention had secured his release. The secretary was blamed for the whole escapade. The wife was returned to her husband, because the Magnificent had insisted with family loyalty which bordered on arrogance that no woman could possibly prefer another man once she was wed to a Medici. The innocence of Pico and the lady was proclaimed far and wide . . . and doubted by all save babes-in-arms! In Florentine taverns citizens still wagered on whether or not the Medici knew the true state of affairs. General opinion held that he loved his brilliant young friend too well to be deprived of his stimulating and audacious conversation for such a frivolous pretext.

Francesca lifted her chin and focussed her smile on the Magnificent, who surrendered himself willingly to the charm.

"May I beg a boon from the most powerful personage in all Florence?" The entreaty sounded demure, but she felt sure of the sudden power which the veils of femininity had endowed her with amid that all-masculine company. Momentarily she held them on the chain of her beauty. She had never before played the real woman to so large an audience and now suddenly perceived that the differences of sex were not just physical but also strangely mystic.

As Franco, she had to rival these others in originality or daring to sustain the advantage that rare good looks present. But, as Francesca, her talent and bravado were of minimal importance. She had no need to compete with masculinity: merely to appear passive and dominated by it so that she might employ her beauty to rule—a subtle thrall that most men found hard to throw off.

She could not despise her true sexuality. As precious as the one for gold was the alchemical formula which represented a complete human being. The balancing of male and female within one individual and the recognition of those aspects could bring about the understanding not only of one's own nature, but also of other people's.

Now it was as the dear dead—whom she scarcely dared remember—had predicted: wife to a noble gentleman, with beauty to bewitch even the most powerful. Yet her heart knew the irony of this situation and just which devious paths had brought her to a state that was certainly something quite different in its actuality. Only she, Guido, and perhaps the silent Anna were aware of it. Yet, who knows, Francesca reflected, perhaps all situations that may appear similarly ideal have some curious reality at their core. She could not believe she was entirely individual in her experiences. The concept brought comfort . . . but also skepticism about all those dreams which had been imbibed with the milk of sheltered childhood.

Lorenzo gazed at the wonderful face, raised both jewel-laden hands to his mouth, and made no effort to release them.

Francesca's own smile deepened. As Franco she had learned just how much the Magnificent—a conscientious but unfaithful husband who adored his children—doted on women. Latterly he had confided to his intimates that his very private performances no longer did justice to his appetite and promises. He blamed the inherited gout for this diminishing prowess but still continued his amorous pursuits.

The hoarse voice contained unmistakable ardour. "Madonna, I wish I were king"—his companions hid their grins at this: In the republic he was king in all but name . . . something his enemies fretted at—"and you were Esther as in the Bible tale. I vow that whatever those enchanting eyes demanded—be it half the kingdom—the republic of Florence would belong to you. My dear Guido"—but his gaze did not seek out the husband—"I hope your bride has the nature of an angel, for else you will indulge her so completely that even you will turn into her slave."

Francesca glanced at Guido. He wore the smile of a man content . . . and something else: It had been part of her protection to study her tormentor so that she might discover ways of suffering less, and she understood that he revelled in their secret and unnatural relationship which no other man could know or comprehend.

"Then you will forgive him for marrying a nobody?" she persisted.

"Forgive him," Lorenzo echoed. "Never. I should like the Council of Seventy to banish him . . . provided that he wasn't allowed to take you with him."

Francesca's smile dissolved into seriousness, but Lorenzo clasped her hands even more fervently. "How can I forgive him for imprisoning the most perfect creature in all Italy? Now I have to find my little Maddalena another husband. That'll please her, for Guido's austerity frightened her. You, madonna, contain the magic fire to melt his ice. I do not bear him a grudge for seeking a wife outside my family . . . but now he has ruined my reputation: for it is said that *I* possess what is best in Florence. By *his* marriage di Cuono alone holds the epitome of flawless treasure."

Then Lorenzo smiled. "You mustn't expect me to forgive him that, madonna." He extended one hand to Guido. "Come, you know I jest. You are as ever my friend, and your wife will be my goddess."

Guido inclined his head so that the fall of raven hair shadowed his pallor and the ironic twist of his mouth.

Lorenzo rubbed his eyes with a velvet sleeve and stared at Francesca. "Pico is right. How much you resemble that scamp, Franco. I wonder if you can say where he has taken his talents and mischief: to Il Moro in Milan like da Vinci, or to my old enemy, His Holiness, who wants someone to decorate that new chapel . . ."

She bowed her head and whispered, "I don't know. I was only his model."

Lorenzo eased himself into a chair, and the crease of pain across his forehead showed that the gout nagged his limbs. "Nay, sweet madonna, you are his sister for sure and fear to admit it lest you receive the punishment he richly deserves. Who your family was I can't guess. Perhaps some gentleman fathered you both on a humble wench. Certainly he was without honour failing to acknowledge such beautiful and healthy children. But, you have nothing to do with your brother's misdemeanours. Indeed, your perfect beauty proclaims your virtue, eh, Poliziano . . . eh, Pulci?"

As if these gentlemen had not been her friends only a few months back Francesca allowed them to kiss her hand. The self-assuredness and exuberance of the Medici ex-tutor and the roguishly amusing poet were somewhat diminished as if impeded by the lady's trailing skirts.

Poliziano—finery shabby as ever despite his patron's generosity—peered earnestly into Francesca's eyes. She tried hard not to laugh, for learned as he was dear Poliziano did not realize that he'd once wrangled with her over his own version of Platonic doctrine . . . or that she had set them all alaughing by dubbing his, Ficino's, and Pico's eclectic philosophy, which borrowed from classical Greece, the Hebrew Cabala, alchemy, astrology, superstition, the Church's teachings . . . and Heaven alone knew what else . . . "as tasty as a dish of mixed boiled meats from Bologna, and twice as indigestible!"

Angelo Poliziano nodded vigorously. "It is a concept that the ancient Greeks held dear, and the artists of our city do well to rediscover. Botticelli's goddesses are as much goodness and love incarnate as paintings of the Mother of God, or Christ and the Apostles . . ."

"Don't you agree we inhabit a wondrous era, madonna?" Pulci interrupted, grinning merrily at the lady, who was struggling to control her usual flow of words beneath an unworn cloak of feminine modesty. "Under the Medici's aegis, beauty and learning have been reborn. Man seems about to unlock the very door of the mysteries. The best of Classic thought mingles with our own tongue, and our Maecenas leads us in writing verses in the people's Italian, so that all may understand, enjoy, and emulate. The stars were certainly in a fortunate conjunction at Lorenzo's birth . . ."

"Oh, you Florentines!" Pico pounced on his usual argument with cheerful alacrity. "Always believing in the stars and the planets . . . practically deciding whether or no to visit the privy by horoscope. How can you be so credulous as to believe in astrology? Wait till my great work on this nonscience is completed and . . ."

"For my part"—Pulci waved his wine goblet—"I believe only in wine. He who shares my faith will be saved."

His audience laughed, but he continued. "Enough of our customary verbal battles. We bore the lovely lady, and Daniello has not yet paid his homage to the city's new goddess."

As if the Divine Hand had just re-created light, Daniello della Sera stepped from the shadows by the window. His blond hair shone like a halo above a short blue cloak. He kissed Francesca's hand with formal grace.

"You can do better than that," Lorenzo urged. "Kiss her lips. She will soon be your sister, and you can take advantage of that."

Francesca gave a little gasp as Daniello's warm mouth pressed hers for the briefest second. She inhaled the wine on his breath and the odour of his body. Her eyes grew soft and gentle as if responding to a lover's embrace. For a fraction out of time she yielded to the man who had once been the nucleus of her future. Yet, his expression remained coldly aloof. The smile never reached his eyes. No mystic spark ignited because they had once exchanged rings. The Narni diamond still winked at the light from his right hand, and in a cassone upstairs, among the meager possessions that belonged to Franco, lay the gimmal ring.

"Madonna, it gives me pleasure to know you and wish you joy." Then, with more eagerness, "Do you really not know where Franco has fled?"

She shook her head, unreasonably envious of her other self whom Daniello evidently preferred. The vagabond youth had been closer to his heart than a beautiful lady. He and Guido embraced affectionately.

"I have recently visited Casa di Cuono, and your sister sends her greeting and wants me to write a full description of her new sister-in-law. She deems it unpleasing of you to fail to invite her here."

Guido, who had marked his wife's expression during Daniello's salute, began to chuckle. "I fear the two ladies will be rivals for all men's admiration. How go your nuptial arrangements?"

"Well enough," della Sera replied without any enthusiasm.

Lorenzo and the others roared their mirth. "Gentlemen, where is your gallantry?" the Medici expostulated. "One of you is wedded to this exquisite creature, and the other is about to marry a sublime dark goddess, yet neither of you shows the least appetite for love."

He rose and placed a hand on Francesca's narrow waist. "I hope when you are alone Guido treats you with more attention. How else will your union be fruitful?" He chuckled. "I trust these secret months of marriage have been spent in the bedchamber."

Francesca blushed but did not answer. She felt slighted by Lorenzo's familiarity. Men in his position did not treat their peers' wives so lightly in company. She perceived that though Guido had raised her to his status in the public eye, his own friends considered her no more than his light o' love, and their admiration contained little respect. I will have to prove this new nobility, she thought somberly, since I cannot claim to be a lady by birth. No doubt my humiliation gives Guido further pleasure.

The merry supper party confirmed her suspicions. The company did not regard her as mistress of the establishment but as their host's beautiful toy, and they showed no embarrassment while singing some of Lorenzo's bawdier verses. Francesca sat silent, her cheeks carmine. She knew the songs well enough, but the role of womanhood lent her chagrin at hearing them, which obviously amused Guido.

Later, when everyone had retired, and Anna had unbound Francesca's hair and clad her in an embroidered silk night shift, the Medici came to the bedchamber to gossip with Guido. Anna scurried from the room, and her mistress had another opportunity to realize that Lorenzo would not intrude so casually if he thought her to be of a heritage similar to his wife's . . . whose own outraged piety had forced her husband to talk with his friends well out of her earshot.

Francesca darted between the curtains and clambered into

the high bed, as Lorenzo called: "How cruel you are, lady, to deprive us of your beauty. It is fortunate that your picture hangs downstairs so that we may remind ourselves of what our eyes have been denied." Then he quoted from his own verses: "Fair is youth and void of sorrow: But it hourly fades away: Youths and maids, enjoy today: Nought you know about tomorrow."

The men slipped into their own talk as if there were no one to overhear them.

"What else brings you this way?" Guido asked, his sharp, white features looking monkish above the black velvet bedgown trimmed with speckled lynx.

Lorenzo sighed painfully. "This damned gout gets worse and sends me once again to the warm springs of Santa Caterina. I pray the holy saint's powers bring some relief, for the willow medicine the doctors prescribe eases the pain for only a short while. Anyway, sweet friend, I'm tired of city life, intrigues, and politics."

"Is that why you're putting so much money into land beyond the city's walls? Daniello told me something of your purchases while we were at supper."

"Such as the di Cuonos have no idea how lucky they are to be landowners. The value of land increases wealth, whereas banking diminishes it. We're no longer living in my grandfather's time when the pickings from lending gold were rich. Do you realize three of the Medici banks have shut down in as many years?"

"You have a general manager to supervise this business. Why concern yourself?"

"Sassetti's good enough," Lorenzo said doubtfully. "But he will keep running to me with complaints about the indiscipline among branch managers. I have an idea this is a reflection of his own lack of discipline. If only he'd refrain from coming to me with all the petty details. It's his way of shelving responsibility, so that whatever goes wrong he can extricate himself by saying that the final decision wasn't his! People think I'm as rich as Croesus but forget that sixty percent of my wealth goes annually in taxation. My informants tell me that there is a scandal abroad which says I milk public funds to boost the bank's decreasing coffers. Why blame me when the Monte can't always pay out the dowries due?"

Guido's voice contained amusement. "My dear Lorenzo, I'm too much your friend to ask outright if this has anything to do with Medici banking strategems."

Francesca, listening amid the curtained darkness, considered the rumours had more than a speck of truth in their foundation.

The Medici yawned and stretched so that the brown silk gown fell back from his muscular forearms. "Banking is so much tied up with politics nowadays."

"And so you use your bank to further your political aims," Guido remarked shrewdly.

"It can't be avoided. I had to pay out enormous sums when I went down to see Ferrante in Naples . . . but that way we secured a peace of some sort. Now all I want is to complete my play *San Giovanni e San Paulo*—it's got some bloodthirsty scenes which'll be fun to stage—talk with my friends, contemplate the beauty of the countryside . . . and naturally make love to my mistress."

"You have the power to do what you want."

"No, Guido, that is not true. Power brings too much responsibility. Frankly I must look to the good of the Florentines so that my own family may prosper, but I abhor intrigue."

"Do you?" Guido smiled. "What about that business with the Turks?"

"What do you mean?" Lorenzo asked guardedly.

Francesca leaned on one elbow to hear the conversation more clearly.

"Some say you invited the Emperor Mohammed's army to invade Italy."

"A monstrous lie! What was my reason?"

"To draw Ferrante's son, Alfonso, and his soldiers away from our doorstep."

"The Turkish invasion even forced Sixtus to extend the swift hand of friendship to Florence," Lorenzo commented. "Italian couldn't fight Italian with the infidel running wild in the country. And, Alfonso and his mercenaries did go hurrying out of Siena to rout the Turks at Otranto. Even better than that—to my mind—they didn't return to prowl round Florence." Then, he sighed wearily. "It's always the way: Under attack we are united no matter what our differences. Immediately the danger is averted, the conniving for power and land recommences. Sixtus is still trying to steal more territories for his bastard Riario. Hence his alliance with Venice against us. Now they're as thick as the thieves they undoubtedly are!"

Guido's laughter was the rasp of a fingernail on silk. "It did mean that you and Ferrante became allies again in order to block His Holiness. How long will this beautiful friendship last?"

"Until the wind changes, or Sixtus offers him some more advantageous deal," Lorenzo retorted. "You can't trust the king of Naples any more than you can trust the fidelity of a hot young wife in the company of a lecherous monk! No sooner do I manage to bring about one peace than another conspiracy starts behind my back. Italy is not yet a land of total chaos . . . but how long will it be before some foreign monarch with a trumped-up blood claim and a hunger to extend his sovereignty marches into the peninsula and seizes a state or two? I tell you, Guido, only unity between the leaders of the republics and kingdoms can prevent the catastrophe."

Guido yawned. "That way no one can gain supremacy, which I deem to be bad. *I* have never believed in equality or democracy, but *you* carefully avoided explaining why the Turks attacked at such a propitious moment . . . well, from your point of view. You must admit they didn't give that butcher, Alfonso, much of a fight before disengaging."

To Francesca, Lorenzo's chuckle sounded uncertain as if he'd been caught without his trunk hose. "You're a clever dog, Guido, even though you pretend to relish only pleasure. You share similar suspicions to our sinister Milanese friend, Ridolfo."

Wrapped in the warm darkness of the coverlet Francesca shivered at the sound of that name, and she again grieved for Taddeo in the hands of that prince of darkness.

"I'll let you into a secret since now it can do little harm. Also it has left me with a puzzle," Lorenzo admitted. "Not too long before the invasion a young fellow with fiery locks and a red-pepper temper to match sought my private ear. He called himself Raffo and would say nothing of his family, although that firebrand is a Florentine as sure as I am. Built like a bull . . . square and stocky . . . but with fine hands which proclaim some noble ancestry. Perhaps he's the bold, bad runaway son of a *magnati* family. Who can say? His attitude reminded me somewhat of Franco . . . only it was hot and reckless, whereas our young painter friend always seemed cool in his daring.

"This Raffo had only one eye, blue and hot like the heart of a flame. The Turks had put out the other one when they captured him at sea. It seems his irascibility and fighting spirit won him his freedom as well as Mohammed's favour. The Turk, desirous of expanding trade and with a broad-viewed glance to the future, sent Raffo as an envoy to inquire if there was any way he might be of service to prove this goodwill . . ."

Francesca's mind was a vortex. Surely this man the Medici described was her brother, alive as she always believed him to be. Praise be to God for sparing one male Narni . . . thus, the dynasty would not die out. If she could find him, then he would aid her escape. Together they might even clear the name they both shared yet dared not utter. She pressed her fist to her mouth to prevent herself crying out in hope.

"It was Raffo who suggested I use the emperor's offer to draw Florentine enemies from our gates. Truly, I thought to hear no more of the absurd scheme . . . and then the Turks attacked so opportunely. If I could find young Raffo I'd reward him."

"He has disappeared?"

"That's the mystery. Perhaps he returned to Constantinople, but he had a hunger to join the Genovese Colombo. That'd take him to Isabella's court. I pray Raffo's quick tongue does not throw him into the clutches of the Inquisition. God, what terrors that holy Catholic she-devil perpetrates in the name of the God of love . . ."

Francesca's newborn hope struggled against the tide of despair and all but drowned. If only she were still Franco she could go forth to seek her brother . . . but now there was no choice but to pray that Raffaello would come back to Florence. So enmeshed in her own snarled thoughts it was a few minutes before Francesca heard her husband discussing his own plans.

"We must go to Florence for Cosima's wedding. We shall return with you after your treatment. I've a new home for my bride, which I trust will be to her liking . . ."

Francesca wondered what the smiling voice intended. She knew him well enough to fear this nuptial gift had a double edge.

Lorenzo embraced Guido, then slapped him on the shoulder. "I shall leave you to your loving, you fortunate, lusty

dog! May I hope that in my honour tonight you'll thrust
forth a fine heir."

When Guido climbed into their bed, his wife feigned
sleep. She sensed him looking down into her face for a long
moment and then heard him turn on his side and begin the
even breathing of sleep . . .

Madonna of the Topaz

FRANCESCA'S NEW PALAZZO in the city was so much a surprise
that she swooned as she approached its portals. It was Daniello who prevented her falling from the white palfrey with
the crimson-and-gold tooled leather saddle and harness. He
carried the supine figure through the spacious court and into
the hall to set her down on a carved wooden daybed beside
the long window. Francesca's faint was so deep she never felt
his hands, or the soft warm sweep of golden hair which
brushed her cheek and mingled with her own . . . so she
never knew that her childhood dream of this handsome
prince bearing her in his arms had come true . . . but, alack,
the dream realized often proves very different from the
dream envisaged . . .

"I believe you will feel at home now," Guido had remarked . . . and their companions wondered at his rare
solicitude, but his wife knew he mocked her. They rode
through the Porta al Prato, past the apprentices playing at
calcio. It seemed impossible that she had been one of those
grubby, foul-tongued urchins kicking, punching, and yelling
in a brutal game of football where the sole rule was to win.
And now she was riding with the Medici and his intimates
surrounded by a bodyguard whose livery bore the golden

pill emblem which brought folk running to cry: "*Palle . . . palle . . .* Good health to our Lorenzo . . ."

The rank smell of the river and the clamour of the narrow streets assailed her senses and evoked a thousand memories of her days as the boy Franco. Country folk vied with each other in their cries to attract customers for their morning fresh wares.

"Good fennel. Come buy my juicy fennel. Sweeten your salads . . . comfort your bellies . . ."

"Lavender Lavender. Fresh cool lavender for your clean chemise. Strew it on your pillow and dream sweet . . ."

Even more stridently: "Fragrant peaches. Golden and juicy oh . . . soothing and delicious as a maiden's plump warm breasts . . ."

At the sight of Francesca on horseback, her glory of hair half concealed under a dashing black hat with a swathe of double cloth hanging to one side and pinned to her shoulder by a great golden brooch studded with agates, the ballad singers began offering up tokens of admiration in the hope of receiving a coin from the noble gentlemen for their impudence.

". . . Oh, thou of the milk-white face, the winds are hushed as thou passest by. All the stars caress thee with their beams. Thou art the fair rose of the garden . . ." From all sides in a motley of different keys came the chorus: "Beautiful, O dear and beautiful, who made thy eyes? Who made them so amorous? . . ."

In the wake of the laughing riders, singers, beggars, and urchins fought to pick up the scattered coins. The company divided as Lorenzo led his bodyguard and servitors towards the *Signoria.* "I must see what new trouble is brewing," he called back cheerfully. "Until our next meeting, madonna, a sweet adieu." And he removed his hat so that the damp air caught his dark hair and ruffled it without respect for the greatness of its owner.

Francesca's heart beat a little more quickly at being back in the beloved city. She could almost feel its own inner pulse throbbing in unison . . . and the surge of exhilaration dared her to think of escape and holding her head proud-high . . . until she saw the house in the White Lion quarter . . .

The original crests on the doorposts had been replaced. Now the blue and white terra-cotta plaques from the della Robbia workshop bore torch emblems, not flower-ringed towers . . . and the gonfalon fluttering in the damp air was scarlet and black, not green and gold.

Thus she returned to her father's house . . . as the wife of his destroyer . . .

When she unwillingly floated to the surface of consciousness—her soul still gasping to drown itself in oblivion—Francesca was first aware of the sharp scent of vinegar from the soaking cloths pressed to her temples and wrists. Gradually her vision cleared and she could see that the vast rooms had been refurbished, although some of the furniture was faintly familiar. Her expert eyes discovered that Ghirlandajo's workshop had been employed to renovate Uccello's pastoral fresco which decorated the walls of the main salon.

Automatic memory impelled her eyes to the leash of white greyhounds in one corner. On childhood tiptoes she had just been able to reach up and stroke their aristocratic heads. It had been her own private test of growth on each visit to the city to find out just where she stood in relation to the figures in the fresco. . . .

She had grown accustomed to the knowledge that she would never again see those greyhounds or enter the palazzo. In fact, when past circumstances had forced her to this quarter of the city she would walk by quickly with her eyes averted . . . until her conscious mind ceased to remember what it was she tried so hard to forget.

Now it all came flooding back . . . too intensely to be

contained by that fragile girl. Guido had never seen his wife really weep and watched as the tears coursed down her cheeks like the rains of spring, and the high-ceilinged chamber echoed with her sobs.

Their companions exchanged questioning glances. "Shall I summon Leoni, Lorenzo's physician?" Poliziano asked. "Your lady is definitely sick. Perhaps the journey overtaxed her, but sometimes the *moria* starts like this."

Guido shook his head and called out for one of the servants. "Hey, Tommasso! Sluggard, run to Lucca Landucci, the apothecary at the sign of the Star on the corner of Via Tornabuoni. Tell him my lady needs a calming draught. Be quick, numbskull!"

Then he motioned to Anna. "Take your mistress to the bedchamber and put her to bed . . ." and the slave almost carried the sobbing, shuddering girl up the curving stairway.

Daniello pursed his lips and spoke only into Guido's ear. "Is she with child?"

"I doubt it," came the laconic reply.

His friend smiled and slapped him on the shoulder. "Just because she hasn't been yours for long enough, old fellow, doesn't mean that she might not be. I'm not traducing your lady, but she has not dwelt in a garden as cultivated and secluded as the maidens of our own families."

Guido shrugged and raised one dark ironic eyebrow. "Perhaps. You and the whole of Florence are entitled to think what you will, but I vow my wife came to me a virgin."

"Quite so," Daniello said soothingly. "We are not peasants to start examining bed sheets."

Landucci sent round a syrup made from poppy heads, its acrid flavour disguised by Madeira sugar and cinnamon. After swallowing it Francesca fell into a dream-tossed slumber inhabited by phantoms of the past.

Each day she dwelt in that palazzo she knew the fates mocked her. Her hatred for Guido magnified, and as she controlled her desire to destroy her tormentor, something within her weakened like a flame pressed to near-extinction by the weight of a cold draught . . .

Her appearance altered. She grew more slender, and the skin lost its golden bloom among the shadows to become the palest ivory which displayed the aristocratic boning beneath. Clad in the costly raiment her husband insisted upon, Madonna Francesca, wife to Guido di Cuono, began to resemble some golden madonna. The exquisite face—as impassive as a statue's, yet with the hauteur of a queen—concealed the tumult of emotion which racked her soul. Because of the large single topaz she always wore at her throat, no matter how many other jewels adorned her perfection, she became known in the city as the "Madonna of the Topaz" . . . as if she had some place in the litany eulogizing female virtue, and Guido laughed with noisy contempt when he recounted this title to Francesca.

"So, my dear, your purity is proclaimed abroad for all to wonder at. Now, don't go acting in any way which might besmirch it. Unassailable chastity is sometimes the target of lechers."

"Your family's name cannot be soiled by my presence," she returned coldly.

Guido's intimates treated her with a new respect which bordered on reverence. The Red Lily had been a palpitating flesh-and-blood creature on canvas but in reality she acquired the aura of a genuine goddess. Francesca grew accustomed to being stared at in silent veneration when she went to attend Mass at Santa Maria Fiore. Even the apprentices, and ruffianos, and women-ogling gallants hanging about the square refrained from hissing their admiration in this lady's direction. For her own eyes met theirs—not with the boldness of a flirt—but with the scorn of a being beyond mundane emotion.

The detachment she exuded caused people to believe in

her extreme piety. So much so that the central pillar of polite—and dull—Florentine society, Madonna Clarice, invited Guido's bride to visit her in the palazzo on the Via Larga.

For Francesca this proved an extraordinary hour where she sat mutely attentive to Lorenzo's good wife expound the plans they had made for their children's future. These same children, whom young Franco had sketched and then romped with, sat close to their visitor's glittering skirts, studying her with candid curiosity.

The eldest girl was named Lucrezia, and Francesca wondered with irony whether or not this plain child had been called after Lorenzo's clever and beloved mother, or his equally beloved mistress. The lovely Donati still held his heart's strings—even though now and again he meandered from the course of faithful adoration. In order to erase old hatreds the Medici had affianced this daughter to Giacopo Salviati: a relative of the infamous archbishop. If the ruler of our state can do this, Francesca reflected gravely, why is it I still maintain my loathing for my family's butchers? Yet, she perceived that the victor could afford such gracious acts, whereas the totally vanquished could not. Besides her own wish for vengeance now had a more immediate basis.

Dear little Contessina, with the enchanting lisp, was to marry into the *magnati* family of Ridolfi . . . thus securing another valuable ally within Florence.

"Our heir, Piero"—Madonna Clarice smiled on her eleven-year-old son—"will naturally marry into *my* family, the Orsini. Nobody in Florence has a lineage to compare with ours. Little Alfonsina will make him an admirable wife."

"She's all right for a mere girl," the subject of the proud mother's remarks said. "But she cries as easily as a pat of butter melts in the sun."

As haughty as his mamma, Francesca noted, but too frivolous and openmouthed to bear a close resemblance to his

father. Let's hope Lorenzo lives for many years. The boy
examined her with bold eyes, and then pulled his youngest
sister's long russet curls. In return Maddalena neatly pinched
the flesh on his calf. Her fate was still unsealed, and Francesca assumed that Lorenzo's original intention of affiancing
her to Guido had been one more ruse to secure the di Cuono
loyalty, as well as gaining him easier access to the voluptuous
Cosima. Now the Medici was searching beyond Florence for
a suitable alliance for Maddalena.

"For Giovanni, Lorenzo hopes that one day he will wear
a cardinal's hat . . . who knows where that might lead?"
Clarice's rather protuberant watery eyes gleamed triumphantly as they surveyed this second son, who was skimming
through a volume of Ovid with no apparent difficulty. "Although still young, he is diligent and studious, and it would
be a valuable move to link our family with the Church.
Indeed it is through the children that 'Our House' will become a renowned dynasty . . ."

Fighting puppylike on a rug gained after the Turkish rout,
the Medici babies, Giuliano and Giulio, seemed more like
twins than cousins. Lorenzo was bringing up the murdered
Giuliano's bastard, Giulio, among his own brood, and these
two little boys had been born in that same fateful year.

"What will you do with these bonny rascals?" Francesca
inquired, holding out jewelled fingers to the boys, who
pulled themselves upright, shouting gleefully as they clutched
at their lovely playmate.

"Now then, boys, let Madonna Francesca be," Clarice reproved, and the children rolled back to their amiable tus-
sling. "We have no firm plans for them as yet, but not
unnaturally Lorenzo wants something great for his nephew.
Just you wait until you hold your own babe to your breast,
my dear, and then you will weave schemes so that your
blood continues in honour."

Aie . . . aie . . . Francesca's heart keened. Once my own

dear papa had plans, and all we foolish mortals must go on dreaming whether or not destiny allows them to come to fruition. Yet, who could argue with this daughter of the Orsini, who remained so sure and smug? And Francesca was constrained to listen to how Madonna Clarice had forced Lorenzo to send the scandalously unchristian-minded Poliziano from their household.

"But what did my tenderhearted husband do? Install that Angelo in a villa of his own where he can spout his ideas freely and tempt all the young men into folly. I swear this Neoplatonic nonsense is heresy . . ."

Francesca's silence was taken for agreement. As she took her leave, Madonna Clarice remarked with a condescension that intended kindness: "My dear child, you certainly appear to prove the exception: that some people can rise above their original background, especially if they hold their tongues. But, pray remember to guard yourself more strictly than any nun from becoming the subject of gossip."

No doubt she believed that the sudden flame which invaded her visitor's cheeks was due to humility. It was fortunate that the good woman could not read Francesca's thoughts which were richly larded with the obscenities she'd picked up during her apprenticeship.

Balls of all the saints! she seethed, no wonder Lorenzo has mistresses. No woman should be permitted to be so self-righteously virtuous, and sit in judgment. If she'd experienced one fraction of my life she'd sing a different tune. Then Francesca sighed. What was the point? If her fate had travelled its appointed course she too would probably have shared such prejudices. Experience of a very rarified sort of existence entitled Madonna Clarice to her cant, snobbery, and piety. The only cruel blow life had dealt was that she had never won her husband's love. There were grey hairs woven into the faded red tresses, and the fine clear skin was threaded with tiny broken veins, and the small mouth was folded in a sour unfulfilled expression. There again, perhaps Lorenzo's wife had never believed in or longed for his love. She had been bred and tutored to marry an important personage: Passionate love was not considered an integral part of such useful unions. In this respect the Narnis had been different, and now Francesca could appreciate that her father's hope for an elevating and loving match was an overromantic dream which must have clashed with what his mind knew to be the truth of all expedient marriages.

Despite Francesca's outward display of coldness she retained an innate desire for affection and camaraderie. Once life had been precarious but she had friends to visit, share a bottle with, or just exchange opinions with. Now she was secure in that she did not have to worry about earning her bread and keep, but most of her time was spent in idle solitude, with Anna shadowing her every movement or glance.

Often at night, Francesca tried to imagine what it might be like to have Daniello there beside her as if the dream had not been smashed by reality. This was not so much mental adultery as a longing for an agape marriage: the spiritual linking of two people. Her whole being shrank from the idea of physical communion now she had encountered it in Guido's terms, and she knew a certain revulsion for her own body because of how it had been abused.

Daniello seemed unaware of this unspoken adoration, but Francesca had ample opportunity to gaze on his Adonis-like countenance for he was a constant visitor to the palazzo in the White Lion quarter. Sometimes he would attempt a stilted conversation with her while he waited for Guido to finish instructing the house steward, Umberto. Daniello would mumble about the damp weather and the state of the streets . . . but there were none of the affectionate smiles or easy words he had bestowed on young Franco. Francesca was forced to the conclusion that not only was Daniello shy of females, but being of *magnati* stock looked down on her as a common creature even though she bore the noble name of his bride-to-be.

Her nights were less and less disturbed by the presence of Guido, for he had embarked on a nocturnal voyage of unbridled gaiety, which began to mark his austere features with two deep lines between nose and the corners of the thin mouth and darkly pouched the skin beneath his eyes.

"We must do our roistering before sweet Cosima comes to the city," Guido explained to the Medici, whose gout did not permit him to join them on all their revels. "For then poor Daniello will have to settle to this solemn business of matrimony and breeding, and thus to a sober life. This is to be his final carnival of youth . . ."

Lorenzo merely laughed and wished them joy of their frolic with a warning to beware of the Eight should their night prowling become too unruly and provoke complaints from the more sober stayabed citizens. Only his eloquent eyes hinted at the ambiguity contained in the newly wed Guido's words.

Francesca's own existence had stiflingly narrow boundaries. She was not permitted to superintend the household in which she was merely an ornament, nor could she seek out her old acquaintances without revealing her identity. Despite Madonna Clarice's patronage few ladies came to visit her, since her antecedents were scandalously doubtful . . . and the few that did come openly displayed their curiosity about her mysterious past, or quite unblushingly questioned her as to whether or no her womb contained a di Cuono scion. Controlling her desire to spit out some of Ghirlandajo's more choice ruderies Francesca sat, hands folded, eyes downcast, and lips uttering only the politest monosyllables . . . until her visitors retired discomfited and puzzled, gossiping amongst themselves that ". . . Guido's bride is most unfriendly. Looks and acts like some French princess, no matter what gutter she really sprang from. Mark my words, that modesty will soon break down and expose her for the brazen hussy she must be . . ."

They eyed with anxiety the many husbands and grown-up sons who chose to renew their acquaintanceship with Guido in order to examine more closely the Madonna of the Topaz and test the much-vaunted virtue. In order to avoid these admirers Francesca chose to remain in her bedchamber, staring out of the window, listlessly reading . . . and occasionally sketching memories with charcoal. These drawings had always to be committed to the fire lest any casual eye recognize their style.

The fine mizzle prevented her sitting in the courtyard, and her only real diversion was attending Mass, which she did regularly just to gain respite from her prison. Only rarely did she venture to the goldsmith's on the Ponte Vecchio or the apothecary for some trivial purchase, and then always accompanied by watch-bitch Anna. The merchants brought their wares to the palazzo for her to choose cloth for gowns, jackets and hoods, or bright silk stockings, or the elaborate and scented French gloves which were the newest fashion.

At first there had been some thrills in being able to buy whatever she fancied, but after a short while the makers of dresses, shoes, laces, and other gewgaws who besieged her began to seem like a plague of locusts. Besides what did it matter that she could change her raiment four times a day? For there was nowhere she could go to display this abundance of finery, and nobody whose opinion she valued to admire her.

Having discovered her at drawing Guido twice escorted her to Ghirlandajo's workshop and Botticelli's studio to admire the works under production. Francesca's appearance caused the babble of abuse and banter to dwindle to reverent silence. She could only compliment the artists without exposing how much she knew of the techniques that went into their work. Privately, Guido made no pretense of taking her there for her pleasure: It was a refined form of torture to show her the world she had once known, been happy and at home in . . . and was now banished from forever by her transformation into his wife.

Sandro was deeply involved in a painting to commemorate Lorenzo's personal triumph in coming to terms—however temporarily—with the king of Naples. Amid stutters, blushes, and agonizing pauses, while he struggled to find words, Botticelli attempted to explain his theme to the exquisite young woman with the steadfast violet eyes. She had never seen him so ill at ease. He liked a pretty face and figure and made much show of his prowess with drabs, but confronted by what seemed to him a true lady he was as tongue-tied as any cloister-dweller. There had always been rumours of dearest Sandro being a sodomite, but Francesca had known him too well to believe them. Now she could see it was his uncertainty with respectable females which had probably produced such calumny. That his beautiful visitor had once been a co-artist's model, and the Red Lily, did not relax him. Since none of the painting fraternity had ever met the creature other than on Franco's canvas, her reappearance as the Madonna of the Topaz seemed as miraculous as Venus rising from the foam.

"It's to be of Pallas and the Centaur, madonna," Sandro muttered finally, standing awkwardly before the canvas.

"And what do you intend by that, Sandro . Botticelli?" Francesca asked gravely, but her eyes contained a bewitching light which seemed to dazzle him so that he blinked wonderingly as if watching the sun rise above the rim of the earth.

"You are so like him . . . and yet . . . oh, never mind . . ." he trailed to a stop, and then continued his explanation: "It symbolizes wisdom overcoming brute disorder. But, I still need the right face for my Pallas . . ." and he stared hard at Francesca who lowered her gaze.

Two days later the painter called at Guido's home and begged an audience with Francesca. She smiled while he screwed up his eyes to discover faults among the frescoes. At last he muttered: "This renovation is well enough done, I suppose. Still needs young Franco's graceful airy touches to bring out its full flowering . . . but that's all in the past."

"What is it you require?" Francesca prompted her guest who downed cup after cup of Trebbiano as if he hoped to discover his courage at the bottom. He became more at ease when Daniello and Guido joined them.

"Ah, gentlemen, God give you both happiness . . . although He must already have done so by sending such a flower into your midst. I have something to ask of Guido, and . . . ahem . . . his lady wife."

From a paint-daubed sleeve Botticelli drew out a careful sketch of a head. "This is how I visualize my Pallas," he explained, and there was a plea in his bulbous eyes as he looked from Francesca to Guido.

Her husband's voice was as soft as cat's fur: "My love, it is your likeness. Now you will become immortal at the hands of one of our greatest painters."

"No . . . no," Botticelli protested adamantly. "The lady is already immortalized. I merely seek the serenity of her expression. Please, madonna, do not deny my canvas your virtue. Just assent to this sketch, and I shall work from it, memory and dreams, and not trouble you till the painting is done when you may give me your honest opinion of it."

Francesca smiled with unsteady lips. "You honour me. I gladly agree if it is not against my lord's wish." She looked at Guido and saw by the lickerish expression in his eyes that he experienced pleasure because here again was proof that he owned a much coveted possession.

He clapped Daniello's back gaily. "Well, brother-to-be, what say you? Shall I cede Sandro the right to make free with my lady's face?"

"It cannot do any harm," Daniello observed dispassionately. "When we are all dust who will be able to name the original of Pallas' face?"

Thus Francesca's features gained a freedom and a futurity their owner could never hope for . . . But she was the only one to know that Botticelli had already captured her image . . . for the della Seras' inspection . . . but that was already ashes ago . . .

Threads of Destiny

THREE NIGHTS before Cosima was due to come to town, Francesca was woken by raucous voices and discordant music. She leaned on one elbow and stared sleepily into the hollow darkness. Perhaps outside, a group of tardy revellers were weaving their unsteady way homeward accompanying themselves on horn and timbrel. Her sense of freedom derived from the awareness that Guido did not occupy the bed. She pattered to the window, the marble floor striking cold against her bare soles.

She pushed open the shutters. It was very late. Moonset. A blustery sullen wind blew leaves and refuse along the streets and alleys. The motley of rooftops and spires resembled cutout paper patterns, their opaque blackness darker than the sky. A faint travelling pool of light—as if cast by a giant glowworm—dodged in and out of the alleyways . . . disappearing behind one building only to reappear further on in some small piazza. The night watch patrolled the city seeking malefactors. Only outside the great houses did the flambeaux burn all night: reassuring patches of flame keeping total darkness at bay.

The noise did not die away. Francesca realized it came from within the palazzo.

Guido had been away all day to complete arrangements with Daniello at the della Sera house in readiness for his sister, and Francesca began to wonder if Umberto had permitted the servants to take advantage of their master's absence, and their mistress's impotence, to hold a forbidden revel.

Only a few days before the whole of Florence had been plunged into terror when red flames were seen to lick the night sky. Many believed these were an omen for ill. In such cases the superstitious were known to throw themselves into wild excesses believing the end of the world to be drawing nigh. More sober citizens preferred flocking to church to ensure they were on the right side of God. Only when the preachers began taking advantage of so large a congregation did the churches begin emptying. After all people came for reassurance, not to be told their necklines were too low, rouge was the devil's unguent, and that they would be damned for giving short measures!

Francesca kindled a taper and surveyed her reflection in a Venetian hand mirror, decorated with plaits of triple-hued gold and real seashells. In the dim light her eyes were far too large for the translucent face, but the jaw was firm and square beneath the fine skin. She donned a night-robe of emerald watered-silk trimmed with fringed, embroidered ribbons. "This cannot be allowed to continue," she muttered resolutely, "and I shall be obeyed by the servants in a house where I am nominally mistress."

It was chill and damp on the staircase, and the draught caught the hem of the robe and wound it about her ankles. It blew the candle flame so that it appeared to stand on its side. The great hallway was dark and still, and the antique marble heads on their shoulder-high pedestals looked like lurking figures waiting to spring. Beneath the door of a salon, which contained a new harpsichord and some smaller musical instruments, light wavered . . . dimmed . . . and brightened as the shadows of the room's occupants moved across it.

The voices were indistinct behind the heavy door, and the shrill cacophony of ill-played music did not suggest it was made by any of the pupils from Lorenzo de' Medici's new music school. The singing contained little melody but resembled harsh chanting.

The volume of sound increased Francesca's displeasure and diminished timorousness. She pushed open the door and stood on the threshold . . . a slight gleaming figure between the massive carved lintels. She parted her lips, but what her eyes encountered subdued any speech.

There was no need of her presence to quell this dissonance, for the master of the palazzo was at home: sprawled in a wide chair with decorated armrests, a wine-cup in one hand, and the other twisting the honey curls on the head of a page boy of about eleven. Guido's glittering gaze never wavered from the face of a street urchin whose grimy inexpert fingers plucked the strings of the lyre Francesca sometimes played, and who was bawling out the ribald version of a popular ballad. Francesca knew her husband to be very drunk. His face had the waxy pallor of death . . . only his lips worked unceasingly and were sheened with saliva.

On a daybed in the corner, oblivious to the others, lounged the golden Daniello. Kissing his mouth with monstrous passion was the deformed Altoviti: notorious in Florentine society, for although he belonged to a respected *magnati* family this dwarf had been convicted of sodomy and violence against street youths whom he had tempted with promises of food, clothes, or gold. Wherever there was vice Altoviti came into his own. Now his misshapen limbs seemed to be sapping the beauty and symmetry of the della Sera heir . . . as if Altoviti were some imp from Hell trying to drag an angel into the abyss.

Daniello's cheeks were crimson. His eyes were glazed. He was totally besotted . . . and a willing victim.

The child at Guido's feet was the first to notice the girl.

He uttered a scream and then began to giggle softly, shielding his mouth with one hand and glancing up at his master. With a shuddering jar the music ceased. All eyes rested on Francesca.

Dear Mother of God, save me . . . She wished she'd never intruded upon this unholy gathering. How simple it would be for them to kill her to prevent her repeating abroad what she witnessed.

Guido rose clumsily to his feet and pushed the boy out of his way. It seemed a very long while before he crossed the floor to his wife. Despite his drunkenness he moved as smoothly as one of the tigers in the *Signoria*'s menagerie. Francesca saw Daniello's foolish slack grin as he tried to focus his eyes. Something within her snapped . . . as if Lachesis had just cut through one of the threads of her fate . . . and she remembered the words of Matteo della Sera at her betrothal: "Sometimes a handsome face and figure offer no real manhood . . ."

The impossible dream she had always harboured within her died in a welter of agony. It would have been far worse than the forced marriage to Guido to have lived through the dream of girlhood coming true, and then discover just how unlike her idealized hero Daniello della Sera really was.

For a fraction out of time Francesca rejoiced that all the people she loved were dead . . . and could not see how their plans flew off course like an ill-fletched arrow.

She smelled the wine on his breath and the sweat of his body as Guido stood before her. He flexed his long pale fingers in an absent way as if testing their strength.

"Well, madonna?" His voice was perfectly level, and she understood he was quite unperturbed by her discovery. After all she only continued to live by his sufferance. "This is no place for you. Get you to our bed."

The words that welled to her lips died stillborn. There were none to govern such a situation. Daniello smiled at her

stupidly. Altoviti's saturnine features twisted into a leer, and
the two boys wore grins of easy contempt . . .

She had stumbled down into hell . . .

Francesca fled and heard the peals of laughter chasing her
up the stairs. Much, much later, when the wraith of morning
began to blanch the sky, Guido came to her bed with his
perverse appetite whetted by her new knowledge . . . and he
made her part of his beastliness until she wished for her own
death.

Yet full day came. A damp grey pall. And Francesca hard-
ened her resolve to find a way to flee from Guido where he
could not use his influence to have her brought back. If she
doubted there was any such thing as a divine soul to be
damned, she still held to her belief that the spark of life
could be doused under too many unbearable experiences.

Her husband treated her with distant mocking respect,
making no allusion to his world of night, and she veiled her
thoughts so that he might not see into her mind. She could
understand this marriage gave him an alibi in the face of any
slander, nor need he fear the outraged interference of her
relatives as would certainly have occurred if he had wed a
girl of his own background: Then, of course, there would
have been scandal.

Later that day Guido and Daniello rode from the city to
collect Cosima. The three would not return for as many days.
For the first time since her marriage Francesca was free to
attempt to put her plan into operation. She wrote a few lines
on a sheet of paper: "If you recall one who sought your aid,
learned to paint but not to pray, and always wore a topaz, be
at the laying of the foundations of the Guarnieri Palazzo
tomorrow one hour before Vespers."

Without signing it she sealed the paper and wrote on the
outside in bold letters "For Fra Sandro." She handed it to
Anna with the directive: "Deliver this to the monastery of
San Marco, and return straight to me."

Francesca did not fear Anna's undoing the paper, for it was most unlikely that the slave could read, and even if she could she would not be able to comprehend or communicate the contents.

Waiting for the next day was an exercise in patience. Francesca rose early to attend Mass. Returning from the Duomo she had to pass the small house with the iron balcony. Automatically she looked upwards, but of course little Fiametta of the gentle heart could no longer gaze on the world from that window. Recalling her affection, Francesca decided it might be pleasant to see Matteo Panetti once more: just in case she found a way to leave the city too quickly to revisit old haunts and acquaintances . . . and perhaps, too, to let him benefit from her present material advancement.

At the palazzo she broke her fast with a bowl of white bread steeped in fresh milk, flavoured with Madeira sugar and a dash of fine ground powder from the fruit of the nutmeg tree.

Then Francesca asked Anna to rearrange her hair in the new curling style which accentuated her femininity as did her clothes. Under the street cloak of laurel-green heavy velvet she wore a skirt of scarlet satin lavishly embroidered in black ribbon and fastened with tiny silver buttons which were also featured on the gold tissue blouse with its slashed black sleeves. The pattens, besides protecting the hem of her gown and feet from the damp and mud, gave her height and the appearance of even greater fragility, for she was forced to make tiny gliding steps.

"I am going to choose some wool for a warm cloak. It will be less tedious than sitting indoors waiting for a host of merchants." Anna accepted this casual statement with her usual phlegm.

Panetti's premises were on the Via dei Ferravecchi, and resembled a private dwelling more than a shop, for in accordance with the strict regulations set down by the Calimala no street display was permitted. Only the sign of a white sheep on a bright red field showed that this was indeed a wool stapler's business. The internal government of the major guild had existed over a hundred years and had been successfully instigated and obeyed so that the serious business of the wool trade might flourish no matter what disruptions occurred within civil government.

Next door in noisy opposition stood Masi's copperware shop, its entrance almost concealed behind festoons of urns, pots, and dishes. From within the shouts and laughter . . . and the lack of rhythmic tapping of hammers . . . told that the apprentices were taking advantage of their master's absence to play at dice . . . and they'd probably even sent out to the Panico for some jars of cervisia to wet their throats.

Francesca was glad to leave the morning clamour and bustle of burghers and artisans thronging the narrow way. It was quiet and orderly within. Here, the apprentices were hard at work sorting, fulling, pressing, or cutting the rough cloth imported from the three permitted sources: France, Flanders, and England. Conversation was carried out in whispers and related only to the craft. Who knew at what precise moment a notary might appear to check that all the guild's statutes were being observed? No games of chance were permitted, lest they cause indiscipline, or worse—some discrepancy—in the account books.

Matteo Panetti had the honour and responsibility of being one of the Calimala's four consuls for six months, and wore his badge of office with pride. He did not look up immediately when Francesca entered but continued to superintend the labelling of the wool with the guild's official seal, so that his assistants could roll it into a bale of double linen stamped with the Calimala's emblem.

He seemed older than she remembered: His hair was sparse and grey, but his voice still had its forthright ring as he called: "Freddi, now bring me that piece of English cloth so we can compare the colour of the dye before the daylight loses its best . . ."

Then the tired, reddened eyes widened with amazement, as Francesca approached. "Good day, Matteo Panetti"—she kept her voice as high as possible—"I've heard you have a fine selection of cloth suitable for a lady's cloak. Why do you stare so? Is aught amiss?"

"Nay, madonna." He sounded confused. "Your beauty dazzles me and brings to memory another time which was both happy and full of pain." He crossed himself, and then asked: "Have you a brother?"

"Not in this city," she replied truthfully. "Did you know someone of my likeness?"

"I recognize you as the Madonna of the Topaz, the wife of Guido di Cuono, but close up you resemble quite a different person. Anyway it's an honour for my establishment to be graced by your visit. I wish my daughter were alive to see you: She loved fashion and finery." He sighed . . . and then added with a lively interest in business, "But what may I show you?"

"I want the finest, lightest wool, but of some unusual hue, which hasn't yet taken the whole city by the ears. I don't mind setting a fashion, but I dislike following one."

"Bring me the Parma," Panetti commanded the hovering Freddi, who returned staggering beneath a felt-covered bale.

"Now this is something special." The wool stapler shook out the cloth. "It is called Parma after the violets which grow there in spring. We perfected the dye only recently by using *guado*—that rich blue the Medici often favours— with *oricello*. Feel the texture: so warm and yet so light." He held the wool close to his customer. "It should really be called after your eyes, madonna, if you'll forgive my boldness. If you wear this wool there'll be such a clamour for it that we'll never be able to supply the demand. It'll bring in more profit than three of the other lines rolled together."

Francesca smiled and draped the cloth about her hair and shoulders, so that her eyes deepened as they reflected the wool's hue. The workers gathered round to stare and murmur their admiration.

"I like this," she said positively. "My cloakmaker will line it with rich green satin, and I trust it will start a new fashion like the goat's hair petticoats . . . a sort of rich woman's rusticity. Send me round the entire bolt."

Matteo Panetti rubbed his hands gleefully, but was forced to add in honesty, "It's very costly, madonna, and much more than you need for a cloak."

In reply Francesca opened a silk purse. "Here are sixty gold pieces. No," she added firmly, as he began to protest that this was too much, "I have a fancy for the Parma cloth, and an equal fancy to pay you this price. Good day, Matteo Panetti. May our paths always cross in happiness."

The man stood staring after the departing woman, even as his employees burst into an incredulous babble about their customer's beauty and extravagance. Something in the lady's last remark rang the bell of reminiscence in Panetti's mind. " 'Tis quite impossible," he repeated over and over, "but she has something of Franco in her manner and appearance."

Twilight was gathering in shadowy patches on street corners when Francesca made her way to where the Guarnieri family had elected to erect their new mansion. Anna followed close, keeping an anxious eye open for cutpurses. Her mistress had sensibly masked her brilliant finery with a cloak held against her figure, and the lovely face was shadowed by the hood which fell well forward. Only a very astute observer could have detected her identity.

Around the trenches on which would one day stand a proud palazzo were grouped the builders, joiners, and masons . . . as well as inquisitive local tradesmen. There were the usual knots of foreign sightseers, many of these Flemish wool merchants taking full opportunity of a business trip to examine all the wonders of the Pearl of the Arno.

Francesca recognized as English a lean-jawed, freckle-faced man, and she was curious to see how he behaved. She had always heard they were a barbarous race . . . made into very devils from travel and study in Italy, and dimly she recalled the bloodthirsty tales her papa had told her about the exploits of the English mercenary Sir John Hawkwood. There were rumours flying from that wet northerly island that the new young king had been slain together with his brother by a usurping regent uncle called Richard. Francesca had overheard Lorenzo remarking humorously to Ficino: "If the English weren't English I'd swear that Sixtus ran their country: They're such a tricky bunch. They seem to be forever warring about which king should rule, and the two factions are symbolized by a white or a red rose—sweet conceits to disguise the stench of carnage."

However, this English tourist seemed as quiet as a peasant visiting the city on market day. He watched curiously as local folk brought their children, arrayed in their best, so that they might cast into the trenches copper coins or tiny plaques inscribed with their names for good fortune and remembrance. Out of custom, and also that Anna would think this was her reason for being there, Francesca threw into the pit a small bunch of Damascus roses she had been carrying as an antidote to the evil miasma rising from open drains. Then she positioned herself on the very edge of the crowd.

Close to her she heard a coarse country accent mutter: "Why are you always so afflicted with ill-favoured servitors, madonna?"

Francesca knew the halting voice and turned slowly to look down into the stained features of Taddeo. Never had his hideous visage appeared more lovable, and she just managed to stifle her sob of delight with a gloved hand.

"We mustn't be seen talking, my friend," he cautioned.

"Did Fra Sandro send you?"

He shook his head, and though the smile resembled a

grisly grimace to others, she knew it meant he was happy at their reunion. "I have sought you since I returned to the city. It's been hard to steal a word with you."

She noticed that he was well and warmly dressed and that his feet were encased in stout boots. "So you managed to escape from that Milanese devil? Have you employment?"

"Aye, and one that permits me to watch over Franco."

"Oh, Taddeo." She clasped her hands. The enormous eyes darkened with despair. "If only you could help me. I cannot tell you what I suffer at the hands of Guido. Yet if you were to come to my aid he would kill us as easily as he grinds an ant beneath his foot . . ."

For a second he placed a hand on her cloak. "Hush, madonna, pretend I am an importuning beggar so that I may leave. Your servant eyes us with suspicion. Do not despair. If there is a route of escape you shall travel it. I vow it by the days and nights in the cave, and also by the most secret gathering of Fontelucente. Remember they swore to aid you."

She opened her lips to reply and then glimpsed the faint puzzlement on Anna's face. "Begone, you rogue!" she said sharply. "I have no alms to give to those who refuse to work. Take your ugliness away before I call the guard . . ."

A few heads turned to see what had caused the small commotion but saw only a hunched figure shuffling into an alleyway, and the slim autocratic figure of a woman in a cloak shaking her head and repeating indignantly in the direction of an unanswering servant: "Shocking. What can the authorities be thinking of to allow such vermin to roam our streets?"

"Daughter, is it not good to give to the afflicted and needy?" the gentle question was uttered in another voice she recognized. The Dominican stood beside her, and she loved his yellowish face with its high creased forehead and sorrowful brown eyes.

Francesca bowed her head. "Aye, father. I beg you to consider the supplication of this petitioner."

He glanced at the costly raiment between the folds of the cloak and the jewels in her ears far brighter than the tears sheening her eyes, and he smiled with faint derision. "You appear to lack for nothing."

"I lack for all," she murmured. "I was forced into this marriage, and my sanity remains in jeopardy so long as I live in my husband's house. He is not only my sworn foe but the devil's minion. I beg you to help me."

"What happened to that bold young painter who stabbed the priest? Can he not aid you?"

"God rest his soul."

"Painter's or priest's?" Sandro inquired drily. "But Benedetto lives. The wound was not fatal. The bitterness in his heart gives him a tongue which sears all sinners. He has come into our midst and is an ardent disciple of Fra Girolamo. He speaks against women and the appetites of the flesh and admits he learned the awful truth about carnality through love of a fair strumpet who drove him near to perdition."

Francesca smiled faintly. "You are speaking both to the fair strumpet, and her protector—according to Benedetto's half-knowledge. I swear I did not try to murder him. That was my husband's work. Did you know what had befallen me?"

"Of course. The hows and wherefores are unknown to me, but I glimpsed your triumphant entry into the city."

"Did you recognize me so easily?"

"My eyes are not deceived by changes of apparel. I see the soul of the wearer. You are young, Franco, and also a woman burdened by much misery." There was compassion in his statement. "The only escape I can suggest is for you to enter a cloister. If you fear to be completely cut off from the world you once knew you might choose the Carmelite order at Santa Maddalena. Go there and ask for Sister Agnes, for you knew her in another time, which is not so long past in years as in experience. They do say that one day she will be the abbess. Under her protection and example your soul might regain tranquillity and acceptance."

He studied the shadowed features and shook his head doubtfully. "My solution does not appeal to you, I know. Once before you turned against the idea. You preferred the world. Well, my daughter, you have seen what that entails. Now that it proves too hard to bear, you wish to flee it but only on your own terms."

"It is not as I was taught to believe it to be," she retorted fiercely.

"It never can be that. We teach of the best and pray that a fragment of reality sometimes measures up to it."

"Could Guido prevent my entering a convent?"

"Not easily. Consider my suggestion carefully, and send me word when you decide. In the meanwhile I shall pray for your enlightenment. God protect you."

Her mouth drooped, and then she straightened her shoulders as if accepting a heavy load. "God be with you too, Fra Sandro, and all thanks for coming to see me."

He drew a cross on her pale forehead and then melted into the enclosing dusk.

"Come," Francesca ordered Anna, who followed submissively. It mattered little to her mistress if the slave had understood what had been said by the priest. If by some remote chance, Anna managed to convey the words to Guido, the possibility of his wife's entering a convent would provoke his mirth rather than fury . . .

Wearily Francesca walked homeward, one question tormenting her mind: the world or the cloister? She knew she wanted the world . . . hungered for it . . . needed it. It was the very proof that the Narnis were not totally extinct at the hand of their enemies. Yet she could not deal with the world she had been forced into.

If only . . . ah, if only . . . Life seemed composed of those two little words . . . but, if only the Medici's Raffo were indeed her brother, and he returned once more to Florence she might seek him, reveal her identity, and throw herself on his protection. He sounded bold enough for any scheme . . . besides they were bound by blood and suffering. Together they could flee, not only the city, but perhaps the whole of Italy. Guido would not catch them. Completely alone she knew she could not outwit her husband.

A harsh, grunting noise interrupted her reverie. Francesca stopped and turned round. Struggling in the grip of a villainous-looking fellow, clad in stinking skin garments, was her slave Anna. The woman lashed out with her large callused hands, but the man pinned her arms behind her back and kept one filthy paw across her mouth. Anna ceased to fight and her grey eyes dilated with terror. Francesca opened her own mouth to scream, and then noted the band of six ruffians emerging from the gloom. Although the small piazza was surrounded by tall, shuttered houses it was unlikely that any worthy merchant citizen would risk his own life or property in order to rescue two helpless females.

"And if you do call out, fair madonna, the Eight will only find two women with their throats torn out. We should prefer a more friendly encounter, eh lads?"

The large-built man, who spoke in the flat tones of a countryside *villano*, was evidently the leader of this band of footpads. He drew near to Francesca. She began to laugh without any mirth, for she knew his voice too well to fear him.

Francesca shook back the hood and allowed the cloak to fall open to reveal the bejewelled gown, and the wealth of gleaming hair. She heard the men begin panting as if in an act of lust, and then let the little dagger she carried in her sleeve slide downward until the flesh-warmed hilt rested lightly in her right palm . . .

"And how do you intend to demonstrate your friendship?" she allowed her voice to drift back to its former husky tones.

The leader peered into her face. "Ho there!" He called one of his men forward. "Bring the link so I may examine our prize."

A torch of tow and pitch was thrust forward. Francesca and her assailant stood in the circle of darting light, whilst the others were no more than a ring of dark silhouettes. He peered down into her face, and her own eyes surveyed him indifferently. Although the features were coarsened and aged before their time she knew him, but now his left arm was bereft of its hand.

"So you are after losing the other," she mocked. "For certainly the left must have been lopped off for thieving as required by the law of talion. An eye for an eye . . . and the hand of a robber to stop his using it against his fellows."

Beyond the light the men began cursing. "Impudent whore! Silence that mouth! Take her jewels. Strip her, and let us have some sport on that haughty piece of flesh!"

Their leader waved his hand to signal them back, and they obeyed, grumbling in their throats like hunting dogs denied their kill. Francesca held up her dagger and laughed again, and the face fixed on hers grew haggard and ashen.

"God grant you grace, Berto," she greeted derisively, "but I gather you gain yours from the nether kingdom, so may the Devil bring you to hell and receive your soul, where it belongs, you snivelling, cowardly cur . . ."

With the filthy, rag-swathed stump he shielded his eyes from her unwavering gaze, and then held out his right hand in cornu: the two extended fingers with their black bitten nails quivering uncontrollably.

"Witch!" he groaned as one in agony. "It cannot be thee, surely." He used the familiar term of childhood, and for one small instant Francesca saw a flash of an idyllic time past as if the curtain of blighted hopes had been rent aside. Then the sunlit memory was quite gone.

The other men moved uneasily together, staring at their normally brutal leader, so completely and inexplicably cowed, and at the vision before him who sparkled even as some unearthly visitation.

"What's up with you, cully?" one of the companions ventured.

"She's a *strega*," Berto muttered, and the men made the sign of the cross and struggled to recite hasty *Aves*.

"Here. Something to remember me by . . . that is, if you ever can forget." Her low voice tormented the darkness. "Take my dagger. It has jewels aplenty. Now, free my slave, so that we may continue our way homeward. But never forget that I hold your identity in my brain and can release it to my lord and the Magnificent at any time, and then you will know what it is to be hunted down and fear every man's eye and hand."

Strange, I am enjoying this position of power, she mused, and over part of my childhood too . . . but he was even then my humble lackey.

"Franca . . ." Berto moaned. " 'Tis not you but your spirit returned from the dead and borrowed by enchantment . . . Franca . . ."

"Aye, returned from the dead certainly," she retorted. "You never came to help me then, did you? I've been to hell and back again a few times now, so do not attempt to fright me with your violence . . . or your threats of robbery, or rape, or murder, for I care not, don't you understand? Here, take the dagger. A fine one, and from Pistoia as I promised you."

But Berto let it fall clattering on the stones, as if contact with the steel seared his flesh.

"Let them go free," he commanded hoarsely. "There are

rich pickings to be had elsewhere. We do not have to have truck with a pack of witches." He spat defiantly at Francesca's feet.

Slowly she replaced the hood and fastened her cloak. Anna's captor released her, and the slave stood glowering at him, rubbing her numbed wrists.

"Come, Anna," Francesca commanded once more, and then with a salute of her gloved hand she added: "Farewell, Berto. You and I shall meet in hell. Remember all the rest of your miserable life what was and never will be . . ."

The link died to darkness. The two women walked away without looking back. When they entered the warmth and light of the palazzo the servants came running. Above the di Cuono livery their faces were chalky and anxious, for it was a full dark evening . . . and rare for any woman—even a street drab—to venture out without a man's protection . . . but totally unprecedented for their master's wife.

"There's nothing wrong," Francesca told Umberto who settled her into a cushion-backed chair with a beaker of warm spiced wine to sip. "Just an unexceptional encounter with would-be thieves. Give Anna some Chianti for she suffered more than I." She smiled gravely at the slave and noted that the grey eyes for once contained a decipherable expression: Somewhat bewildered she read fear in those luminous depths.

Later, clad in a loose bedgown of figured blue velvet and seated before the bedroom fire of pine cones, Francesca allowed Anna to comb down her hair with a carved double-sided ivory comb. The slave had once more cloaked herself in complete blankness. Francesca's eyelids fluttered shut, and she relaxed, lulled by the rhythmic gentle tug against her tresses, the scented heat, and the fatigue of events. "A day of reunions," she murmured. "But to little purpose."

Before she slept Francesca thought of Taddeo. But what could he do even with the best intent? No, there was nothing for her but to remain Guido's prisoner, or voluntarily take on the captivity of the veil . . .

"...more bitter than death..."

A GLIMMER-GOLD DAY . . . as if the silver sky were a sea sequined with sun-flecked waves. It would end in rain, but in the meantime the drear November morning had borrowed its light from summer's granary. As splendid as strutting peacocks two groups of young men stretched a scented garland of the last yellow roses and myrtle blossom entwined with spangled ribbons across the street outside the palazzo di Cuono.

The air was a mosaic of different sounds . . . the chatter of wedding guests and spectators . . . the raucous laughter of beggars, apprentices, and street balladeers, who loitered hoping for a distribution of coins, wine, and viands to encourage them to follow the bridal procession with honeyed words and choruses (occasionally, the father too mean or forgetful to ensure such precautions had escorted his daughter to her marriage pursued by catcalls showering doubt on the girl's virginity and the bridegroom's sanity!) . . . the lilting whistling notes of a street musician's ocarina merging with the more formal tones of the viols and flutes being played inside the palazzo.

The atmosphere vibrated with expectancy. Everyone enjoyed a wedding, despite the new mode for as much fun and debauchery as possible without the shackle of matrimony. Young men, much taken with this old Roman custom, considered women as the very devil, but their fathers, who wanted legitimate grandchildren, painted femalekind as the receptacle of all virtue. Her scolding tongue could be silenced with a blow or a sharp word. Train her in obedience from the beginning so that she knew you were master . . . and a husband might indulge his taste for something more exotic in the bedchamber out of sight of home and spouse. Newly married men rejoiced to witness another bachelor lose his freedom . . . bachelors rejoiced that the victim was someone else . . . maidens rejoiced with fluttering hearts hoping that their own nuptials were not too far off . . . parents rejoiced that tradition was being followed . . . and all the nefarious brethren of the streets rejoiced that here were so many plump chickens ready to be plucked of their fine feathers. A thief might do as well out of a fashionable wedding as at carnival: for Florentines liked to put their fortunes on their backs!

As the sun emerges from behind a bank of cloud so came forth the bride from the massive stone house. She was a slender vision clad in cloth of silver. The tight low bodice showed off two-thirds of the proud full bosom, and the trailing sleeves lined with white satin accentuated the delicate paleness of hands which clasped a bouquet of myrtle and roses. The curling dark hair was unbound save for a chaplet of myrtle and undulated about her back and breasts. A skillful application of rouge to lips and cheekbones emphasized the skin's alabaster perfection: This was none of the bold artifice that gave rise to the presently popular saying: She who whitewashes her house wishes to let it!

Cosima was very beautiful. She stepped towards the fragile barrier, smiling openly at the audacious compliments which welled above the music.

". . . made of such fine flax it's no wonder she found a lordly young fellow to spin it . . ."

". . . ah, to be Bacchus entangled in a net with that Aphrodite—I shouldn't mind facing a phalanx of angry husbands! . . ."

The bride's huge dark eyes examined the rows of young men in their wedding finery. Custom deemed she must give her nosegay to the man she considered handsomest. After a moment of smiling hesitation Cosima presented it to a tall, dark man whose mulberry-red attire was lavishly trimmed with a small fortune in pearls and gems. He bowed low before her, kissed the rosy fingertips, and then held the flowers against his heart . . . to the delight of the onlookers.

Francesca, who led the bevy of matrons and maidens escorting the bride, failed to see Daniello, clad in blue and silver, his hair an angel's halo, cut through the wedding garland with a dagger so that he might meet his bride . . . her own eyes fixed on the bouquet's new owner, and her breathing grew rapid and nervous. The wedding of Daniello della Sera to Cosima di Cuono was indeed honoured: for not only did the Medici and his wife attend, but among dignitaries such as the papal legate, the Venetian ambassador, and a Turkish envoy came Il Moro's representative from Milan: Messer Ridolfo di Salvestro.

Daniello lifted Cosima into the saddle of a wonderfully harnessed black horse, and the Medici gallantly assisted Francesca to mount the white palfrey. She was conscious of the subtle pressure of his hand on hers, and the smile which deepened the lines around his eyes. It was evident that Lorenzo was attempting a new conquest. Cosima bestowed a ravishing smile on him, but Lorenzo's attention was otherwise engaged. Her eyes poured venom on Francesca who had to stifle a grin as she recalled the same hostility in other circumstances.

It seemed to her there was one verse in the Old Testament which might have been written for Cosima. Her memory groped and discovered it among the Preacher's words: ". . . And I find more bitter than death the woman whose heart is snares and nets, and her hands as bands; whoso pleaseth God shall escape from her, but the sinner shall be taken by her."

Francesca's own unhappiness at Daniello's betrothal to Cosima had dissolved to become bitter triumph for the wedding. She could secretly rejoice that the lovely girl who had been instrumental in destroying the Narnis was to be coupled with this handsome degenerate. She doubted that Cosima's voracious sensual appetite would find fulfillment in his arms. With each new figure in the dance of life and death Francesca perceived that fate made mock of all individuals. It gave her some satisfaction to realize that she had not been singled out to be tortured by destiny's cruel humour.

The bridal cavalcade rode off in a jingle of harness and a clatter of hooves, preceded by trumpeters, their glistening instruments decorated with square pennons bearing the red lily on a white ground. Above the triumphant fanfares heralding the bride rose the shouts of congratulations . . . and as ever when the Medici and Madonna Clarice came into view surrounded by their bodyguard the loyal cries of "*Palle . . . Palle . . .*"

Cosima was flanked by a laughing and chattering Daniello and Guido, and Francesca rode a little behind among the dark-haired di Cuono aunts and cousins, and the much blonder della Seras. Daniello's elder married sister, Veronica, shared his golden beauty, but her blue eyes were glazed china which gave her a remote, doll-like appearance. She, like all the other fine ladies, treated Guido's wife with icy politeness, but Francesca was neither vexed nor insulted . . . merely relieved not to have to join in their giggling gossip which had much in common with peasant women on such occasions: just how well the groom would acquit himself in the bride's bed!

Her eyes roamed among the guests, and a tiny smile shaped irony on her lips. Riding among the lesser folks were three of her very own relatives, although they certainly did not recognize her. Like a family of white-faced weasels, Uncle Maximo di Aquia, cousins Lionello and Nannina wore supercilious smiles . . . and their best finery. Evidently, father and son had some part in drawing up the legal details of this great alliance and so were included among the guests. When they presented themselves at the palazzo, it had soothed Francesca's scarred heart a little to see them bow before her and pay their respects in obsequious voices. She had asked after Maximo's wife in the same patronizing manner so much favoured by Madonna Clarice, and the man had replied carelessly, "Oh, she's been dead many months. An ailing woman who was a burden to her family."

To Francesca's relentless gaze he was looking rather mangy, for now it was his son who had all the bright-eyed cunning of the young weasel, and she had enjoyed their discomfort when she persisted: "But did not someone tell me that your late wife was connected to a noble Florentine family? Let me see if I can recall their name ..."

Three narrow faces had tinged dull red, and Lionello hastily interrupted without knowing what irony was contained in his answer. "Nay, madonna, we are just ordinary folk with no more claim to a *magnati* heritage than they tell me you had before your marriage." He had given an ingratiating smile, and his lips shone with saliva. Francesca sensed the lechery in his thoughts, for surely those eyes were trying to visualize what she looked like unclad in the image of the Red Lily.

And she had relished remarking to Guido just within their earshot: "Tell me, husband, do you place all your trust in those lawyers? To me they have a singularly unethical appearance."

Guido considered his wife to be as astute as any wise man, and she knew that despite his stout assertions of the di Aquias' reliability the seed of doubt had been planted in his mind, and in the future he would choose to consult some other legal practitioner. Thus her advancement gave her an opportunity to pay back some of their nastier slights, and she was glad that Aunt Riccarda had been liberated. Let Heaven comfort her for all the misery she had endured ...

Guido reined in his horse so that he could whisper in Francesca's ear: "Wife, I trust you did your duty by informing my sister what joy awaits her."

She retorted swiftly, "I wished sweet Cosima as much happiness from her marriage as I experience from mine."

To a casual onlooker Guido di Cuono placing his hand over Madonna Francesca's seemed a charming loverlike gesture, only she felt the pain as he twisted her gloved flesh.

The trumpets sounded from above the *loggia* of the Bigallo, where on appointed days foundlings were displayed. The sun shone on Ghiberti's bronze doors to the Baptistry. For a brief moment Francesca's spirit transcended all problems as it worshiped the sublime artistry. Surely such work entitled these portals to be the entrance to Heaven.

One man gazing on the rapt features of this girl simply clad in cloth of gold, compared her perfection with Ghiberti's figure of Eve being drawn from the sleeping Adam's side. Francesca turned her head and caught his glance.

The spell was broken. As if no people, noise, or mirth existed between them, Messer Ridolfo's eyes held hers, and she could not doubt that he guessed her true identity. He doffed his plumed hat and bowed towards her, a formal smile on his lips, but the dark eyes still burned as she always remembered them.

He cannot harm me, her mind insisted as she followed Cosima into San Giovanni. It was her allotted task to arrange the consecrated veil—the symbol of chastity—over Cosima's dark glory. The two beauties stared at each other, and then Cosima gave a defiant laugh.

"I never imagined my wedding veil would be handled by an artist's model."

The ceremony was a lighthearted affair . . . despite the solemn intoning of the priest and sweet singing of the choir. It was evident Daniello had drunk a good deal to fortify himself for this ordeal, for he had some difficulty in placing the ring on his bride's finger which caused her a paroxysm of ill-concealed giggles . . . to the merriment of the younger folk and the scandalized whispers of their elders.

Francesca did not let her eyes return to Messer Ridolfo, and from under her lashes she saw Lorenzo gazing ardently at her, waiting for her glance to meet his so that he might produce one of his rare winning smiles. She concentrated her own attention on the bridal couple and allowed the agonizing memory of Andrea to tear at her vitals. Here was the woman he had adored and vowed to wed . . . the mother of his son . . . the betrayer of his family . . . marrying the man his little sister had been pledged to.

Francesca thought of another, an even more beautiful girl who had loved him, and was also a bride . . . but Sister Agnes was the espoused of Christ. She did not wear jewelled finery or a filmy veil but the unadorned white habit of the Carmelites, and her features were stamped with indelible purity and suffering . . . for the heart that had belonged to Carlotta Corbizzi clung steadfastly to her love, and each day she prayed for the salvation of his soul.

Holding to Fra Sandro's counsel Francesca had visited the convent of Santa Maddalena the following day, attended by Anna . . . and also Tommaso, whom Umberto had insisted on sending with them for protection. She left the servants in the bleak silent courtyard where not even an echo of the bustle from the nearby Via Colonna penetrated. Francesca wandered the chapter house while she waited for Sister Agnes. There was one large unadorned wall, and she filled in the time meditating on how Franco might have executed a commission to decorate it.

Inspired by curiosity at the rare visit of a beautiful, worldly woman, several of the sisters found an excuse to tiptoe into the chapter. Painting and drawing faces had given Francesca much insight on the true character of their owners . . . and she was taken aback to read some of these Carmelites' countenances. For even within this cloistered world where each minute of the day and night was controlled by the ordinance of prayer there were traces of cupidity, sloth, and lasciviousness.

Then a small grin illuminated her lovely face as she remembered a passage from the *Decameron*. Ah, it was one of the tales which had delighted the Company of the Cauldron when she recited it. The one about Masetto who feigned dumbness and became a gardener in a convent where all the nuns took it in turn to lie with him until he scarce had strength to work. Besides sly wit there was wisdom in this story, for Boccaccio had well understood that not all who take religious vows are suited to a monastic life. She repeated the well-worn phrases beneath her breath: ". . . there be many men and women foolish enough to believe that, whenas the white fillet is bound about a girl's head and the black cowl clapped upon her back, she is no longer a woman and is no longer sensible of feminine appetites, as if the making her a nun had changed her to stone; and if perchance they here aught contrary to this their belief, they are much incensed as if a very great and heinous misdeed had been committed against nature . . ."

She was still smiling when a voice from the past whispered: "You wish to speak with me?"

Francesca turned, and without thought of concealing her own identity, breathed: "Carlotta."

A bright flush as if caused by some sharp pain invaded the perfect pallor, and the eyes brightened . . . the moisture standing out and then overflowing in two salt drops. "I am Sister Agnes." There was a rebuke in the hushed tone.

Francesca cast herself on her knees, at the young nun's feet. She caught the cold, white hand in her jewelled clasp and gazed upwards, her eyes full of supplication, as if before the Virgin's shrine.

"Really you must not kneel, lady," the nun implored, and then like a tiny night animal ensnared she cried: "Franca. Little Franca." She began to cry.

Slowly, Francesca rose to her feet, and embraced the sobbing girl. "No, no, sweet Sister Agnes, I did not come to make you weep." She realized that Carlotta had become a nun to escape memory, and her own sudden resurrection had callously destroyed this fragile defense.

She could not sully this girl's ears with her own miserable experiences. "Now I understand," Francesca murmured tenderly when the tears had ceased. "I cannot hide here. It would destroy your peace . . . besides it would cure nothing within me. Seeing you, gentle sister, makes me aware of how strong I must be. I cannot believe it is Divine will—if such exists—that I find sanctuary in a religious life."

"You must believe. God, how beautiful you've grown." Sister Agnes smiled wonderingly. "That you survived so much peril and hardship convinces me that God, His Son, and the Holy Virgin are watching over you, shielding you from real harm. Go in peace, and I shall pray each day that you find solace and happiness in the world where you belong. Live, live . . ." and the gentle voice became impassioned. "Live for us, who have lost everything, Franca. Live, so that we may believe . . ."

Francesca emerged from her memories just as the bridal pair began moving towards the center doors. She and Guido followed. The light seemed very bright after the candlelit gloom of the church, but the sun had concealed itself behind thickening clouds, and the damp breeze irritably plucking at skirts proclaimed that rain was not far off.

Traditionally brides were supposed to walk home after the ceremony, but this custom had fallen into disuse. As a concession to it, Cosima walked across the square to where guests and horses waited. As the first drops of rain fell they mingled with the thick shower of rose petals which were cast upon bride and groom.

Lorenzo stepped forward, murmured something to Daniello who nodded and smiled, and in full view of the multitude kissed Cosima on the lips. He extended a hand to Francesca, whom he also embraced. She felt the pressure of his lips demanding the surrender of her own, but she kept hers coldly clamped, and her violet eyes stared up at him unflinchingly.

Lorenzo laughed. Francesca's resistance whetted his ardour just as much as her sister-in-law's compliance. "That's what's called keeping it in the family," various wits in the crowd remarked, and there were bursts of delighted laughter. The Medici escorted the two sisters to their horses.

"Ladies," he said gallantly. "You are both nonpareil. Cosima is the moon. Francesca the sun. Although our Pico insists we make our own destinies I must maintain that our basic characters are conditioned by the planets which rule the houses of our birth. Cosima was born under the Crab and is as varying in her moods as the cycle of the moon. Whereas Francesca, governed by the sun, is fixed, fiery, and indomitable in her splendour."

A long time ago another man had told her this, and Francesca's eyes slid covertly towards Ridolfo di Salvestro to find him still watching her.

The ragged mob had swollen to a huge crowd outside the palazzo. One and all greeted the wedding party rapturously: they had been well-primed with copper coins, Chianti, cervisia, new bread, sausage . . . and the ordinary man's best delight: cheese. Now, without doubt, Madonna Cosima was the most chaste and beautiful bride . . . only to be compared with fine cheese—a compliment indeed! Daniello was the handsomest, bravest, and most virile of bridegrooms, with male seed pouring from his loins . . . and the entire di Cuono and della Sera clans were so steeped in virtue that there was little left for anyone else in the world! Even the papal legate received applause, which astonished him, for it was the habit of most ordinary Florentines to jeer openly at the Holy Father's representative.

The banquet and celebrations lasted for three days. Two hundred calves . . . numerous kids, peacocks, and hares . . . plus a thousand capons, geese, and pheasants . . . and a fish-pond of trout . . . were transformed by the Medici's own cooks not only into succulent dishes, which would pleasure even the most jaded palate, but also into confections to delight the eye. Some animals and birds appeared whole, while others were fashioned into palaces, churches, or caverns filled with treasure. Marzipan and fruits were cunningly contrived into the di Cuono and della Sera emblems, and there were realistic sugar images of the bride and groom. Innumerable casks of Tuscan and Rhenish wine were emptied, and the fountain in the court played Trebbiano instead of water.

The tables were decked with gold, silver, and Venetian glassware set on damask cloths garlanded with fresh leaves and flowers. The walls were hung with new tapestries costing five hundred gold florins apiece, and represented the labours of Hercules in bright silks and glittering threads.

The entire palazzo and its formal gardens rang with laughter, music, and conversation and were filled with the rich aroma of food and the rare scents worn by guests. While they rested from dancing the company were entertained by musicians and singers from the Medici's school of harmony performing Poliziano's magnificent opera *Orfeo*. The Company of the Trowel, wearing fantastic costumes, presented two plays: one sacred, but with a befitting theme —the "Wedding at Cena" . . . and the other a very near-the-knuckle comedy by Plautus. The religious piece caused a good deal of amusement, for, when the wine miraculously appeared in the jars, one of the actors made a wry face and exclaimed: "Poor quality! Not at all like the stuff we drank at Cosima's and Daniello's wedding!"

It all seemed a long way from the stipulated custom of little music, two courses at dinner, and the segregation of the sexes. At the bride's table were fifty young men and women, flirting without restraint, despite marriage or betrothal. Cosima herself sat between Daniello and the Medici, but seemed to give the latter more of her attention, while the bridegroom, flushed and boisterous, exchanged broad jokes with

Guido, Pico, and Poliziano. From an adjacent table Altoviti inclined his head towards Francesca in a mocking bow.

The only person not delighted by this cheerful break with tradition was Madonna Clarice, who murmured in shocked tones to Francesca: "My dear, at this rate, I shouldn't be at all surprised if they ignore the Sacrament and actually consummate their union the first night!"

Francesca hid her smile behind the fan Cosima had given her—again breaking a custom, for the bride was not permitted to give costly presents to her friends and relatives. The silk, ivory, and gold fan was very charming, painted with a voluptuous Venus lolling nakedly among cupids and satyrs . . . and, as Matteo della Sera, remarked: "Asking for all the trouble she was bound to find herself in!"

He sat on Francesca's left, and the sight of him—older but much as she remembered—brought back the past. He gazed at her for some minutes, his large brow wrinkled in puzzlement. "I feel I know you . . . oh no, not just because of the painting that Guido so proudly displays. You have eyes like I've only once before glimpsed, but I cannot recall where."

"Perhaps you dreamed me," she replied steadily, "dreamed that we were bound to meet at a wedding. It sometimes happens that we feel we are experiencing something that occurred before . . ."

He smiled and shook his head. "I do not know, but I realize that I and the gentleman on your right are the most favoured men in Florence."

Unwillingly she turned to acknowledge the smile of her other neighbour. Eating with the same deft movements of a golden fork as she recalled was Messer Ridolfo.

"We have not met before," she challenged.

"Not in this life," Ridolfo's quiet voice answered. "But you are as the fates promised, so the rest must come true . . . or do you not believe that?"

"I believe many things." Her voice was fierce. "I believe

in a man of night who brought destruction on an innocent family in their house blessed by Easter because he was involved in the conspiracy their small daughter overheard."

"I cannot alter what you believe, madonna," he said gravely. "But I can give you the truth even if I cannot convince you of it. The man of night rode to that house of death to warn its occupants but got there too late. His heart was torn with fury and anguish at the slaughter of the innocents, and he mourned all his days for the girl he had vowed to wed."

Later when they danced together, linked by Francesca's lace kerchief, their conversation drowned by the music of viols and pipes, Francesca demanded: "And why did this man of night ride out there?" It was as if in the midst of the music and the dipping, whirling movements they were the only two people in the world.

"To warn the head of that house and his loving, but foolish, heir that a plot had gone awry, and some of those implicated were going to escape blame by taking swift revenge."

There was a pause while they separated to join the parallel rows of men and women performing intricate steps . . . then with a swirl of silks the women returned to their partners' fingertips.

"And of the servant with the purple-marked face?" Francesca queried, breathless from the dance, and thinking at the same time: Even if all he says is true it is too late for me to be rescued . . . even by him. These facts do not untie my marriage knot. The Medici would have no ear for anyone who raked up old miseries and interfered with friendships. Besides, great men do not like to admit they have been duped . . . better to allow one miscarriage of justice than lose face . . .

"He was well enough treated when once his secret had been wrested from loyal but obstinate jaws. Sometimes pain can prove expedient. He bears me no grudge, since he at least believes in my innocence. I gave him a task close to his heart: to seek out his friend, watch over her from a distance, and inform me of her movements . . . which is why I am so opportunely in your city to accept Guido's kind invitation. Did I not always say della Sera could not be yours?"

She shrugged indifferently. "Nor shall I be yours. Fate always lies. Do you know how I come to be as you see me now?"

"By treachery. A man who can arrange the destruction of an entire estate can easily trap a foolhardy young artist."

"So you always knew?"

"At first I but suspected, and then I knew that the feelings you inspired within me could not be caused by man."

Francesca laughed harshly so that he glanced down at her face. His mouth grew bitter and his eyes hard as onyx. "Aye, lady, I have heard many clandestine things about Guido. I do not doubt you are unhappy."

"And shall continue so." She threw him a bright savage look and curtsied as the music ceased.

That was their only dance, yet all the while she danced with the Medici, Daniello, Guido or the score of men who begged for that favour (Lionello she had great pleasure in contemptuously refusing), Ridolfo's narrow dark gaze marked her.

The women retired to help the bride disrobe for the first night. Cosima, as skittish as an unbroken colt, danced and sang about the newly decorated bedchamber, while old Bianca, scolding and panting, tried to comb the unruly hair. She will not find her husband as passionate as Andrea, Francesca mused, remembering . . . while the other ladies grouped themselves around the great nuptial bed, exchanging sly, amused glances, and sharp digs in the ribs—except in the case of Madonna Clarice, whose cheeks were scarlet with indignation.

The nurse—like the good country soul she was—waved male and female mandrake roots bound with myrtle over the sheets, while Cosima shouted with merriment.

"We shall do well enough without that, old witch. Am I not beautiful enough to make him hot with passion?"

"It is to help you conceive," Bianca insisted gravely.

"How dull it would be to lie here just with the intent of conception," Cosima answered with a saucy wink, and the younger women tittered. "Well, sisters-in-law, it is your duty to put on my nightgown . . . but, I trust, Veronica, your brother will not insist on my keeping it on for long."

Veronica smiled aimlessly—as she did in answer to any remark—and she and Francesca pulled off the chemise to reveal Cosima's warm and perfect nakedness, and then slid the embroidered bedgown the nurse had aired before the fire over the curving form.

Cosima stared at Francesca. "Guido's wife, I know your eyes and mouth. They remind me of two people. Is that possible?"

"With you, Cosima," she replied, "all things become possible. I wish you a sweet night."

The men carried the groom into the room. He had to be helped into bed by Guido, for he was more than a little drunk.

"Bear up, Daniello," Lorenzo commanded, "else one of us will gladly have to take over your task."

Side by side on the pillows rested a raven and a golden head. Cosima smiled provocatively at the Medici and at her husband, to whom she snuggled closer . . . and then to the delighted shock of the witnesses she kissed him full on the lips.

"Bravo!" Lorenzo and Guido shouted encouragingly, and Altoviti called out: "Go to it, Daniello . . ."

Then the Medici remembered his wife and added without much conviction: "Remember, not until tomorrow night."

The nurse brought a silver loving cup full of hippocras. Cosima sipped a little, but the bridegroom downed the entire contents.

"Come now," Guido remonstrated, laughing. "Wine forges desire but ruins the hammer's action on the anvil. For the honour of both our families, Daniello, I trust you can satisfy my sister and of course get her with child."

Francesca found Ridolfo at her elbow. There was disgust on his face. "This horseplay does not bode well for the act of love."

"It is the custom," she replied carelessly. "Afterwards the younger men will gather to play dice outside their chamber and listen for the noises within. They are put to bed to do one thing after all, and their relatives and friends hope for it to be well done."

"In Roman times," Ridolfo observed, "nut shells were scattered outside the bridal chamber, so that anyone walking by could not hear secret matters."

"I can well believe that Madonna Clarice is a Roman," Francesca returned, laughing. "Look on her face. She is going to tell her husband a harsh thing or two later when they are alone."

Ridolfo did smile at the sight of her mirth, and then savagery pulled at his features as if his thoughts caused him pain. "Tell me, madonna, was your own bridal night celebrated according to this pattern?"

Francesca laughed and he stared down at her without understanding. "Nay, sir, it was celebrated after a fashion unknown to the people in this chamber."

In the morning Cosima's features, which Francesca could read well, did not speak of fulfillment, and Daniello began drinking as soon as he rose.

Late in the darkening afternoon Francesca wandered into the garden to cool her wine-inflamed cheeks. Indoors the young folk had started to play at hoodman blind, which of course always ended in the exchange of a kiss. Guido and

Daniello were sitting with some sparks playing *tarocchi*
. . . Ridolfo played at chess with Marsilio Ficino while Pico
and Poliziano watched and argued.

She was glad of the new violet cloak which had aroused
the envy and admiration Matteo Panetti had foreseen. It was
cold in the bare pergola for the breeze could play un-
hampered by foliage among the stone arches. There were
some noises close by, and Francesca assumed that a couple
had sought the shadowed solitude of the artfully placed seat:
for surely that was a female giggle, and the voice had the
hoarse intonation of masculinity. Then came the prolonged
unmistakable sound of a kiss. She did not wish to intrude
upon some clandestine loving but couldn't help her curiosity.

She peeped around a pillar but did not have to worry
about being observed for the couple were too busy. Cosima,
clad in one of her bridal gowns, was being granted the satisfaction she so much sought. Her male companion, his hands
and loins hidden by the glimmering skirt, was none other
than Lorenzo de Medici.

What fools, Francesca whispered to herself . . . and then
thought coldly: They are not so foolish. Who would tell
on the Medici? And besides Daniello has too little interest
in females to be the scrap jealous or hurt that he was already a cuckold. Probably he'd be relieved if Cosima might
be fatigued by efforts other than his.

A squall of angry rain broke from the sky, and Francesca
hurried indoors to see the man and woman return singly:
Cosima's face was flushed, and tendrils of dark hair had
escaped its ornaments, but she looked even more beautiful.
Lorenzo appeared rather worn. The bride went immediately
to her husband and stood behind him, caressing his golden
locks. He looked up from his cards to smile. "Welcome, my
love. Perhaps you can bring me luck. Your brother seems
to have all the good fortune."

Then Ridolfo joined their game, and Francesca wandered
over to watch. The mulberry-clad figure won and won,

until the group of players and watchers murmured at such luck.

"Indeed sir, you are the very devil with cards," Guido said, a rare flush on his cheekbones.

Ridolfo smiled. "The cards have a will of their own, but they recognize their master. They are like women."

Francesca looked away, guessing that his eyes sought hers . . .

The Sixth Deadly Sin

FOURTEEN EIGHTY-THREE dawned with all the signs of being a momentous year, yet Francesca had no reason to believe it held forth any promise of change for her.

Two of the lions in the city's menagerie became sick, which all Florence considered a bad omen, especially with regard to the war being waged in Lombardy. Crafty Sixtus had changed sides yet again and joined Naples, Florence, and their allies against the Venetians. The evil-looking fellow with one hand who had been hired to help feed the wild beasts was blamed for the lions' ill-health and dismissed.

To cheer the populace—and also take their mind off the rising cost of corn and beans—the Medici held a great Easter fete. This took the form of a hunt in the Piazza della Signoria. Although the rain abated for the day it was not an overwhelming success, for the lions—perhaps out of sympathy for their sick brothers—lacked spirit. One raised enough enthusiasm and a mangy paw to kill a dog . . . but the stags and buffaloes provided for their sport received no hurt . . . despite the screams of encouragement and derision, rising from the crowds massed on platforms, which had been erected at great cost along the house fronts.

One unforeseen event was a buffalo killing three men.

That the people should not be too disappointed a tasteless novelty was introduced—which the respectable saw as a sign that Florence was fast falling into the decadence of ancient Rome: Without giving thought to the presence of women and children a stallion was loosed with a mare . . .

In April came a total eclipse of the moon, and inexplicably three people fell dead in the streets. Rain pelted nonstop for one month until the Florentines seriously doubted the arrival of summer. Only when the statue of Our Lady of Impruneta was paraded through the city did the fine weather commence.

It was a time of miracles. Francesca concluded this fresh crop of holy wonders had their origins in the general uncertainty that always troubled folk in time of war. When matters went well why bother your head with religion? Now they looked desperately for Divine help . . . as if they knew that their leaders were as much pawns of an uncontrollable power as themselves. There were frequent accounts of bells ringing of their own accord, people being miraculously healed, the Virgin appearing at numerous lonely grottoes . . . and of course the usual selection of statues changing colour, bleeding, or weeping. The babe who refused to suckle on Good Friday was considered a model of piety.

The direct result of man's own inhumanity were the tragic huddles of folk passing through the city, fleeing from war and famine in Lombardy, and seeking some security in the Romagna. Francesca's heart went out to these victims . . . the pinched bluish faces of the babes . . . men and women broken and old before their maturity . . . emaciated mules bowed down under bedding, cooking utensils, and stoves . . . all that could be salvaged in the path of war.

Soberly she considered her own lot. Happiness and freedom eluded her, but at least she was fed and housed. Guido did not pester her too often with his vile attentions, and she knew he had two new pages in his personal retinue—as vicious and insolent as they were pretty. Still he could dress them in gold and lace, pamper them with sweetmeats and scents, present them with songbirds, and do what he wished, just so long as he left her alone!

It was a time for miracles nearer home too. Cosima was pregnant. Although Daniello was showered with congratulations on his swift prowess, his sister-in-law silently doubted that the babe's hair would be corn yellow. Cosima's condition made her fretful, and sometimes too sick to leave her bedchamber, and her beautiful face and figure became lumpy overswiftly. Mature matrons spoke knowingly of this being the way with first pregnancies! Daniello, provenly relieved from further marital duties, took up his old life and was rarely seen at home. He made no secret to Francesca of his horror of female moans, moods, and ailments, and his dislike of the sight of all creatures pregnant. He spent much time in the palazzo di Cuono, which gave Cosima further reason to pour venom on her sister-in-law whose attractions she blamed for Daniello's absence. Whenever she visited her brother she openly railed at him for marrying a ne'er-do-well artist's strumpet sister and begged him to put aside the barren creature and take a more noble wife.

"See, how scrawny she is. Those hips are as flat as a boy's and will never bear you a son. It's all very well for Botticelli to make an exhibition of *her* face." The painting of Pallas and the Centaur had received wide acclaim, and Francesca had wept with delight when she accepted an invitation to see it complete. Once again the Florentines had cause to admire her beauty. "Besides, I wager she's cuckolding you left, right, and center . . . My Daniello's always hanging round here, and he doesn't bring much strength or enthusiasm home to my bed . . . and Lorenzo appears bewitched into sending her costly gifts."

Delighted with Francesca's appreciation of beauty and deprived of Cosima's constant company, Lorenzo never lacked an opportunity to send her anything from a dwarf rose tree in a majolica pot, decorated with eyes to ward off evil, to a silver-gilt saltcellar, fashioned as a gryphon. Cosima refrained from mentioning the jewels he had given her, especially the thick pearl choker which had greeted the announcement of her pregnancy.

Guido was merely amused by her vindictive outburst, and commented, "Look to your own virtue, little sister. We cannot all be as fecund as you."

Yet, Francesca was gnawed by the terror that he might soon begin to demand a child, and if she did not accede to his wish he would certainly erase her from life. Whenever she went out, her eyes searched the passersby for someone fitting Raffo's description. Then, she overheard the Medici remark to Guido he had word the red-haired adventurer, Raffo, had encountered Columbus which would probably involve him in a perilous expedition . . . and she recognized despondently that she might never have an opportunity of knowing if he were indeed her brother. Sometimes she glimpsed Taddeo, but by no flicker of a facial muscle did he betray recognition, and Francesca was comforted that he did not desert her. Messer Ridolfo visited the palazzo soon after the rains stopped to bid Guido farewell.

"Louis XI of France is dead," he explained. "Il Moro is sending me to pay Milan's respects to the young King Charles."

"They say he is an ugly youth," Guido said, "with a mind full of romantic notions about the glories of battle. The French are so old-fashioned!"

"Lodovico believes in making allies rather than enemies so that when his regency ends, and the young Duke Gian Galeazzo comes to power, he will rule a strong dukedom."

Guido laughed. "I doubt Il Moro will relinquish his position easily. And I doubt, dear Ridolfo, that your visit to France is out of straightforward courtesy." Francesca was surprised to realize her husband interested himself in such matters. His was a wilier character than she'd imagined, and this increased her fear of him.

"Farewell, beautiful madonna," Ridolfo kissed her fingers, and a tremor travelled along the veins in her arm, echoing an afternoon when she was still an innocent girl. "Remember to hold fast only to the truth. I shall try not to be abroad too long."

She regarded his absence with relief mixed with disappointment. Relief that his presence would not stir up memory and doubts, and disappointment that the curious power he emanated could not deliver her from Guido. She felt he had not fulfilled an unspoken vow to be her help.

The death of French Louis had a detrimental effect on the Medici's bank in Lyons. The depositors panicked and began to withdraw their funds. This crisis of confidence caused a reorganization in the Medici banking empire . . . and deepened the grimness of Lorenzo's features.

It was hot in the city. The narrow streets stank. Mists of flies hovered everywhere so that the still air seemed to buzz. Francesca was forever plagued by itching mosquito and flea bites. She felt too listless to do more than sit by the fountain in the court, listen to its cool music, and unenthusiastically net a green silken purse. Dear Gostanza had been right: her charge never became interested in needlework.

Cosima, exhausted by the heat, insisted on going to Buonventura, for she imagined that Daniello would accompany her. Instead he sent his young wife off in a marvellously woven litter, with Veronica for a confidante, and an escort of servitors, telling them to let him know when Cosima's time arrived . . . and how his father did, for the old man was also at Buonventura recovering from a seizure.

Before she departed Cosima deposited something in her brother's charge, Mario, now a mischievous toddler, and her old nurse, Bianca.

"Why do you leave him here?" Francesca protested. "Your brother dislikes him, and the child screams with fear whenever Guido comes near. Does Daniello object to the boy?"

"No . . . no more than he does to my pet monkey.

Nothing disturbs my golden husband. I'm sure he intends that I have fifteen children around my skirts . . . but I'm tired of Mario's crying. It makes my poor head ache worse," Cosima said fractiously. "People of your background are used to brats, and it'll keep you from boredom."

"The child is not a toy," Francesca argued. "He is a human being. Better put him in the Foundlings Hospital or give him to a holy order than simply dump him where he isn't welcome."

"Guido may do what he wishes. Perhaps when *my* babe is born Mario will be company for it."

Mario was the most exquisite of children, and people seeing him with Francesca remarked slyly: "Oho, so that's the way it is: the babe is her bastard. Look how alike they are. Wonder who the father was . . . certainly not Guido, or else he'd legitimize the boy."

Indeed he was so much a Narni that Francesca mourned and rejoiced at one time. Anna would have nothing to do with the clever, lively boy, and Francesca could identify loathing on the woman's face. But, she did not blame the slave: after all, it was his arrival that cost her both speech and beauty. When the child sat on his aunt's lap, the slave kept to the farthest corner and stared at her mistress with unfathomable fear.

Only old Bianca was content, for at last she had found a lady prepared to listen while she extolled Mario's virtues . . . a lady who apparently adored him more than his own mamma (whose identity she did not reveal!). Francesca lost herself in happy hours teaching Mario all she could recall from childhood. There were the funny little songs her own father had taught her, to which his grandson now clapped chubby hands . . . tales of St. Francis and the beasts . . . and baby words like *pappo* for bread . . . *bombo* for wine . . . *ciccia* for meat . . . and *far la nanna* for going to sleep. She dandled him on her knee, played bopeep through her jewelled fingers, taught him to pray, and to wrestle, and drew pictures of creatures for him to name . . . and altogether spoiled him.

Mario's presence kept Guido from her, and often he would complain that he could smell the child on her gown. She was slow to understand that Guido was jealous of the attention and gentleness she bestowed on the child who was nephew to them both. He had never known her tenderness and now often jested in company: "Well, madonna, I can see I'll have to redouble my efforts in your bed for I'll get no peace until you have a babe of your own to lick and fondle . . . like a whelping bitch . . ."

Francesca feared that as much as she feared the future for Mario. Now that he was in the palazzo she could not try to escape unless she could ensure his well-being. Bianca would gladly die for him, she knew, but that would not bring him the good life he ought to know.

With Mario in mind she slipped out one afternoon alone, having told Anna she was going to rest because her menses were giving her pain and set her to a pile of mending. Francesca went straight to the Via dei Servi to a tiny dark shop which smelled of wax and was festooned with multitudes of waxen images, arms, legs, hands, feet, hearts, and babes. It was crowded with honest folk purchasing these miniatures to hang in church in order to gain the Virgin's protective or healing powers.

The entrance of so fashionable and beautiful a lady caused a stir. All eyes turned towards her, momentarily their owners forgetting the purpose of their own visit. The greater folk normally scoffed at such superstitious practices . . . and sent their servants for purchases at the wax shop. It took the owner quite a few minutes to understand Francesca's request for a model of a little boy who somewhat resembled herself in colouring and features, for he was so overwhelmed by her appearance.

"Of course, madonna, right away," the man mumbled,

wiping his hands on an apron streaked with varied colour wax.

An old grandmother patted Francesca's arm and muttered comfortingly between broken teeth, "There, there, little lady, you must not fret if a babe does not enter your womb straightaway. The Virgin will send you one in good time, especially now you're going to dedicate the wax boy to Her."

Francesca thanked her gravely and let the curious gathering think what they wanted. When the image was ready, she took it to the Church of the Annunziata. In the chapel with the silver altar was a painting of the Annunciation, and Francesca stared up at the Virgin's face with wondering eyes: for everyone said that the head had been painted by a divine hand while the artist slept. Suspended beside the altar were countless wax offerings, and reverently Francesca placed Mario's image among them.

Then she sank to her knees and began to pray: "Dear Mother of God, it is long since I asked you for anything. I do not care what befalls me but pray you will guard the life and soul of Andrea's son, Mario. He is so beautiful, and now he dwells in such an evil house. I fear my husband will either harm him or corrupt his innocence . . ."

When she had done praying she gazed again upon the calm face of the young girl, blessed above all women, who had endured the agony of seeing her God-given son crucified so that mankind might be redeemed . . .

It was stifling hot and very bright when she left the cool splendour of the church. The shadows were lengthening, but the sky above was cobalt blue, and the stone buildings were tinged warm gold. Francesca walked swiftly across the piazza and stopped briefly to watch two youths stripped to their trunk hose practise wrestling . . . the smaller balancing on his opponent's feet. Whoever fell first would be the loser.

"Whore! Lump of flesh with eyes. Get you gone from this

place!" Francesca assumed the tirade came from some merchant scolding a tardy maidservant . . . but the insults did not cease. She half turned to see a white-faced monk standing beside her . . . the dark cowl giving his features the shadows of a skull. He continued hissing abuse, until Francesca felt her cheeks flame with anger. What right had this prating fellow to address a respectable woman so . . . and then she saw that the eyes sunk in livid hollows were the eyes of Benedetto, and her glance softened. She extended a hand: "May the God you confess to bring you enlightenment. Go in peace, brother, I am not what you believe . . ."

"Blaspheming witch!" he screamed.

Passersby stopped to listen, shrug, and walk on. One indignant, plump matron sent her husband across and he mumbled gruffly: "Madonna, do not harken to him. He is deranged. He wanders up and down these streets cursing our young women, especially those who are pregnant. He is harmless and to be pitied."

Francesca stood her ground. Benedetto could not hurt her, but she understood he was torturing himself.

"Dear friend," she tried again, "let us go into the atrium of the church and talk quietly."

"Whore!" he spat in her face and then held a crucifix before him.

She wiped the spittle from her cheek and off the bodice of her gown, recalling with sadness that once he had pressed such moisture into her mouth . . . how strange that the same element could mean two such different things.

Before Francesca could walk on, a young man, clad in claret, with long dark curls and an unusual beard, dashed forward. He struck the priest on the mouth. Bright blood streaked the white chin. Benedetto blinked like someone regaining consciousness, and his voice became as mild as when he used to speak with Lauretta. "I have no quarrel with you, sir. Why did you strike me?"

"For vilifying a goddess," the stranger declared passionately. "You dared to sully her ears with your coarse words."

Once again, Benedetto turned on Francesca hurling maledictions. "Curse her! Let those eyes rot! May those lips be encrusted with sores to show the corruption within her, for she brings infection to every man in her path. Let the whore be burned!"

This was too much for the young man in red. He knocked the priest senseless with a sharp blow to the chin and then stood over his victim, panting from exertion. He turned to Francesca with a comic mixture of alarm and triumph in his brown eyes, and with concern he noticed her pallor and that she was trembling.

"Sir," she said breathlessly, "you will be in dire trouble for striking a priest. Get you gone before you are discovered."

"I refuse to leave you here alone," he protested. "Madonna, believe me, I am an honourable man, and intend you no harm. My name is Davide Ben Ezra, and my grandparents' home is but a few paces from here. Let me escort you there so you may recover."

His limpid eyes had the trusting gaze of a child who believes dreams can come true and has received no lasting hurt from the world. She doubted if he'd ever before struck anyone.

Davide took her hand and led her into a labyrinth of sweating alleys, made dark as evening by the overhanging upper stories of the tall houses. The customary miasma pervading all such narrow ways was tempered by a delicious aroma of cooking. Francesca wrinkled her nose appreciatively: good, yet unlike the normal macaroni, garlic, and tomato . . . nor the pungent *baccalà* which always proclaimed Friday in artisan districts.

She had not explored the ghetto during her previous existence and only once before had spoken to a Jew. Nofri had brought Solomon to Castelfiore for a few days. They were both studying at Padua, but the older man was more interested in magic than medicine. He had spent many hours discussing the intricacies of the Cabala, the Zohar, and the ten sephiroth with Vincenzo. Only when they sat down to eat did Francesca see the differing customs enjoined by his faith. He was forbidden pork . . . nor could he take other meat unless it was slaughtered in a particular way . . . and even then this could not be eaten with cheese or milk. Certainly his was a complicated religion. To Tullia's supreme indignation—and ever after she termed him as Maestro Nofri's Heathen—Solomon ate frugally of a little trout and that from a plate he'd brought with him. Before he broke bread and drank wine, he spoke some words in a strange chanting tongue, and Vincenzo de Narni listened enraptured to the Hebrew prayers.

Francesca, as a little child, had thought their guest was performing magic, and she peeped into the wine-cup to see if the contents had turned to gold . . . but it still resembled dark wine with winking bubbles playing on its surface.

"I but thank the Lord our God for the fruit of the vine and the earth," Solomon explained to Madonna Ginevra, who was both impressed by his piety and doubtful whether a good Catholic should entertain a Jew. After the meal Francesca had climbed upon his knee and, lulled by the rising and falling cadence of his complicated discourse, had fallen asleep against his beard. Gostanza had scrubbed her face with cold water before bed. "Lest any Jewish contagion contaminate your immortal soul," she said, making the sign of the cross over the washing water.

Now Francesca stared eagerly around and found her concept of the Jew's appearance to be mistaken. They were not all dark-haired or olive-skinned. Indeed many were fairer than herself. Davide looked almost like a jester in the bright attire which accentuated his slight stature, for despite the heat most men were clad in the ankle-length *lucco* of somber wool.

More extraordinary to Francesca was that all men—even

the youngest—were bearded, and they left their sidelocks uncut: for these were dedicated to God. This long hair swayed about narrow, serious faces in two beguiling glossy ringlets. Not one among them was bareheaded. Some favoured a fashionable, feather-trimmed hat like Davide's, but most preferred little silken skullcaps that she remembered Solomon always wearing.

Everyone appeared in a great hurry. There were only a few maidens about, carrying covered baskets. Their long hair flowed free, and they kept huge, plum-dark eyes lowered as they passed the men. Francesca was amazed by the modesty of their attire: in every case the cloth was fine, the golden ornaments costly and tasteful . . . but the sleeves revealed only fingertips, and the necklines only a fraction of white neck, as concealing as any nun could wish for . . . and certainly not the current fashion among sprightly Florentine girls looking out for admirers. They threw lash-veiled glances at Davide . . . and Francesca. She was aware that her brilliantly embroidered gown, which simulated hand-painted flowers and clouds of butterflies, with its low bodice, must look very bizarre.

"There are only a few hours left until the Sabbath begins," Davide explained. "When the first stars show then all work is ended. No more cooking may be done, so everything must be ready. The girls are coming from the baker with Sabbath twists of white bread."

Before he pushed open a thick double door with an iron-ring handle, Davide touched a small carved container affixed slantwise to the righthand doorpost and then kissed his fingertips.

"What does that signify?" she asked.

"It is a mezuzah," Davide said. "The Bible commands our people thus: 'And thou shalt write them upon the doorposts of thy house.' It contains a parchment on which are written the laws of God, and the prayer best known to all Jews, which starts 'Hear, O Israel, the Lord our God, the

Lord is One.' When we leave the house we also salute it. Rabbis say it is to remind a man to guide his family according to the Law, and to deal justly with his fellows outside the house."

"Like an amulet against evil," Francesca murmured. She stepped down into the cool gloom. Because of the unpretentious building she had prepared for a humble interior, but the ornate silverware was of the finest work, and there were many books and folios spread on the carved chests and shelves. A long table was prepared for the evening meal: silver cups and plates, a wonderfully pierced spice box, and candlesticks with pure white wax candles. The bread was covered by an embroidered cloth. All was in perfect polished order. This was the home of people who revered living and learning.

Francesca was acutely aware of the absence of religious pictures, statues, or the normal votive shrine, with its flickering light or nosegay, dedicated to the Virgin, which most households contained, unless they had their own chapel. What was it Papa had told her? The Jews were forbidden by their Law to make images of God, lest it be construed as idolatry.

"Davide, you are late." The voice belonged to an old man who looked up from a book. Beneath heavy white brows he had two deep-set blue eyes which examined Francesca keenly. If she had wanted to paint Moses well stricken in years Francesca would have chosen Davide's grandfather for her model.

"Grandfather, I tarried to help this lady. Madonna, this is Rabbi Eleazer."

Francesca curtsied and then held out her fingers, but the Rabbi shook his head. "Be welcome, but I may not touch you."

She looked across at Davide who smiled reassuringly. "It is forbidden for the orthodox men of our faith to touch a woman—be she Jewess or Gentile. Even when they dance at their wedding the couple are divided by a handkerchief. More often the men dance together."

An old lady emerged from another room, carrying a dish of honey and almond cakes. "Enough religious instruction, Davide, bid our visitor sit down and drink a glass of wine."

The face was as wrinkled as a walnut but the eyes were full of humour and her hair still glossy and brown. She put a dry, bony hand on Francesca's cheek. "You are amazed at my hair, eh?" and she cackled with laughter. "Another of our customs. When we wed, our girlhood hair is cut and made into a wig to cover our head. This was the colour of my youth."

Rabbi Eleazer's wife peered at her guest. "It's a crime that such beauty should not belong to one of our people. What say you, Davide?"

Davide Ben Ezra blushed and nodded.

"Woman," the Rabbi said sternly, "you prattle too much. I am going to the synagogue to see all is in order for the service. Davide, follow me."

With a courteous nod of his head towards Francesca the old man departed.

"Are you to become a rabbi, Davide?" she asked curiously.

He sighed. "It seems so, but I prefer to be a poet."

"Such foolishness," the grandmother scoffed. "To be a teacher of our people is an honour and a blessing. Besides we have no son to follow your grandfather. His mantle must fall on you."

Before Francesca had time to wonder the grandmother produced a plate of spiced fish cakes, some thick slices of white bread and slivers of cucumber in vinegar. "I can tell you are hungry. Eat."

She wanted to protest, but the food tempted her appetite. For the first time in many months Francesca ate with relish, while the grandmother nodded with a benign satisfaction that things were as she predicted.

Francesca smacked her lips and then wiped the crumbs and grease from them with a clean linen napkin. "There," she smiled, "I feel restored."

"Are your parents dead?" Davide began uncertainly.

She nodded and then asked hastily to prevent further questions about herself, "Are you an orphan?"

"Our only child, Rebecca, died when Davide was born." The old woman twisted a lock of his dark hair tenderly. "So the Almighty blessed us with a life for her life. His father is too occupied to pay him much attention, except for giving him too much money to spend on trifles like these clothes, and besides Reuben's ways are not our ways. He does not hold with book learning. He would have the boy become a Marrano."

"Father considers if I became converted I should have a better chance in the world beyond the ghetto." Davide's voice was bitter. "He is a usurer. We Jews are not permitted many livelihoods through the Church's edicts so have to fulfill the tasks forbidden to Christians: like lending money at twenty to thirty percent interest."

"Go to, Davide!" Francesca retorted. "Cloaked under the acceptable name of banking that's precisely what the Medici and some of his friends do. The Church encourages us in hypocrisy so its leader doesn't feel too alone! As to your being converted: You'd never really be thought of as Christian. They would still call you a Marrano!"

The grandmother laughed. "Men will not thank you for your wisdom."

Francesca shrugged. "People are ever hated for the truth. I can tell by your accents that you were not always Florentines. Where did you come from?"

Davide's face had taken on thoughtful lines while she spoke, and he answered: "A long time ago my mother's family fled from England, after the massacre of the Jews in a city called York. They tried to make a home among the cities along the Rhine—where my father's people originated. Alas, there Jews are hated, persecuted, and slain. So, some came into Italy while others went on to Spain."

"Where they prospered and were happy," the grandmother interrupted, "until the Inquisition started in seventy-eight. Since then I have no word from our relatives in Seville. Either they have been forced to abjure their faith or else burned to death. It is ever thus with our people. Sometimes it may seem we have found a haven, like here. Then a sudden storm blows up and drives us out. If we grow fat, believing we are safe, we cannot understand the persecution when it breaks out. Also, some of us accumulate too many possessions to flee in the night, and think that the wealth will be a shield. On the contrary the gold is often a spur to our foes. Kill a Jew and take his riches! Nobody speaks out against such practices. Can you imagine what it is like to belong nowhere, and every man your enemy, madonna?" the old woman demanded.

Francesca met the bitter glance fearlessly. "Yes, lady, I can, and alone, without any solace from a faith which at least binds you to a wandering community."

"That's impossible!" Davide argued.

"Be quiet, boy," his grandmother admonished. "You do not yet know how to read faces. She knows."

"I must go." Francesca rose unwillingly. "I am happy here. I should like to come again."

The grandmother shook her head. "It is best if you don't. Guido di Cuono is no friend of Jews. His family have frequently borrowed money from our people, and when settlement falls due they send in men with whips and fierce dogs to drive us from town."

Shame suffused Francesca's cheeks. "I did not know you recognized me."

"The Madonna of the Topaz who rose from nowhere cannot go about this city unrecognized. Peace be with you.

I am sorry we cannot meet again. Davide will escort you. But, hurry back, boy, for your grandfather will blame me if you are late at the service."

Davide Ben Ezra talked all the way back to the White Lion area. Francesca could not help laughing at his intensity and the way ideas tumbled over each other in a rush to exhibit themselves. "I do not know if you are a great poet, Davide," she said, when they parted. "But I do know that you talk more than any person I've ever met. Thank you for being my champion, but, as you live, strike no more priests."

"I shall remember meeting you forever," he whispered and stood in the starlight, long after she had disappeared from his sight, staring down at the hand she had patted.

It was stifling in the hallway as if an unseasonal fire had been lit in one of the salons. Francesca was taken aback by the curious sights and sounds which met her. The normal evening quiet was punctuated by thin wild shrieks as from a dog caught in a snare. There were bursts of laughter and also the unmistakable crackle of burning logs. Rocking back and forth on the bottom stair was Bianca, her flabby face marked with a livid bruise. She sobbed without tears. Further up the staircase, sentinel of the shadows, stood Anna, twisting her hands, and with something like a smile on her features.

Francesca darted forward and seized the nurse's shoulder. "What has happened, goody?"

"Mario . . . oh Mario . . ." Bianca moaned, and one palsied hand pointed to the closed door of the main salon.

Anna tried to bar Francesca's path, but with a strength born of anxiety she pushed the slave aside and flung open the door.

"Welcome, madonna. While you've been out a-pleasuring some paramour, we've been playing a little game," Guido said indolently. He was lounging in a chair a distance from the blazing fire, the buttons of his doublet undone, and a whip hanging idly from his fingers . . . as he watched his two pages sport before the hearth.

The scream of rage exploded from Francesca's throat and mingled with Mario's wails. For the small boy was being tossed from one youth to the other in imminent danger of falling into the flames. He was badly bruised and one plump arm had an inflamed scorch mark.

"We are just toasting him a little," Guido continued smoothly. "We must not let him get ideas that he is anything but a worthless lump of flesh because he keeps to a fine lady's chamber . . ."

She seized the whip, darted forward, and snatched Mario from the grasp of one of the lads, while lashing out at the other. His astonished bellow of rage and pain spoke of her strength and aim.

Mario screamed and struggled. He was burning hot, and wet from sweat and urine. Above the squirming little body Francesca faced her husband and the flush-faced pages, who glowered their defiance, eyes flickering to their master, like dogs just waiting for the word to attack. At that moment she did not fear anyone.

"You cannot live long, Guido," her voice rang out. "And I do not care if I have to die to bring you to hell."

The amusement twisting his mouth froze to an expression of cold contempt.

Francesca carried the child to her room, cleaned him, and put a honey-based salve on the burn. Then she wrapped him in a blanket and gave him sugar to suck. He whimpered a little, but with his eyes firmly fixed in her direction, he dropped into sleep.

That night she sat before her chamber door, a knife in her lap, her eyes watchful . . . as she waited. But Guido had gone out to continue his revels: He could take vengeance in his own time and much preferred his victim to be tormented by the delay. At first light, Francesca woke Bianca who had been dozing in a chair beside the sleeping child.

"Here are his clothes, more than enough gold for your journey, and a note for Madonna Cosima. Tell her what occurred and that you and Mario must stay at Buonventura." Francesca knew her written words might startle Cosima into obedience: "If ever you knew joy in Andrea's arms, keep his son from Guido's clutches."

"Be first out of the city gates," Francesca continued. "Get a ride in a country cart, but be wise and do not tell anyone you have money or are connected with an important family. Go now."

"Madonna, madonna," the woman implored. "You are as good and brave as any saint. But I fear for you. He does not care for those who thwart him. Think of your slave's face. Come with us."

Francesca's head ached, and her eyes were enormous in the exhausted pallid face which had taken on the hard lines of fury. "No, you would be in danger if I accompanied you. He would be sure to follow after. I love Mario, more than my life. Keep him safe, and pray God we meet again."

She dressed the sleepy child and kissed his soft face a dozen times. Still carrying him, she led Bianca downstairs and then entrusted the boy to the nurse's arms.

Francesca threw herself on the bed . . .

At midday she was woken by Anna who held a large bouquet of flame roses. A scroll of paper was attached by a pretty but ill-tied ribbon. Francesca stared up at the slave who had been so desensitized by Guido's cruelty that she had been able to triumph while a helpless creature was tortured. Francesca could neither harangue nor pity the woman.

She buried her nose in the scented clusters before undoing the paper on which was inscribed in a fair flowing hand "for Madonna Francesca di Cuono."

Davide Ben Ezra had written: "Madonna, although it is forbidden to write on the Sabbath I have ignored such laws to send you the most beautiful words ever penned in tribute to fair women. Your loveliness inspires me with the knowledge that I am not skillful enough to compose a poem in your honour." He had copied out a selection of verses from the Song of Solomon.

Francesca did not notice Guido until she finished reading. She feared his smiling face and quiet manner.

"So, it is a Jewish dog you have sniffing round your skirts. I do not care that my wife should link her body with one of that circumsized race, lest it bring deformity on my own progeny."

"Guido!" she cried. "You do not believe that of me for one second. You must know this epistle comes from a foolish boy whose mind is in a realm of poetry. He intends no disrespect . . ."

"What I believe and how I act are often very different, Francesca," he said softly. "Now I am going to teach that Hebrew a lesson none of his ilk . . . or you . . . will forget."

She flung herself at him, but he slipped aside so that her body jolted against the slammed door, and she fell, winded, to the ground. Bruised and weeping, Francesca changed her gown and, ignoring Anna's attempts to help her, she brushed her own hair but did not bother to arrange it. The violet cloak covered her simple attire and flowing hair, and then Francesca hurried unattended through the streets.

At the Medici palazzo she learned Madonna Clarice was gone to the country for a visit and Lorenzo was now alone in the gardens after receiving a representative of the Eight. The Medici servants hid their grins as the beautiful girl ran through the archway which led to the paved sheltered walk preferred by their master. So now Madonna Francesca was his new toy . . . and very nice too!

The short-sighted eyes recognized the violet cloak, and the hoarse voice exclaimed: "Cosima, my darling, what are you doing back here?"

"She does wear a similar cape," Francesca replied breathlessly, "but you have mistaken the lady."

"Francesca, I am honoured that you come to me alone."

He kissed her fingers but did not attempt to release them, and his dark gaze examined her dishevellment. "You are pale, but even more enchanting with your hair loose. Is something amiss?"

"You have much power," the amethyst eyes were enormous with pleading. "Can you do something for me?"

"In exchange for a kiss, I'll do whatever you ask."

She ignored the price but continued. "Guido is set on destroying a young Jew who has written me a note. Davide Ben Ezra is harmless. His people are honourable and learned. But you know how vicious Guido can be. For God's sake, Lorenzo, intervene."

The Medici drew her close and rested his chin on her warm tumbled hair. "It is too late. Nothing can prevent the Florentine rabble when it is incensed."

"What do you mean?"

"Young Ben Ezra was discovered by Guido and Daniello in Or San Michele. They tried to stop his defiling a statue of Our Lady, but the boy seemed quite mad and threw filth on the figures, and scratched out the Babe's eyes."

"I don't believe it."

"One of the Eight has just reported the whole sorry business to me. Guido, Daniello, and their attendants dragged him outside, but a crowd gathered, before they could take him to the Podesta. The people started throwing stones. I'm afraid they put out the young man's eyes, and his body was crushed between two blocks of masonry . . ."

Francesca almost swooned, and her weight collapsed against the Medici who supported her with eager arms. She recalled dark, sparkling eyes, which were full of dreams and laughter, and the merry lips which talked ceaselessly . . . and now Davide was . . . and her mind flashed up an image of Andrea's mangled remains. There was no doubt in her mind that Guido had staged the entire scene playing on the prejudice of the crowd to finish off what he had started.

"Lorenzo," she whispered, "Guido caused this . . ."

"Hush, my darling," he replied gently. "So what does one young Jew matter in the scheme of things? Your husband was right to be jealous. I doubt that he will react in like manner should I declare my passion for you. I have ensured the Guard protect the moneylenders though, for the Eight were worried lest the crowd start a Jew hunt, which would disrupt trade. Come now, Francesca, we shall go indoors, drink some wine, and relax . . ."

He clasped her to him and buried his lips on hers. Distraught, she did not at once react. When she realized what Lorenzo was doing to her, strength returned redoubled by fury, and she hit and scratched at his face until he released her.

"You dare to embrace me," she screamed, "when you have allowed so many of my dear ones to be foully slain."

The Medici looked at her long and steadily. "Madonna, you forget yourself, and also who you address. To judge by your scandalous behaviour Guido was right to take justice—however rough—into his own two hands. Evidently the Jew meant a lot to you. I deem that most unseemly in the wife of one of my friends. Unchastity should not be proclaimed so that all may mock a man for marrying beneath him. I think I must suggest that your husband take you to the country where you may recover your manners. Good day, madonna."

Like one demented, who must continue until the madness is spent, Francesca sped into the Ghetto. The door of Rabbi Eleazer's house was ajar, and she stumbled in. Surrounded by a thick crowd of mourners were the grandparents and the father. They sat on the ground, their clothes rent, ash on their heads, and the air was filled with wailing.

The grandmother looked up at the figure, strangely bright in that gloom, and she pointed a bony condemning finger. "Go," she shrieked. "This is the Abode of the Dead that we call Sheol. The living have no place here. While you live, remember that you are an instrument of death . . ."

The Path to Fulfillment

MEMORY GUIDED her feet along the dark and secret ways. Brambles clutched at her skirts, but she pushed onwards, leading the docile white palfrey on a slack rein. Down the hill—behind her in space and time—stood the charred remains of a happy world, but the wilderness reclaiming the formal gardens, orchards, and vineyards sent out tendrils of green to carpet the broken flags and softly drape the blackened stones.

The deep pool of Fontelucente reflected a moonless lavender twilight, and the cooling air already contained an acrid hint of early autumn. Francesca was far less frightened of encountering any witches in this loneliness than returning to Casa Cuono.

It was a week since they'd left the city so hurriedly that she had been unable to get some message to Taddeo. Francesca prayed he would discover where she'd gone . . . but if he did, what purpose would it serve? Each day now she sensed Guido's thoughts grow more murderous, for he felt unable to return to his life in Florence possessed of a wife who had incurred the Medici's wrath. She feared one drunken night he and his painted boys and their snarling mastiffs would tear her to bloody pieces.

Despite his physical possession of her Guido could not slake his lust or jealousy: for he could not quench that vibrant flame which mocked him as it burned. Never before had he owned something which he couldn't completely control, and the challenge of Francesca's spirit was driving him towards a final act of violence.

She could content herself that no matter what befell her at least Mario was far from his hands. Desperation and the memory of Taddeo's words impelled her to where she had been initiated into the mysteries of La Vecchia. In the late afternoon when the Western horizon was an amber sea, she had managed to elude Anna's vigilance, and while the stable lads played at knucklebones in a dusty court, she saddled up the horse and galloped into the green vastness.

If the witches would not let her bide among them she had a story ready for her return: of a pilgrimage to a shrine a few miles from Casa Cuono. This wayside statue had attracted multitudes because it miraculously turned from blue to red . . . besides answering people's prayers. Francesca had a shrewd notion that its alteration in colour had a lot to do with climate: from her experience with frescoes she had noted that temperature sometimes had the oddest effect on certain shades.

She tethered the white mare to a tree and wrapped in the violet cloak she stole into the thicket to wait for darkness.

One by one the worshipers of Diana Aradia arrived. They were not all identical with Francesca's memory, for time and the authorities had reaped their harvest, but others had joined to make up the number. She watched them divest themselves of clothes which proclaimed their differing stations in life as well as their urban or rustic origins . . . and then the witches half-clad themselves in animal pelts.

It was time for her to join them. She removed clothes and boots and covered her pale nakedness with the cloak. As she walked through the damp lush greenery her nose was assailed with the heavy garlic scent of Jack-by-the-hedge as it bruised underfoot. Automatically she made her way to the natural throne in the clearing, and the group let her pass in silence. Francesca stood and addressed them and the star-filled dark.

"I am the child of Aradia, whose secret you vowed to keep. Here is your sign." She threw off the cape and turned to reveal the small star burned on to her smooth curved buttock.

A fine woman with black hair streaming over her breasts

and back gently seated Francesca on the stone, and then handed her the silver-bladed axe with the dark bone handle.

"This is the symbol of authority. You are our Lady's envoy, and for this night have sovereignty over us. How may we serve you?"

With one accord the witches knelt before her, their eyes gleaming on beauty unadorned but for a topaz at her throat. Fearlessly, Francesca answered them. "I must flee from my husband, who otherwise will kill me. I shall not profane this hallowed place with an account of his deeds, but he is an evil man in the sight of all those who hold life to be sacred."

Helped to his feet by a near-emaciated youth, the old man with the milk-blue eyes of a seer spoke in a cracked high voice: "While we feast we shall consider your request, and then tell you our design."

They brought her food and the first draught from the wine chalice but took their own repast a distance away. Afterwards they regrouped about her feet, and the old man began: "Lady, we have scried by starlight on witch water, and we see you can never break free from your husband . . ."

"But, I must . . ." Her impassioned cry rang through the quiet place like a tocsin.

"Hush, lady, be still. You have not heard all. The power deems that only death can sever you from him. We have woven a spell so that this man must soon meet destruction."

The black-haired woman stepped close. "Here is hempen rope, lady, over which we have performed our magic. Whisper the man's name in my ear."

Francesca obeyed wonderingly and then watched as the witch began to make knots in the rope, while her companions chanted in a strange tongue.

"You must conceal this in his bedchamber," the woman instructed. "Soon these knots will begin to cut off his powers: no semen will flow from his manhood . . . no urine from his bladder . . . and then the spittle will dry up . . and lastly breath will cease. He will die slowly, lady, and in great agony. This I swear."

Francesca put the knotted rope in her cloak. She felt no weakening of her resolve. Pity was spent. All she wished was that she had strength enough to perform the deed with steel, but perhaps that would be too quick.

"No, lady," the old man read her thoughts. "He must die without your being blamed. For you must live and fulfill your destiny. Let the witches' ladder do your bidding."

Then the women anointed her body so that she might join in La Volta. As she leapt and circled in the chain of dancers it seemed she had whirled backwards in time. They danced their measures to panpipes and the wild carolling of their own voices. Francesca flung back her head and felt her hair flowing cold along her spine: Above, the stars spun like dancers on the floor of night.

When it was done, each one kissed her lips as a token of shared embraces.

She left them to their revel . . .

Guido was drunk, sprawled out on a rug before the fireplace, one arm about a page boy's neck, the other hand tilting a wine flagon to his lips. It was chill in the hall, and the flames made only a small circle of warmth.

The wine dripped down Guido's pointed white chin and stained the fine tawny doublet. "Well, whore," he yelled in greeting, "which peasant have you been under a hedge with?"

I shall not have to endure him much longer, her mind insisted, and she tried to mount the stairs. Guido staggered to his feet and blocked her way.

"You have not answered. Why deprive us of your charming company so swiftly? My friends will think you don't care for them—that is most unflattering."

"I doubt any of you mind my feelings," she retorted. "As to where I've been: on a childhood pilgrimage."

With difficulty, he focussed his eyes made stupid by the wine. "I trust it has not rendered you overvirtuous," Guido sneered, "for I have a mind to join you in our bed."

Francesca hastened upstairs. In the bedchamber she succeeded in hiding the hempen rope behind the arras just before Anna entered to help her disrobe. The slave's eyes widened at the mud and strands of grass caught on her mistress's garments, and the green staining the narrow arched feet.

Guido did come to her. She did not know whether wine, too much play with his ganymedes, or the witches' ladder caused his inability to become erect. Impotence increased his fury, and he struck at her, yelling all the while: "Whoring witch, it is your doing." Francesca read fear in his eyes, and her satisfaction compensated much for pain and misery.

Over the next two days Guido's fury and drunkenness increased. He would not let Francesca out of his sight for a moment, and she was forced to spend her time in the company of his minions.

She sat with her eyes fixed on him while he read a note delivered by a servant from Buonventura. "Sorceress!" he screamed suddenly, waving the paper in her face. "Cosima has miscarried, after receiving some words from you. She vows you cursed her womb!"

The violet gaze held him without flinching. "I have put a curse on your entire family many times," she mocked. "As to her womb: Let Daniello fill it if he can, or if not I am sure the Medici will oblige once again."

He struck her face and then resumed his own chair. She cradled her hot cheek against a cold hand, and then noted the younger page pull at Guido's arm and whisper. Then Guido laughed: "Why not, little Pedro. She has plenty of other finery. Francesca, give the child your topaz. He has a fancy for it."

Her hands flew to her neck. "No. He may have anything you have given me, but the topaz is mine."

"That is most ungenerous, madonna." Guido came towards her, and his pale fingers grabbed at the jewel.

She struck and scratched at his hands with all her force, and the pages seeing their master thus attacked rushed to his defense. She felt their blows on her breasts and belly but still kept hold of the topaz.

Then, through the din came a voice which made them all turn towards the door.

"Good even, Guido di Cuono, I trust I don't intrude, but it is still many miles to the city and full dark. I should be grateful for your hospitality this night. Good evening, madonna, I hope all is well."

As if he had been carved from night and inspired with breath Ridolfo di Salvestro stepped forward, smiling and bowing, his mulberry clothes immaculate, only his boots dulled with white dust.

The pages' clawing hands slid to their velvet-encased sides, and Guido released Francesca. "You are welcome, Messer Ridolfo," he said breathlessly, and then: "Get you to bed, sweetheart. It is late. We shall probably indulge in some serious drinking, and I want to hear Messer Ridolfo's account of his journeys."

Francesca straightened her hair and gown and tremulously smiled at the guest. He bowed over her hand without smiling, and she felt his eyes question her bruised face.

Much, much later, when night held the chill of death, Francesca heard a step outside her door. She cowered in the bed, dreading Guido's entrance. But, it was Messer Ridolfo who stood framed in the doorway. Anna appeared behind him, and he turned calmly and said: "Woman, your master is unwell. I think he has drunk a draught too much. Go down and attend to him."

She obeyed, and Ridolfo closed the door behind her.

"It is done, Franca." He addressed her by the name of childhood. "Put on some clothes and a cloak. Taddeo waits for us outside with the horses. Bring nothing from this house. I have a kingdom and its treasures awaiting you."

Francesca stared across at him without comprehension. "What do you mean coming into this room?" she protested.

"I mean"—he smiled quietly—"why, I mean, madonna, to abduct you—whether you be willing or no."

"And Guido?"

"He will not aid you. I told your slave he has drunk his fill . . . and his last, too. Soon, he will find himself unable to move . . . the secretions of his body will dry up . . . then speech will become impossible . . . and then . . ." he shrugged.

"You have poisoned him?" she cried aghast.

"Aye. Do you mourn such a monster?"

She shook her head, and her eyes sought the arras. Perhaps Messer Ridolfo's arrival had been their work too.

"Why did you come here?" she demanded, as he threw some clothes onto the bed and drew the curtains to give her privacy while she dressed.

"I had word from Taddeo that you had disappeared, so I rode immediately to Florence, to discover that his secret information service had found you at Casa Cuono in danger. Are you ready? Then, you must drink this."

He poured some wine into a cup and into it sprinkled grains of white powder which he took from a minute gold box.

"More poison?"

"Only if taken in large amounts."

They did not descend through the main hall, which was filled with the hum of agitated voices . . . but instead sought the stairway down from Cosima's old room.

"Where are we going?" Francesca whispered, and the

strength ebbed from her limbs so that Messer Ridolfo had to lift her in his arms.

"To Paradise, little madonna. Now you are free, and destiny has written you are to be mine."

She tried vainly to argue, but her eyes began to dim. Only vaguely did she recognize Taddeo holding the horses' reins, as unconsciousness imprisoned her senses . . .

Francesca awoke in a chamber more beautiful and bright than anything she had ever seen. Fur rugs were scattered upon the tiled floors, and wondrous paintings decorated the walls. In the middle of the room was a large blue pool on which drifted brilliant flower heads. There was a marble table with a golden mirror, jewelled and alabaster pots of unguents and instruments in ivory and gold for beautifying the nails. Beside the pool stood a huge dish of fruit, a golden ewer, and some wine goblets.

She turned her head at the soft sounds of female voices and laughter. This was a language she couldn't understand. Two slim, brown girls ran to the daybed and began to undress her. Francesca could not hide her amazement at their clothes. Their lower limbs were barely concealed by near-transparent baggy trunk hose . . . tiny blouses of a similar rose-hued material covered their breasts and arms . . . while their smooth bellies were absolutely bare but for a jewel at the navel. Dark eyes were painted with green and blue, and the smooth loose tresses were adorned with gold and pearls.

Francesca tried to push them away, but with gentle firmness which brooked little argument the two Turkish slave girls drew her to the pool and forced her to descend into its warm scented waters.

After a while it began to seem like some delicious dream, and she allowed them to bathe her, wash her hair, perfume her body, and dress her in a white and gold silk gown, which might have been made especially for her. Then they led her into another chamber, as fine as the former but containing a huge bed instead of the bathing pool.

On a table stood golden baskets of sweetmeats and fruit and flagons of wine. Francesca sank into a chair and waited with nervous impatience. As soon as Messer Ridolfo appeared in fresh mulberry finery she demanded: "Where am I?"

"In Paradise." He smiled, and bowed. "Welcome, madonna. That is the name I give to my house. We are within the Duchy of Milan, and this entire palazzo was purchased and furnished with you in mind. Until I found you again it was a mausoleum to a dead dream. Only now it is as I had planned: the home of my bride who will be the mother of my sons."

"No," Francesca returned. "It is enough to have been married once. Besides what will the world say if the widow of one day's standing remarried her husband's murderer?"

"That poison is all but unknown in Italy, so your husband will be assumed to have died from his excesses, and we shall keep our secret for a reasonable time if that's what you prefer. But, do you really not want to become my wife, Franca?"

"I intend to belong to no man." There was vehemence and fear in her voice, and the violet eyes were wild. "If you try to force me, I think I should rather take the dagger you wear and plunge it into my own heart."

Messer Ridolfo made no comment. "You must be tired still from the journey. We rode like the North Wind. I have never seen Taddeo so content. Tomorrow you shall talk with him and discuss the future. Meanwhile, madonna, taste some of these delicacies. They come from the lands ruled by the Turk, as do many things in this house."

"Including those lovely servants?" she inquired, biting into a soft jelly which tasted of rose petals and was filled with nuts. "Ah . . . this is good. May I take some more?"

"By all means." Ridolfo pushed the basket towards her

and contented himself with drinking a little white wine. "The girls were bought from a harem, and only know about beautifying themselves and pleasing men . . ."

"I am sure you have tested their skills," Francesca remarked acidly and then wondered why she felt indignant.

Ridolfo smiled at her tone, but inquired politely: "Are you feeling better, Franca?"

She began to laugh and couldn't understand why. "I feel lightheaded as if I had drunk too much. My limbs seem to float, and I want to laugh. Can it be the result of those fumes rising from the dishes?"

"They are just herbs being burned to sweeten and warm the air. Perhaps you have eaten too many dainties."

Francesca giggled helplessly and wondered at herself. "My dear friend, it is not possible to be made to laugh by such things as honey and nuts. What other ingredients do your sweets contain?"

"The loukhoum, halva, and manzul are made with what the Arabs call hashish el kif—a sticky substance obtained from a plant with medicinal and euphoriant properties."

"Oh," Francesca responded vaguely. The room seemed to dance and divide into a rainbow of colours before her eyes. It was not unpleasant, but she wished she felt more in control of herself . . . as things were she might say or do anything.

It took her a few seconds to realize that Messer Ridolfo had risen from his chair and was holding her in his arms. "No," she whispered, "I won't let you kiss me. I never want to know a man."

Her voice sounded to her own ears as if it came from a long way off. Messer Ridolfo's laughter was lighthearted. "My poor darling," he said, "you are made for love, and I shall prove that to you. I'm afraid I have been wicked: hashish el kif has many wondrous powers—one of these is acting as an aphrodisiac, especially on unwilling ladies. I trust, Franca, that by the time you have recovered from its influence, you will forgive me."

She tried to struggle as he carried her to the bed and unhooked her gown. Francesca felt the soft warm air on her nakedness, as she lay, defenseless and so very beautiful that the man could only gaze on her in wonder before kissing her hand with genuine reverence.

"My darling, your eyes are still filled with terror. After all, little Franca, you have already been married. I vow that for tonight anyway I shall be as considerate as a bridegroom with a brand new virgin."

Francesca turned away her head as Ridolfo began to kiss her unresponsive lips. "You must give me a little encouragement, other than your loveliness," he reproved, "else I shall conclude you do not care for me at all."

His own passionate hands and lips began to explore her body, and Francesca found herself relaxing. Her lips parted, and her eyes grew luminous and gentle. His hair looked very black against her white flesh. Suddenly she gave a sharp indignant cry and jerked away from him.

"Eyes of God!" Ridolfo exclaimed. "Madonna, you are a virgin. How can this be?"

In a remote voice which permitted her to speak the unutterable, Francesca explained. At last she gave a weary smile: "I am still a virgin, although my body is defiled."

Ridolfo's eyes blazed, and his fists clenched. "You are not defiled, for your spirit is as clean and pure as fire. Why did I allow him to die with such little pain?" he muttered between his teeth. "By God, if I had him here, I'd . . ."

She began to laugh merrily at his fury. "Aye, sir, if you had him here, then I should not be in your bed."

He gazed on her laughing features with disbelief. "Franca . . . Franca . . . you have returned to me. I told you once that I would be the first man you ever knew. I loved you then. In great torment I learned to love you even more.

Now you have the same expression you wore when first we met. Please be mine, and I shall teach you to love me."

Initiation into the great secret was a little bewildering and painful, for he would not release her until she too had learned about ecstasy. Then they lay close, hands entwined, watching the growing darkness which covered them like a soft blanket.

"I am sure you should be clad to answer such a question," Ridolfo teased, kissing her throat, "but, Madonna Francesca, despite your unseemly but becoming nakedness, will you be my wife?"

"Shall we really be happy?" Her voice contained wistfulness. "It is long since I have known what that means."

He leaned on an elbow to stare gravely onto her beauty. "I swear on my life and honour that we shall be happy . . . but, my darling little Franca, I cannot erase the past. All I can do is promise you a future without shadows."

She stretched upwards, pulled him down onto her breast, and then stared into those eyes of night she had once feared. Tears gathered in her own eyes. "Oh, Ridolfo, Ridolfo," she whispered, "I am already happy in your love. Now I can look forward . . . forward . . ."

They clung tightly to each other and Francesca knew she was falling in love . . .

Books Consulted

A Florentine Diary, Luca Landucci
The Civilization of the Renaissance in Italy, Jacob Burckhardt
Daily Life in Florence, Lucas Durreton
Autobiography of Benvenuto Cellini
The Italian City Republics, D. Waley
Life in Italy at the Time of the Medici, John Gage
The Renaissance, Walter Pater
Princes of the Renaissance, Orville Prescott
Florence, Edward Hutton
History of World Costume, Carolyn Bradley
The Decameron, Boccaccio
The Penguin Book of the Renaissance, J. H. Plumb
History of Florence, Ferdinand Schevill
The Social World of the Florentine Humanists, Lauro Martines
The Story of Art, E. H. Gombrich
The Renaissance, George Bull
The Prince, Niccolò Machiavelli
Everyday Life in Renaissance Times, E. R. Chamberlain
Made in the Renaissance, Christine Price
They Saw It Happen in Europe, Charles R. Routh
The Fifteenth Century, Margaret Aston
The Lives of Painters, Giorgi Vasari
Italian Gardens, Villas and Palaces, G. Masson
A Traveller in Italy, H. V. Morton

Date Due

MAY 9 '73	OCT 16 '75	MR 03 '95
MAY 27 '73	SEP 12 '76	MAR 0 1999
MAY 22 1973	OCT 1 2 1979	
MAY 27 '73	SEP 2 '8	
JUN 25 '73	AUG 1 4 1984	
AUG 11 '73	JE 24 '87	
OCT 14 '73	JUN 1 9 1987	
OCT 26 '73	JE 25 '87	
NOV 16 '73	DE 15 '89	
JAN 30 '74		
MAR 5 74		
APR 8 1975		